Need You To CHOOSE ME

>>>>> BLUEBONNET CREEK SERIES <<<<<

ANNA B. DOE

Need You To CHOOSE ME

ANNA B. DOE

Copyright © 2025 by Anna B. Doe
All rights reserved.
ISBN 978-953-8511-47-9

Need You To Choose Me by Anna B. Doe
Publisher: Wild Heart Publishing d.o.o.
Lukarišće, Croatia, 2025
Print on demand

Copyediting by Once Upon A Typo
Proofreading by Sisters Get Lit.erary Author Services
Cover Design by Qamber Designs
Cover Photography by Wander Aguiar Photography
Cover Models: Cassie & Andrew
Publisher: Wild Heart Publishing d.o.o.

Without in any way limiting the author's exclusive rights under copyright, any use of this publication to "train" generative artificial intelligence (AI) technologies to generate text is expressly prohibited. The author reserves all rights to license uses of this work for generative AI training and development of machine learning language models.

This is a work of fiction, created without use of AI technology. Any names, characters, places or incidents are products of the author's imagination and used in a fictitious manner. Any resemblance to actual people, places, or events is purely coincidental or fictional.

No part of this book may be reproduced in any form or by any electronic or mechanical means, including information storage and retrieval systems, without written permission from the author, except for the use of brief quotations in a book review.

❀ Created with Vellum

For my readers.
Thank you for sticking with me when I wasn't at my best.

She didn't want love,
she wanted to be loved-
and that
was entirely different.
- Atticus

One night, no names, no kissing had seemed like a good idea until I got a big, fat plus sign on a pregnancy test, and I have no idea who my baby daddy is.

I'm determined to raise my baby on my own, but then *he* waltzes into my classroom to drop off his son.

Blake Walker.

The newly retired linebacker and single dad is even more gorgeous now than the night we spent together, and now that he knows I'm pregnant with his baby, he's adamant to do right by us.

I promised myself I won't be somebody's responsibility. However, Blake's a man who doesn't back down, especially when it comes to his family.

As if this town isn't small enough, he moves into the house across the street, and his presence is impossible to ignore. Blake is everything I never expected, and all three Walker boys are slowly working their way into my heart, but I can't get used to it.

He wanted our baby, and I wouldn't settle for anything less than a man who chooses me...

Chapter 1

SAVANNAH

March

"Double whiskey on the rocks," I say to the bartender as I slide onto the first open barstool.

The guy gives me a curious look, but he doesn't comment as he grabs a glass, throwing a few cubes of ice in it before placing it on the bar in front of me and pouring my drink.

The moment he starts to lift the bottle, I wrap my fingers around the cool glass, toss my head back, and down the drink.

My eyes squeeze shut as the alcohol burns down my throat, making tears prickle under my eyelids.

Shit, this is strong.

But I needed strong.

More than that, I needed to feel numb tonight.

And this was the only way I knew how to do it.

Blinking my eyes open, I wave to the guy for a refill.

I was determined to get drunk tonight.

Maybe that would help erase the last few days from my memory.

Or at least alleviate this sharp ache inside my chest.

Because today was the day I put my grandmother, my only living family, to rest.

It still felt surreal. Even at seventy-five years old, Grams was one of the most vibrant people I knew. I loved her to pieces, although some days, she drove me crazy with how independent she was. How damn stubborn. That woman was energetic, opinionated, loud, and generally didn't take shit from anybody.

How could a person like that be gone?

One day, she was here telling me I should ditch my piece-of-shit boyfriend and find myself a nice man who would treat me well so I could focus on him and stop bossing her around already, and the next, I found her lifeless body lying in her bed.

A heart attack.

My throat grows tight as the image of her pale face flashes in my mind, and more tears gather in my eyes.

She was right, though.

Mark was a piece of shit.

Not just that, he was a lying, *cheating* piece of shit.

Which was the second reason I was drinking tonight.

I didn't think it was too much to expect my boyfriend of four years to attend my grandmother's funeral, but I guess I shouldn't be surprised Mark told me he couldn't come because he was too busy at work. To say he and Grams didn't get along would be an understatement. So I did it all alone. Yes, my friends were there, as was half of Bluebonnet. After all, Grams was very loved in our little community, but that wasn't nearly the same.

Now that she was gone, I was on my own.

Completely and utterly alone.

The funeral and the wake were a blur of emotions and people as I tried my best to keep myself from falling apart. I couldn't break down in front of my small town. My family was enough of a spectacle as it was.

But then everybody left, and it was somehow even worse. It

felt like the walls of my childhood home were narrowing down on me. Asphyxiating me. I couldn't stay there. I needed to get away. I needed to *breathe*. I needed to forget. I needed somebody familiar.

I needed Mark.

So, I figured I'd go and visit him. The two-hour drive cleared my mind a little, but when I got to Houston, his house was empty. So I decided to drive to his office instead. Mr. Rodriguez, one of the security guards I got to know in the past, was at the front desk. After a quick chat, he let me go up to Mark's office.

The hallway was quiet as I walked; the plush rug carpets muffled the sound of my clinking heels. I was in such a hurry to leave I didn't even bother changing after the funeral. Most of the offices were in the dark, his colleagues long gone by now.

Except his.

The door to Mark's office was ajar, light peeking through the small crack.

I pushed the door open just as a loud moan came from the room.

My body froze as I slowly lifted my gaze and took in the image in front of me. An unfamiliar blonde was bent over Mark's desk, his tall figure standing over hers, his face sweaty, cheeks red as he pounded into her from behind.

Just thinking about it made my stomach roll and the bile rise up my throat.

I told you so.

I could hear Grams say those words loud and clear to me in my mind. Grams wasn't one to pull punches, and she hated Mark. Hell, she hated all of my ex-boyfriends. Always claimed none of them were good enough for me, but what if she was wrong? What if it wasn't them? What if it was me? What if I was the problem? What if I was broken? What if I was unlovable?

Do you seriously think somebody could love you? You were a means to an end, Savvy. You had one purpose, and you blew it. If I knew how much trouble you were going to be, I would have gotten rid of you while I had the chance, but now I'm stuck with you.

The hateful words from my past are like a slap to my face. Grabbing my glass, I chug it, only to choke on the bitter liquid.

Shit.

I bend forward as I try to catch my breath when I feel a hand pat against my back. "Easy now."

The low, raspy voice has the hair at my nape standing at attention. Following the sound, I turn to the side, but my vision is too blurry to see clearly. All I can do is feel. Feel a big hand soothe up and down my back, making the goosebumps rise on my skin. Feel the warm body sitting next to me, his knee brushing against mine. Smell the spicy scent of an unfamiliar man's cologne.

Finally, I stop coughing and manage to catch my breath. Blinking a few times, the guy's face comes into focus, and my mouth goes dry, but for a completely different reason.

Holy shit, this man is gorgeous.

And tall. So damn tall. You could see it even when he was sitting. How did I miss him taking the chair next to mine, I'll never understand. Because there was nothing subtle about this man. I was pretty sure when he entered the room, everybody knew it. My tongue darts out, sliding over my dry lips as I stare at him.

It wasn't just his physical appearance either. There is a silent intensity shining in his light eyes as he watches me. Blue or gray? It was hard to tell in the dimly lit room. His dark hair is rich, the ends curling around his ears, and a neatly trimmed beard is covering his jaw. He's dressed in simple jeans and a blue polo shirt that reveals his firm bicep with a full sleeve of tattoos adorning his tanned skin.

His brows pull together, a few lines marring his forehead. "You okay, Blondie?"

Hearing that nickname snaps me back into reality. Feeling embarrassed, I look away, searching for the bartender. "Fine."

The guy is serving the customer on the other side of the bar. I lift my hand, signaling for another round, and he nods in acknowledgment.

"Do you really think that's a wise idea?" my companion continues without missing a beat.

Seriously? Is this guy for real?

Annoyance rises under my skin. I didn't come here for a lecture; I came here to forget, and he was making it impossible. I tilt my head to the side to find him watching me, his long fingers wrapped around a glass of rich brown liquid. "Who are you? My dad?"

Those astute eyes lock on me, and it takes everything in me not to shudder. "I could probably be."

I let out a snort just as the bartender appears with my refill. "You're not that old, buddy."

At this angle, I could see a few lines on his face, mostly around his eyes and on his forehead, but he was far from old. Older? Probably. He had what? Eight years on me? Ten tops, which would put him in his mid-thirties. Definitely not more than that.

What the hell was a guy like that doing at a random hotel bar in the middle of nowhere Texas? He didn't seem like the country type. Even with the beard and messy hair, he was still too clean-cut for this place. And there was no hint of a Southern accent either. A passerby. Maybe on business?

My eyes dart down to his glass and the hand wrapped around it. No ring. Or line where one was supposed to be.

Why the hell are you looking at his ring finger? I chastise myself as the bartender refills my glass. *Get a grip, girl.*

"Some days I feel that old." He tips his chin in my direction. "What is a gorgeous woman like you doing drinking all by herself?"

His question brings Mark back to the forefront of my mind, and the anger that's been simmering under the surface of hurt comes back swinging.

"Lying, cheating *ex*-boyfriend," I grit through my clenched teeth.

That's better, though. Because if I focused on Mark, I could forget the empty hollowness that losing Grams left inside of me.

"Huh, so I guess we're the same."

It takes me a moment to register his words. My head whips in the direction of the handsome stranger, my mouth falling open. "What?"

"Today, I signed two of the most important documents in my life. Including finalizing the divorce from my lying, cheating *ex*-wife."

Wife? He was married? Scratch that, she cheated on him? Was she nuts? Why would somebody cheat on a man like *that*? If I was coming home to that man every night, I couldn't imagine myself even glancing at another guy, much less cheating on him.

He lifts his glass before he downs his drink in one go, something dark and dangerous flashing in those light irises. Contrary to me, he doesn't seem the least bit affected by the alcohol.

My throat bobs as I swallow, following his lead.

He waves at the bartender for another round. Once our glasses are filled, he clinks it against mine. "To better luck in love?"

I let out a strangled laugh, running my fingers through my

hair. "Yeah, I think not. I've had my fair share of it, and I'm officially done with love. Hell, I'm done with *men*."

His brow quirks up. "That bad?"

I can feel his gaze roam over my face, taking in every little detail. I shift in my seat, suddenly feeling self-conscious under his sharp eyes that don't seem to miss anything. The motion makes my knee bump against his under the table, and a jolt of electricity shoots through my body at the small touch.

He must feel it, too, because I can see his pupils dilate.

He lifts his glass to his mouth, not once breaking the contact between us as he takes a slow sip of his drink.

My gaze falls to his mouth. One amber droplet clinging to that full lip. His tongue darts out, and my heart starts to race inside my chest as I watch him sweep it off his lip.

"We're closing in fifteen," the bartender says as he grabs our glasses, breaking us out of our staring contest.

I look down, a strand of hair slipping from behind my ear like a shield. "Well, that's a bummer."

Taking my bag from the table, I push to my feet. My belly feels warm from all the drinks I had. In hindsight, it might not have been the best idea to drink so much because I still had a good hour's drive in front of me before I got back home.

Home to my empty house and my memories of Grams.

The stranger gets up and stops in front of me.

I tilt my head back to find him observing me with a silent intensity. It's like he can see into my very soul. Those light irises have grown darker, the shade of the sky just before the storm hits.

My stomach twists, warmth spreading through me, but it doesn't have anything to do with the alcohol and everything to do with this man standing in front of me.

He lifts his hand, and I suck in a breath, bracing for the contact. His fingers gently brush the lock of my hair behind my ear as his gaze falls on my mouth. His jaw works as he just stares at me, and my thighs clench together as neediness pulses through me. A need I haven't felt in so long, it leaves me breathless for a second.

"You want to get out of here?" he asks in that gruff voice that makes goosebumps rise on my skin.

My heart starts beating faster, my palms turning sweaty.

He can't mean...

But he does.

Oh, how he does.

My teeth sink into my lower lip.

I should say no. That would be the most logical answer. I wasn't one for hookups. I was a good girl who followed the rules. I was the type of girl who went on at least three dates before sleeping with a man.

And where did that get you? A little voice at the back of my head challenges. *Dating losers who can't make you come, only to cheat on you and leave you brokenhearted, that's where.*

This man wasn't a loser. I don't know how I knew it. I simply did. And I was pretty sure he knew how to treat a woman. There was this air around him. Confidence oozed off of him in waves. Besides, what did I have to lose? I had nobody waiting for me back at home, only memories and those I did not want to face. We were both available and newly single.

One night.

It would be one night where I could forget everything and just be.

Then I can go back to my boring, ordinary life in Bluebonnet Creek.

What would be the harm in that?

"Okay," I whisper softly, the words barely audible.

Surprise flashes on his face but is quickly replaced by need. "You sure, Blondie?"

There it was. That nickname. I shouldn't like it. But damn it, I did. There was just something in the way he said it, like a lover's caress.

I nod softly. "Let's go."

He stands still for a second longer as if he's giving me a chance to change my mind before his hand drops and takes mine, our fingers interlocking. My heartbeat echoes in my eardrums as he leads me out of the bar and into the hallway. The elevator is just about to close when his hand shoots up, and we manage to scramble inside, along with an older couple. My palm grows damp while they eye us with interest.

Do they know? Can they see we're two strangers who are about to hook up? And if they do, why do I care? I'll never see them again. Just like I'll never see this man again after tonight. It didn't matter.

I look away, my eyes fixing on our reflection in the mirror.

Now that we're standing under the bright lights, I can finally see him clearly. He looks larger than life, towering over me a good foot, his wide shoulders taking a good portion of the tight space. His warm fingers are still safely clasped around mine. He's dark to my light. He runs his fingers through his hair, making the thick locks unruly around his head, and his skin has a glow to it of a man who spends time out under the sun. Nothing like my fair skin that burns the moment I step out of my house.

We look good together, more than good really. We look like a couple.

Don't go there, I remind myself. *You're not a couple. You're just hooking up; that's all.*

He must feel me watching because his gaze meets mine, and the fire blazing in his irises makes me shudder. It's like he's devouring me with his gaze alone, and suddenly, the elevator seems too small, the air too thick, his hand on mine too hot.

The ride to his floor seems to last forever, but when the bell finally chimes, I barely get to say goodbye before he pulls me out into the hallway and marches toward his room. He presses the card against the lock, and the light barely shines green before I'm ushered into a dark room.

The door falls shut, and he spins us around. All the air is kicked out of my lungs as my back touches the hardwood. Soft light is peeking through the curtain over his shoulder, but then he's in front of me, and he's the only thing I can see. The only thing I can *feel*.

"You're so fucking gorgeous, Blondie," he rasps. Those large palms frame my face, tilting my head back as his thumb skims over my lower lip. "I saw you the moment I stepped into the bar, and I couldn't take my eyes off of you."

He leans down, but before he can press his mouth against mine, I turn my head to the side so his lips brush against my cheek, his beard sending shivers as he kisses down the side of my neck and back up. My arms wrap around his neck, fingers sinking into that lush hair to pull him back.

"No kissing on the lips," I whisper softly as his eyes meet mine. "One night. No names. No kissing."

My heart is beating so hard it feels like it'll break out of my chest as I wait for his reaction.

Those were my rules, and if he didn't want to follow them, well... Tough luck.

Those full lips tempted me so badly, but I knew kissing him would be a mistake. It would feel too personal, and I couldn't deal with that. I don't know what it was about this man, but I knew he had the potential to break what little of my heart was left intact, and I couldn't allow that.

I was broken too many times by too many people. I would not allow another person to once again have this power over me.

And it started today.

With this man.

Those silver eyes darken like the sky just before the storm. The time seems to be ticking down slowly as he weighs my words, and for a second, I think he'll reject me.

I'm about to tell him this was a mistake, but he's faster.

Before I can blink, he flips me over. I brace my hands against the door as his lips trace the column of my neck, and that raspy voice whispers in my ear, "Whatever you want, Blondie."

His body envelopes mine, the warmth of his skin seeping into me as his hard cock presses against the small of my back.

Holy shit, he's big.

Way bigger than I thought.

And so damn hard.

My thighs clench in anticipation as his hands slide down my sides and onto my stomach, pulling me closer to him. My dress rides up my legs, his rock-hard length nestles between my ass cheeks, and I can feel him groan.

"Fuck, that dress has been driving me crazy all night long." His palms slide lower. "Those fucking legs and shoes. I could see them wrapped around my waist, your heels digging into my ass as I pounded into you until I could hear you scream my name. I guess hearing you scream will have to be enough." His hand moves to the inside of my thigh, slipping upward until he reaches my center. "*Shit*, you're so wet for me already, Blondie." My eyes fall shut, and I roll my hips against his hand, needing more friction, needing to satiate this ache inside my pussy. "So fucking needy too. When was the last time your ex made you come?"

Too long. I shake my head. *It's been way too long since a man has given me pleasure.*

"I don't want to talk about my ex," I breathe as I loop one hand back, my fingers playing with the soft curls at the back of his neck.

"Then what do you want?"

I look over my shoulder, and even in the darkness of the room, I can feel his intense stare on me. My teeth scrape over my lower lip. "I want your dick inside me. I want to feel you so deep that I'll forget everything else."

Erase everybody else.

He smirks, his fingers tracing my chin. "Don't worry, love. After I'm done with you, you won't remember any douchebag from your past. But first..."

In one swift movement, he turns me so I'm facing him, and grabs the hem of my dress, pulling it over my head and tossing it aside. He drinks me in, his eyes scanning every inch of my exposed skin before he nudges me down on my knees. "First, you've gotta earn it."

My tongue darts out as it slides over my lower lip. He holds my gaze silently, the fire blazing in those silvery eyes matching the one burning inside of me. Without breaking our contact, I slowly lift my hands, unbuttoning his jeans, and pulling his hard length out.

My mouth waters at the sight of him, my panties growing damp as I wrap my fingers around his dick, slowly working his length with my hand.

"Blondie..." he growls softly. His fingers gather my long hair, and he wraps it around his wrist, tugging my head back ever so slightly. I can feel the slight sting on my scalp as he tilts my head back. "Open that pretty mouth and suck my cock like the good girl I know you are."

Shit.

Nobody ever talked to me like that, but a part of me liked it. It liked it a lot.

My lips part, and I suck the tip of his dick. He softly hisses as I work his length, taking more of him into my mouth with each bob of my head, until I'm so full I can hardly breathe. He's barely halfway inside me when my eyes start to water. There is no way I could ever take all of him, but I'm sure going to try.

"Fucking hell, Blondie," he groans.

My tongue swipes over the underside of him as I pull back. I flick my tongue over his tip, tasting the saltiness of his precum on my tongue as my hand works at his base. His cock twitches in my palm as I slide down, taking him even deeper into my mouth, the hand on my nape guiding my every movement.

"Such a good girl," he rasps. His hooded eyes hold mine hostage as he keeps me in place, just where the pleasure and pain meet for a few seconds longer.

I press my legs together, but it doesn't help alleviate the ache building inside of me.

"*Shit.* I'm not coming just yet." He tugs my head back, his dick popping out of my mouth before his hands slide under my arms, and he hoists me up into his arms and carries me to bed.

He lays me down, my chest rising and falling as I watch him take his clothes off quickly until he's gloriously naked in front of me.

The faint light coming from the window illuminates his toned body: each muscle defined to perfection, six-pack abs, that delicious V that's leading to his hard cock... It's unlike anything I've ever seen before. He's glorious, honed like a statue of a Greek god, only he's not. He's real and warm, and he's mine.

For tonight.

He grabs my ankles, pulling me to the edge of the bed. "Rise." The commanding tone of his voice leaves no room for argument and has chills spreading over my skin.

I lift my hips, and he slides my panties down before unhooking my bra and getting to his knees.

"What are you... *Shit.*"

His fingers wrap around my waist, pulling me closer as he slides my knees over his shoulders and buries his face in my pussy. There is no finesse to it, just raw need as his tongue laps at my center. He hums appreciatively, his tongue swirling and sucking. My fingers grip his hair as his tongue dips into me, his beard scratching against my inner thighs.

"Yes, more. I need—" I let out a loud moan, my head falling back as the first wave of pleasure makes my body quake.

His shoulders shake, or maybe that's just me. Maybe I'm the one shaking as he continues licking at me until I slowly come down from the high before pulling back. His thumb rubs at the inside of my knee as he licks at his lips, that heated gaze taking in my naked body.

"You have the prettiest cunt I've ever seen, Blondie. Ever tasted."

I let out a shaky breath, my chest rising and falling rapidly. He holds my gaze as he presses his mouth against my navel and then slowly kisses his way up, each touch sending another shiver through my body.

A self-satisfied smirk pops on his mouth. "So fucking responsive."

My hands slide over his wide shoulders as he nuzzles his head into my chest, sucking one nipple into his mouth just as his hot cock settles between my thighs.

My fingers dig into his muscles. "I need you to stop teasing me, a-and..." my voice stutters as he slides into me in one long thrust. I'm so freaking wet, he enters me without any resistance whatsoever. My nails dig into his back as he rocks his hips against me.

"Shit, you're so fucking tight, Blondie. So wet for me, so warm, but so damn tight."

He grabs my knee, pulling my legs further apart so he can sink deeper.

My eyes fall shut as he stretches me further, a shaky breath falling off my lips at the fullness as he slowly fills me. I lift my hips, needing more. God, I was so clo—

"Eyes on me, Blondie," he growls, his body freezing.

I blink my eyes open to find that hungry gaze watching me intently. "I want to see the moment you fall apart, so if you want me to make you come, you better keep your eyes on me. You want me to make you come, right?"

I nod my head silently. I wanted it more than I wanted my next breath.

"Good girl." His biceps flex as he presses his hands against the sides of my head. "Now, wrap your legs around me."

My teeth sink into my lower lip as I do what he says.

He lets out a loud groan as my heels dig into his skin. I'm pretty sure it'll leave a mark, but he doesn't seem to care one bit as he starts to move.

His thrusts become stronger, more frantic. My pussy tightens around him, and I'm so close. So freaking close—I slide my hand down, and find my clit, rubbing at the sensitive bud.

"Fuck, yeah. Touch yourself for me, sweetheart."

With each thrust, I can feel him, feel the place where we're connected. Warm and hard.

Those burning irises don't leave mine as his muscles flex under my palms. My pussy tightens around him as another orgasm slams into my body. With one final thrust, he comes inside me, his body falling onto mine.

Our ragged breaths mingle together as we come down from the high. He easily flips us over, his hand brushing my hair back.

I try to pull back from him, but he doesn't let me go, his lips press against the top of my head. "Stay."

I shouldn't stay. I knew better than that.

But he felt so nice. So warm.

I close my eyes.

One moment.

Just one moment to catch my breath, and then I'll leave.

The first thing I see when I open my eyes is the sun slowly peeking through the curtains. I let out a soft groan. My head is throbbing, and the bright light isn't helping.

What the hell was I doing last night?

Closing my eyes, I turn away from the brightness only to bump into a solid wall of muscles. I look up and then up some more, the sleeping face of an unfamiliar man staring back at me.

The memories of last night flash in quick, blurry succession —one after the other. Drinking with the sexy stranger. Leaving the bar. Agreeing to one night.

"*Holy shit.*"

I slept with him. Not just that, I had the best sex of my life with this guy, and I didn't even know his name.

One night. No names. No kissing.

Even in his sleep, he had that scowl etched between his brows, and my fingers itched to smooth it out.

Get a grip, Sav.

I needed to get out of here and fast.

I hold my breath until I disentangle from his warm body and get out of the bed. The process is slow, but he's still firmly asleep as I quickly start gathering my clothes and pulling them on. Once I'm done, I run my fingers through my hair.

I'm pretty sure I look like a mess, but that's what I get for hooking up with a handsome stranger.

Handsome, dirty-talking, grumpy stranger that made me feel unlike any other man before.

With one last look at the man sleeping in the bed, I turn around and get the hell out of there.

Chapter 2

SAVANNAH

April

"I'm going to grab another box!" I yell over my shoulder as I go toward the door. Miguel's trunk is half empty, but there is another batch waiting at Becky's family's house. I'm just grabbing a box when I feel my phone vibrate in my pocket. Cursing silently, I switch the box to one hand and pull out my phone, but the damn thing falls out of my grasp, so I have to crouch down and grab it.

"Hello?"

"Savannah, hi. Do you have a moment to talk?"

"Mr. Miles, hi," I breathe, slightly winded. "Sure. How is it going?"

"Good. I just stopped at your house like you asked me to, and everything looks good."

My brows pull together. "Really? You sure?"

From the corner of my eye, I can see a flash of red.

"What are—" Becky stops when she sees me talking on the phone and mouths, "Sorry." I give her a reassuring smile as I listen to my landlord.

"Yes, I tightened the pipe, but everything looks okay. So I wouldn't worry about it."

"Okay, thank you so much for doing that, Mr. Miles."

We say our goodbyes, and I slide my phone back in place.

"What was that about?" Becky glances at me as she grabs her own box.

"There was a leak in my bathroom, so I asked my landlord to give it a look, but he claims everything is in order. But for a few days I've been noticing little patches of water after I shower, and it's not where the door is, but more to the side? I don't know."

"That is weird. Do you want me to see if Miguel or my brother can look into it?" she asks as we make our way into the house.

"No, it's fine. He said he tightened the pipe, so I hope that will fix it."

I knew they had their hands full, and I didn't want to add my problems to theirs on top of everything.

"Are you sure? It's no prob—"

"What did I tell you about carrying those?" Miguel glares at Becky as he descends the stairs, his hands landing on the box in her arms. He tries to pull it out of her grasp, but she isn't letting go.

"I can carry it just fine by myself," she protests, puffing at a strand of hair that fell from the messy knot on top of her head.

"But why would you carry it when you have me to do it for you?" He flexes his arms pointedly. "I'm not working on those just to look pretty, Red."

I move past them into the kitchen and exchange a look with Kate, who just shrugs, and continues putting away the dishes into their designated spot. Being childhood friends, I guess she was used to their antics by now.

"I thought you were working on those so your coach wouldn't rip you a new one?" Becky quirks an eyebrow.

"Besides, don't you have to get your ass in the truck and go pick up that enormous couch you wanted?" She bats her eyelashes innocently as she pulls the box closer to her chest and carries it to the counter.

The frown between Miguel's brows deepens as he watches her every move like a hawk.

The two of them used to be high school sweethearts, but they broke up in college, only to be reunited this past summer since Kate and Emmett, their mutual friends, were getting married, and they were supposed to be the maid of honor and the best man. Now, not even a year later, Becky and Miguel were back together, engaged and moving into their brand-new home they purchased a few weeks ago. Still, after all that time and everything they've been through, some things didn't change.

Miguel turns to Kate and then me, pointing his finger at us. "Don't let her carry any more heavy boxes."

Becky rolls her eyes. "You're insufferable, Fernandez."

Miguel marches to Becky and grabs her face before plastering his mouth to hers. He devours her as if they're all alone in the room. My cheeks heat from intruding on their moment, so I look away.

I was glad that my friend had finally found her happiness, but I couldn't deny that a part of me felt jealous. Both Becky and Kate were loved and cherished by their partners, so why couldn't I find somebody like that?

Do you really think somebody can love you, Savvy?

My throat tightens as it always does when those intrusive thoughts cross my mind. I press my hand against my rolling stomach, the bile rising up my throat. I've been feeling nauseated for days now and even threw up a few times.

Did I catch a bug?

It didn't feel like a stomach bug, but I couldn't exactly pinpoint what was wrong with me. Maybe it was the fact that the end of the school year was just around the corner, and things were more hectic than usual. Which I didn't mind per se. Staying busy helped keep my mind on what needed to be done instead of everything that had happened in the last few months. Like the fact that Grams was gone, and she left me her house. A house I haven't set one foot in since her funeral.

The image of Grams' still body lying in her bed pops into my mind, and a cold sweat washes over me.

Don't think about it, Sav.

Focus on here and now. On helping your friend move in so she can start her life with the man she loves.

"I'll see you in a little bit," I can hear Miguel whisper to Becky. His large palms are still cradling her cheeks, and I can't help but remember another set of hands. Hands that were framing my face, roaming my body, and bringing me pleasure unlike anything I'd ever experienced before.

"Don't lift heavy things," Miguel repeats, snapping me out of my thoughts.

Seriously, Sav? I shake my head, pushing the memories of *that* night to the back of my head.

Not giving her a chance for a swift comeback, Miguel leaves the room.

Becky's teeth sink into her lower lip as she stares after him.

Kate nudges her with her hip as she opens one of the drawers and puts a couple of pots inside. "What's up with him?"

Panic shines in Becky's eyes. She quickly schools her features, but there is no hiding her pink cheeks. "What do you mean?"

"You know what I mean." Kate gives her a knowing look. "He's been on your ass for carrying those boxes all day long. It kind of reminds me of how Emmett was when..." The pot falls into the drawer with a loud *bang*. Kate's lips part in a perfect 'o' as she straightens to her full height and points her finger at Becky. "*Oh my God!*"

I look between the two women, clearly missing something. "What?"

"Oh my God!" Kate repeats, shaking her head.

A guilty expression flashes on Becky's face as she nibbles at her lip.

"Will somebody explain what the hell's going on?"

"She's pregnant!"

She's... I turn to Becky. "What?!"

If possible, Becky's face turns even redder. "I'm going to kill him."

"You are! Oh my God, Becky!" Kate rushes toward her best friend, pulling her in a hug. "Congratulations! How long?"

"Eighteen weeks," Becky pulls back and smooths her hand over her shirt, revealing a small bump. "It wasn't that we didn't want to tell you guys, we just wanted to make sure that everything was okay. We were actually planning to invite everybody over once we were moved in to share the news, but then Miguel had to go and ruin it with his constant worrying!"

"He's just being overprotective." Kate waves her off. "You better get used to it; it only gets worse from here on out."

Becky turns from Kate to me. "You guys aren't angry at me?"

"Of course not!" I go to her and wrap my arms around her. "This is amazing news, Becky. I'm so happy for you. After everything you've been through, you guys deserve this. When did you find out?"

A relieved smile spreads over her lips. "After the Super Bowl." She turns to Kate. "You remember how we were talking about Kaylee and how you got a go ahead from your doctor and all? Well, that's when it clicked that I hadn't had my period in a while, and when I told Miguel he just freaked."

Becky's comment has me pausing.

Because when was the last time I had my period?

My period was usually all over the place. Sometimes, a few days early; other months, a few days late. It was unpredictable, to say the least, but it always came.

Not last month, though.

I frantically search my mind for the last time I had to buy tampons. Or hell, the last time I had cramps. My cramps were so strong some days that I could barely function, and oftentimes, if I didn't take some pain reliever, I ended up spending that first day in bed.

Kate and Becky are still talking, their voices a distant buzz in my mind. I turn my back to them, trying to focus.

I remember having to leave school early in late February because my period snuck up on me, and I was in so much pain I could barely think. That was shortly before Grams...

I shake my head. *I was not going there.*

But if that was the last time I had cramps, that would mean I didn't have my period for two months.

No. I lift my shaky hand, running it through my hair. *That couldn't be right. Because if I didn't have my period for the last two months, that would mean that...*

"Anyway, he all but dragged me into the store, and we bought the pregnancy test. How somebody hadn't seen us, I'll never understand, but here we are. Then the next morning I thought it was all just a dream, so I sent him to the next town over to buy a few more tests just to make sure I was actually pregnant." Becky shakes her head, a soft smile playing on her mouth. "After I took the third one, he confiscated the rest of them away from me so I wouldn't get tempted to do it again. But the whole situation just felt surreal and..."

"Do you have any of those left?"

Both women turn toward me, matching confused expressions on their faces at my interruption.

"Yeah." Becky's brows pull together. "They're up in the bathroom. I remember putting them under the sink last ni—"

I spin on my heels, not waiting for her to finish.

This isn't real.

It can't be real.

"Sav?"

Taking two steps at a time, I climb to the second floor and start pulling the door open until I find Rebecca's bedroom. I'm loudly panting as I cross the space. Once I'm in the bathroom, I crouch down and yank open the cabinet under the sink, and sure enough, just like Becky said, a stack of five pregnancy tests is sitting there.

My throat bobs as I swallow.

Slowly, I grab one box in my hand and get to my feet. My gaze meets my frantic reflection in the mirror. I look like a madwoman—hair wild, face pale, pupils dilated.

This is all just in my head, right?

It had to be.

I was just late.

That's all.

It wouldn't be the first or the last time it happened.

It was just stress.

There is no way I could be pregnant.

Those stormy eyes boring into mine flash in my mind, reminding me of that night.

We used a condom, right?

Everything was blurry, but we had to have used it.

I couldn't use hormonal birth control, so I always made sure the guy wore a condom.

My grip on the box tightens, crumpling the paper.

Don't be a ninny, Sav. It's just a plastic stick.

A plastic stick that can change my whole life.

But I couldn't not know.

I rip into the box with shaky hands. It takes me a couple of tries before I manage to open it, and the pregnancy test falls into the sink. Taking it in my hands, I flip it from one side to the other until I figure out what to do.

Letting out a shaky breath, I squeeze the plastic stick and go to the toilet.

There is a loud knock on the door. "Sav?"

Becky.

Doing my best to tune my friend out, I concentrate on the task at hand. It seems like it takes forever before I finally manage to pee. Closing the lid, I place the test on the counter and wash up. That damn thing sitting next to me like a ticking time bomb.

"Savannah!" More knocking. "What the hell? What's going on? Are you okay?"

My time was running out. Sliding my fingers through my hair, I force myself to look at the stick.

"Becky, maybe she needs a moment," Kate chastises.

"She had her moment." The door handle rustles as somebody, Becky probably, bangs against it. "If you don't open this door immediately, I'm going to knock the..."

The door bursts open, and Rebecca stumbles into the bathroom, clearly startled by the whole ordeal.

Hazel eyes find mine, assessing me. "What are you doing? You just stormed out—"

Her gaze falls to the counter.

On the test sitting there.

The big, fat plus sign shines brightly, although it's barely been a minute since I took it, if that.

Rebecca's mouth falls open as she stares at it before her head shoots up. "That's not mine."

"N-no."

"You?"

I shrug helplessly, still unable to wrap my head around it.

"What's going o—" Kate peeks over Rebecca's shoulder, looking around the room, until she, too, spots the test. "*Oh!*"

"B-but... how? When?" Becky stutters, her eyes growing wide. "Please don't tell me it's with that douchebag of your ex. You cannot possibly be linked to that tool for the rest of your life."

"No." I shake my head adamantly. "You have to have sex in order to end up pregnant."

"Well, that test clearly states you had sex!" Rebecca snorts.

There is no judgment in her voice, only pure curiosity. Still, I feel my cheeks heat at the accusation.

"Not with Mark. He..." My throat bobs as I swallow. "It's not Mark's."

I watch as Becky blinks a few times as she processes my words. "Not— What?!"

I wince softly.

If this is how she reacted when she found out, what will other people say? My throat burns just thinking about it.

My family's been the talk of the town one too many times in the past. But it's not like I can keep this hidden forever. People will find out, and there will be gossip. This is Bluebonnet Creek, Texas, after all. There were some lovely people living here, but this was a small town and being pregnant and single wasn't common. There would be questions and dirty looks.

Like mother, like daughter, the little voice at the back of my head taunts.

My vision turns blurry as my stomach rolls, and I run toward the toilet, dry heaving.

"*Shit,*" Becky curses as I fall to my knees and start throwing up, my loud retching filling the room.

This can't be happening. It just can't.

I grip the toilet seat as I throw up, my stomach convulsing in pain, my throat burning.

What the hell have I done?

I squeeze my eyes shut as I fight the retching, and I can feel tears fall down my cheeks.

Pregnant.

I'm pregnant.

My hair is pulled back, and something cold touches my neck, making me shudder as a hand soothes up and down my back. Becky's gentle voice registers in my mind. "It's going to be okay."

But it won't.

You think you're so much better than me, Savvy? You just wait and see. The apple doesn't fall far from the tree.

The hateful words from the past ring in my head—the words I thought I had forgotten in the last fifteen years, but, apparently, I was wrong.

I shake my head, pushing them back into the box and lock them inside.

I was nothing—*nothing*—like her.

I never would be.

We stay like that until my stomach is empty, and I'm drained, physically and emotionally. Kate hands me a new towel, and I wipe at my sweaty face.

"Are you okay?" Becky asks, brushing a damp strand out of my face.

I shake my head silently.

Becky and Kate exchange a look before my best friend asks gently, "Who's your baby's father, Sav?"

Rough fingertips skimming my skin.

A hard body pressed into mine.

A heated look holding me hostage as that low growl sent a course of electricity running all the way to my core.

Eyes on me, Blondie.

Just remembering it sends a shudder through me. Some days, I still dreamed of him. Of the way he held me as we slept together. I knew I should have left as soon as the deed was done, but it was too tempting to stay, to get lost in his embrace and forget all of my insecurities and worries. *He* was too tempting.

"I..." My tongue darts out, sliding over my lower lip. "I don't know."

Becky's brows furrow. "What do you mean, you don't know?"

"Exactly what I said."

I was pregnant, and I had no idea who my baby's daddy was.

"It was a hookup. I stopped at this hotel bar after I found Mark, well..." I wave my hand, not in the mood to bring him up again, especially not considering the murderous look in my best friend's eyes. Becky never liked my ex, and even less after I told her what happened when I went to visit him in Houston. "Anyway. This guy was sitting next to me, we started talking and one thing led to another and..."

"You didn't catch his name?"

"I didn't want to know his name," I correct, letting my hand drop. The motion knocks over the test, it falls down face first, the plus sign laughing at me. "It was supposed to be one night."

Only now, it wasn't. Not any longer.

Why is this happening to me?

"Hey." Rebecca's arms wrap around me, pulling me into a hug. "It's going to be okay. You're not alone in this; you have us."

"She's right," Kate chimes in. She joins us, her hand landing on my forearm. "We've gotcha. Anything you need. We'll help you."

"Thanks, girls. I really appreciate that."

Becky pulls back, nibbling at her lower lip before asking tentatively, "Do you have any idea what you wanna do?"

My hand slides down to my stomach, and I swear I can feel a flutter inside my belly. Rationally, I knew it was way too soon for the baby to move, but the idea gave me comfort.

A baby.

My baby.

Something of my own. Something I wanted so desperately my whole life, but never dared to hope for. Somebody to call mine.

I had it. For a little while, it was Grams and me. Our own little family.

Losing her, the only person who truly loved me, wrecked me to my core.

Could she see it wherever she was right now? Did she realize that she left me all alone, and this was some kind of sign?

Emotions swell inside of me at the thought of Grams. My eyes burn, my throat grows tight. What would she say to this whole thing? Would she be disappointed in me?

As soon as the thought crosses my mind, I push it back.

No, not Grams. She would have my back.

"I think..." I start, but my voice comes out groggy, so I clear my throat before trying again. "I wanna keep it."

Chapter 3

BLAKE

August

The flicker of blonde shines in the sunlight.

I narrow my eyes as I take in the woman, my heartbeat rising as recognition sets in. "Blondie?"

She turns around, eyes the color of the summer sky widening in surprise at being caught sneaking out.

Before I can think twice about it, my fingers wrap around her wrist and tug her to me. "Where do you think you're going?"

"Home," *she whispers, her teeth sinking into her lower lip.*

My gaze falls to her mouth, wishing I could have a little taste. What would she do if I leaned in and kissed her? Would she pull me in or push me away?

I'm seriously contemplating testing my theory, but she takes a step back. "You knew the rules."

One night. No names. No kissing.

Yes, I knew the fucking rules, and I cursed myself for agreeing to them in the first place. We weren't some stupid kids playing games.

"Fuck the rules!" I yell, reaching for her, but it's too late. She's already gone.

I sit upright, my heart hammering against my rib cage as I scan the bare room—*my new bedroom*. I run my palm over my face and rub at the stubble covering my jaw when the alarm clock catches my attention.

7:15 a.m.

"*Fuck.*"

Pushing back the covers, I jump out of bed and make my way down the quiet hallway.

All summer long, Levi's been waking up at the crack of dawn, along with me, but the day school starts, of course, he has to sleep in.

Slipping into his room, I go straight to the bed. The covers are hanging off the mattress, and one of his arms is tossed over his head, his mouth open as he breathes.

"Levi, buddy." I give him a gentle shake. "Time to wake up."

His eyelids flutter open, sleepiness still clinging to his gray irises. "Dad?" he croaks out, rubbing at his face. "What time is it?"

"Late. I need you to put some clothes on, and we have to get to school."

Levi groans. "Don't wanna."

His protest has me chuckling. "I'm afraid school's not optional. C'mon." I help him sit upright and grab his clothes from the chair where I put them last night. Thank God for that. "Here. I'm going to wake up your brother while you dress."

Levi grumbles something but starts to change, so I call that a win while I go to the other side of the hallway and knock on the door before peeking into Daniel's room. "Daniel, time to wake up. We're already late."

My oldest grumbles loudly in protest and tugs the covers over his head. "I'm not going."

"Yes, you are. You have five minutes to get up; don't make me drag you out."

I wait for a heartbeat, but there is no answer.

"Five minutes," I repeat as I exit the room, leaving the door open.

I go back to my bedroom and quickly put on some clothes. Going to the bathroom, I splash some water on my face and brush my teeth. When I get out, I can hear both kids moving around, so I make my way downstairs and grab them each a protein bar, just as there are footsteps coming down the stairs.

Thank fuck.

"C'mon, boys, we really have to hurry up," I call out as I go toward the door.

Not like that was helping anything.

We were late.

And it was only the first day of school.

"I'm seriously killing this single dad thing," I mutter to myself as I watch Levi rush down the stairs, his backpack bouncing on his shoulders.

I couldn't believe that he was already starting school.

Seriously, where did the time fly? It feels like only yesterday I brought him home from the hospital.

"Put your shoes on," I say gently, my gaze darting up the stairs. "Where is your brother?"

"In his room."

"Dan—" I start to yell when my *sixteen*-year-old appears at the top of the stairs, a scowl that's become a permanent feature between his brows greeting me.

"I'm here," he grumbles. "You don't have to yell."

"I need to yell because we have to get on the road. We're late."

But my son likes to test my patience these days because he just sticks his hands in the pocket of his black hoodie. Why did he think wearing a hoodie in August in Texas was a good idea, I'll never understand. Then again, if he wanted to sweat his ass off, who was I to object? There were many more important things to fight about, and this wasn't making the list.

"Well, if we just stayed in Austin and not moved to the middle of nowhere, I could have taken a bus," he mutters as he descends the stairs, stopping so we're eye to eye. "Or you know, if you actually bought me a car, I could use that license I have and drive myself to school."

Keep your cool, I coach myself, sucking in a long breath. *He just wants to rile you up. There is no sense in fighting with him.*

"Well, we live in Bluebonnet now, which means you have to drive. And having a car is a responsibility." I quirk my brow at him. "Something you've shown me time and again, in this past year, you're not ready for. Once you start acting maturely, we can reopen the topic of you getting that car."

Daniel snorts. "Sure, *Dad*."

Don't let him provoke you.

I press my lips in a tight line as I watch him put on his shoes, and then finally, *finally*, we're out of the house.

Locking the door behind me, I run my hand over my face as I watch my sons climb into my truck.

It's fine. I can do this. I can totally do this.

Since Bluebonnet Creek is a minuscule town, there is only one school that's divided by different grades, something that goes in my favor right about now.

"Don't cause any trouble," I glance toward Daniel as I pull in front of the high school, but he's too busy typing away on his phone to pay me any attention. "Dan—"

"Yeah." He locks his phone and opens the door. "Whatever."

"I'll see you"—he slips out and shuts the door behind himself—"later."

Running my fingers through my hair, I watch Daniel walk into the school, not once looking back. Letting my hand drop, I put my truck into drive and make my way to the parking lot.

Since we are running seriously late, I walk Levi into school. The security guard takes my information and gives me instructions on how to get to Levi's classroom. With a nod in thanks, I place my hand on his back and urge him forward.

"What if they don't like me?" Levi asks, his voice so soft it's barely audible.

I look down to find the first traces of uncertainty written on his face.

Shit.

Screw being late; making sure my son was okay will always be the most important thing. I place my hand on his shoulder and crouch down so we're on the same level. Levi bites the inside of his cheek and glances down at his feet.

Am I doing the right thing?

The question that's been haunting me for the last few months comes back to the forefront of my mind.

While Daniel started to talk back and lash out after his mom left, Levi did the complete opposite. He closed off, became more uncertain, and a little bit clingy when it came to me. It was as if he thought that I would do the same thing. I figured retiring and moving to a new place—a smaller, more family-oriented place—would be the solution, but what if I was wrong? What if this move ends up bringing more anxiety to my kids?

Fuck, this single-parent thing is hard.

"Levi, look at me," I say gently. Pushing back my own

insecurities, I wait for him to lift his head and face me. "Where is this coming from?"

"I don't know anybody. What if they don't like me?"

"It's the first day. First grade. Nobody knows anybody." This was a stretch considering the size of this town, but what was a little white lie if it was going to make him feel better? "Besides, you're a cool kid. They'd be silly not to like you. And you'll see Gage later at recess. You liked playing with Gage, right?"

Miguel and his brother Aaron helped me move some furniture this past weekend, while Mrs. Fernandez and Rebecca watched the kids. Miguel's fiancée was heavily pregnant and due in a few weeks, and Miguel was spending more time here than in Austin these days, not wanting to risk a chance of her going into labor without him there.

"I did." Levi nods. "Why can't I be in class with him?"

I chuckle softly. "Because he's a year older than you, buddy."

"Well, I wanna be older." Levi purses his lips, which only makes me laugh harder. "Then I could be in the same class with Gage."

"And just this morning you were saying you don't want to go to school." I shake my head. "C'mon, let's get you to class." Pushing upright, I slide my hand over his back, giving him a reassuring rub as we continue walking down the hallway. "I've heard you have a really nice teacher. Her name is Miss Parker, and apparently, she's the best in the whole town."

Levi looks up at me. "Is she?"

"That's what the lady at the office said."

"Is she old? Mrs. Andrews was old, and she was mean."

Mrs. Andrews was his kindergarten teacher last year, and to say he didn't like her would be an understatement.

"I don't know, buddy. I didn't get a chance to meet Miss

Parker. But if people say she's the best, I would hope there is a reason for it, right?"

"I guess so."

"How about this? You be brave and go in there, and when I pick you up from school later today, we'll go to Scoops for ice cream. What do you say? Do we have a deal?"

He tilts his head back, his eyes lighting up. "For real? We can go and get ice cream?"

The way he asks, the clear surprise and sheer joy at the idea, has my chest tightening. But why wouldn't he be surprised? I couldn't remember when the last time was I took him to get ice cream or anything really. While I tried to spend as much time as possible with my kids, things came up more often than I'd like to admit. Practice would run late, one of my teammates would ask me for help with one thing or another, or I had to do PR or an interview or *something*. There was always something, and my kids were the ones who had to deal with canceled plans and broken promises.

This is why you're here. So you can focus on them. So you can have more moments like this.

"For real," I reassure him, ruffling his unruly hair.

He pumps his little hand. "Yes! I can't wait."

Chuckling, I lift my hand and knock on the door. Turning the doorknob, I urge Levi in front of me.

"Let's g—" My voice trails off as I look up, and my eyes land on the blonde woman in front of me.

She turns toward the door, her attention on my son as she smiles brightly at him. "Well, hello there. It's so ni—"

"Blondie."

She glances up, her eyes widening when they land on mine.

Holy shit, it really is her.

All the air is knocked out of my lungs as I stare at eyes as bright as the sky on a sunny day. The same eyes that were haunting my dreams even though I'd only seen them once before—months ago—when we shared that one passionate night that most days seemed more like a mirage than reality.

It was crazy. I was thirty-five, recently divorced, and a single dad. Hookup days were long behind me, but damn, something about that woman drew me to her from the very first moment I laid my eyes on her.

She was gorgeous, but that wasn't it. I've met my fair share of gorgeous women over the years. I was married to one, and never before have I been as captivated as I was when I saw Blondie.

And then, as if she wasn't tempting enough, she threw me a challenge.

One night. No names. No kissing.

I loved and despised the idea. I didn't have time for dating, not with two kids who needed me. Not when I just bought a house in a small town and prepared to uproot their lives. Did I even know *how* to date? It's been ages since I did it. Besides, who even dates at thirty-five? But there was something about this woman that drew me to her. It was the combination of innocence and allure around her, the sorrow I could see shining in her irises, and the spunky attitude that slipped out every once in a while. She was a walking, talking contradiction, and I couldn't get enough of her.

So I agreed.

I had her, but the next morning, when I woke up, my bed was empty. The only sign that she was even there was her sweet scent lingering on my bedsheets.

But now she was here.

Not just that, but she was my son's teacher?

My heart is beating wildly inside my rib cage as I stand still in the doorway, too afraid to even blink because what if I do, and she disappears?

Blondie.

My mystery girl.

Here.

In Bluebonnet Creek, Texas.

What were the odds?

I take her in slowly.

That gorgeous face I couldn't get out of my head was completely drained of color.

Those full breasts peeking delicately from the cleavage of her white and blue floral dress rising and falling rapidly.

The curve of her waist.

The small bump.

Her hand slides to her middle as if she wants to hide it from me.

My stomach sinks as my brain slowly processes every little detail, and my whole world tilts on its axis.

Fuck my life.

My head shoots up, cold sweat washing over me as I meet those panic-filled eyes.

She's pregnant?

"What—" My voice comes out rough, but before I can ask anything, Levi tugs at my hand, demanding my attention.

I glance at my son, still too stunned to think clearly.

Blondie is here. She's here, and she's pregnant. And based on her bump, she's around four months? Maybe five. Which means...

The bile rises up my throat just when Levi whispers so loudly that the whole classroom can hear him. "She's not old!"

Fuck.

Blondie lets out a strangled sound that has me looking up. Red floods her cheeks, her teeth biting her lower lip, as she's trying to hide her smile.

No, she was most definitely not old.

I was screwed.

Completely and utterly screwed.

Her gaze meets mine for a moment before she shifts her attention to my son. "And you must be Levi, right?"

"Yes." Levi eyes her carefully and tilts his head to the side, a lock of his hair falling into his eyes. "And you're Miss Parker?"

He tries to blow it out of the way, but it's useless. I should have probably found time to take him to the hairdresser, but between all the other things and the move, I completely spaced out. Just another reason why I was failing at this whole single dad thing.

"That's correct. Why do—"

"You look pretty," Levi says, flashing her a toothless grin.

She looks stunned for a moment. If the situation were different, I might be embarrassed, but this was the woman I couldn't take my eyes off of since the first moment I entered the room that night. Levi was most definitely his father's son in that regard.

"Well, thank you." She tucks a strand of her hair behind her ear. "Why don't you go and take your seat, Levi? It's the one in the last row."

Levi nods once and hurries to his seat without a backward glance. At least he seemed content.

Blondie straightens to her full height, which is a good foot shorter than my six-five, her hand sliding to the underside of her belly.

"Blondie..."

Her head whips in my direction as if she just realized I'm still here.

I rub my hand over my jaw as I try to come up with the right thing to say, but there is just too much that's swirling inside of my head. So many questions I want to ask her, starting with the most important one—whose baby is she carrying?

"*Miss Parker*," she says sternly, crossing her arms over her chest.

The motion should be defensive, but it only presses her tits closer, giving me a better look at her cleavage. They were nice before, but pregnancy only made them more alluring.

Shit, get a grip, dude. You're in a classroom full of children, for fuck's sake.

"We have to talk."

Her fingers grip her arms so tight her knuckles turn white, but her voice is steady as she says, "If there is anything you want to discuss you can ask for a parent-teacher conference."

I open my mouth to protest, but she stops me. "I have a class to get to. And please, try not to be late next time, Mr. Walker."

Class, right.

I move closer. Her eyes widen, but she doesn't back away.

"This isn't done, *Miss Parker*. Not in the least," I whisper so only she can hear me, my voice saccharine sweet. "We'll continue this conversation later." My eyes skim over her body one last time, pausing on her stomach before I meet her gaze. "It seems we have a lot to discuss."

Her throat bobs as she swallows, but she doesn't try to deny it.

Yeah, I didn't think so.

Waving at Levi, I turn on my heels and get the hell out.

With each step I take, one thought keeps echoing in my mind.

Blondie—*my Blondie*—is here.

And she is pregnant.

How the fuck did that happen?

The old-fashioned way, that's how.

I try to remember that night. Did we use protection? I thought we did, but then again, her current state would suggest otherwise. And before her, it had been a while since I used condoms. A while since I had sex, really.

Maybe it's not even yours, the little voice at the back of my head whispers. *Maybe she got back with her ex. Or maybe she found somebody else.*

Then why would she react this way at seeing me?

And that wasn't just a surprise at running into somebody you hadn't expected or didn't want to see again, no there was a trace of fear shining in those blue depths too. The protective way that she hugged her bump.

Why would she do that if the baby wasn't mine? It made no sense whatsoever.

I run my hand over my face. I could feel the soft throbbing building behind my temples as my mind still tried to process what had just happened.

With one last glance at school, I put my car in reverse and head out of the parking lot.

I would get to the bottom of this.

She was working here, it's not like she could just up and leave.

"I didn't expect to see you here," Aaron Fernandez says in the way of greeting when I get out of my truck. A man our age who's standing next to him says something, and Aaron nods, patting him on the back before he starts walking toward me. "What brings you here, Walker? Don't tell me you're already bored of retirement and are looking for a job."

I let out a snort. "Highly unlikely."

I was good at a lot of things, but I was no rancher.

"Shame." Silent amusement dances in my friend's gaze, but

his face remains serious. "I think it would be entertaining to see you try to get your ass on a horse."

"Entertaining for you, maybe." I look around the clearing noticing a few ranch hands mingling around. I didn't think this through very well. "You have a few minutes for me?"

Some days it was hard to remember that other people had jobs and obligations while I was retired at the ripe age of thirty-five and had no freaking idea what to do with my life.

"Sure thing." He tilts his head toward the barn. "Let's go inside."

Not waiting for an answer, he starts walking toward the building, and I follow after him to the small office attached to the barn.

While I might have been friends with Miguel first, since we played two seasons together in the NFL, Aaron and I clicked the moment we met last year when Miguel invited the boys and me to spend Thanksgiving with his family. I'm not sure if it was the fact that we were closer in age or that we were both single dads. Either way, I was glad that I had somebody I could talk to and who could understand things I was dealing with.

Not that Aaron would ever get a girl he barely knew pregnant. No, he was too serious, too stoic, too responsible for something like that. Unlike me.

"Want a drink?" Aaron crouches in front of the little fridge that's sitting in the corner of the room. "I have water, Coke..."

"Do you have something stronger?"

Aaron's brows shoot up, but he doesn't say anything as he closes the fridge and walks to the shelf. Turning two glasses around, he grabs one of the bottles standing there. Jack. The amber liquid gleams in the sun that peeks through the window, and the memories of that night emerge in my head.

The way those lush honey curls swayed as Blondie tilted her

head back to down her drink. The smell of Jack on her breath as we were mere inches apart.

One night. No names. No kissing.

A glass *clinks* against the desk when Aaron places it in front of me, snapping me out of my thoughts. I wrap my fingers around it and down it in one go, letting the alcohol burn on its way down to my stomach.

"Will you finally tell me what happened that drew you to drink before noon?" Aaron asks as he slides into the chair opposite me.

"What do you know about Miss Parker?"

Fuck, I still don't know her name.

Aaron's brows furrow in confusion. "Miss Parker? You mean Savannah Parker?"

"Savannah Parker," I whisper, testing the sound of it on my tongue. My fingers curl around the glass as her name echoes in my head, in tune with the wild beat of my heart.

Sa-va-nnah. Sa-va-nnah. Sa-va-nnah.

"Is she Levi's teacher?"

"Yes. What do you know about her?"

Aaron shrugs. "Not much. She teaches first grade. Gage was in her class last year, and he liked her. She also runs a reading group for kids at Reading Nook. Cheryl usually takes —" Aaron's words trail off. He runs his hand through his hair, a dark expression passing over his face. "She used to take Gage there."

I feel a pang of guilt at stirring the painful memories. Aaron's wife died last year in a car accident. I didn't know the details, but Miguel said that Aaron hasn't been the same ever since.

While taking a pull of his drink, Aaron's dark eyes fix on mine. "Why are you asking about Savannah? Did something happen today?"

"No, nothing happened, I just..." I rub my hand over my jaw. "Do you know if she's seeing anybody?"

"If you wanted to get some town gossip, you should have gone to the café or something." If possible, that scowl deepens even more. "But seriously, what's with the twenty questions about Savannah Parker?"

I run my fingers through my hair, letting out a long breath. "You remember when I came here back in March?"

Aaron nods. "What about it?"

"Well after I left the ranch, I didn't go home."

My friend's brows pull together. "You didn't?"

I shake my head, the memories of that day coming back. "I got on the road and started toward Austin, but everything that had been going on got the better of me, so I decided to make a pit stop. I just needed a moment to breathe, and since I knew Mrs. Maxwell would stay the night with the boys... Anyway, that's where I met her."

The image of Blondie—Savannah—from that day flashes in my mind.

So beautiful she took my breath away.

"She was..." I shake my head. The sadness in her eyes that was erased with one comment from me, bringing out that fiery temper she'd been leashing in tightly. "Unlike any other woman I'd ever met. Not that I've met many women since I got married, but there was just something about her that drew me in. So we chatted and had a few drinks. When the bartender told us he was closing, I invited her to my room, and well..." I shrug, letting my hand drop. "She didn't want to exchange names, and when I woke up, she was no longer there." My throat bobs. "Until I saw her again today when I dropped Levi at school."

"Damn, man." Aaron shakes his head. "That's so messed..." His voice trails off as he narrows his eyes at me. "Wait, when did you say you guys hooked up?"

"End of March."

"March," he whispers, and I watch his face intently. "Because I saw her last week at the store and..." His eyes widen, mouth falling open. "She's pregnant. That's why you've been asking all these questions. She's pregnant, and you think..."

"It could be mine," I finish, some of the weight falling off my chest.

So I wasn't completely crazy to think this could be my baby after all.

"*Damn.*" Aaron grabs the bottle of Jack and pours us each a new drink, taking a long pull from his glass. "Did she tell you that?"

I shake my head. "No. I wanted to talk, but there was a classroom full of kids there, including Levi, so I left."

Aaron nods. "What are you going to do about it?"

"Try to talk to her. See what she has to say."

"And if the kid is yours?"

My mouth goes dry at his question, my stomach tightening with nerves.

It felt like I was thrown back in time, and I was that eighteen-year-old kid again sitting in the bathroom with my girlfriend watching the big, fat plus sign sealing my fate.

Only I wasn't that eighteen-year-old kid. Not any longer. And Savannah was not Reina. I don't know how I knew it, but I was sure of that one thing.

"Then I'll do everything in my power to make this right."

I meet Aaron's grim face.

"I guess now is as good a time as any..."

A chill goes down my spine. "What?"

"Savannah is Becky's friend."

Becky's...

"As in Miguel's Becky?"

"The very one."

My heart does a little jump inside my chest. "You're shitting me."

"I'm afraid not."

Becky's friend.

Savannah was...

"Fuck my life." I run my hand over my face. "Miguel wasn't joking when he said this town is too fucking small."

Aaron just silently lifts his glass in the air. "Welcome to Bluebonnet Creek, my friend."

Chapter 4

SAVANNAH

Blake Walker.

That was his name.

Blake Walker.

The father of my unborn child.

My heart is thundering inside my chest as I stare at the screen, still trying to wrap my head around it.

It took everything in me to gather my wits and focus on my job once he left the classroom. I'm still not sure how I managed to do it. The whole morning was a blur of events as I was counting down the minutes until I could get the kids off to the cafeteria for lunch and get a few minutes to myself.

And now I had it.

After all these months, I finally had a name to put to the man who changed my life in one night.

I often thought about him since I found out I was pregnant. I even went back to that bar a few times in hopes I might run into him, but of course he never showed up. Why would he? The main reason why I agreed to our little arrangement was because I was sure he was just passing through, and I wouldn't have to see him again.

I wondered what I'd do if I knew his name.

Would I be able to find him? How would he react? Would he want the baby? Would he ask me not to have it, or would he want to be involved?

There were so many questions. So many possibilities. And only one reality.

Until today.

Until he walked into my classroom and changed everything.

With shaky hands I grab my phone and press the call button. I hold my breath as the phone rings in my ear for what seems like forever until my best friend picks up.

"Sav?" Becky asks, a trace of worry in her voice. "What's going on? Are you okay? Shouldn't you be—"

"He's here," I whisper softly.

There is a pause for a heartbeat. "He? What are you talking about? Who's here?"

"*He's* here, Becky!" I hiss, all the uncertainty and fear I've been pushing down since I saw him is bubbling to the surface, and there is no holding it back any longer. "The guy I hooked up with. He's here. In Bluebonnet Creek."

"Your baby daddy?" she yells so loudly I have to pull the phone away from my ear. "Shit! How? When? Where? I don't understand. Didn't you say that he was just some random guy you met at a bar?"

"That's what I thought, but he's here. As in he *lives* here." My fingers curl around the phone to the point of pain as the panic rises inside my chest. "What the hell should I do, Becky? What if he thinks I did it on purpose? What if he thinks I tricked him in some way? What if he doesn't want my child? But what if he does? Or worse, what if he tries to take my baby from me? He can't do that, right?"

The words spill out of me in a rush, and with each question I can feel my throat constrict tighter, making it hard to breathe, until the only thing I can hear is the sound of my thundering heart echoing in my eardrums.

"Sav? Take a deep breath for me, okay? You're having a panic attack."

My eyes water as I suck in a gulp full of air.

"I d-don't know wh-what to d-do," I wheeze out.

"Breathe. I just need you to breathe. This isn't good for the baby."

I nod, forcing myself to slowly let the air out of my lungs, and breathe in once again, slower this time.

In and out.

In and out.

Slowly.

Steadily.

"I don't know what to do, Becky," I say softly, once I've regained some of my composure.

"We'll figure it out. Where did you see him?"

"School." I run my shaky fingers through my hair. "He dropped off his kid for school, and, well..."

My phone starts buzzing with an incoming call. I pull it away and check the screen.

Mr. Miles.

"Shit, I'm sorry. I have to take this. I'll call you later."

"Sav, you can't leave—"

"I'm sorry, but I really have to answer this. There was water in my bathroom once again this morning. I'll call you later, bye!"

I don't give her a chance to protest before I disconnect the call and answer my phone. "Hi, Mr. Miles, did you get a chance to stop by my place and take a look at that leak?"

"Hey, Savannah," Mr. Miles says, his gruff voice making the hair on my nape rise. "Can you come to the cottage?"

"I— What happened?" I ask, my fingers gripping the phone tighter.

"You were right about the pipe. It must have burst completely since you left because the whole cottage is flooded."

The whole cottage...

"Flooded?" I shake my head. "No. That's impossible. There was only a small puddle when I left."

My home.

"I'm so sorry, Savannah. We'll get it fixed, but the damage..." He lets out a long sigh. "Can you leave work early? Grab your stuff."

Grab my stuff. Because my home is flooded.

Maybe he's exaggerating? Maybe it isn't that bad, and it can be fixed. It's only been a few hours since I left.

"I... Y-yeah. I'll be there."

Hanging up the phone, I quickly grab my stuff and go to the admin office to tell them I need to leave early. Thankfully, they're really understanding and manage to find a substitute teacher quickly, so I leave before lunch is done.

My fingers are gripping the steering wheel, my knuckles completely drained of color. I try to keep to the speed limit as I drive back home. My mind is reeling with all the possible scenarios, each one worse than the last, making the knot in my throat grow tighter.

The moment I take a turn onto my street, my gaze snaps to my house. There are a few cars parked in front of it, so I pull up to the curb, quickly unbuckle my seat belt, and get out just as Mr. Miles steps out on the porch with another man.

I hurry toward them. Mr. Miles looks up when I climb the steps and offers me a sad smile.

"I got here as soon as I could," I say in a way of greeting.

"I'm so sorry this happened, Savannah. We'll help you gather your things."

My throat bobs as I try to swallow the lump down. "It can't be that bad?"

"I'm afraid so. George went to look at the bathroom and determined the pipes were old and rusted. The whole thing needs to be replaced, along with the floors, since they were damaged from the water. While that happens, you can't be here."

He wants me to leave?

"How long will that take?" I run my shaky fingers through my hair, feeling completely lost. "Where should I go in the meantime?"

I couldn't just pick up my things and leave the place that's been my home.

There is no missing the pity in Mr. Miles' eyes. "It'll probably be a few months. Based on the first look, they'll need to replace the whole piping system in the house before we can fix the damage to the floors and walls. And that takes time and money."

"B-but..."

He couldn't be serious.

But he was. I could see it on his face. There was no changing this.

Mr. Miles places his hand on my shoulder and gives me a soft rub. "Did you sell your grandmother's house?"

"I..." I shake my head. "No."

"Then, that'd be a perfect solution. I always wondered why you didn't ask to move out after Poppy died. God rest her soul."

That knot is back in my throat, tighter than ever.

There was a reason for my decision, but he didn't need to know that. Nobody did.

"C'mon"—he places his hand on my back and gives me a fatherly pat—"let's get your things."

I let him lead me into the place that was my home. They weren't joking about the damage to the cottage. The place is wrecked. There is water all the way to my ankles, and you can see the hardwood floors already lifting at certain parts.

I direct Mr. Miles to the kitchen to grab some of the stuff I have there, while I make my way to the bedroom, which looks the worst since it's the closest to the bathroom. The water also entered my closet, destroying some of the stuff I had stashed in boxes on the floor. Thankfully, most of it is salvageable, so I work quickly to pack everything.

It takes us a good hour and a few trips to my car before it's full.

"That's it." Mr. Miles closes the trunk and dusts off his hands.

All my stuff—my whole life—could fit in one car.

I don't know why, but that realization makes me sad.

"It's going to be okay." Mr. Miles shoots me a soft smile. "I'll keep you updated on the repairs, but if you'd rather stay at your grandma's house permanently, let me know."

Did I have a choice?

God only knew how long the repairs would last. It could be months. And I had a baby on the way. A baby that would be here soon and needed a place to call home.

The day I found out I was pregnant I promised myself I'd do better. That I would make sure my baby had everything I didn't, and that started with a home. I couldn't go breaking my promises before he or she was even here.

As the reality of the situation dawns on me, the anxiety starts building inside my chest. My heart races faster, the furious thumping echoing in my eardrums as my vision turns blurry, and I sway on my feet.

"Savannah, are you okay?"

I blink a few times, clearing my sight, and nod. "Fine. It's just been a long day."

The older man gives me a soft smile. "Try to get some rest. It's not good that you're working so hard when you're pregnant."

I let out a humorless chuckle. As if I had a choice.

"I'll be fine. Don't worry, but I think I won't be coming back." My hand settles on my stomach as I look over his shoulder at the house that was my home for the last few years, giving it one final glance. "This baby is coming soon, and I have to prepare everything. Moving back doesn't make any sense."

Mr. Miles nods. "I would imagine so." He lets out a sigh. "It'll be hard to find a tenant as good as you. I'll call you the next time I'm here so I can return your deposit since none of this was your fault."

"Thank you. I really appreciate it."

And I did. Baby stuff was expensive, and I've been trying to save as much as possible to order what I'll need. I guess it was a good thing that I still haven't bought anything since it would have probably been destroyed today. A small blessing really.

With a promise to talk soon, I slide in my car and suck in a long breath before grabbing my water bottle and taking a long pull. Only when I feel slightly calmer, do I start my car.

The drive to my grandmother's place is short. It was one of the plus sides when I originally rented it. Grams was getting up in age, and I wanted to be close by so I could get to her quickly if she needed me. Not that she appreciated it. That woman was stubborn as hell.

The corner of my mouth tips upward, and a jab of pain pierces through my chest. It was bittersweet thinking about her. Grams was the woman who raised me. My only family. It felt like there was a gaping hole inside my chest the day she died, and nothing could fill it.

That was the reason why I hadn't stepped foot into her house since she died. It just hurt too much.

But now I don't have a choice.

Bluebonnet Creek was a small town, and the housing market was even smaller. Besides, I didn't have money to spare. Not with the baby on the way.

My fingers tighten around the steering wheel, and I suck in a sharp breath, my old silver Volvo slowly coming to a stop.

"You can do this, Sav," I say to myself as I kill the engine. Willing my fingers to open the door, I place one foot in front of the other as I get out of the car and look at the house.

The two-story craftsman style house that's been my home for the better part of my life has definitely seen better days. I'm not sure if it was money, or the fact that Grams was set in her ways, probably a little bit of both, but even to an untrained eye, I could see all the things that needed fixing.

The paint was worn off, and the shutters were rusty. The flowers my grandmother loved so much have all dried out, and I was pretty sure the whole front porch would need replacing.

Just thinking about all of the expenses made me sweat.

This was so not in my budget.

But I didn't have a choice, did I?

It was either this or sleeping in the car.

There is a soft flutter in my belly. I drop my hand against my stomach, rubbing at the place where I could feel that flutter. Not a kick, not yet, but the pregnancy book I was reading said that it could be the baby moving. Or gas.

"I'll make this right, Munchkin," I whisper to the baby. "I mean if all these people on the internet can renovate a house on their own, why couldn't we? You *will* have a home to go to once you're here. I promise." Taking a step toward the house, I say with more conviction, "I promise."

And it was a promise I meant to keep no matter what.

I knew all too well what it was like not to have a place to call home.

For the first eight years of my life, I moved around more

times than some people moved in their whole life. Mom would uproot and move us every few months, the change usually went hand in hand with whoever her boyfriend was at a time.

But I wasn't my mother.

I refused to be like her.

Not now, not ever.

"Miss Parker!"

The hairs at my nape prickle at attention at the sound of the familiar voice. Slowly, I turn around to find Levi Walker rushing toward me, and behind him is none other than his father.

My baby's father.

And if it's to be judged by the look he's shooting my way, he wants to murder me.

Chapter 5

BLAKE

It really is her.

I stare over the roof of my truck at the woman standing across the street, too dumbfounded to move.

What the hell is she doing here?

All that golden hair is shining under the bright sun. At some point after I left, she pulled it in a knot on top of her head, but a few strands have slipped and are now curling around her pale face. She's still dressed in that tight dress that hugs her body, accentuating every fucking curve to perfection.

When I went to pick up Levi, I was determined to talk to Savannah and get to the bottom of this, but then another woman brought the kids to the pickup line, and when I asked about *Miss Parker*, they told me she had an emergency and had to leave early.

Emergency, my ass.

She was avoiding me.

I knew it.

And I was right.

Only now she's here.

"Too fucking small."

But at least this time, living in a small town went in my

favor. Miss Parker could try to avoid me, but our paths would meet at some point.

While I'm trying to figure out my next move, Levi runs across the street, not even bothering to check if a car is coming.

"*Fuck.*"

This kid is going to be the death of me.

I rush after him as he suddenly stops in front of Savannah, and even from here, I can hear him chatting a mile a minute, something that hasn't happened in the last year. Ever since his mother left, Levi hasn't been himself. He's shyer, almost guarded in a way, with everybody, especially strangers, but apparently not Miss Parker.

"It is you, Miss Parker! I thought so when I saw your hair. Why didn't you come back to class? I didn't really like Mrs. Dawson. You'll be coming back tomorrow, right?"

Wait... what?

Savannah tucks a strand of her hair behind her ear as she warily glances toward me. "Umm... Yes, I'll be back in class tomorrow."

"Great!" Levi all but beams at her. "Everybody was worried when you didn't come to get us after lunch. We asked Mrs. Dawson, and she said that you had an emergency, and then she wanted us to write. It was boring." He tilts his head to the side. "Do you live here?"

"I—"

I come to a stop behind him, my hands falling on his shoulders. "Levi, you can't run off like that. And you shouldn't be bugging people."

"I'm not bugging. I'm talking to Miss Parker!" He rolls his eyes as if that makes it better before he turns his attention back to her. "So do you live here?"

Live here? Nobody in their sane mind would live here.

I glance over her shoulder.

The place was falling apart. I'd noticed it that day I came to check on our house, and the place had only gotten worse in the last few months. I was pretty sure that the steps leading to the front porch couldn't take the weight of a regular adult; forget about a grown-ass man.

"Yes, I do, actually."

My head whips in her direction.

She couldn't be serious.

I open my mouth, but Levi is faster. "Really? That means you're our neighbor!"

Like hell.

"Levi." I give his shoulders a squeeze. "Why don't you go into the house and grab a snack? I have to talk to Miss Parker about something."

Savannah's throat bobs as she swallows, but she doesn't try to protest.

Good.

I was getting my answers, and I was getting them now.

"But Dad..." He tries to protest, but I leave him no room for argument.

"Levi. Home. And make sure to check the road before crossing it this time around."

"Fine." He stomps his foot and glares at me before turning his attention to Savannah. "I'll see you tomorrow, Miss Parker. You promise?"

The corner of her mouth tilts upward. "I'll see you tomorrow, Levi."

With a wave goodbye, he runs back home. I keep an eye on him, only returning my attention to Savannah when I know he's safely inside our house.

Crossing my arms over my chest, I slowly turn toward the woman next to me. The little color that was left on her face disappears, and her throat visibly bobs as she swallows.

"Mr. Walker, I—"

"Blake." I take a step closer, and she has to tilt her head back to keep eye contact. "I think after everything that has happened between us, Blondie, the least you can do is call me by my name."

Her tongue darts out, sliding over her lower lip. "I don't see how that makes any difference."

"I think it makes all the difference." Another step closer. Her intoxicating scent reaches my nostrils. It's sweet and flowery with just a little bit of bite to it. It's perfect for the woman in front of me. My finger slips under her chin, and I tilt it up, tracing the outline of her mouth with my thumb. "Tell me, Savannah, is the baby you're carrying mine?"

Different emotions flicker across her face. Fear, anxiety, and finally resignation as she gives me the faintest of nods. "Yes, the baby is yours."

The weight that's been sitting on my shoulders since the moment I saw her this morning finally lifts, and it feels like I can breathe again.

Mine.

The baby is mine.

I knew it.

The moment I saw her, I knew it. I'm not sure how or why, but I knew that baby was mine. Still, hearing her say those words out loud...

"I never wanted to hide it from you," she hurries to add. "I tried to call the hotel after I found out, but they wouldn't tell me anything. I even went back to that bar in hopes of running into you, but you never showed up. If I had any info to go off of... If I just knew your name, I would have found you and told you what happened."

I slide my thumb over her lips. Savannah sucks in a sharp breath, those doe-eyes fixing on me.

"I know. I believe you."

I watch as a shudder goes through her. Her shoulders sag, and for a second, she closes her eyes, letting out a long breath.

Why the hell did we think not sharing names was a good idea? It seemed reasonable at the time to give the night a little bit of mystery and excitement, and I needed that. But what a fucking disaster it turned out to be in the end. Five months. I've lost five months with this woman.

"Why run away from school?"

Her eyes snap open, fire blazing in those blue irises. "I wasn't running away today. There really was an emergency that I had to deal with. And I'll admit, maybe a teeny-tiny part of me was relieved I didn't have to face you just yet, but I *would* have told you. That being said, I want you to know I don't expect anything from you. I don't want your money or anything like that."

"You... what?" I blink, my whole body going still. She couldn't be serious, could she?

"I would have told you. It was never my intention to keep the baby a secret from you, but since it was my decision to continue with the pregnancy, I'm ready to take one hundred percent of the responsibility. I don't want your money, and if you don't want to, you don't have to be in the baby's life. I mean it; you don't have to worry about it."

"I don't have to worry about it?" I feel like a parrot, repeating everything she says, but my brain is still trying to process the implications of what she's saying.

She thinks I will just walk away? After she told me that this baby is mine? She just expects me to turn around and leave them to fend for themselves?

"Yes, we'll be fine." She nods once, the determination written all over her face. It's as if she made her decision, and there wasn't anything swaying her mind. "I planned to raise this baby on my own anyway, so the fact that you live here doesn't have to change anything. We can both continue with our lives as we did before."

As we did...

"Are you fucking kidding me?" I grind my teeth together, and it takes everything in me to keep my cool.

Does she seriously think so little of me? Sure, we don't really know each other all that well, but damn it. Did she seriously think I would walk around this town and pretend like I didn't know her? Pretend like the kid she's carrying isn't mine? What does she think will happen if we run into each other in town or in a store? That I'd just ignore them and go on my merry way?

Hell to the no.

"No," I say softly, but it's like she doesn't hear me at all because she simply continues.

"It's honestly better this way. I think it would be—" Savannah stops mid-sentence, and I can see the moment my words register in her mind because her mouth falls open. "What did you say?"

"No."

She blinks and takes a step back, her arm sliding to her stomach. "What do you mean, 'no?'"

As if she wants to protect the baby.

Our baby.

From me.

Fuck. That.

"Just like I said, Blondie. No." I take a step closer, and she retreats until her back touches her car. I let my palms brace against the warm metal, caging her in. "There will be no continuing with our lives as usual. No fucking pretending like you're just my son's teacher, no pretending that I don't know every fucking inch of your body. This baby is as much mine as it is yours. So, no. I don't agree with this bullshit. I don't know about what kind of men you've dealt with in the past, but I'm not some asshole that walks away from his responsibilities."

Savannah flinches slightly at my words.

What the—

"Then what do you suggest?" she asks, lifting her chin up a notch, her voice strong, although I can see apprehension on her face.

I watched her a moment longer, trying to see if I'd imagined it, but she schooled her features well. Not that I'm surprised. I saw it that night we met. This woman has built walls as tight as Fort Knox around herself, but every now and then, traces of that softness hiding beneath them would show. I saw it that day, and I saw it again now. Just a glimpse, but it was there. And I wanted to see more. I wanted to get to know her better. I wanted to be there for her and for our baby.

"We should get married."

The words fall off my tongue before I can think better of them.

It's impulsive and crazy, but the moment they're out in the open, I know it's the right thing to do. The past was repeating itself, but while all I could feel back in college was immense pressure and uncertainty about marrying Reina, now things were different.

I was different.

I've come a long way from that eighteen-year-old boy from the suburbs of Baltimore. And Savannah wasn't Reina, not even close. We'd figure this out. I know we would. It might take time, and there are the boys to consider, but—

"Are you insane?" Savannah hisses, looking left and right as if she's scared somebody might have heard me.

"What? It's the perfect solution."

"Perfect solution for whom?" She shakes her head. "No. I'm not your *responsibility*, Walker."

Her palm connects to my chest, pushing me back as she grabs her suitcase and pulls it toward the house. When she gets to the steps, she grabs the handle.

"Sav—" I start to yell, just as there is a loud *crack*.

Fuck.

She stumbles, the suitcase falling from her hand as she tries to reach for the railing and steady herself, but it's useless.

I run to her, my arm sliding around her and pulling her against my chest as the step beneath her breaks. I can feel her heart thunder against my hand, the erratic beat matching my own.

"*Holy...*"

Her body is shaking in my arms, so I tighten my hold on her. I put her down on the ground and turn her around so she's facing me. Those blue eyes are wide like saucers as she stares at me blankly.

"Are you okay?" I cup her cheek as I take in her body, making sure she didn't get hurt.

She blinks, turning her attention to the big hole in the step. "I almost fell."

"That house is a death trap. Just another reason why you should marry me. I don't want you living here."

My words snap Savannah from her daze. Her head turns in my direction, her eyes shooting daggers my way. "I'm *not* marrying you. And want it or not, this place is my home."

Stubborn, infuriating...

I grind my teeth together. I could see that she was still scared and upset about the whole situation, and any added stress wasn't good for her or the baby. "And what will you do when the baby starts walking around?"

She takes a step back, breaking the connection between us. "Well, it's a good thing that we're far, far away from that problem, isn't it?"

"Savannah..."

"I'll deal with it. The house just needs a little love, that's all." I open my mouth to protest, but she shoots me a glare. "It will be *fixed* by the time the baby comes."

With that, she spins on her heels and starts to reach for the suitcase, but this time, I see it coming. Placing my hands on her shoulders, I gently move her out of my way. "Don't you dare touch it."

"I don't need—"

"I don't care, Blondie. You're not carrying that damn thing up the stairs that are already breaking down. Hell..." I eye the floorboards covering the front porch for a second before I lift her up.

"What the hell do you think you're doing?" she asks as I lift her over the steps and put her onto the porch. I hold my breath as I wait for a heartbeat and then another one, just in case, before I let go.

"Get your ass inside. I'll bring in your things."

She crosses her arms over her chest and gives me her best teacher look. Although, it doesn't have the effect she wants because I can feel my dick twitch in interest as she glares at me. "Blake Walker, you'll do no such thing."

"Oh, yes, I will. You're not carrying shit around when you're pregnant."

"Well, I'll have you know I was doing just fine on my own so far."

"Glad to hear that, but now I'm here, and I don't want to hear a word about it."

Her lips part, and I move forward. Since she's standing on the porch, it puts her at the perfect height for me to look her in the eyes. "I swear to God, Savannah, if I hear you protest one more time, I'm going to shut that stubborn mouth with my own."

She closes her mouth immediately, pink spreading over her

cheeks as her gaze drops to my lips for a split second before she looks away.

"Get inside, Blondie," I mutter, my voice coming out rough.

This time she doesn't try to protest.

Letting out a long breath, I watch her as she turns around and pulls the key out of her bag, sliding it into the lock. Once she's safely inside, at least I hope the inside is better than the outside, I grab the suitcase and test the second step. It groans at my weight but doesn't break, so I quickly make my way up and into the house.

Savannah's footsteps echo inside the dark house. I leave the suitcase by the door and go back to the car. It takes me a few trips, but finally her car is empty just as she comes from down the hallway.

"Do you need me to carry anything upstairs?"

She glances toward the stairs, her throat bobbing as she swallows. "No, this is fine."

"Blondie…"

"There is a guest room downstairs. I'll just use that until I figure things out." Those blue eyes find mine. "You should probably go home. Levi is there alone."

"Daniel is also home." At her quizzical look, I explain. "My other son. He's sixteen."

"Oh…" Her lips part, and the initial surprise on her face is replaced by uncertainty. She ducks her head, a strand of hair falling from the bun and shielding her from me. "I didn't realize you had two sons."

"Yeah, it's just the three of us. Well, and Mrs. Maxwell. She's going to be around occasionally. She helps me around the house and takes care of the boys when I travel."

Tucking the runaway strand behind her ear, she nods. "I should get to work. I have to at least clean up a little bit and settle in."

She was dismissing me.

I wanted to tell her I could help and convince her that it would be best for everybody involved if she would just move in with us, but I could see the determination on her face mixed with exhaustion.

"Thank you for your help. I appreciate it."

"No problem." I start for the door and exit the house. "Our earlier conversation isn't done, Blondie. I was serious when I said I wanted to ma—"

"And what about your kids, Blake?" Savannah interrupts me.

My mouth falls open. I close it as I turn around to face her.

Her lips are pressed into a tight line, her expression unyielding. "How are you going to explain an unfamiliar woman in their home, huh?"

She had me, and she knew it. Daniel and Levi didn't know about what happened. God only knew how they'd react once they found out Savannah was pregnant. They've gone through so many changes in the last year, and they were still processing it. We all were.

I run my hand over my face and through my hair.

"I thought so." She grabs the door. "I have nothing to think about, Blake. My answer will stay no."

With that, she shuts her front door in my face and turns the lock for good measure.

Fucking hell.

Chapter 6

SAVANNAH

"You're such a brat, Savvy. Did you seriously have to go to the school nurse?" Mom mutters as she pushes me into our apartment—or, better said, her boyfriend's apartment.

"I didn't go," I protest and stumble forward, grabbing the table and steadying myself. Barely. "My teacher sent me when I threw up."

"Noisy little bitch." Mom's eyes meet mine, and I can see anger shining in them. "You're a fucking responsibility I never should have had. I should have gotten rid of you when I had the chance so you wouldn't drag me down. But did I do it? No. Of course not. I thought you'd be useful and your daddy would take care of us, but what a fucking joke that was. He knew how big of a nuisance you'd be even before you were born, so he left. Go to your room. I don't want to get whatever stomach bug you have. Rick won't appreciate it."

With that, she pushes me into the closet that is dubbed as my room and slams the door, the loud bang making the wall rattle.

I suck in a sharp breath, my eyes flying open. My breathing is ragged as I look around the room, and it takes me a moment to realize where I am.

Grams' house.

I came to Grams' house since my cottage was flooded. I was in her guest room, one of the rare rooms I managed to make habitable after everything that happened yesterday, and then I crashed. But apparently, even utter exhaustion couldn't stop the past from coming back to haunt me.

I run my hand over my face. My shirt clings to my body as I look at the old-fashioned alarm clock and check the time. It was barely after six. I still had a little time before I had to get up.

Sighing, I start to lower back into bed when I hear it.

Bang-bang-bang.

"What in the ever—"

So it wasn't just the nightmare that woke me up after all. But who the hell was making so much noise this early in the morning? It's been a while since I came here, but yesterday, I didn't see any construction on any of the nearby houses. Unless you count the giant hole currently on my front steps that needs fixing—

"Fucking hell."

Pushing the blanket off of me, I slide off the bed and slip my feet into my flip-flops. The moment I open the door to my temporary bedroom, the banging becomes louder.

Much, much louder.

I unlock the door and pull it open to find a crouched figure standing in front of my steps, wide shoulders stretching the material of a dark blue shirt.

"What the hell do you think you're doing?" I ask, my fingers gripping the door handle as Blake slowly looks up.

Goosebumps rise on my skin at the slow perusal. Time seems to slow down as his eyes take me in from the tips of my dark red toes all the way to my face, the gray of his irises turning darker as his gaze lands on mine.

I feel exposed under his watchful eyes. Naked. His gaze is like a touch.

Just thinking about it has a shiver going through me. My nipples harden, the aching tips pressing against the worn cotton. The shirt seemed oversized when I put it on last night, but right now I realize just how wrong I was. I can feel the edge of it teasing the curve of my ass and leaving my legs bare.

And I'm not the only one who notices just how utterly inappropriate this attire is.

"Good morning, Blondie," Blake rasps as he straightens to his full height. "Did you sleep well?"

The nightmare I had pops in my mind. You didn't have to have a PhD in psychology to understand what brought up the old memories from my childhood. But they were the last thing I wanted to think about, so I pushed them back and focused on the man in front of me.

"I would have slept better if the loud banging didn't wake me up." I cross my arms over my chest. "What do you think you're doing, Walker?"

Blake's gaze falls to my chest, and I realize my mistake. Cheeks reddening, I let my hands drop and snap my fingers. "My eyes are up here."

Blake lifts his gaze, taking his sweet time. The corner of his mouth tips upward unapologetically. "I just couldn't help but notice a few more changes that's all."

"Can you get your mind out of the gutter?" Yes, my boobs had gotten bigger since I had gotten pregnant, but this wasn't the time or place to talk about that. Hell, there were zero reasons for us to talk about it at all. "What are you doing here, Blake?"

"I came to secure the steps, so you don't fall and break your leg. This will have to do until I get the material and fix it."

"Material for what?"

"To fix your porch, of course."

To fix my...

"I don't need you to fix my porch, Blake. Or anything else, for that matter. I'll figure it out."

His fingers curl around the railing, and he places his foot on the step, putting some weight on it as he climbs up. "Have you ever fixed a porch?"

"I— Well, no. I can't say I have, but I'm pretty sure I can figure it out."

His lips press in a tight line. "That's the thing, you don't have to figure it out."

"Yes, I do. Because if I don't, nobody else will do it for me."

"Savannah," he growls, clearly irritated. Good, that made two of us.

"I have to get ready for work."

Not giving him time to protest, I turn around and slip back inside, shutting the door behind me.

I can hear Blake curse from the other side of the door.

Why was he being so stubborn? Couldn't he just leave me alone and continue with his life? Apparently not.

"Stubborn, infuriating man," I mutter to myself as I go to the bathroom.

After a quick shower, I make my way to my room to put on some clothes. The whole ordeal was starting to become a bigger challenge every morning. Now that my bump was visible and growing bigger, most of my old clothes didn't fit, and since I refuse to spend any money on maternity clothes that I won't need later on, I've been sticking to wearing my maxi dresses. I'm just finishing putting on some makeup to cover the bags under my eyes when I can hear a knock on the door.

Huffing in annoyance, I march to the door and pull it open.

"What the hell do you—" The words die on my lips when I spot the redhead on my doorstep. "Becky?"

My best friend raises her brows. "Were you expecting somebody else?"

"I—" I glance over her shoulder, but the front porch is empty, a floorboard covering the broken step. "No." Shaking my head, I shift my attention to her. "But what are you doing here? How did you know where to find me?"

Becky glares at me and pushes into my house, her big belly leading the way. In the last few weeks, she's grown double in size, but while most women looked all swollen and tired at this stage of pregnancy, Becky was still glowing.

"Apparently I have to find out that you *moved* from your neighbor because you don't have the audacity to answer your damn phone!" She turns around and crosses her arms over her chest. "What the hell, Sav?"

I wince softly at the accusation. "I'm sorry. I forgot and left my phone in my car yesterday when I got here."

More like I refused to leave the house in case Blake was lurking around and waiting for me.

"We have to talk." Becky lets out a sigh and drops her hands. "About what happened yesterday."

"I know, and I wasn't avoiding you. I genuinely left my phone in the car. A lot has been going on, and I just..." I run my fingers through my hair, feeling that familiar anxiety rising inside my chest and making it hard to breathe. "I don't know what the hell to do, Becky. I was finally getting to a good place, and now my cottage is flooded, and now *he's* here. Not just that, he has a kid." Blake's comment from last night rings in my mind. "*Kids*. He has two kids, and he's aggravating and headstrong, and apparently since my luck is so bad, he lives just across this fucking street, and now that he knows about Munchkin, he sees us as some fucking responsibility that he has to take care of, and I—"

"What?"

"Yes, if I remember correctly, his exact words were, 'I don't know about what kind of men you've dealt with in the past, but I'm not some asshole that walks away from his responsibilities,'" I mock in Blake's deep baritone. "Oh, and that was after he dropped the bomb that we should get married."

"He did what?!" Becky's mouth falls open. "Fucking Blake Walker."

"Tell me abou—" My shoulders go rigid as her words register in my mind. "What?"

I go back over our conversation, but I don't remember saying his name.

Becky gives me a knowing look. "I'm right, aren't I? Blake is the father of your baby?"

I shake my head, my mouth going dry. "How do you—"

"Yesterday, you said that he brought his kid to your class. Levi is in first grade, and, well, there aren't that many new people moving to Bluebonnet to begin with."

"I don't understand," I whisper; my words are barely audible over the buzzing in my ears.

Becky knew him—all this time. Becky knew the father of my child.

How is that even possible?

"Blake used to play for the Lonestars with Miguel," Becky explains, her hands landing on my shoulders. "Say something, Sav."

"How is this possible?"

Of all the people in this world, and I hook up with one of Miguel's teammates? Somebody must be playing a trick on me. There isn't another explanation.

"I keep saying that this town is too damn small, but this is on a whole other level." Becky snorts, her face turning serious. "What are you going to do?"

Wasn't that a million-dollar question?

There were a lot of unknowns surrounding Blake, except one.

"I know what I'm not going to do."

"Oh?" Becky quirks her brow.

"I'm not marrying him, that's for damn sure."

Chapter 7

BLAKE

"Mrs. Maxwell!" Levi yells as he runs into the kitchen and throws himself at the older woman. "You're finally here."

I feel that familiar ache in my chest at those words. While Levi was always big on showing his love toward people he cared about, recently, since Reina left, there's been this need inside of him to keep them close by and reassure himself they won't leave him as well. A part of me hated her for making him so insecure. It was one thing to leave me if she wasn't happy, but to leave our boys without a second glance? Fuck that.

"You missed me, Levi?" Mrs. Maxwell smiles at him, patting his head affectionately.

"Yes." He tilts his head back and grins at her. "Did you bring me any cookies?"

"All you think about are cookies, young man," she scoffs, but I can see the amusement shining in her eyes. "I did not, but I can bake some today."

"Yes!" Levi pumps his hand excitedly. "The chocolate chip ones?"

"Is there any other kind?"

"Nope."

"How about you eat your breakfast first?" I suggest, placing the cup of coffee on the counter. "We have to get going soon. Where's Daniel?"

"Dunno." Levi shrugs and slides onto the barstool at the counter just as Mrs. Maxwell places a plate with some eggs and bacon in front of him. "He didn't come out of his room."

I shake my head, trying to keep my irritation at bay. "Eat, I'll go check in—" I turn on my heels when a shadow appears in the doorway.

Daniel's eyes lock on mine for a heartbeat, the tension building between the two of us. I was trying my best to be understanding and give him time to come to terms with everything that was going on, but he sure was testing my patience.

"Well, look who finally decided to join us," Mrs. Maxwell says, breaking the uncomfortable silence.

Placing the second plate on the counter, she goes to him and jabs him playfully in the side. "Is that any way to greet an old lady?"

Daniel's shoulders relax as he shifts his attention to Mrs. Maxwell, the corner of his mouth lifting a notch. It's the closest he's come to smiling in ages. "I don't see any old ladies around here. But it's good to see you, Mrs. M."

"Daniel Walker!" Mrs. Maxwell places her hand against her chest in a dramatic fashion. "Coming from the grump himself. I have to admit, I'm surprised." Letting her hand drop, she pushes him toward the chair. "Come on, sit and eat. You need to get to school."

Daniel doesn't try to protest as Mrs. Maxwell steers him toward the chair. For all the bullshit he pulls with me, he's always respectful when it comes to her. Not surprising, considering she's been working for us since the moment I got my first NFL contract and was somewhat of a grandmother figure for both of my boys;

something they both desperately needed. Reina didn't talk to her parents even before she got pregnant, and my mother died when Daniel was only five, so he didn't remember her that well.

"How have you boys been? Did the move go well?" she asks as she joins them at the table.

"It would have been better if we didn't move at all," Daniel grumbles, jabbing his fork into his food as he pointedly looks at his plate.

"I like it," Levi grins. "My new teacher is really nice, and she's pretty too."

His words have me almost choking on my drink.

"Is she now?" Mrs. Maxwell inquires, thankfully completely oblivious to my mishap.

"Mm-hmm…" He nods, his head bending down and a lock of hair falling in his face. "Way better than my old teacher."

"Well, that's great news to hear. Bluebonnet is a really nice town, so much to do." She brushes the runaway lock back. "Like get a haircut." Those dark eyes fix on me over the rim of her glasses, making me squirm in my seat. It's like I'm ten all over again. "Seriously, Blake?"

"What?" I lift my hand and rub at my jaw, feeling the sharp bristles scratching at my palm. "Between the move and everything, there was not much time."

She shakes her head. "You have to make time. People will talk."

"Yeah, well, they can talk all they want."

I think they'll have much more interesting things to talk about soon enough, but I don't bother pointing it out.

Although I'd been tossing and turning for most of the night, thinking over Savannah's words over and over again, I had yet to figure out how to tell the boys about her. About the baby. I didn't know how to bring it up or properly explain what had happened without destroying the fragile relationship I had with them.

But Savannah was right, until I told them, I couldn't do right by her. One'd think that at thirty-five, I'd have my shit in order, but they'd be wrong.

"Finish that up, boys." Mrs. Maxwell claps her hands, snapping me out of my thoughts. "We have to go if we don't want to be late." She turns to me, drying her hands on a towel. "Do you need anything else while we're out?"

"Oh, it's fine." I open the dishwasher and put away my cup. "I'll take them to school."

When I straighten, I find her staring at me, her brows pulled together. "You will?"

"Umm... Yeah."

"You never take them to school," she points out.

Her words make me stop in my tracks.

She's right.

I never took the boys to school. By the time they'd be ready, I was already at the Lonestars facilities going through my workout, dissecting plays, or working on our next game plan. And even on the days I didn't have to be at the facilities, there were other things that needed to be done.

Was it even surprising that I had a shitty relationship with my kids?

Bile burns my throat, but I force it down.

You're trying to do right by them now, I remind myself, but that little voice at the back of my head that's been haunting me for a while is relentless.

Do you seriously think you can do right by them and *Savannah?*

"Now I do. Besides, I need to grab some things in town."

Mrs. Maxwell watches me for a second longer before she

nods. "Sounds good. I'll get to setting up the kitchen and get those cookies started in the meantime."

"Thanks, Mrs. M."

The boys finish their breakfast and clean up their mess before going to grab their things. Not even ten minutes later, we're out of the house.

"Wanna drive?" I ask Daniel.

He glances at me, his face impassive. "Does that mean I get my own car?"

Seriously, this kid...

"That means you get to practice driving," I extend my hand toward him, the keys a silent offering. Daniel watches them for a moment. Just when I think he'll brush me off, he takes them.

"Whatever, might as well drive."

Shaking my head, I help Levi get into the back before sliding into the passenger's seat, just as Daniel starts the truck. I keep my mouth shut as he drives. His expression is serious, his whole focus on the road. He was a good driver for his age, not that I was surprised. Daniel is smart and has so much potential, however, he is easily influenced by other kids. He pulled a lot of shit in the last year, and while I wanted to trust him, I needed to see that he was willing to put in the effort to make a change.

"Park the truck over there," I point at the open space in the school parking lot.

"Don't you want to drop Levi off first?"

I shake my head. "I'll walk him to the door."

After a couple of tries, he maneuvers the truck into the space and kills the engine. He hands me the keys before we get out, and the boys grab their things.

"I'll see you later," Daniel mutters, and he's gone before Levi can even put his backpack on.

Glancing over my shoulder, I watch as Daniel marches

across the parking lot toward school, not paying any attention to the kids lingering around.

Sighing, I look at Levi. "You ready?"

"Yeah. Dad?" He looks up at me, nibbling at his lip. "Do you think Miss Parker will be in school today?"

"I don't see why not, buddy."

Levi nods, his fingers wrapping around the straps of his backpack. "I really want her to be there. She's fun. Not like that other teacher."

My hand falls on Levi's shoulder, and I look down at my son. He seemed happy. Would that still be the case once he found out about Savannah and the baby?

"You really seem to like her, huh?" I ask tentatively.

"She's the best." His grin grows even bigger. "Miss Parker!"

It's like there is an invisible string between us, pulling us together. Savannah tilts her head to the side, her honey hair shining in the morning light. One strand slips from her braid, so she tucks it behind her ear as she nods at whatever the woman is saying before turning her attention in my direction. Today she's dressed in another dress; this one is too big on her, helping conceal the bump I know is hiding underneath. My fingers itch to touch her and reassure myself that our previous encounters weren't just a fluke.

This morning, she came out of her house dressed in an oversized shirt that barely covered anything and made me want to do all sorts of things to her. My cock stirs at the image in my head. Those long, toned legs that I wanted to feel wrapped around my waist once again. Her flushed cheeks and all that messy blonde hair...

Fuck my life.

The last thing I needed was a freaking boner—in school of all places. What was I? Twelve again?

Levi comes to a halt in front of Savannah and grins up at her. "Morning, Miss Parker. You came today!"

She shifts her attention to my son and smiles at him. Even if I didn't like her up until this moment, I'd like her for this: for giving my son attention and making him feel like he's the center of her world. I knew it wasn't just Levi; she probably treated all of the kids she taught the same way, but she's been the first person in a long time that he was compelled to open up to.

"Good morning, Levi. I promised I'd come, didn't I?"

"Yes, you did. But sometimes people don't keep their promises."

Savannah pauses for a moment, her face softening slightly. "No, they don't. That's why I always make sure to do my best to keep my word."

"And I'll always keep my promises, too." Levi nods once, his expression way more serious than any six-year-old ever should be. But then his gaze darts in the direction of a few kids. "Kyle!" He grabs the straps of his backpack and runs toward a dark-haired boy. Only when he's halfway there does he turn around and smile at me. "Bye, Dad!"

"I'll see you later, bud," I call back, as I come to a stop in front of Savannah. "Miss Parker."

That frown between her brows deepens as she glares at me. For somebody who insisted on calling her Miss Parker, she sure as hell didn't seem happy when I did it. Still, she schools her features quickly, that mask of indifference falling in place. "Mr. Walker. It's nice to see you came on time today. Now if you'll excuse me—"

She starts to turn around, but I grab her wrist. Surprise flashes in her blue irises, her cheeks turning pink.

"Are you still angry about the porch? Because I'm not going to apologize for keeping you from getting hurt."

Savannah presses her lips in a tight line. "Are you going to apologize for keeping things from me?"

Keeping things? My brows pull together in confusion. "What are you—"

"Professional football player?" She pulls her hand out of my grasp. "Really, Blake?"

Well, shit.

Did she look me up? Or did somebody tell her?

I guess now it didn't matter how she found out, just that she did. And she was clearly pissed.

"*Ex*-football player," I correct. "I retired after last season before we met."

She crosses her arms over her chest. "Is that supposed to make me feel better?"

Dammit.

"Blondie, I..." I open my mouth, but no words come out. What was there to say really?

"This thing between us? It can only work if we're honest with each other."

I run my hand over my face. "I know. I didn't mean to keep it a secret. I just..."

But didn't I? I liked the fact that she didn't know I was a professional football player. I liked the anonymity. I liked that I didn't have to worry about if she was trying to deceive me because she could get something out of me. That night she liked the man she saw, not all the zeroes in my bank account, or the attention she'd get if we were seen together.

"You just did," she finishes, shaking her head. "I can't do this."

Icy chills go down my spine. "What do you want me to do?"

"I want—" She looks away, her tongue darting out to slide over her lower lip as she carefully weighs her words. "I want you to give me space. I have so much on my plate right now;

between the school and the move, I just... I need time to process"—she waves her hand—"all of this, and you being here doesn't make this easy."

"You want me to leave you alone?" I say, feeling the irritation growing inside of me. "You can't ask me that. I've never—"

"Walked away from your responsibility?" she finishes, those blue eyes fixing on mine. Frustration and something that looks so much like sadness and hurt, playing on her face.

"Yes!" I run my fingers through my hair.

Savannah flinches, and this time, she doesn't even try to cover it.

"Blondie..."

"No." She lifts her hand and takes a step back. "I don't want to hear it. I need to get to my job."

With one last look in my direction, she spins on her high heels and goes toward the door. This time, I don't try to stop her.

"Fucking hell."

I messed this up.

And I messed it up badly.

What's another fuckup in a row?

Since there was nothing that I could do about it, not now that she was angry and busy with work, I headed back to the parking lot.

Might as well deal with shit that I can change.

Just as I slide into my car, my phone pings with a text message.

MIGUEL:
Got time to spot me?

Or I could sweat out my frustration with the whole situation.

BLAKE:
I'll be there in 15.

"So how are things going?" Miguel asks from above me, watching me carefully.

"Fine," I breathe, pushing the bar up, the weight making my muscles scream in protest. This was our fourth and final round, and I'd asked him to put more weight on than usual.

"The boys doing okay?"

I roll my eyes and grit through clenched teeth. "Great."

Miguel snorts. "You don't sound great. And you've been acting like a freaking grumpy asshole more than usual. I guess now I know why you're such good friends with my brother."

I fumble at the mention of Aaron, the bar almost slipping from my hands, but I manage to catch it at the very last second and correct myself. My palms are sweaty, so I tighten my grip on it.

Did he hear about my visit yesterday? Does he know about Savannah? Was that the reason for all the questions?

"Shit, you okay?"

No, I wasn't okay. I was freaking pissed. At Savannah, at myself, at everything, and I didn't know what to do.

"Peachy."

Pushing through the last few reps, I put the bar in place and grab the towel hanging from the bench next to mine as I sit upright, rubbing at my sweaty face.

"What the hell's going on? I thought coming here was what you wanted, but you don't seem happy."

"It is. I just have a lot on my mind." Instead of answering his question, I decide to change the subject. "What's the best place to buy stuff to fix a porch around here?"

Not just the porch, but a whole freaking house. I guess the porch would have to be a good start since I highly doubted that Savannah would give me a key to her place, and I don't think breaking into her home will buy me any points. But I had to do *something*.

Miguel frowns. "Why do you need to fix a porch? Yours seemed fine."

"I'm not fixing my porch."

"Then whose porch are you fixing?" he asks just as the door to the gym opens and Rebecca strolls inside, her gaze landing on me.

"Savannah's." She props her hands on her hips. The gesture should look stern, but with her big belly protruding in front of her, it looks funny. Or it would have if she wasn't shooting me a death glare. "Marriage? Seriously, Walker?"

I wince inwardly at her accusing tone.

So, that's how she found out who I am.

It made sense; they were friends after all.

Well, I guess it was just a matter of time. People would find out sooner or later the whole story, which is why I had to figure out how to tell Daniel and Levi before they heard it from somewhere else.

"Marriage?" Miguel looks from me to his fiancée. "What marriage?"

Becky tilts her head in my direction. "Oh, ask your friend. I'm also interested to hear what he has to say."

Two pairs of eyes turn to me, one pissed off, the other one confused. This was going great.

"I hooked up with Savannah back in March, and well..."

Miguel's eyes widen as he stares at me. "You did not. You're shitting me, right?" He turns to Becky before he shifts his attention to me. "But that would mean that…"

I can see his brain work as he does the math.

"*Holy shit.* You're—"

"Sav's baby daddy?" Becky finishes for him. "Well, yes, he is. And his grand solution to the problem? Telling her they should get married."

I wince at the jab.

"It wasn't like that."

"Oh, no?" Becky lifts her brows. "You didn't tell her you guys should get hitched?"

"Well, I did, but… It wasn't like that. I mean, it was, but I also like her and…"

I run my hand over my face.

I was messing this up.

Badly.

Becky shakes her head. "Oh, trust me, I understand it perfectly. But seriously, what were you thinking?"

"I was thinking that she's carrying my child that I didn't know about until now, and she was just about to move into a hellhole," I snap, done with the twenty questions.

"So you weren't actually thinking."

No, I wasn't. That was the problem. I was reacting, trying to come up with a solution to this mess of a situation we were in.

"Is it so wrong that I want to take care of her? She's pregnant with my kid, for fuck's sake." I run my fingers through my hair, pushing it back. The pent-up tension that's been building over the last few days, and which I thought I'd somehow sweat out of my system in the last hour, is back in full force.

"Is that the only reason why you suggested that? Because she's pregnant?"

"I—" I open my mouth, but no words come out.

I like Savannah. I liked her that first day we met. Not only was she a gorgeous woman, but something about her, her sass, and her kindness, made looking away impossible.

"Savannah is..." Becky shakes her head as if she's at a loss for words.

"Stubborn? Too freaking independent for her own good?"

"Guarded," she finishes finally. "Not that you can blame her. She's been hurt too many times by the people she loved, and she doesn't open up easily."

My fingers clench into a fist by my side. "Her ex?"

I could still remember the sorrow on her face that day we met when she told me about her ex. Was he the one who hurt her? Or was there somebody else?

"Her ex was an ass, sure, but I think she was with him because he was safe. She knew he wasn't for her, and he wouldn't be able to hurt her. Not really."

I grind my teeth. The idea of Savannah with some unknown guy got on my nerves. I didn't like it. I didn't like it one bit. "You're not making any sense."

Becky shrugs. "It's not my story to tell."

"Then what's the point of all of this?"

"My point is that you're different. You're the father of her child, and you do have the power to hurt her." She moves closer and jabs her finger into my chest. "And if you do that, you'll have to deal with me. Do I make myself clear?"

"Red," Miguel comes behind her, his hands resting on her waist. "Blake is a good guy, remember?"

"And Savannah is my friend," she says, not moving her gaze from me. "She loves that baby more than life itself. I won't let anybody take that away from her or upset her in the process, which is apparently what you've been doing the last few days."

"Then what do you expect me to do?"

Because I needed to do something. I couldn't just sit still. I'd go crazy.

"Give her time. She's been dealing with a lot, and she needs time to process everything. The stress isn't good for her or the baby."

There it was again.

What the hell did she mean by "she's been dealing with a lot?" Was something happening I should know about? Was it her or the baby? And was this whole thing only making it worse? Shit, I hate this. I was a fixer. I took care of people in my life; it's just who I was. Knowing that there was something Savannah was dealing with and not being able to do anything...

"I know." I run my hands over my face. "Fuck, I know. The last thing I want is to add more to her plate."

"What are you going to do?" Miguel asks softly.

"Let her come to me, I guess?" I could understand how all of this could be too much for a person. The last thing I wanted to do was make her feel more stressed out. Besides, I had shit of my own to deal with. "I don't know. I have to figure out a way to tell the boys before they hear it from somebody else. And I'm going to fix that freaking house. She's pregnant; she shouldn't have to deal with all of this on her own. She *won't* have to deal with all of this on her own. I take care of what's mine."

And she and that baby?

Want it or not, they were mine.

Chapter 8

SAVANNAH

"We're done for today, guys! Don't forget to do your homework, and remember, football practice is kicking off this Friday, so if you want to participate, make sure to bring in this paper signed by your parents, okay?" I lift the paper in the air. "You can grab them at my table."

A chorus of agreement spreads through the room as kids collect their things and grab their backpacks. Some of them stop by my table before we head for the exit where there is a line of cars already waiting.

Between parents wanting to get out of here as soon as possible, and kids pumped to be done with classes, the school pickup is always hectic. I chat with the parents, and even a few grandparents as kids slide into the cars before waving them off.

Closing the door, I turn around just in time for a black truck to pull in front of me. My stomach tightens with nerves while I wait for it to come to a stop. The window rolls down, and the older woman sitting behind the steering wheel smiles at me.

Letting out a long breath, I push back my disappointment that it's not the certain tall former football player.

You told him to leave you alone, I remind myself. *This is for the best.*

"Hello, Miss Parker. You look pretty like a peach today, my dear!"

I chuckle nervously at the comment. "You're too kind, Mrs. Maxwell."

"Nonsense." She shifts her attention to Levi. "I hope this little one didn't give you any trouble."

"Not at all. Levi is one of my best students." I wink at him. "He's pretty amazing."

I wasn't even exaggerating. Levi was such a nice kid, well-mannered, kind, and really smart. Everything a teacher could ever ask for in a student.

Levi's grin widens, and he puffs out his chest. "Hear that, Mrs. M.? I'm amazing."

The corners of her eyes crinkle as she chuckles. "Of course you are."

I pull open the back door, and Levi climbs up. "I'll see you tomorrow, Miss Parker?"

"Until tomorrow, Levi."

"Have a good one!" Mrs. Maxwell says as she pulls from the curb.

It takes me an additional fifteen minutes before all the kids are collected, and I can finally return to my classroom. I tidy the space a little, making sure everything is in order for tomorrow before my gaze falls on my desk. There is a bunch of work that has yet to be done. I have papers to grade, class plans to write, and I need to figure out what to do about the practice, but my stomach rumbles loudly, reminding me I should probably grab something to eat.

No, not something.

Apples.

An apple pie or cobbler with cinnamon and vanilla ice cream.

Just the idea has my mouth watering, and my stomach

grumbles once again, which is weird because I don't usually even like cinnamon.

"Okay, okay, I hear you, Munchkin," I chuckle softly and lay my hand on my bump, giving it a soft rub.

At twenty weeks, I've only recently started to show, and I got to the point where I couldn't button my pants. It made this whole situation that more real.

I gather my things and go to my car. The drive to Reading Nook takes only a few minutes. The small bell rings when I push on the door, and the sweet scent of baked goods and coffee fills my lungs.

"I'll be out in a second," a female voice calls from the kitchen.

"No rush," I yell back, taking in the familiar space. The small café and bookshop were decorated in peachy and dark wooden tones that fit our little town perfectly. The music was softly playing in the background, tuned in to the local country station. The whole place has a homey vibe that I simply adore.

A few tables were filled with people. Old Mr. Maverick was sitting at his usual spot, reading newspapers. A group of teens was giggling as they watched something on their phones, and then there were Mrs. Miller and Mrs. Tyson sitting in their spying corner.

They spot me instantly and wave me over. "Savannah! How are you doing, my dear?" Mrs. Miller asks as I join them. "We heard about your house. Are you okay? Do you need help with anything?"

I wince softly. Of course they heard about the house. Nothing could stay hidden for long in Bluebonnet Creek.

"No, I'm fine, but thank you. I'm just sad things turned out the way they did, and the cottage got destroyed."

"I've been telling Marcus that he needs to take better care of his property. Didn't I tell him that, Trish?"

Mrs. Miller nods, her lips pursed. "You sure did, Millie."

"Damn right. But did he listen?" Mrs. Tyson tsks unhappily and taps my hand affectionately. "If you need any help, you let us know. Okay?"

My heart swells at their kindness. The two of them were pushing eighty, and Mrs. Miller was even using a walking stick, but I knew that if I asked, they'd help me in a heartbeat; that was the beauty of living in a small town. People might be nosy as hell, more often than not, but they took care of their own.

"I'm good, really, but I appreciate it."

"You moved into your grandmother's house?"

"That's right, ma'am."

"I told you." Mrs. Miller glances at her friend. "I saw Charlotte today at the store, and she told me she saw lights there and people moving around. At first, she thought somebody was breaking in, but then she saw your car."

Mrs. Tyson scoffs. "That one always had a flair for dramatics. We haven't had a robbery for longer than I've been born, and it's been a hot minute since that happened."

I bite the inside of my cheek, trying to hide my amusement at their banter. One thing was for sure: there was never a dull moment between the two of them.

Mrs. Miller gives me a knowing look. "I'm happy to hear that, though. Your grandmother would love to know that you and your baby will make that house your home instead of having it sit empty. That woman loved you so much."

That familiar pang of sadness hits me at the mention of my grandmother. I didn't think it would ever go away, not fully, but it wasn't as intense as it used to be.

"Yeah, she would." I thought living in her house would be hard, and on occasion, it was. I still couldn't bring myself to go to her room. However, I also started to remember the good times we had together, of which there were many. "There are some things that need fixing, but we'll get there."

"You really shouldn't be lifting things now that you're pregnant," Mrs. Tyson points out before glancing at Mrs. Miller. "Trish, didn't you say your nephew is coming?"

"Yes, he just called me yesterday to confirm it." Her eyes shine brightly as they fix on me, and I know what will come out of her mouth before she even opens her lips. "You know, if you need help moving something, I'm sure he'd be more than happy to help while he's visiting."

"Oh, no, that's fine. I'm not really lifting anything." I shake my head before she can get any ideas. "I'm focusing on just clearing out stuff and unpacking."

This wasn't the first time they'd tried to set me up since they found out I was pregnant, and I feared it wouldn't be the last. I wanted to keep my pregnancy to myself for as long as possible, but since those first weeks were pretty rough, with me throwing up constantly, people quickly caught up. They all assumed the baby was my ex's, and we split up, and I didn't try to correct them because I thought it'd be just Munchkin and me, only…

This baby is as much mine as it is yours. So, no. I don't agree with this bullshit.

Blake's words ring in my head, and I can feel a knot form in my throat. This whole situation was such a mess, and I had no idea how I'd deal with it.

"You guys could still go out and grab a coffee," Mrs. Miller points out, breaking me out of my thoughts. "He can't very well spend all his time with me. I'm too old to entertain him."

"You're not old, Mrs. Miller!"

Just then the kitchen door squeaks open, and Jessica appears at the counter, a smile pops up on her face when she sees me. "Savannah! How are you doing?"

"Good, I—" The smell of apples and cinnamon reaches my

nostrils, and my stomach grumbles, reminding me of the reason I came here. "It's like you're reading my mind."

I turn to Mrs. Miller and Mrs. Tyson. "I'm off to grab some of those desserts while they're still warm, but I'll see you ladies for the book club?"

"Of course."

I turn around and go toward the counter, thinking I was pretty sleek about the whole situation, when Mrs. Miller calls out, "Think about what I said!"

Yeah, how about no? I had my hands full as it is. I didn't want to add a man to the mix.

Jessica fights a smile, one of her brows quirking. "Do I wanna ask?"

"Nope." I shake my head. "Can I have some of those apple cobblers? They smell divine."

"Oh, a craving?" Jessica asks as she grabs a box and starts putting the pastries inside.

"Maybe? It's weird. I don't even like cinnamon, but it smells so good, and I can't get it out of my mind."

"We can't have that. Here." She puts the box on the counter. "Anything else?"

Jessica's been working part-time at Reading Nook while attending a local community college and was also part of our monthly book club, so we knew each other pretty well.

"No, I think I'm good. How have you been? Did your date go well?"

She sighs. "It was okay; nothing too spectacular."

"That sucks."

"Yeah, it is what it is, I guess."

We chat for a few more minutes before I grab my order and get back on the road. My feet were killing me after a whole day, and I couldn't wait to sit down on my porch, lift my legs up, and eat that cobbler.

It doesn't take me long to get to Grams' house. *My house.* It was still hard to think of it as my home. The sun is low on the horizon, the last golden rays illuminating the two-story house as I park in front of it and slide out, grabbing my things.

I look at the place with a critical eye. The house was run down with color peeling and wood creaking with every step, but I could see the beauty it once held, and I planned to bring it back to what it once used to be—with shiny white walls, cherry red shutters, and flowers. Grams loved flowers.

Entering the house, I drop my things in the living room and beeline for the kitchen, where I grab the spoon. Too giddy to wait any longer, I open the box, dip my spoon into the cobbler, and take a big bite. My eyes fall shut as I slowly chew, savoring the delicious taste.

"Damn, that's good."

Box in hand, I pad back outside so I can sit on the swing and enjoy some peace and qui—

My brows furrow as I come to a sudden stop.

Something's not right.

I pull my brows together as I look around, trying to figure out what exactly caught my attention. Everything seemed to be in order. The swing was in the corner, throw pillows tossed around. The plants I bought are sitting on the side, waiting for me to put them in their place.

"You're imagining thi—" I shake my head at myself and go toward the swing when it hits me.

The quiet.

The floorboards weren't creaking.

That's what was missing.

My gaze falls to the porch, my eyes narrowing as I move a few steps to one side before I go a few steps to the other.

Still nothing.

And did they look darker somehow?

I turn around, my gaze still glued to the floor. If one of my neighbors were to come out and see me, they'd think I was crazy.

Maybe I was.

Because who over-fixates on floorboards out of all things? And yet...

My gaze falls on the steps.

The steps without those damn boards that Blake put on them so I wouldn't fall.

They were gone.

My head snaps up, eyes zeroing in on the house across the street. "I'm going to kill him."

Chapter 9

BLAKE

"Where the hell is she?" I mutter as I narrow my gaze on the window, which is conveniently looking at the street and the house on the other side.

Her car wasn't in the driveway like normal. She usually came home after work around four. I knew because I might have been looking out the window. Was it creepy? Yes. Did I fucking care? Not really.

Just because I was giving her time to get used to all of this while I figured out how to break down the news to the boys didn't mean that I was giving up or that I didn't care about her or the baby. Besides, knowing how stubborn Savannah was, I wouldn't be surprised if I saw her carrying some heavy shit around once again, and the last thing I wanted was for her to get hurt. But I'd do the same thing even if an old lady lived across the street.

Who're you trying to fool, Walker?

"Where is who?"

My head snaps in Levi's direction as my heart kicks up a notch at being caught. So much for not attracting attention.

"Umm... Nobody." I glance down at the castle. "You're doing so good, buddy."

"I can't find the right piece." Levi tilts his head and glares at all the scattered pieces on the coffee table. "Do you see it, Dad?"

"Let's see..." I turn my focus on the Lego bricks, grateful that he was easily distracted. For now. "Looking for this?"

"Yes!"

His tongue peeks out of the side of his mouth as he places the piece in place and turns his attention back to the instructions.

Now that he's entertained once again, I glance toward the window and that empty driveway.

What if something happened to her, and that was the reason she was late? I didn't have her phone number, and nobody knew that the baby was mine. Even if something happened to either of them, I wouldn't be able to know. I wouldn't be able to be there for her.

Just the thought of it made my heart race and my palms turn sweaty as the anxiety inside me grew.

Fuck this.

I slide my hand into my pocket and pull out my phone. It takes me only a second to find the right number.

BLAKE:
> Did you hear from Savannah today?

I watch the screen, my fingers tightening around my phone to the point my knuckles have drained of color as I will the answer to appear.

It feels like forever before three little dots flash on the screen.

BECKY:
> Was I supposed to?

BLAKE:
> She's not home.

BECKY: Are you spying on her?

BLAKE: I'm not spying. She lives right across the street. It's not like I'm blind.

BECKY: Mm-hmm... Sure thing, buddy.

BLAKE: Seriously, where is she?

BECKY: Probably working? You do realize teachers mainly do their work after school is done for the day, right?

I guess I never thought much about that, but it made sense.

BLAKE: You should give me her number so I can check in with her. Just in case.

BECKY: I'm not giving you her number.

I grind my teeth, feeling the irritation rising.

I hate this. I hated the not knowing. I hated that I couldn't help her. I hated the thought of her all alone in that big ass house. I hated feeling this useless.

BECKY: What happened to letting her come to you?

BLAKE: It disappeared when she didn't come home at her usual time.

"Dad, what's for dinner?"

Locking my phone, I turn my attention to my son. "Mrs. Maxwell prepared tacos. You hungry?"

"A little."

"Okay, I'll go and get started on that. How does that sound?"

"Good. I'll try to finish this before dinner."

"Sounds like a plan."

Pushing to my feet, I slide my phone into my back pocket as I make my way to the kitchen, just as there is a loud knock.

I stop in my tracks, my gaze darting to the door.

I wait for a heartbeat, thinking I might have imagined it since nobody ever comes here except for Mrs. Maxwell, and she has a key when I hear it again.

Somebody was definitely knocking.

Making my way to the door, I unlock it, only to come to a stop when I see the person standing in front of me.

"Blondie?" My brows pull together. "What's wrong?"

My eyes scan her body, thinking I'm imagining it, but no, it's her, here in the flesh. And she looks... fine? Better than fine, if I'm being honest. Her cheeks have a healthy flush to them, and her dress is hugging every single one of those delicious curves—

"My porch isn't creaking."

Well, fuck.

I guess there went the hope that she might not notice. I'm surprised it took her this long to figure it out in the first place, still, I play along.

"Your porch isn't creaking?" I repeat, tilting my head to the side.

Savannah grinds her teeth. "No, Blake. My porch isn't creaking. Do you have any idea why that might be?"

I shrug, making sure my expression stays impassive. "No clue whatsoever."

"Bullshit." She moves closer, jabbing her finger into my chest. "You fixed it, didn't you?"

"You're imagining things, Blondie."

She lets out a frustrated huff. "You can't keep fixing things for me, Blake."

"I can fix whatever the hell I want." The words are out before I can think better of them.

Great, just great.

"It's my house!" she protests.

"Exactly." I take a step forward, closing the distance between us. The soft, flowery scent reaches my nostrils, sweet and sexy and so much like her. I want to lean down and try to find the source of it so I can bury my head there and inhale it deep into my lungs. Inhale her. "Since you're the one who's demanding to live there, I get the right to insist the place doesn't fall apart, and you don't get hurt. Would you rather I pay somebody else to do it? Because I will."

"What? No." She shakes her head. "Absolutely not. You'll not pay anybody for anything."

I cross my arms over my chest and give her a pointed look. "Then I'll fix it."

Her fingers curl into fists by her sides. "Why are you being so stubborn about this?"

I let out an unamused laughter. "I'm the stubborn one? Out of the two of us, who's the one who's refusing any sort of help?"

"Ugh, fine." She stomps her foot, and before I know it, she's spinning on her heels and marching back to her house. "Do whatever the hell you want."

She was fine, alright.

"I plan to," I call out, unable to resist it, the corner of my mouth twitching upward.

Savannah shoots me a death glare over her shoulder, and it

takes all of me not to burst into laughter. I don't think she would appreciate it.

I don't know what it was about this woman that made me want to act like a freaking teenager, all so I could get a reaction out of her, but she did.

I stay on my porch, watching her until she's safely inside her house, before turning around and going inside myself.

I'm just locking the door when I look up and spot Daniel standing on top of the stairs, watching me with a contemplative expression on his face.

"Hey, what are you doing there?"

"Hungry." He glances at the door before his attention returns to me. "Who was that?"

Shit.

"Our neighbor."

How much did he hear? I go back over my conversation with Savannah. We didn't mention the baby, but still...

I have to tell them.

I tried a couple of times, but every time I opened my mouth, it was like I couldn't find the right words. How the hell was I supposed to explain to them what happened? Levi wouldn't understand it, but Daniel... he would understand it perfectly. Which was exactly what I was afraid of.

His eyes narrow slightly. "What did she want?"

"Something about her porch?" I shrug, trying to play it off and start toward the kitchen, changing the subject before he can ask any more questions. "I was actually just going to start dinner. We have tacos. How does that sound?"

"Fine."

Levi joins us a little while later, and the two of them set the table while I finish the food. Meanwhile, Levi chats about school and his new friends, including a boy he wanted to invite over.

I was grateful that he seemed to be doing well and adapted so quickly, then again, this was Levi. Up until Reina left, he was always a cheerful and happy kid with lots of friends.

I glance toward my oldest son as we sit at the table to eat. "How is school?"

"Fine." He shrugs, shoving a big bite of taco in his mouth.

"Make any new friends yet?"

"No." He rolls his eyes. "They're all weird."

"Kyle's not weird!" Levi defends instantly.

"Well, all the kids in my school are weirdos. And their accent is so thick I can barely understand them."

"You should give them a chance, Daniel."

"Why would I do that?" He looks up, anger flashing in his irises as he glares at me. "They don't seem to have a problem with judging me. So why should I give them a chance?"

"If you came with that attitude, I can't say I'm surprised."

"Whatever, I don't care about what they say. I don't need friends like them anyway. Besides, I'll be going to college soon."

I don't point out that he has to graduate high school first in order to do that. Daniel was a smart kid, but since starting high school he barely put in any effort whatsoever. He kept getting in with the wrong crowd, which didn't help motivate him to do better in school.

"Any extracurricular activities you'll be picking out?"

"Like what? Horseback riding?" he snorts. "Yeah, I think not."

"I'll be playing football."

My head snaps up, and I look at Levi, who's shoving a huge bite of taco into his mouth, his hands sticky with the sauce.

"You wanna play football?"

Contrary to some of my teammates and colleagues, I didn't put pressure on my kids to play football. Daniel used to insist we play catch when he was younger. It was like he was obsessed with it. We could stay out in our backyard for hours just tossing the ball. He wanted to play peewee football, and for a kid, he had a really good arm on him, and he was wicked fast. Then, one day, he just stopped. I'm not sure what happened exactly. Did he lose interest? Or did I just become too busy and told him no one too many times, so he simply gave up? Probably the latter. Either way, around eight he stopped playing and hadn't picked up a ball since.

Levi, on the other hand, never showed much interest in playing. He liked to watch me out on the field, but to actually be the one with the ball? Not that kid.

Levi nods, licking his fingers. "Yes, there is practice on Friday after school. Kyle is coming, too." His gaze fixes on me. "Will you come and watch me, Dad?"

"Sure thing, buddy." Levi's grin grows bigger as he grabs another taco. "You know you can pick whatever you want, right? It doesn't have to be football. You can do a different sport or activity."

The last thing I wanted was for either of my kids to think they had to play football in order to get my attention.

Levi's brows furrow at my comment, the trace of that stubbornness I was familiar with coming to the surface. "I know, but I wanna play football, just like you. I can play, right?"

"Of course." I ruffle his hair. He really needed a haircut. I added a mental note to take him soon. "I wouldn't miss it."

The chair screeches, drawing my attention as Daniel pushes from his seat and grabs his plate. "I'm going to my room."

Avoiding my gaze, he puts the plate in the dishwasher before he leaves the kitchen.

"He's angry again," Levi says, grabbing his glass.

All the canceled appearances pop in my mind. How many times had I told him I'd come to his school event or game, but I never showed up?

Too many to count.

"He's angry at me and with reason."

And before this whole thing is done, he would get even angrier. I just hoped that I'd get a chance to make this right.

For Savannah and our baby.

For Levi.

For Daniel.

Chapter 10

BLAKE

"Hey, Mrs. M." I knock on the kitchen doorway, the sweet scent of vanilla filling the space making my stomach growl. "What are you up to?"

"I'm baking some cookies. I figured I'd leave you boys something sweet over the weekend." She looks up, watching me over the rim of her glasses. "Need me to do anything else before I go and pick Levi up?"

"I'll be picking him up today."

"You will?" Her brows quirk up, surprise evident in her voice.

I had originally planned to do more things on my own, including dropping the kids at school and picking them up. Still with everything that happened with Savannah, I asked Mrs. Maxwell if she could do it temporarily, until we settled in, to which she agreed.

"Yeah, Levi has football practice, so he asked me to come and watch."

If possible, her brows rise even higher. "Levi? Playing football?"

I let out a soft chuckle and grab one of the baked cookies,

popping it into my mouth. "I was surprised, as well, but he said one of his friends is joining the team, so he wanted to do it also."

"We'll see how that goes." Mrs. Maxwell says diplomatically, returning to her cookie dough. "Levi seems to be adapting well. I don't remember the last time he was so excited about going to school."

"He is, isn't he? He's been asking me to go and play with Kyle, and school has barely started. It makes me feel less guilty for uprooting their lives."

My gaze darts to the window and the house across the street. That unsettling feeling growing inside of me and making it hard to breathe. I seriously needed to tell the boys about Savannah and the baby. But it was so damn hard knowing how fragile our life here was. Levi was settling in nicely. Will the news upset him? She was his teacher, after all. And Daniel... Daniel was still struggling as it was. I didn't know if he could take one more blow. If our relationship could take one more blow.

"Blake?" My head snaps up, and I turn to find Mrs. Maxwell giving me a curious gaze. "Are you okay?"

I run my hand over my face, my stubble prickling my fingertips. "Just a lot on my mind."

She tilts her head to the side, quiet for a moment, as if she's weighing her words. "Does it have anything to do with the fact that you've been fixing the house across the street this week?"

Shit.

I guess it was too much to expect that she wouldn't notice it. Not when she was spending every morning here. She never asked any questions, but it was silly to think that just because she didn't comment on anything, she didn't know what was going on around the house.

"I'm just trying to be neighborly; that's it."

"Mm-hmm... neighborly," she hums, not buying it in the slightest. I look away, my gaze falling on the clock on the wall.

"Shit. I really have to get going."

"Try not to meddle too much?"

I grab one more cookie, which earns me a glare from Mrs. Maxwell. "When did I ever?"

"Of course not," Mrs. Maxwell mutters dryly and rolls her eyes. "Be nice."

"I'm always nice."

"I know that but try to be extra nice to whichever poor soul is doing this job."

I scoff. "You're exaggerating, Mrs. M."

"I'm doing no such thing." Mrs. Maxwell props her hands on her hips. "I know you as well as I do my sons, Blake Walker. Did you or did you not scare the poor man who was coaching Daniel's football team a few years ago to the grave?"

I cross my arms over my chest defensively. "The guy was useless."

The look she shoots my way would send a lesser man running. Thankfully, I was used to this kind of behavior by now. "Like I said, be *nice*."

"Yeah, yeah. I'll be nice as long as the person who's coaching is doing a good job of it."

Mrs. Maxwell tsks. "Why do I feel like this has disaster written all over it?"

"Now, you're the one exaggerating, Mrs. Maxwell."

"We'll see about that." She waves her hand dismissively. "Off with you. I'm going to finish these cookies and then prep some dinner."

"You're the best."

With a wave in her direction, I make my way out of the house and jump into the truck. My gaze fixes on Savannah's house as I pull out of the driveway. Savannah's car was nowhere in sight, then again, school hadn't let out yet. Would I get a chance to see her? Just the thought of it has excitement swirling inside of me, and I press my foot against the gas. The short interaction we had the other night wasn't nearly enough. I wanted to be patient and give her the time she needed, but damn it, that wasn't in my nature. I wanted to be there for her. I wanted to take care of her and make sure she was alright. I messed up so many things in my life, and I didn't want to mess this up, too.

It was unnerving. I don't remember the last time I was this excited to see a woman. Probably not since college, but there was just something about Savannah that drew me in.

Before I know it, the school appears in front of me. I bypass the pickup line and go straight for the parking lot. The entire time, I look for a flash of blonde hair, only to come up empty. I try to swallow down my disappointment as I park the truck. The sound of the kids yelling greets me the moment I push open the door.

Great, I was late, and they've already started.

I follow the cacophony of noises toward the smaller football field, my eyes taking in the space. A few parents, mostly moms, are sitting in the stands talking amongst each other.

One of them spots me instantly, and then a few more curious gazes turn in my direction. Tilting my head in greeting, I find an open space on the bleachers, sit down, and shift my attention toward the field. The kids are running drills, jogging from one side of the field to the other, each of them holding a football tucked in the crook of their elbow. When they get to the yard line, they bend down to touch it before running back to the start and moving one-yard line further.

Levi is standing between a boy and a girl his age. His teeth are gritted as he runs, cheeks red from straining.

I lean my elbows against my knees, bending forward as I

watch them. The group has only ten kids, seven boys and three girls, but I guess when you have a town the size of Bluebonnet Creek, it's not really that surprising.

The loud whistle pierces the air, making the kids turn around. "Okay, guys, that was amazing. How about you pair up, and we'll work on some tossing drills?"

That voice.

The hair at my nape rises as I turn around and just stare at Savannah. She's standing on the sidelines, dressed in a pair of leggings and a baggy tee that does little to hide her bump, a clipboard in her hand. A deep purple ball cap is sitting on top of her head, shielding her face, her blonde ponytail swaying with each movement as she pairs the kids and gives them instructions.

"What the hell is she doing here?" I mutter softly, my gaze locked on her as I watch her interact with the kids. The way she lowers down to talk to them. Her hand falls to the top of their heads, ruffling their hair or patting them on the shoulder. Easy, natural, motherly.

I can't take my eyes off of her. This was her element, and she was excelling at it.

A little girl tosses the ball to the boy opposite her, the ball barely reaching the kid, making me wince.

Savannah tells something to the girl and jots down a note on her clipboard before moving away to the next kid.

"That's not how it's done!" I yell loudly.

Even from here, I can see her shoulders stiffen. Slowly, she turns around, and although her ball cap is throwing a shadow over her face, I can feel her glare fixing on me.

Pushing from the wooden bench, I make my way to her until I'm standing right in front of her.

"What the he— *heck* do you think you're doing?" she hisses softly, tilting her head back.

The corner of my mouth twitches upward at the anger flashing in her eyes and making my own blood boil in answer. I wanted to lean down and press my mouth against hers so I could erase the annoyance from her face and hear her moan my name. I wanted to know how she'd taste and feel like against me.

"The better question is, Blondie, what the heck are you doing?"

"I'm trying to coach football, *Mr. Walker*. Now if you'd turn around, get your behind seated in the bleachers section and stay quiet, maybe I could actually do that."

Like hell, I will.

I cross my arms over my chest. "You were doing it wrong."

She grinds her teeth. "And what, pray tell, was I doing wrong?"

I tilt my head to the side in the direction of the girl. "Her stance is all wrong. You didn't correct her."

Savannah steps closer, so our bodies are practically touching, her finger jabbing into my chest. "Number one, I didn't correct her because it's our first practice, and I'm trying to see what I'm working with here. Number two, they're *six*. We're not getting ready to play at the Super Bowl. And she's not freaking Tom Brady."

"And how do you know anything about Brady?" I pull my brows together, the irritation spiking.

"Everybody knows about Tom Brady." Her gaze darts over my shoulder, cheeks turning pink. She lowers her voice. "Now sit down, Walker. You're making a scene."

"Not until you tell me why the hell you are doing this."

She's pregnant, for fuck's sake. She should be slowing down, not taking on more obligations. Obligations that could get her hurt.

Savannah presses her lips together, that pink turning into a deep red. "Because," she grits, jabbing her finger into my chest, "there is nobody who wants to do it, and the kids like it. Besides, it's *peewee* football. Now, sit. Down. I don't need you hulking over me."

"Blondie..."

"People are watching, *kids* are watching."

I lift my gaze, and sure enough, all eyes were on us—kids and parents included.

Fuck, she's right.

Not waiting for an answer, she spins on the balls of her feet and goes back to the kids. Like a glutton for punishment, I watch her retreating back, the sway of her hips, the curve of her ass...

Get a grip, Walker. You're here to watch your kid's practice, not his teacher's sexy ass.

Shaking my head, I turn my attention to the field just to catch Levi waving at me, a big smile on his lips. I wave right back and go back to my spot on the bleachers.

The practice resumes, and this time, Savannah actually corrects the kid she's talking to, although her own stance could use some work. Something I could totally teach her, if—

"Hi there. I don't think we've met?"

I turn around at the sound of the sultry voice to find a blonde woman standing next to me. Her hair is so pale it almost looks white, nothing like Savannah's golden strands. Her brown eyes have more makeup on than some women wear when they're going partying. And then there is the dress and heels. Why would somebody wear high heels to a football practice? Especially a *kid's* football practice?

"Umm, I don't think so."

I start to turn my attention back to the field, but she slips on the bench next to me so close her leg is touching mine.

What the hell?

"I'm pretty sure I'd remember your face. Are you new in town?"

"Yes, we just moved here."

"Well, that's nice. Welcome to Bluebonnet Creek..." She lets her sentence hang in the air, waiting for me to finish it.

"Blake."

"It's so nice to meet you, Blake. I'm Lucy Donovan." She tilts her head to the kids. "Which one's yours?"

Just then Savannah stops next to Levi. "The one with Bl—" I catch myself at the very last second and clear my throat. "The one next to Miss Parker."

I might not want to hide the fact that Savannah and I knew each other, but I wasn't about to blurt out our business in front of a stranger. Especially a stranger who's her student's parent.

Levi looks over his shoulder and beams at her, his mouth moving quickly as he chats away. Her arm rests on his shoulder, and she nods at whatever he says, which only makes him smile harder, and I can feel my chest tighten.

My boy was hungry for female attention. And apparently, it wasn't just any female attention. He liked Savannah.

"Oh, my David is just across from him." She points in the general direction of the kids. "I don't know why she paired him up with that girl when he's so talented at football."

Oh, so her kid was the one throwing the ball with too much force to the poor girl.

Why am I not surprised?

"If good players don't practice with weaker ones, they'll never get better," I say non-committedly because what was there to say?

The woman—Lacy? Luce? No, Lucy—lets out a long sigh. "I guess there is that. Your wife isn't coming today?"

My head whips toward her at the sudden change of subject, but she blinks innocently, an easy smile plastered on her face.

"I don't have a wife." Before she can ask anything else, I turn my attention back to the field, just in time to see her kid throw the ball. But instead of using the force in his arm, his whole body shifts, making the trajectory of the ball curve.

Right toward Savannah.

"*Shit!*"

I'm on my feet before I know what I'm doing. Thankfully, the field is small, so I cross the distance in no time whatsoever. Savannah's eyes widen as she sees the ball coming, her face draining of all color. I jump at the ball at the very last second, my palms burning from the impact as my body rolls to the ground. The fall is hard, knocking the air out of my lungs and making my ears ring.

Fucking hell.

I blink a few times and start to push upright when Savannah's face appears above me. "Are you okay?"

My body falls back in surprise as she leans over me. She takes me in, scanning my body for any injuries; her blue eyes wide as she nibbles at her lip. She cups my cheek, her thumb skimming over my skin, and sending a shiver run down my spine. The scent of flowers, fields, and sun surrounds me instantly. *Fuck, she smells nice.*

"Blake? Talk to me. Did you hit your head? Should I call a doctor? Maybe you have a concussion and—"

"I'm fine," I say, my voice coming out rough as I push upright. Her hand slips down, and I miss her touch almost instantly.

"Are you sure? You fell down really hard—"

"I'm sure. This isn't my first rodeo." I push to my feet and extend my hand to help her upright, but I don't let go of her fingers instantly. "It's cute you're worried about me, Blondie."

Her lips part. "I'm n-not..." she stutters but is saved by one of the kids.

"That was so cool! You were so fast."

I turn around to find the boy—David—watching me with excitement dancing in his eyes. "And you jumped so high. I want to be able to do that."

My fingers clench around the ball as I fight my need to yell at the kid.

He's just a child, I remind myself. *Just a kid. He didn't know better.*

"I had to be fast because otherwise the ball could have hit somebody, and they would have ended up hurt." I look around the group, noticing all the kids' attention is on me. "In football, we don't throw the ball around without thinking. You have to visualize where you want it to go."

"Visualize?" a little girl asks, her brows furrowing in confusion.

"Yes, football isn't just about how strong one can throw the ball, but you have to see the field. You have to know where your teammates are, what their strengths and weaknesses are, and who will be able to get that ball to the end zone so you can win. But in order to do that, you need to know how to do it properly." I lift the ball in the air. "Who wants me to show you?"

Little hands shoot up in the air eagerly.

But before I can say anything else, Savannah steps in front of me, those blue eyes blazing as she glares at me and hisses softly, so only I can hear. "What are you doing?"

I cross my arms over my chest. "I'm going to teach these kids how to properly throw a ball, so somebody doesn't get a concussion in the process."

"You can't do that."

"And why not?"

"Well..." She tucks a strand of her hair behind her ear. "You're not the coach. I am."

I quirk my brow at her. "And what exactly is your experience?"

She opens her mouth, but no words come out.

"I'm a retired NFL player. Who better to teach these kids how to play football than me?"

I move closer, that intoxicating flowery scent filling all my senses. My eyes fall to those full lips, and I can feel my muscles tighten in response to her nearness.

"You know this would be the perfect solution, Blondie," I whisper, my voice coming out raspy. "I know the game. I have experience playing and working with kids. Lonestars occasionally organized summer camps for kids, and we'd go there and help around. So this wouldn't be anything new for me. Let me help you with this."

Plus, helping her meant spending more time with her. Getting to know her. Which is a win-win in my playbook.

I watch those pretty blue eyes widen slightly. They fall to my mouth before she lifts her gaze to meet mine, tongue darting out to sweep over her lower lip.

Fuck, she's killing me.

"Blondie..."

"Dad, are you going to coach football?" Levi asks as he joins us, glancing between Savannah and me.

The corner of my mouth tips upward. "You'll have to ask Miss Parker. She doesn't think I'm good enough."

Savannah glares at me. "I didn't say that."

Levi takes her hand, drawing her attention to himself. "He's the best, Miss Parker! He played in the NFL, and he even won the ring last year. Right, Dad? Did you tell her about the ring?"

A different kind of ring pops into my mind, and I'm not the only one. Savannah takes a step back, a mask of indifference slipping firmly in place. "Fine, but you'll have to take it up with the principal."

"Blo—"

She shoots me a death glare, so I press my lips together.

"Okay, *Miss Parker*. I can do that."

I'll do whatever I have to if it means I get to have this time with her.

Chapter 11

SAVANNAH

"This was exactly what I needed," Becky sighs after taking a long sip of iced tea. "Remind me again, why did I think walking around town in this heat was a good idea?"

Today, Bluebonnet was celebrating its Founder's Day, and just like every year, the town council decided to make a big deal out of it. Small businesses put out stands along Main Street and the gazebo; there were different games and attractions scattered throughout our little town, and later in the evening, there would even be a mini-concert, and a party organized on the high school football field.

Everybody and their mother were here. If people weren't working, they were mingling around, and there were a bunch of folks from surrounding towns as well.

I originally planned to use this extra day off to catch up on some housework, but Becky would have none of it.

"Don't ask me. If it were up to me, I'd be back in my house."

So far, I've only managed to tackle the first floor, and even that was just some basic cleaning and moving in. I had yet to step foot on the second floor or make any drastic changes, like taking down the wallpaper or putting a new coat of paint on. Or deciding which pieces of furniture I'll keep, and which needed replacing. Just thinking about my never-ending to-do list gave me an anxiety attack.

"Working your ass off, so it's not like it would be different from any other day. At least this way, you get to relax and have some fun."

"Maybe just a little bit."

"I'll give you a little bit." She shoves me away playfully. "I'm amazing company."

"And so humble, too."

But the truth was, I was enjoying spending time with my friend for a change. Both our lives had been crazy these past few weeks, and they were only bound to become crazier once our kids arrived.

Blinking, I start to turn toward Becky, when I spot two women watching me from a few tables away. My eyes narrow as I try to place them, but they quickly look away.

Becky shifts in her seat, and winces softly, drawing my attention.

"You okay?" I ask, eyeing her carefully.

She slides her hand to the small of her back, and her face twists in a grimace.

"My back just hurts, but honestly, that's nothing new. I swear if this kid doesn't come out soon, I'll scream."

"It should be any day now, no?"

"Yeah. I'm so ready for it, plus, Miguel's still in pre-season, so I'm hoping he'll be able to make it to the birth like we planned. We'll hear what our doctor tells us tomorrow at our appointment."

"Didn't you go just the other day?" I could have sworn she mentioned they went in for a checkup the last time we talked.

"We did, but they're way more frequent now that the baby is almost here. When's your next appointment?"

"It's next week."

A mix of excitement and fear swells inside my chest, but those feelings were my new normal since I saw that plus sign on the pregnancy test. So many things could go wrong, but I refused to let the fear win over me. The only thing that mattered was that my baby was okay, the rest I could deal with.

I slide my hand to the side of my belly, rubbing at the hard bump.

"I can't believe that I'm almost halfway there."

"Enjoy it while you can since this is the best part. Once you enter those final weeks, you'll be one swollen, painful, cranky, emotional mess." There is a short pause as she bites the inside of her cheek. "Your appointment. Do you want me to come or is B—"

"I thought it was you two!"

Becky and I turn in unison to find Jessica standing by our table.

"Hey, Jess!" I look behind her, but there is nobody there. "What are you up to?"

"I'm just meeting with some friends, but I saw you guys and wanted to say hi."

"Any exciting plans?" Becky asks, sitting upright.

"Nothing as exciting as Sav's life apparently." Jessica crosses her hands over her chest. "You've been keeping secrets from us."

An icy chill runs down my spine at her words.

"Wh-what?"

She couldn't know, could she? Nobody except Becky knew about Blake and me, so—

She smirks. "You've been the talk of the town—"

My heart starts beating faster, the sound echoing in my eardrums and muffling Jessica's words. I curl my fingers, but my palms are sweaty.

This couldn't be happening.

Is that what those looks have been about?

How did they find out? The whole situation was hard on its own; I didn't want people to meddle in my life...

"What new coach?" Becky's question snaps me out of my thoughts.

Coach?

Her eyes narrow at me. "You're not coaching the peewee football, but then who—" Her mouth falls open as the realization sets in. "No way! Walker? He's the new coach?"

I open my mouth, but no words come out. What is there to say, really?

"Yes, and apparently that's not it." Jessica wiggles her brows knowingly. "Some kid threw the ball and almost knocked Savannah over, but he ran across the field and stopped it from hitting her. It was quite a gesture."

Becky turns to me. "Did he now?"

"Stop it. It wasn't like that." I roll my eyes. "He was just showing off."

The corner of Becky's mouth tips upward. "Mm-hmm... I wonder why."

I shoot her a warning glare, that only makes her grin grow wider.

"People seem to like the idea of having a former NFL player coaching peewee football. I know my dad's excited. He couldn't stop talking about it during our dinner the other night." Jessica winces softly, and hurries to add, "Not that you weren't doing a good job..."

"But I'm not a former NFL player." I let out a loud snort. Jessica's dad was the elementary school principal. I was hoping he'd agree with me that having Blake coach peewee football was absurd, but he couldn't stop gushing over him. "I'm sure that's the only reason why parents like him so much."

Even saying parents was stretching it. It was *moms* who liked it. And not because of his football knowledge. They liked *him.* The bleachers were packed during the last practice, and I could barely hear myself think from their constant chatting and sighing every time he came close enough so they could ogle him. It was embarrassing. They were grown-ass women, for God's sake! Not just that, a good majority of them were married.

And I could do nothing but stand on the sidelines and watch it all unfold since, while my principal was ecstatic to have Blake on board, he still wanted me to be there to supervise practice and make him feel welcome. As if he needed me to do that when he had a whole freaking fan club there.

"Jealous, Sav?"

My head snaps up only to find Becky smirking at me. "Jealous?" I glare at her. "Of what exactly?"

"Oh, I don't know. You tell me."

"Please. They're acting like preteen girls who just saw the lead singer of their favorite boy band."

Jessica bursts into laughter. "I can totally see that being the case. Lucy Donovan was in the shop the other day, and she already had a plan on how to win him over."

I grind my teeth together, feeling that spike of irritation rising to the surface as the image of the gorgeous woman shamelessly flirting with Blake after practice flashes in my head. She was recently divorced and wasn't even hiding that she was on the lookout for a new husband, and in her head, Blake was perfect for her.

Only I was pregnant with his baby.

Wonder what she would say if she knew that little tidbit.

An elbow connects to my side. "Not jealous, huh?" Becky wiggles her brows.

"Stop it," I hiss, but it's already too late.

"Wait." Jessica glances between the two of us. "What am I missing?"

"What do you mean?" I tuck a strand of my hair behind my

ear, trying to seem as inconspicuous as possible, but Jessica isn't buying it. "You're not missing anything."

"I know I'm missing *something*."

"You're imagining it." I shake my head, scanning the crowd for a way out when I spot a familiar face. *Thank God!* "Hey, there is Miguel!"

Just then, he turns around to say something over his shoulder, and I see the person who's standing behind him.

And it's none other than the man we were talking about only a few seconds ago.

Because that's just my luck.

Blake shakes his head at whatever Miguel says before looking away.

Right. At. Me.

There is no missing the look of surprise on his face as his eyes land on mine, and I swear I can feel a jolt of awareness shoot down my spine as we stare at one another from a distance.

Shit, shit, shit.

How is this my luck?

It's like an invisible string connects us, and every time we'd enter within a couple of miles radius from one another, it would tug us together.

My tongue darts out, sliding over my dry lips as my heart starts beating harder, dulling the noises around me while his gaze holds me hostage.

"Sav, you okay?"

"What is *he* doing here?" I hiss softly, turning my attention to Becky. "Did you know he would be here?"

Becky lifts her arms in defense. "Nope, it was just supposed to be Miguel, Aaron, and Gage. I would have told you if I knew."

"Shit." I run my fingers through my hair.

What the hell was I supposed to do now?

I couldn't very well run away now that he saw me, no matter how tempting the idea was. I guess I should have expected it. After all, he's friends with Miguel. What were the odds of our paths not crossing? Pretty much nonexistent.

"Not missing anything, huh?" Jess asks, drawing my attention. "Seriously, what's the deal with you and the coach? You've been acting all weird."

"You're delusional. I'm not acting weird," I protest quickly.

Too quickly.

"Miss Parker."

The hair at the back of my neck prickles at attention at the sound of that low baritone. I bite the inside of my cheek, sucking in a sharp breath. Both Becky and Jessica just watch me with matching amused expressions on their faces.

Traitors.

"Delusional, huh?" Jessica smirks. I glare at her, but it doesn't faze her in the least. Instead, she smiles sweetly and greets Blake. "Coach. It's nice to see you here. Are you enjoying our small town?"

His brows furrow in confusion, but he nods. "Yes, Levi heard about the fair at school and asked me if we could come." Those dark gray eyes turn to me, and I can feel the goosebumps rise on my skin as he oh-so-slowly moves his gaze up. "Are you having fun, *Miss Parker?*"

"I was until a few moments ago."

Before you showed up.

He doesn't miss the silent jab, the corner of his mouth tipping upward. "Well, my day just got better. You look nice today."

Color rises up my cheeks at his words. They were completely inappropriate, something I'm pretty sure my friends didn't miss and will bring up the first chance they get. I'm just about to tell him that when a little body connects with his side.

"Dad! Dad!" Levi tugs at his arm. "Gage and I want to go to the haunted house. Can we? Pretty please?"

Blake looks down at his son. "Umm... yeah, buddy, sure thing."

"Yes!" Levi fist bumps excitedly, and turns around, which is when he spots me. "Hi, Miss Parker! Do you wanna go to the haunted house with us?"

Blake and I in the darkness alone?

"Oh, no, I'm good."

As a matter of fact, I was ready to leave. Somewhere far, far away from here. From *him*. Not like that was possible since the man seemed to be everywhere I went.

Blake turns to me, his arms crossing over his chest, making the tattoos on his forearms stand out. My throat goes dry as I watch those muscles flex. How is it possible that he can make a motion so mundane look so sexy? It doesn't seem fair.

"Don't tell me you're afraid, Miss Parker?"

"What?" I look up from Blake's arm to find him giving me a knowing smirk. My eyes narrow at him as I tuck a strand of my hair behind my ear. "Of course not, don't be ridiculous."

As soon as the words leave my mouth, I know I said the wrong thing.

"Prove it." Blake grins at me. "Come with us."

"Yes, Miss Parker!" Levi chimes in immediately. "You should come with us. It'll be so much fun. And if you're afraid, my dad can take care of you."

Levi's innocent words make me choke in surprise.

"I-I don't..." I stutter, trying to come up with something to get out of this mess, only to come up empty.

Becky snorts, or maybe it's Jessica, but before I can tell them exactly what I think about their reaction, Levi grabs my hand.

"C'mon. The haunted house is this way."

I look over my shoulder, trying to signal my friends to save me, only to catch Jessica and Becky high-fiving one another.

I'm so going to get back at them for this.

"Gage, let's go!" Levi yells, letting go of my hand, just as another one slides to the small of my back.

A bigger hand.

Much warmer.

A man's hand.

Blake's tall frame falls in step behind me. "C'mon, it's not going to be that bad. I don't bite." He leans down, his mouth brushing against the shell of my ear. "Except if you ask nicely."

A shudder goes through me as his warm breath tickles my skin. Blake chuckles, his thumb rubbing at the small of my back. I don't get a chance to answer because the next thing I know, we're standing in front of the haunted house.

There is no line, so Blake pulls out a wallet and hands the guy a few bills. On autopilot, I start to do the same, but Blake covers my hand with his. "Put that away."

"What? Absolutely not." There was no way I was letting him pay for me like this was some kind of date.

Because it wasn't.

"Blondie." The way he says my name sounds more like a growl. "I already took care of it, so put it away."

That hand is once again at the small of my back, giving me a gentle, yet firm, push toward the door, where the two boys have already disappeared to.

I turn over my shoulder to glare at him. "You can't pay for me, Walker. I can pay my own way. I've been doing it for years."

"I didn't say you couldn't." Blake's fingers slide through the small opening on the back of my dress and rub at my skin. I suck in a sharp breath as a shiver runs down my spine. Then he moves closer, his warm breath tickling the side of my face as he whispers, "Are you generally this stubborn, or is it just me you have a problem with?"

Seriously, what was it with that man and touching?

"I'm not being stubborn; I'm just saying it as it is," I mutter and hurry up, breaking the contact between Blake and me.

The boys giggle in the darkness, followed by somebody's scream, and a loud, bone-chilling cackle coming from the hidden speaker spreads through the room. My heart thunders loudly, sweat coating my palms.

It's just a silly haunted house, Sav. It's all fake.

Still, my eyes take in the darkness in front of me. They placed strategic lights through the space, shadows dancing and giving the room an eerie look. Very realistic cobwebs stuck to the corners are hung from the ceiling. Skeletons are placed against the walls, bats hanging on thin strings, and there is even an open coffin sitting in the corner of the room.

"Then what is the problem?" Blake continues as we move deeper into the house.

"It's not appropriate."

A loud, screeching noise makes me jump in surprise.

Blake bumps into me from behind, his palms landing on my shoulders. "You okay, Blondie?"

"Fine." I shake my head as I start walking again. Blake extends his hand, removing whatever is hanging from the ceiling so I can pass. "You're the father of one of my students."

"I'm also the father of your child," he mutters, not missing a beat.

Why did he have to be so rational?

"They don't know that."

"But they'll eventually find out. Besides, why do you care what other people think?"

"I know, it's just..."

How do I explain it to him?

I knew he was right. There was no avoiding it. But I wasn't ready for the fallout once that information got out.

My family's been gossiped about so many times over the years. I've worked so hard to put my past behind me, only to once again end up the center of attention, and now it was my own damn fault. And I wasn't the only one to consider. There were Blake's kids. Our baby. One wrong move and all our lives will be altered irrevocably.

"Blondie?"

"Nothing." I shake my head, walking past him.

And right into a skeleton.

Only this one is alive.

Bloodshot eyes meet mine as the person lifts his arms as if he's going to grab me, just as a piercing sound spreads through the room, followed by children's laughter and rushing footsteps.

"Holy fucking shi—" I turn around and collide with a firm, warm chest. One I recognize immediately, so I burrow my head into the soft cotton and inhale his spicy scent. My heart is beating wildly inside my rib cage, the sound echoing inside my ears as I try to calm down.

"I've gotcha," Blake murmurs, strong arms wrapping around me and pulling me closer. I could still see the grotesque face and the almost maniacal look in the skeleton's eyes.

"Is it gone?" I whisper softly, my fingers digging into Blake's shirt.

"He's gone." Blake smooths his hand up and down my back in gentle strokes. "You're safe."

I did feel safe.

Now that Blake's arms were around me, I could feel my muscles relax, if only slightly. My heartbeat was calming down, matching the steady rhythm of his heart.

It was crazy. I barely knew the man. And yet, being with him, I felt safer than anywhere else.

"You sure?"

Blake lets out a muffled sound, his chest shaking. "I'm sure, Blondie."

No, not his chest, his whole body.

I pull back, so I can look at him, only to find him fighting laughter.

He was laughing.

At me.

I slip out of his arms, irritation building inside me. "You're the worst!"

"What?" Blake asks, his face is all innocent.

But he can try that on somebody else. Maybe they'll believe him.

"You're laughing at me!"

He doesn't even try to deny it.

"You said you're not afraid of a haunted house."

"I'm not!" I jab him in the chest. "I was just surprised, that's all."

"Mm-hmm..." The corner of his mouth twitches upward. "Or maybe you just wanted to snuggle with me. It's okay, Blondie, I don't mind."

"Snuggle—" My mouth falls open, which only makes him chuckle harder.

The annoying, obnoxious, infuriating man.

That's what he was.

Pressing my lips together, I shake my head. "You know what? Whatever. Think what you will."

"Blondie, don—"

With one final glare at him, I spin around and march for the exit.

Chapter 12

BLAKE

"What's up with that scowl?" Miguel slides next to me, nudging me with his elbow. "I figured you'd be happier since you got to spend some time with Savannah."

"He fucked something up," Aaron chimes in as he takes a sip of his beer, his attention fixed on the boys who're playing hoops on the nearby stand. "She ran out of there like the devil's at her heels and has been glaring at him ever since."

I narrow my eyes at Aaron. "She isn't glaring at me."

"Only because she's been ignoring you for the last hour," Aaron points out.

I guess he had me there. Savannah is standing at another table along with Becky and Katherine Santiago. She and her husband Emmett joined our group while we were in the haunted house, and the women were currently watching how Emmett held his young daughter as they rode on the carousel.

Becky says something that has the woman laughing, and I can't help but feel a jab of jealousy at seeing Savannah so happy. I wanted to be the one who made her smile like that, but I always ended up saying the wrong thing.

"And the scowl is back." Miguel shakes his head. "You two seriously need to figure your shit out before that baby comes."

"Did you tell the boys at least?" I wince softly at Aaron's question, which earns me a disapproving look. "Seriously, dude?"

"There wasn't a right moment."

"There will never be a right moment for something like this." Aaron shakes his head. "The more you prolong it, the worse it will be once the truth comes out."

"I know." I run my hand over my jaw, feeling the frustration growing inside of me. "Fuck, I know. But I can't just come and say, 'Hey, boys, do you want Lucky Charms or Cocoa Puffs? Oh, and yeah, you'll be big brothers in about four months; congrats!'"

Miguel winces softly. "When you put it like that."

"I'll tell them. Trust me, the last thing I want to do is hide any of this, but I just have to figure out the best way to do it."

The best way to preserve the tentative relationship I was trying to build between my boys and me, while at the same time getting a chance to see where this thing with Savannah might lead me. Lead *us*. Where did I want it to lead us? That was the better question.

My gaze darts toward the table where the girls are sitting, only this time they're not alone. There is a tall guy standing between Becky and Savannah, his hand leaning casually against the back of Savannah's chair.

"Who the hell is that?" My fingers clasp into a fist by my side as I watch Savannah tilt her head back so she can look at the dude. She listens intently to whatever he's saying, and then she laughs—freaking laughs.

Something that feels a lot like red, hot anger boils inside my stomach.

Miguel looks at the girls. "That's Nico. We went to school together."

"You went to school with half this town," I mutter, glaring at the guy whose hand has now moved to Savannah's shoulder.

Was there something going on between the two of them?

"Just a handful of people." Miguel narrows his eyes at me, the corner of his mouth lifting in a knowing smirk. "Are you jealous, Walker?"

"Jealous?"

Because a good-looking young guy, somebody that was more her age and didn't have a ton of baggage like me, was touching her?

Hell, yes, I was jealous.

"You totally are jealous," Miguel says as if he can read my mind and bursts into laughter. "I think this is a first."

Reluctantly, I shift my attention to my friend. "What are you talking about?"

"You. I don't think I've ever seen you jealous before."

No, I don't believe he has. Because I wasn't that type of guy. At least, I thought I wasn't. I wasn't even jealous when I found out that Reina was cheating on me. I was hurt that it had to end the way it did, and I was angry that she left our boys the way she did, but I wasn't jealous. Not for a moment.

Until now.

Until I saw this preppy dude flirt with Savannah.

Because something about seeing that guy's hands on her, like they belonged there, annoyed the crap out of me.

I down the rest of my drink. "Shut up, Fernandez."

"What are you guys talking about?" Becky asks as she joins our group.

"Blake's dark mood." Miguel slips his hand around her waist as he pulls her into his side and takes her in. His palm rubs at the side of her belly, his lips brushing against the top of her head. "How are you feeling, Red?"

"The same." She waves him off, those green eyes fixing on me. "Why gloomy?"

"No reason." I look over her shoulder, expecting to see Savannah there, but she's nowhere in sight. "Where is Savannah?"

"So that's the reason for the gloominess." She smirks. "I should have figured as much."

"He got jealous when Nico stopped by."

Becky's elbow connects to Miguel's side, and he lets out a soft yelp. "As if you're one to talk. You men are all the same." She rolls her eyes. "She left for home a little while ago since she was tired."

"Tired?"

"Yes, Blake. Pregnant women get tired. And on that note, I think I'm ready to go home. My feet are killing me."

Miguel doesn't need to be told twice. "C'mon, Red. I promise to give you a foot rub when we get home. How does that sound?"

"Perfect."

They say their goodbyes, already too lost in one another. I watch them walk away slowly, and I can't help but feel a pang of jealousy. He was ten years my junior, and he had his life figured out. He put a ring on his fiancée's finger, and now they were expecting their first baby together.

"You want another drink?" Aaron asks, bringing me out of my thoughts.

"Nah, I'm good." I shake my head. "I think we'll go home too. Make sure Daniel didn't get into any trouble while we were away."

Aaron gives me a knowing look. "Yeah, good luck with that."

Knowing Daniel? I had a feeling I might need it.

Together, we collect the boys who have moved from

shooting hoops to the bumper cars and go back to the parking lot, where we say our goodbyes.

"Did you have fun?" I ask Levi as we get on the road.

"It was the bestest." He smiles sleepily. "Can we go again?"

I let out a soft chuckle. "I'm not sure when the next town fair will be, but sure, we can go."

"Can Kyle come with us the next time?" he asks, his smile growing bigger at the idea. "I think he would like it."

"We'll see, buddy. How about we start with a play date at the park or something?"

"Or he could come to our house, and we can play together with Lego bricks."

"Sure thing; we can ask."

Levi nods. "You'll have to learn how to talk with your hands."

"Talk with my hands?" My brows pull together in confusion.

"Yes. Kyle doesn't hear, so we talk with our hands. Like this."

I look up in the rearview mirror and find him moving his hands.

"What did you just tell me?"

Levi giggles. "My name, silly!"

"You're right, silly me." I make a turn into our neighborhood. "When did you become so smart?"

"I've always been smart, Dad! Duh! I wanna know *all* the signs. Miss Parker is teaching us."

Why didn't that surprise me in the least? Maybe I was wrong, and Savannah knew sign language from before, but she seemed like the type of woman who'd go the extra mile to make her students feel welcome and included.

"You like Miss Parker?"

"Yes." He leans forward in his car seat, his voice dropping lower. "Although she's a big scaredy cat."

The feel of Savannah's body pressed against mine in that haunted house flashes in my mind. Her sweet scent surrounding me. Her fingers clutching at me for dear life. The way she buried her face into my shoulder, her body molding to mine just right. As if she belonged there.

"That she is," I agree softly as I pull in front of our house and kill the engine.

The light is on in the hallway, but the rest of the house is in darkness; nothing unusual since Daniel has probably closed himself in his bedroom and is playing his video games.

Sliding out of the truck, I hold the door open for Levi. "Go upstairs, change into your PJs, and don't forget to brush your teeth." The movement across the street catches my attention. "I'll be up to check on you in a few minutes."

"Okay, Dad!" He rushes past me toward the stairs.

"I mean it, Levi. I'll know if you don't, and then you'll be in trouble."

"Will do!" he yells as he climbs two steps at a time. How he had the energy after spending the whole day outside playing, I had no idea. I was freaking exhausted.

With a sigh, I close the door and cross the street to where Savannah is sitting on the stairs of her front porch; her head tilted back as she watches the sky.

"Running away again, Blondie?"

"It can hardly be called running away when you know where I live."

I join her on the step, my arm brushing against hers. "The only difference is that now I know where to find you."

She tilts her head, those crystal blue eyes meeting mine. She took off her makeup at some point since she got home, her face completely bare but no less beautiful. I liked seeing her like this.

Seeing all the different sides of her that made her the woman she is. And the more I saw the more I wanted to get to know her. Truly know her. Know her ticks and tells. Know how to make her laugh and what made her sad.

I wanted to know every single piece of her: body, mind, and soul.

It was scary. I never wanted anything like that. Not with Reina, or any woman that was there before her.

A lock of hair falls into Savannah's face. She starts to lift her hand, but I'm faster. I curl the silky strand around my finger, testing its softness, before I gently tuck it behind her ear. My knuckles brush against her cheek, and she inhales deeply.

It's like all the air has been sucked out of the space, leaving only the sizzling, pent-up tension that's been building between us since that first night we met.

"I wanted to look for you the moment I woke up that day," I whisper softly. "But you were gone, and I had nothing to go by. I cursed myself so many times for agreeing to your idea."

Those full, pink lips part in surprise. My gaze falls to her mouth. The mouth I've thought about kissing so many times in the last few weeks. I wanted to see if she tasted as good as I imagined she would. If it would feel as good as I thought it would.

I slip my hand under her chin, the tip of my thumb rubbing over her lower lip.

"Blake..."

My name is a breathy whisper on her lips, a prayer and a curse all in one, but she doesn't pull away.

I lean down, closing the distance between us. Just a few inches. That's all that was left between us. Mere inches...

"What the hell is going on here?"

Savannah and I jump apart at the question, turning toward the sound of the voice, I find Daniel coming from the shadows, his hands curled into fists by his sides as he glares at the two of us.

Shit.

Panic slams into me as I try to figure out how much he heard and saw. If it's to be judged by the way he is looking at us, enough.

Then something else clicks.

The direction from which he came. It was from *behind* Savannah's house.

My eyes narrow at him. "What are you doing outside?" I ask, pushing to my feet.

Savannah starts to get up too, so I grab her arm to help steady her, my fingers lingering on her soft skin before turning my attention to my son, whose gaze is locked to that singular point of contact. Reluctantly, I force my fingers to uncurl and let go. "Daniel?"

He looks up slowly. "I was bored, so I went out for a walk." He shrugs, trying to play it off, but there was just something about his stance that wasn't adding up.

"You said you'd stay home," I remind him, crossing my arms over my chest.

Daniel's eyes turn to slits, but he doesn't back down. "I'm here, aren't I?"

"Daniel," I growl in warning. He's been toeing the line since we moved here, trying to test my limits, and I've all but had it with him.

"What?" He lifts his arms in the air and lets them fall by his sides. "I'm here, just chill."

"What I want to know is where you were before."

"Well, what I wanna know is what were you"—he shifts his attention to Savannah—"doing out with her?"

"Miss Parker and I were just talking. Now will you..."

Daniel lets out a snort and stops me before I can finish.

"Talking? You can tell that to Levi. He might believe you." He chuckles, but there is no amusement in his voice, only anger and resentment. "I'm not a kid anymore. You're fucking her."

From the corner of my eye, I can see Savannah flinch at his crude, hurtful words.

My fingers clench into a fist as I take a step closer, trying to keep my voice in check. "Watch your mouth, Daniel. You'll not talk like that about Savannah or any other woman for that matter."

"Now it's Savannah, huh? Done with pretending, *Dad*?" Daniel spits out, anger burning in his gray eyes. "And how should I be talking about her? I'm just stating the truth. It didn't take you long to find somebody new." He turns to Savannah, his eyes scanning her from head to toe. "But Levi's teacher of all people? Seriously? And not just that, she's also pregnant. How can you—" His words trail off, brows pulling together, and I can see his mind work, putting the pieces together. "Holy shit."

"Daniel, I swear to God..."

"It's yours," he mutters, his mouth falling open. "The... The kid, it's yours."

Fuck my life.

Savannah's panicked eyes meet mine.

This was bad.

So, so bad.

My worst-case scenario was playing out in front of me, and there was nothing that I could do to put a stop to it.

"Daniel..." I place my hand on his shoulder, my heartbeat echoing in my ears as I try to find the right words, but Daniel yanks his hand out of my grasp.

His cheeks are red, eyes wild as he glances from me to Savannah and back.

He takes a step back. "You knocked her up?"

"It's not like it seems..."

But it was exactly as it seemed.

I was the father of Savannah's baby.

There was no denying that. I didn't want to deny that.

"You're a fucking liar," Daniel yells. I don't try to stop him when his fists connect with my chest. "You knocked her up. Is that why you were so insistent that we should move here? So you can be with her?"

"He didn't know I was pregnant until you guys moved here," Savannah says softly, her hand reaching for Daniel's forearm.

"Don't touch me," he hisses, pulling his arm back. "Who the hell do you think you are? Just because he's fucking you doesn't give you the right to mess with our lives."

"Daniel..." I grab his arm and pull him back, so he doesn't shove her by accident.

If he wanted to take his frustration out on somebody, it should be me, not Savannah.

"One more word, and I swear to God, you won't like the consequences," I growl softly, my grasp on him tightening in warning. "Just because you're angry at me doesn't give you the right to act this way."

He lifts his chin up, the defiance written all over his face. "Fuck you. Both of you."

Ripping his hand out of my grasp, he spins on the balls of his feet and marches toward the house without another word.

"Fucking hell," I mutter, running my hand through my hair as I watch after him, anger and frustration boiling inside of me.

Not just at Daniel, but also at myself.

I should have told them both the moment I realized Savannah was pregnant with my baby, and none of this would have happened, at least not to this extent.

When I turn toward Savannah, I find her standing a few feet away from me, her arms wrapped around herself as she stares toward my house where Daniel disappeared to, a somber expression on her face.

"I'm so sorry for the way he spoke to you."

"Can you blame him?" Savannah gives her head a little shake before she shifts her gaze to me. "You should go and check in on him."

"I..." I rub my palm over the scruff on my jaw.

The need to stay here with her and make sure she's okay fights with my need to do right by my son. This whole situation is fucked up on so many levels, I couldn't even begin to put it into words.

They deserved better.

Levi.

Daniel.

Savannah.

Our unborn baby.

They all deserved so much better than a man who kept messing up over and over again.

"Go home, Blake," Savannah says softly. "He might be angry, but at the end of the day, he's just a kid. And I think deep down he needs his dad to reassure him that everything will be alright."

There was no judgment on her face, only sadness. And I hated that I was the reason for it. How Savannah could find grace for my son after he said all those things to her, I'll never understand. Most women would be appalled, but not her. Never her.

Instead, she was worried about him.

I scan her face, but that unreadable mask is firmly back in place. "We'll talk later?"

I needed to know that this wasn't the end. That while I might need to sort this whole situation with Daniel out, and I still had to tell Levi, she'd give me a chance to make this right.

She'd give me—give *us*—a chance, period.

Her throat bobs as she swallows and nods. "You know where to find me."

"That I do. Good night, Blondie."

"Night."

She turns around and makes her way inside. I wait to hear the resounding *click* of the lock falling into place before I face my house.

Yes, I hate how this whole situation played out, but I couldn't deny that a part of me was relieved that the truth was finally out in the open.

Now I just had to figure out how to make things right.

With everybody.

Shaking my head, I make my way back home. The house is eerily quiet as I climb up the stairs. Levi's door is open, and he's lying in his bed.

Taking in a long breath, I enter the room. "All done buddy?"

"Yeah," he murmurs, his eyes heavy with sleep. "What's with Daniel? He just ran into his room and slammed the door."

I sit down on the edge of the bed and slick back his hair. "He's angry with me."

"That's nothing new."

"No, I guess it isn't. Sleep tight. I'll go and talk to him."

"Mm-hmm... Night, Dad."

"Night, buddy."

The bed creaks when I push to my feet. I'm just at the door when Levi calls out. "Dad?"

I look over my shoulder at his sleeping frame. "Yeah?"

"Today was lots of fun."

"Today was lots of fun for me, too," I whisper back. He nods, snuggling deeper into the pillow. By the time I close the door of his room, he's already asleep.

Rubbing my palm over my face, I look at the room across the hallway.

You're in this mess because you've tried to avoid this in the first place. It's nobody's fault but your own, so now deal with it.

I let out a sigh and crossed the room. Silence greets me on the other side, and the need to barge in and make sure Daniel is really inside is strong. I didn't forget that he wasn't back home like he said he would be. Then again, did I really get to judge him for not confiding in me when I didn't do the same?

"Daniel?" I knock against the door, listening intently for any sign of life, but there is nothing. "We have to talk about what happened."

More silence.

"Dan—"

Something bangs against the door, making it rattle.

Loudly.

"Leave me alone."

That's promising.

I run my fingers through my hair.

"Fine. Sleep on it, but we're talking about it tomorrow." I wait for a heartbeat, hoping for some kind of response, even if it's another thing thrown at the door, but there is nothing. Sighing, I whisper, "I love you."

Still nothing.

Not that I expected it.

Not from Daniel.

But I was determined to keep saying it.

Maybe one day he'll actually believe me.

Maybe one day he'll forgive me.

Tonight wasn't that day.

Chapter 13

SAVANNAH

My phone buzzes on the table, drawing my attention from the class schedule I was making for next week. Absentmindedly, I grab it and press the answer button, but before I can even open my mouth, Becky begs, "I'll give you anything you want if you can bring me one large, iced coffee from Reading Nook."

Placing my pen down, I lean back, stretching my sore muscles. "While that's a tempting offer, how come you don't go and get it yourself? Weren't you just complaining that you were bored being stuck at home all day?"

"Yeah, well, things have changed..."

There is a beep, and when I pull my phone away from my face, I notice that she switched to a video call.

What the...

I press answer and almost drop my phone when I see the little bundle in a bassinet with the tiniest blue cap pulled over his head.

"Oh my gosh..."

"Sav, meet Jackson Luis Fernandez, your godson."

Tears blur my eyes as I stare at the baby. His skin is slightly red and wrinkled, but he's still the most gorgeous baby I've ever seen.

"He's precious."

"He is, isn't he?" she says softly, her finger gently sliding over Jackson's curled fist. "He came into this world kicking and screaming in the middle of the freaking night. If that's not an indication of what our future will look like, I don't know what is."

I chuckle softly, brushing away a tear that slipped down my cheek. "You'll figure it out. He's amazing. How are you feeling?"

"Like I could use some decent iced coffee. And maybe some of those muffins I love from Reading Nook? Miguel offered to go and get them for me, but I don't want him to leave."

No, I don't believe she would. Not after they just had their first baby.

"No worries, I can get them for you. I was just finishing up at school anyway."

"You're a godsend, Sav."

"We'll see if you think that when I collect on that 'anything' you promised me. Send me the details, and if you need something else. I'll see you guys in a few."

With that, I disconnect the call and start gathering my things. I grab my water bottle from my desk, refill it before leaving school, and jump into my car just as my phone *pings* with a message—the floor and room number.

Putting the car into drive, I rest my hand against my belly. "Time to go meet your friend, Munchkin."

After a quick stop at the Reading Nook to grab Becky's order, I make a pit stop at Walmart, where I buy a few goodies for the new parents and continue to the hospital. Thankfully, there is no traffic, so I get there in a decent amount of time.

Grabbing the basket and the coffee, I slip out of the car and make my way inside.

I still couldn't wrap my mind around it: Becky and Miguel were parents.

It seemed surreal.

Would I feel like that when I give birth?

Most likely.

The nurses smile at me as I pass by, but they don't ask any questions while I go down the hallway. The message says it's the last room on the right, and sure enough, when I come closer, I can hear Becky's soft voice coming through the crack in the door that was left open.

I slow down my steps as I move closer and spot Becky lying in bed, holding her new baby, with Miguel sitting behind her, his arms protectively wrapped around them.

I bite the inside of my cheek as I stand there and watch them. It felt wrong to barge in and intrude on what was clearly a private moment between the three of them.

"He has your nose," Becky whispers, looking over her shoulder at Miguel, who smiles at her, a look of pure adoration on his face.

A knot forms in my throat as I watch them. A perfect little family. It was the only thing I've wanted for as long as I can remember—somebody to call mine.

And I'll have it. Soon enough, I'll have a little person to call mine. But it won't be the same since it'll be just the two of us.

Swallowing the knot in my throat, I turn around. I'll just go to the bathroom and give them a momen—

All the air is knocked out of my lungs as I collide with a firm chest.

Shit.

I tighten my hold on the coffee and basket, so they don't fall.

Warm hands wrap around mine, holding me steady. The calloused fingertips rub at my skin.

Fingertips I was familiar with.

Fingertips that were, only last night, caressing my face as he was leaning down to kiss me when we were interrupted.

"Blondie..."

I raise my gaze and find Blake standing in front of me, surprise written on his face. "What are you doing here?"

"Becky called me and asked me to bring her some iced coffee and muffins."

"Did you say you have muffins?"

I jerk back at the sound of Levi's question, the sudden movement almost making the basket fall. *Again.*

"Gimme that," Blake mutters, taking the basket from my hands before I can protest.

I look down at the small boy, who's watching me expectantly, an "It's a boy!" balloon clasped in his hand.

I tuck a strand of my hair behind my ear. "Umm, yes, I do."

"Can I have one?"

"Levi, that's for Rebecca." Blake shoots Levi a pointed look.

Levi pouts unhappily. "But those are muffins!"

"You know what else I have?" I interject before Blake can protest again. "Some chocolate chip cookies."

Those silver eyes that are so much like his father's shine in excitement. "Can I have that instead? I like chocolate more. Just like my friend Kyle."

I chuckle softly. "You can have them"—he opens his mouth, so I lift my finger—"after you see the baby. We can't touch him with dirty hands."

"Fine, I guess."

By the sigh he lets out, you'd think he has all the weight of the world resting on his small shoulders.

"You guys are here!"

We all turn toward the door to find Miguel standing in the doorway, looking at us.

"And we brought you your things," Blake says as he goes toward Miguel. Shifting the basket to one hand, he pulls him into a hug. "Congrats, man."

"Thanks." Miguel waves us into the room. "C'mon, go inside, he just woke up a little while ago."

"Can I see him?" Levi asks, clearly excited. "We brought him the balloon."

"Why, thank you. Go on in."

Levi slips past him, and I join him, giving Miguel a quick hug. "Congrats, Dad."

"Don't congratulate him. It's not like he did any hard work, he only got to participate in the fun part," Becky mutters as I hand her the coffee. She takes a long pull from the cup and sighs happily. "This is exactly what I needed."

"Maybe she'll start feeling less cranky now," Miguel mock-whispers.

"Oh, stop it." I shove him playfully, my attention going to Levi, who's standing by the bassinet, still holding the balloon.

"He's so tiny," he breathes, his eyes wide as he takes in the baby.

"He is, isn't he."

"Eighteen inches, five pounds and ten ounces," Miguel beams proudly.

Levi leans closer, his mouth falling open. "Look, he's watching me." He looks up at Becky. "Can we play together?"

Becky chuckles softly. "Not just yet, buddy. But soon. Once he's a bit bigger."

His smile falls a little, but he doesn't pull away. "You have to grow fast so we can play together."

My heart swells a little bit inside my chest as I watch this sweet boy interact with the baby.

Munchkin's half-brother.

I move closer, standing just behind Levi. He gazes at the baby, gently playing with his foot. Not that I'm surprised. Levi is an extremely emotional and kind kid, and I could already see that he'll be one of the most popular students in his class.

Will he be equally excited when Munchkin is born? Will he come to visit my baby and gush over his new brother or sister? My stomach clenches just at the thought. I wanted it. I wanted it so badly.

Grazing my teeth over my lower lip, I look up, only to find Blake watching me. My cheeks heat at being caught staring. It's as if he can see right through me, into my very soul, and I wasn't sure how I felt about it.

"Miss Parker, are you also going to have a baby boy?"

The sudden question has me turning my attention to Levi, and I can feel my palms turn clammy with nerves.

Does he know? Did Blake tell him? Did Daniel?

I look up at Blake, only to be greeted by a matching panicked expression as he shakes his head no, and it takes all that's in me not to let out a sigh of relief.

"I don't know."

After everything that happened with Daniel last night, I couldn't fall asleep. I was so anxious about the whole thing, and Daniel's reaction. Would Levi be the same?

The thought of his rejection and potential resentment scared me shitless. Not for me, I could deal with that. I've already dealt with that, but I didn't want my baby to be despised by his or her family if I could help it. I wanted better for Munchkin, but what if that wasn't in the cards? What if they hate me, and by extension they hate my baby?

"How can you not know?" Levi's brows furrow in confusion.

"Well, the baby is still too small, so the doctor can't see it clearly."

Levi thinks about it for a moment before nodding. "I guess that makes sense. When will you be able to see it?"

"In a few weeks. But I think I'll wait until the baby is here. Make it a surprise."

Levi's eyes widen. "Really? You don't wanna know?"

"No, I just want my baby to be healthy, that's all. Like this little guy." Just then, Jackson makes a sound in protest. "Oh, no, no..." I coo gently, rubbing the back of my finger against his clenched fist. His skin is impossibly soft, and he has that newborn smell to him. All I wanna do is bury my head in the crook of his neck and inhale it deeply so it can calm me. "Why are we crying now?"

"Wanna hold him?" Becky asks. "Maybe moving him would help a little."

I glance at her. "You sure?"

"Yeah, go ahead. You have to practice anyway."

"I guess you're right about that. There, there, I've gotcha," I softly whisper as I wrap my hands around the bundle and pull him into my arms. Becky makes a face as she shifts in the bed. "You okay?"

"Just sore, but it'll pass." A smile spreads over her lips as she looks at her son. "It was worth it. *He* was worth it."

"He was." Jackson stops fussing, and those big, dark eyes open and look at me, and my heart melts a little, tears filling my eyes. "He really is perfect."

"Why are you crying, Miss Parker?"

"I'm just emotional, that's all." I sniff a little. "They're happy tears."

If I was this much of a mess now, I couldn't even imagine what it would feel like when I gave birth to my baby.

From the corner of my eye, I can see Becky try to reach for

the basket. Miguel sees it immediately and grabs it, handing it to her. His hand lingers on Becky's, and I can't help the pang of jealousy.

Not at my friends, God knows they deserved this happiness more than anybody else after everything they've been through. What I'm jealous of is the bond and love they share.

Because I want it.

I want to have somebody who'd love me the way Miguel loves Rebecca.

Just then, the door opens, and two older couples peek inside.

Fernandezes and Santiagos.

Both women attended our monthly book club at Reading Nook. They glance at the baby, gushing at the small boy for a moment.

"Oh, Becky, he's beautiful..." Mrs. Fernandez says.

"Just like his momma." Mrs. Santiago moves past me and goes to Becky, kissing her on the cheeks. "Congratulations, honey. How are you feeling? Need me to bring you something?"

"Hey, what about me?" Miguel protests.

"Oh, shush you. You had the easiest part up until now," his mom chides.

"No, I'm fine. Sav already got me everything I need."

The older woman glances at me and gives me a soft smile.

"You wanna hold him?" I ask, stepping closer to Mrs. Fernandez.

"Oh, I don't want to intrude. We just came in to check on you guys. See if you need anything."

"You're not intruding." Becky waves her off as I gently shift the baby from my arms into his grandmother's and take a step back.

"Oh, he's precious," she whispers, just as Mr. Fernandez comes to stand behind her, glancing at the baby over her shoulder.

"His name is Jackson." Becky smiles at them. "Jackson Luis Fernandez."

Miguel's father lifts his head; his mouth opens in clear surprise, eyes slightly misty.

I move out of the way as Miguel goes to join his parents, my eyes glued to them.

A family.

Something I would never have.

When I give birth, it'll be me and my baby. No loving husband that'll hold my hand through the pain and reassure me everything will be okay. No parents who will come to see me, excited to meet their grandchild.

If Grams were here, she would be there. Every step of the way. She would be by my side, just like she always had been. But she, too, is gone.

And there is nobody.

Just me and Munchkin.

And the thought only makes me feel more alone than ever.

Chapter 14

BLAKE

The room is a cacophony of noises once the two older couples join us. Soft coos and gushing over the new mom and the baby fill the space.

But not Savannah.

It's like she pulled away once they came in.

A longing expression appeared on her face, but sadness soon replaced it.

Deep, soul-crushing sadness that was like a punch to my gut.

The need to go to her and wrap my arms around her to make sure that she was okay and reassure her that whatever was troubling her would go away was overwhelming.

But before I can do or say anything, she's already picking up her bag and leaning down to whisper something to Becky.

A worried expression flashes on Rebecca's face, but Savannah forces out a smile and tells her something that must reassure her because she nods, and before I know it, Savannah is slipping out of the room.

Shit.

I glance at Levi, who's watching everything play out from the chair next to the bed. "I'll be back in a bit, okay?"

He nods, his attention going to the door. For a moment, I wonder what he's thinking about, but I know I have to hurry up if I want to catch up to Savannah before she disappears.

Miguel glances at me, but I just shake my head and mouth, "A minute," before slipping out the door just in time to catch a glimpse of golden hair dashing behind the corner.

I hurry after her.

Something about this whole situation felt off. Why did she leave like that? Things were fine only moments ago, and she just left without so much as a goodbye?

No, something wasn't adding up, and I wanted to know what.

The elevator *pings*, and I start to run, my hand jots forward just as the door is about to close.

A blonde head lifts up, tear-stained blue eyes meeting mine.

"Blondie…"

My chest squeezes tightly as I stare at her, my breathing ragged. The elevator door closes behind us, and we start to move.

"Wh-what are you doing here?" Savannah looks away, rubbing at her cheeks.

I gently wrap my fingers around her wrists and pull her hands down. "What's wrong, baby?" I rasp out, the endearment falling off my tongue as natural as breathing.

"Nothing, I'm just tired."

"Bullshit."

She looks up, her eyes widening in surprise at my harsh words. But I won't let her simply brush away the fact that something clearly upset her.

Upset her to the point she was *crying*.

Fuck that.

"Tell me what's wrong," I say, this time more gently.

"It's nothing; just leave it already. I'll be fine."

"You're not fine. What happened out there? You just up and dashed off—"

Just then, the door opens, and before I know it, she slips away.

Fucking hell.

I run my hand through my hair in frustration before starting after her. People give us curious looks, but I ignore them, catching up to Savannah just as she exits the hospital.

"Savannah, what the he—"

She turns around to face me, fire blazing in her tear-stained gaze. Even before she opens her mouth, I know I've crossed a line. I can see the exact moment something in her snaps. It's like the dam broke, and all the feelings she's been pushing back are coming out to the surface, threatening to swallow us both in their intensity, and I could only hope I would be able to stand out the storm.

"You wanna know why I ran away?" she mutters, her lip wobbling slightly as a tear slides down her face, and she points at the door. "Because that in there? It'll never be me. When I go into labor, I'll be all alone. There will be no family to come and see how I'm doing, nobody to help me through those first days and weeks." She hiccups softly. Her hand falls, fingers curling into a fist. "It'll just be me and Munchkin, and I'm scared. I'm scared, and I'm sad, and I feel so freaking guilty for feeling jealous of my best friend. Who does that?"

"Blondie..." I tighten my grip on her, pulling her to me.

Shit, how long has she been keeping all of this to herself?

She shakes her head, her fist connecting to my chest.

"A friend who's been through so much and deserves all of this and then some. I'm crying because I miss my Grams, and I know she would have loved to be here to see all of this, but she's gone, and I have nobody. *Nobody*, Blake."

"Hey, you're not alone," I whisper softly. Tugging her closer, I wrap my arm around her, slipping my finger under her chin, and force her to turn to me. "You're *not* alone. I've gotcha, Blondie. We're in this together. You and me."

She blinks, more tears rolling down her cheeks.

"We can't be in this together. Your kids hate me."

"They don't hate you."

"Daniel does."

Fuck.

I was screwing this up on all fronts and royally.

"He doesn't hate you. If he hates anybody, it's me. I'm the one who keeps throwing changes at him, but he'll come around, just... give him time. I promise you he's a good kid."

Her tongue peeks out, sliding over her lower lip, drawing my gaze to that lush pink mouth. "I don't blame you. You should put them first. I'll put Munchkin first, always."

"I know you will," I say, my throat feeling tight. "You'll be an amazing mother, Blondie. I'll put our baby first, along with Levi and Daniel," I promise. And it was a promise I meant to keep. Rubbing my hand over her lower lip, I slide it to her cheek. "But I'm putting you first, too, Savannah." Leaning down, I press my forehead against hers, that sweet scent of jasmine and something else, something sweet and wild, filling my lungs. "I've gotcha, Sav. You'll never again be alone. I'm here, and I'm not going anywhere, no matter what."

Her lips part, her fingers digging into my shirt. "You don't want me," she whispers, her words barely audible.

"Bullshit." My hand slides to the back of her neck, my fingers tangling in her hair. "I want you. I've wanted you since that first night we met, and I couldn't stop thinking about you since. You've been the only thing that's been on my fucking mind ever since I laid my eyes on you a few weeks ago, Blondie."

She starts to shake her head, but I tighten my hold on her, not letting her move. "I want you. You drive me crazy half the time with your stubbornness and independence, but damn it if it's not the sexiest thing I've ever seen. I want *you*, Savannah."

I move slowly, giving her ample time to pull back, but she doesn't. So I press my mouth to her cheek in a gentle kiss, no more than a fleeting caress. I can taste the saltiness of her tears, my thumb gently massaging her neck.

"I want you, Savannah, but if you don't want this..."

She tilts her head, those bright blue eyes meeting mine as our warm breaths mingle together, but she doesn't take a step back. No, that soft mouth meets mine, and fuck it, she tastes even sweeter than I imagined.

Groaning, I swipe my mouth against hers slowly, not wanting to scare her. Her fingers curl into a fist, tugging me closer, all those luscious curves press against me. She moans softly; that low sound sends a jolt of need through my body. My dick is rock hard as it rubs against her belly.

Sweeping my tongue over her lower lip, I deepen the kiss. I slide my hand to the small of her back, pulling her flush against me as my tongue dives into her mouth.

And holy shit.

This kiss was unlike anything I've ever experienced. Her tongue meets mine in a sensual dance like we've done the same thing a hundred times before, her body fits against mine perfectly. She pulls back, and I nip at her lower lip before tugging her to me again.

There was probably a good reason why we hadn't kissed that first night because if we did, I might not have let her go at all. Because if all I could do was kiss Savannah Parker for the rest of our days, I'd take it.

The sound of the approaching sirens snaps us out of our daze, and Savannah pulls back. I stare at her as I try to catch my breath. There were still traces of tears on her skin, but a healthy glow was back on her cheeks.

"You should go inside." Savannah sinks her teeth into her lower lip, averting her gaze from me. "Levi is waiting for you."

This woman...

Even after everything that has just happened, she still puts my kids first.

"In a minute. Levi is safe with the Fernandezes." Cupping her face, I slide my thumbs over her cheeks, brushing away the tear stains as I wait for her to look at me. "I know this is all messed up, and I know it's not fair, but I need time to figure this out with my kids."

She opens her mouth, but I press my lips against hers, effectively shushing her. "*However*, don't go thinking for a second that this isn't real or that I don't want you. This is what you do to me, Blondie. I'll be there for you for whatever you need. I'll be at every appointment, and I'll give you anything you need. You want me to hold your hand in the delivery room? I can do that. You want me to get the hell out? I can do that too. I'll hate every minute of it, but I'll do whatever you need me to do. Be whoever you need me to be."

Letting my hand slide down, I intertwine our fingers. "We're in this together, Blondie, but I need you to let me in."

Her throat bobs as she swallows, but she nods. "Okay."

I blink, unsure if I heard her correctly. "Yeah?"

"Yes, I..." Her tongue darts out, sliding over her lower lip as she glances away, the words coming out low. "Letting people in doesn't come easy for me."

No, I don't think it does.

This was another small piece of her that made her the woman standing in front of me. I wanted to ask her what happened to make her so guarded, but I had a feeling it would only make her close off again.

Piece by piece.

I was determined to collect them all. I wanted to know every single thing, no matter how small and insignificant, because to me, it wasn't.

She was slowly becoming everything.

And she didn't even realize it.

That's why I couldn't hurry and would have to let her come to me when she was ready to share more about herself. My boys weren't the only ones who needed time to adjust to our new normal.

"When you're ready." I slide my finger under her chin and turn her to face me. "I'll be waiting for you. I'm not going anywhere."

Those big blue eyes stare at me, her throat bobbing visibly.

"C'mon, where did you park your car?"

"Oh, you don't ha—"

"I want to." I stop her before she can even finish, my eyes locking on hers as I tighten my grip on her hand. "I know I don't *have* to. But I *want* to. I want to take care of you and our baby. Do you wanna know why I moved here?"

Savannah blinks, clearly surprised by my subject change but she nods.

I let out a shaky breath. I couldn't expect her to share her past with me if I wasn't willing to do the same.

"For most of my childhood, it was just my mom and I, and we were scraping by. She got pregnant young and did the best she could, but she was a single mom working a low-paying job. So when I got a chance to play pro, I took it, hoping I could do better for my kids and make their lives easier. But in doing so, I missed so many important moments of their lives, and we got to the point that I didn't know my kids, and they didn't know me, and it was all my fault. When Reina left, I knew I had to do something to change that, so I quit football and decided to move here. I want to give Daniel and Levi the father they deserve. I want to be there for my family. That's all I've ever wanted, Savannah. And want it or not, you're also my family, and together, we have to figure out a way to make this work."

She's nibbling at her lower lip as she processes my words, a serious expression on her face.

Finally, after what feels like forever, Savannah nods in agreement. "Okay. It's this way."

She tries to pull away, but I tighten my grip on her hand and indicate that she can lead the way. With another sigh, she starts walking.

Her Volvo is parked relatively close by. The lights flash as she unlocks the door.

She looks at me, tucking a strand of her hair behind her ear. "Could you... Could you not mention this to anybody?"

"My lips are sealed," I promise and pull open the door for her.

"Thank you." She lets out a long sigh, her body visibly relaxing. She slides into the driver's seat, so I take a step back. "Blake?"

"Yes?"

She tucks a strand of hair behind her ear as she looks up. "I have a doctor's appointment next week. Do you..." She lets out a shaky breath. "Do you wanna come?"

Her voice is soft and laced with uncertainty. Seeing her like this breaks something in me.

"I'd love to come."

"Okay." She nods, a tentative smile curling her lips, and I have to grip the door, so I don't lean in and kiss her again. "I'll text you the details."

"Sounds perfect. Do you want to write down my numbe—"

"I have it." She must see my confused expression because she explains. "The school records."

Right.

Savannah turns on the engine and glances at me. "I'll see you later?"

"I... Yeah."

I hold on for a second longer, fighting the need to pull her out of that car and not let go until she believes me completely. Because while she might have started to open up to the idea of this thing between us working out, and me wanting her for her, she doesn't fully trust me. Which was fine. I wasn't afraid to work hard to show her that I mean business.

One day, she wouldn't have a trace of doubt in her mind.

Today wasn't that day.

So I close the door and take a step back. I watch her as she pulls out of the parking spot and drives away before I return to the hospital.

The moment I enter the room, Miguel's gaze finds mine, his brows rising in a silent question. I shake my head. This wasn't the time or place to talk about this. Not that I planned to tell him what happened with Savannah. Not after she asked me to keep it to myself.

But she's gone, and I have nobody. Nobody, Blake.

Looking at the room filled with all these people, I had an inkling of how hard this must have been for her. Seeing her best friend surrounded by her family on one of the most important days of her life couldn't have been easy. Especially knowing that she would never have that.

But I meant what I said; I would do anything she wanted me to. I wanted to be there for her and our baby. I could just hope that she would take me up on the offer.

"Levi, are you ready to go home?"

Levi turns his attention from the window and nods.

"You can stay."

I shake my head. "You guys should spend some time with your family. Besides, Daniel's home alone."

Miguel nods in understanding. "Sure thing." He shifts his attention to Levi and ruffles his hair. "I'll see you soon, little guy?"

"I'm not so little."

"You're right. What was I thinking? Silly me."

Miguel extends his fist, and Levi bumps their knuckles together. We say our goodbyes to the rest of the room, but they're still charmed by the little boy sleeping in his mother's arms, so they barely pay us any attention when we leave.

My mind goes back to Savannah and the olive branch she offered me as I pull out of the parking lot. I knew it couldn't have been easy for her to ask me to come with her to her doctor's appointment. It was obvious that she craved a family of her own, but she was so independent that she hardly let anybody in.

What happened to you, Blondie?

Who hurt you so badly that you won't let anybody close? Was it her ex? For some reason, I couldn't see it. There was something else. Something I didn't know about.

One day.

One day, I was determined to know every single thing about Savannah Parker.

The moment I turned onto our street, my gaze went to Savannah's house, and her silver Volvo parked in front of it.

She made it home safely.

Some of the worry eases off my chest as I park the car in front of our house, and we get out of the truck.

"Dad?" Levi calls out as I open the front door and let him go inside.

"Yeah, buddy?"

I eye him carefully. He's been unusually quiet the whole

drive home; his attention focused on the scenery passing us by when usually he would be chatting my ear off.

"Why do you call Miss Parker Blondie?"

Shit.

I didn't realize he'd overheard our conversation; then again, kids have the tendency to catch and remember the parts we want them to hear the least.

"Umm..." I rubbed the back of my neck, trying to come up with some kind of explanation because I couldn't exactly tell him that the reason I started to use that nickname in the first place was because I didn't know her real name the first time we met.

"Is it because she has blonde hair?"

Sure, we can go with that.

"Yeah, that's right."

I expect him to change the subject, but his gaze is still fixed on me, and the contemplative expression on his face tells me there is something more going on here that's troubling him. "Why did Miss Parker leave so soon today?"

"She was busy, so she had to go," I pause for a moment. "Why do you ask?"

"She looked sad." Levi shrugs. "And then I saw you hugging her through the window."

Shit, shit, shit.

How was I supposed to explain that one?

"I—"

"Are you shitting me? You brought Levi with you to meet your side piece?"

I turn around to find a fuming Daniel standing on top of the stairs and glaring at me. His fingers are curled around the railing, his knuckles white from how hard he's been squeezing it.

"Daniel..." I growl in warning. I've about had it with him and that attitude.

"What, *Dad*?" he all but spits out. "She has no business messing with our lives. Just because you knocked her up doesn't mean shit. She should go to hell and leave us alone." Daniel turns to Levi. "Stay away from that woman. She doesn't give a shit about you; she's just using you to get to Dad."

"She is not using me!" Levi stomps his foot. His face is beet red as he yells at his brother. "You're a liar, Danny. Miss Parker likes me. You're just jealous that everybody here hates you."

"Yeah, right." Daniel snorts. "I don't care what a town of single-minded people thinks. Your dear Miss Parker is more interested in getting into Dad's pants."

Levi glares at Daniel. "You're just being a meany!"

"Did you tell him the ecstatic news?" Daniel turns his attention to me.

I place my hand on Levi's shoulder. "That's enough, Daniel. You'll watch your mouth, or you're grounded."

Daniel starts laughing. "Grounded? For what exactly? Saying the truth? Did you or did you not screw Levi's teacher, and now she's pregnant with your child?"

I suck in a long breath as I try to keep my anger at bay, my voice deadly calm, "Get your ass to the living room."

He opens his mouth, but I point toward the door. "Living room. Now."

Daniel presses his lips into a tight line but does as I say. He descends the stairs slowly and walks past us as he goes to the living room, Levi and me at his heels.

"Sit down."

Levi is the first one to listen, his fingers clasping and unclasping in his lap as Daniel takes his sweet time doing as I asked. Once he finally takes his seat, he bumps into Levi.

"I met Savannah last spring," I say before they can get into it again.

Daniel rolls his eyes. "I'm really not in the mood to listen to your sexual escapades."

I give him a warning look, my voice deadly calm. "You'll listen to whatever I tell you to listen. I've had it with you, Daniel. This kind of behavior is not permitted. I've let it slide, but you've gone too far now. You will not talk about Savannah, or any other person for that matter, in the way you've been doing the last few days. And, trust me, you don't want to cross this line because once you do, there will be no going back."

Daniel grits his teeth. "Of course, you have to go and defend her."

"I'm not defending her. There is nothing to defend. She didn't do anything wrong. *We* didn't do anything wrong. We met the day I went to sign the papers for this house, after your mom and I split up and *after* the divorce was finalized. We met and liked each other." Daniel opens his mouth, but I glare at him, daring him to interrupt me. "I didn't know she lived here, and I didn't know she was going to be Levi's teacher. Neither of us planned things to play out the way they did."

"Tell us something new. Unplanned is your go-to. One would think you'd be smarter and not make the same mistake again."

He thinks I view him as a mistake?

I shake my head, wondering how the hell I can fix this. Was there even any chance of fixing this, or were we too broken for that?

"I made a lot of mistakes in my life, Daniel, but having you, having Levi, and having this baby isn't one of them."

Some of that snarkiness dies down and shame flashes on his face, so he looks away.

"Savannah's baby is your baby?" Levi's soft voice breaks me

out of the staring contest with my older son. There's a frown between his brows as he tries to keep up with the conversation.

"Yes, Savannah's baby is my baby." I let that sit for a little while. "How do you feel about that?"

If possible, that frown between his brows grows even bigger.

I crouch in front of him and place my hand on his knee, giving him a reassuring squeeze. "It's okay if you're not sure how you feel. If you have any questions, you can ask me anytime, you know that? But this doesn't change anything. Savannah is still going to be your teacher, and I'm still your dad."

"And I get a baby brother?"

"Yes, or a baby sister."

"Are you even sure the baby is yours?" Daniel chimes in. "Maybe she's trying to dump another guy's kid on you..."

"The baby is mine," I grit through clenched teeth, leaving no room for discussion. "Savannah didn't know me or what I did when we met, and she didn't bring it up once after she found out. Quite the contrary, actually."

"Will Miss Parker live here with us?" Levi asks suddenly.

Daniel's body stiffens at his words, all the color draining from his face at the idea.

I curse inwardly.

"No, Miss Parker will keep living in her house."

"But then where will the baby live?" His face lights up. "He can sleep in my room! I don't mind sharing."

I chuckle softly, some of the tension easing from my shoulders. "That's really nice of you, buddy. But we'll have to wait and see what happens. There is still a lot of time before the baby comes."

"How long?"

I count back to when we first met, which was late March, so that would mean... "Probably sometime around Christmas."

"Does that mean that Santa will bring us the baby? Like a present?"

"No, Levi," I chuckle softly. "Santa won't bring the baby. We'll take Savannah to the hospital, where she'll give birth to the baby. Like Becky."

Levi's brows furrow in confusion. "How will she give birth?"

"I—" *Fuck.* I scratch my neck as I try to come up with some kind of explanation. This kid was too curious for his own good. "It'll come out of Savannah's belly."

Levi's eyes grow wide. "The baby is in Savannah's belly?"

Before I get a chance to come up with an answer, Daniel pushes to his feet, his knee bumping into the coffee table, as he marches out of the room. I watch the empty doorway for a moment longer, feeling a headache brewing behind my temples.

Before I can do anything, Levi's arms wrap around my neck. "Don't worry, Daddy, I love my baby brother."

"I know you do, buddy."

He beams at me. "I'll be the best big brother."

It's going to be okay.

It had to be okay.

Daniel would come around.

Eventually.

And we'll figure this out.

I press my mouth against the top of his head. "I don't doubt it for a second."

"I can't wait to tell my friends at school. They'll be so—"

Shit.

"Hey, buddy." I place my hand on his shoulders. "You can't tell your friends just yet."

His smile falls immediately. "Why not?"

Seriously, this kid.

"Because we're keeping it as our little secret."

"But I want to tell my friends," he pouts.

"I know, Levi, and you'll tell them, just not yet. Soon, I promise. Okay?"

He crosses his arms over his chest and huffs. "I guess."

He looks so serious; I can't help but chuckle. "You really are the best big brother."

"I know; I'm the bestest!" He pulls back. "I'm going to find something me and my baby brother can play with."

Levi dashes away without a backward glance.

Rubbing my palm over my face, I let out a sigh.

That went well, right?

Chapter 15

SAVANNAH

I place the paper on the stack and stretch my neck, trying to release some of the tension in my muscles. My gaze goes to the other stack, the one that had yet to be graded.

"Tomorrow," I promise myself, letting my hand fall to my bump. "We'll deal with this tomorrow, right, Munchkin?"

There is a little flutter in my belly that has me pausing as I hold my breath, waiting for something... more. But there is nothing.

I shake my head at myself; it was probably just gas.

Sighing, I gather all my things and put them in the tote for tomorrow, but instead of going to bed like I should, I grab my book and go out to the porch. Our monthly book club was soon, and between all the other things, I've barely had time to read. Pulling a blanket on my lap, I settle in and flip through the pages until I find the spot where I left off and start reading.

And because that's just my luck, this month's pick was no other than a sports romance about an injured football player who moved to a small town to heal and a feisty librarian who just happened to run into him while he was swimming in the lake. Completely naked, no less.

I bite into my cheek, pressing my thighs together as she

watches him from behind the tree, the water cascading down his hard, tanned muscles.

Only a different body flashes in my mind.

This one also was built, his chest and arms covered in black ink.

The way those muscles flexed as he sunk into me...

"This book has to be really interesting if it has all of your attention."

I let out a soft yelp in surprise, my head snapping up. My heart is beating wildly inside my chest as I find a grinning Blake watching me over the top of the book. His chest is naked, sweat glistening on his skin, one lone drop sliding down, down...

"See something you like, Blondie?"

Blake's low baritone sends a shiver down my spine. He crosses his arms over his chest, and my head snaps up. Amusement and something else, something darker is playing on his face and making my stomach tighten as he raises his brow in a silent question.

"Wh-what..."

I lift my book, but in my hurry, it falls from my hands and onto my face.

"*Ouch.*"

Before I can react, the book is gone, and Blake's standing there, mere inches from me. His expression is serious as he scans my face. "Are you okay?"

"You scared me!" I protest and reach for my book. "Gimmie that."

Blake shakes his head and pulls it out of my reach. "Oh, no, I wanna see what was so interesting that you didn't hear me coming."

He opens the book and starts reading.

I swallow hard. Maybe he opened some random scene, maybe...

His brows rise, eyes widening the more he reads.

"Blondie." He glances at me. "I really hope this isn't for school."

I jump to my feet and grab the book out of his hand. "Of course it's not for school. It's for my book club."

If possible, his brows arch even higher. "This is what you discuss at book club? Smut?"

Color floods my cheeks, but I refuse to look down. "It's a *romance* novel. Not smut." I cross my arms, clutching the book to my chest. "But even if it were, I don't see how that has anything to do with you."

"I don't know about that." Blake shakes his head, the corner of his mouth twitching upward. "If I knew, I might be tempted to join. I didn't have any idea that reading could be so... educational."

I try to imagine it. But instead of seeing Blake's tall frame in one of the chairs at the Reading Nook as he discusses sex scenes with the ladies of Bluebonnet, a different scene pops into my mind. Blake trying to recreate one of the steamy scenes from the book. Down to the smallest of details. With me.

My mouth goes dry as heat pools in my belly.

"Savannah?"

I blink to find Blake watching me expectedly.

I shake my head, pushing the thoughts out of my mind. "What are you doing here anyway?"

"I was out for a run and saw you sitting on the porch." His eyes scan my face. "So I figured I'd check in on you."

"Oh..." I tuck a strand of my hair behind my ear, suddenly feeling self-conscious. "I'm fine."

I haven't seen Blake in the last few days. Ever since *that* day. The day I fell apart at the hospital, and Blake saw it happen. Not just that, he comforted me. Held me while I cried. He *kissed* me. And I let him.

I'll do whatever you need me to do. Be whoever you need me to be.

I bite into my lower lip.

I swear I could still feel his lips pressed against mine. Feel those calloused fingers on my cheeks as he cupped my face, making me feel safe and not so alone.

And now he was here.

Checking in on me.

"Savannah, look at me."

"I'm fine." I shake my head. "I'm not going to break—"

"I know that." Blake's finger slips under my chin, and he tilts my head back, my eyes meeting his. "But it would be okay even if you broke down because I'd be there to catch you. I told you; I have your back."

A knot forms in my throat, making it hard to breathe.

"Wanna know the truth?" Blake rubs his finger over my lower lip, so I just nod wordlessly. "I'm here because I wanted to see you. That's the truth."

I suck in a shaky breath, not knowing what to say to this. To *him*. I wished this was different. I wished he was an asshole so I could be done with this and go back to my life—just Munchkin and me—but Blake wasn't like that at all, and I didn't know what it meant. Where did that leave us? All I knew was that he was making me feel things I had no business feeling and making me wish for things that would never belong to me.

It scared me shitless.

He scared me shitless.

Those intense eyes bore into mine, and I swear he can see into my very soul. His gaze falls to my lips, his thumb sweeping over it before his palm slips to the back of my neck.

For a second, I wonder if he'll kiss me again. I suck in a breath, my lips parting as he leans down, and his lips brush against my forehead.

My heart flips inside my chest as his fingers dig into my skin, holding on for a long moment before he pulls back.

He lets his hand fall and takes a step back, giving me one final glance. "Goodnight, Savannah."

I lift my hand, rubbing at my lower lip as I watch his retreating back and wonder what the hell am I going to do about all of this.

"Slow down!" I call out, but it's useless. The kids are running excitedly toward the football field. Practice has been the only thing they've talked about the whole day, and there was no stopping them.

My chest is rising and falling rapidly as I try to keep up with them when I hear my name being called. I glance toward the kids who were already on the field before turning around only to spot Mrs. Tyson and Mrs. Miller walking my way hand in hand.

"Savannah, how are you doing, my dear?"

"Good." I glance between the two women. "What brings you ladies around?"

"The new coach's been the talk of the town, so we came to check him out." Mrs. Miller winks at me as they walk past me.

The new...

I follow after them, only to come to a sudden stop once we reach the field. "What in the ever lo—"

I bite my tongue just in time and simply stare at the almost full bleachers.

Something that has *never* happened before. Especially not for practice. And it wasn't even moms this time around, there were a few dads, too. To think all we needed was an ex-NFL player taking the coaching position, and suddenly everybody would be interested in peewee football. Go figure.

A few dads are gathered by the sidelines, talking to Blake. Although he's surrounded by people, he stands out, almost a head taller than most of them, a dark purple ball cap sits on his head and throws shadows over his face.

He tilts his head to the side, nodding slowly at whatever they're talking about, but I swear I can feel his gaze on me, his eyes running over my body. I bite the inside of my cheek as a shudder runs down my spine.

Get a grip, Sav.

I shouldn't let him affect me, but it's like I couldn't help myself. He's been on my mind since he left me standing on my porch the other night.

"You know, if you need an assistant or something, I'd be more than happy to help," I hear one of the dads eagerly say as I move closer to the group, and it takes everything in me not to snort out loud.

There wouldn't even be a peewee team if I hadn't agreed to coach it in the first place because when I asked parents if they'd like to help after the old coach retired, none of them wanted to do it. They all said they didn't have the time. You'd think I was asking them to help me and not to do something nice for their kids.

"You know, I played in college, so—"

"That's cool, dude." Blake slaps him on the shoulder, effectively dismissing him. "But Miss Parker and I have it covered. Practice will start soon so you better get to your seats."

Without waiting for an answer, his hand falls to the small of my back, and he pushes me toward the coach's bench. "I swear if I hear one more word..."

I glance at his annoyed face and can't help but chuckle.

"Oh, you just wait for it. People here love to meddle; then again, I guess you know all about that."

Blake's eyes narrow. "It was just one time, and I corrected you because you were doing it wrong."

"Mm-hmm..." I pat him on the chest. "You just think that. Although seriously, you should take one of them up on the offer and—"

"Hell to the no." Blake's fingers curl around my wrist as he turns to face me. "You're stuck with me."

"Wh-what?" I stutter, my lips parting as the words register in my mind.

"You heard me." Blake smirks, his fingers brushing a strand of my hair behind my ear, the corner of his mouth tipping upward in satisfaction as he leans closer, his voice dropping so only I can hear him. "You're not getting rid of me so easily, Blondie. It's you and me."

He lifts his ball cap and places it on my head.

What the—

"There, perfect." He winks at me and turns around, calling out loudly, "Guys, time to hustle."

Stunned, it takes me a second to process what just happened and gather my wits about me, and by the time I do, Blake's already leading the kids in a series of exercises and stretches.

I look around, lost. "What the hell should I do?"

For a moment, I just stand there as Blake joins the kids in running a few laps around the field. Deciding he doesn't really need me, I let out a sigh and go toward the bleachers where the dads are sitting at the edge of their seats, cheering and tossing suggestions at Blake, while the moms were busy giggling and flipping their hair.

Lucy Donovan spots me, her eyes narrowing as she gives me

a once over, snorts, and shifts her attention to the field, her mouth moving as she whispers something to her companion.

What is her problem?

I'm about to turn around when I spot the lone figure sitting a few rows behind.

Rose O'Neil.

I've met the woman a few times since she moved back to Bluebonnet Creek. She was Becky's age and moved out of Bluebonnet for college, only to come back once her husband didn't make it to the NFL. She usually brought her son Kyle to the reading group for kids in the Reading Nook, and she even joined our reading club a handful of times, but for the most part, she kept to herself.

Her shoulders are tense, hands folded in her lap as she stares out at the field.

On impulse, I decide to join her. "Hey, do you mind some company?"

Rose startles at my question but shakes her head. "No, go ahead."

I sit next to her, my attention going to the field just as Blake has the kids line up so they can run some drills. From the corner of my eye, I can see Rose nibble at her lip.

"You okay?"

She tucks an invisible strand behind her ear and forces out a smile. "Am I that obvious?"

"Not too much."

"I know it's silly, it's just peewee football, but... He's different than the rest of the kids. I don't want his deafness to define him or stand in his way, but at the same time, I can't help but worry about him."

I nod, my hand falling to my bump. "I understand that, but he's doing really well."

Some of that tension seeps out of her. "Is he?"

"I think so, yes. He's made friends, and other kids are excited to make him feel included by learning some of the sign language. I'm not nearly as good as you are, though, but I figured even a little bit will help all of us, although Kyle is very good at reading lips, and I've even heard him speak on a few occasions."

"I really appreciate you doing that, and I know he does as well. I've been really worried when they told me they won't be able to provide him with a one-on-one teacher's aide, but you put in so much effort in helping him..." She shakes her head. "It means the world, really."

I place my palm on hers, giving her a reassuring squeeze. "Of course. If I notice something that might concern me, I'll bring it up, but so far, he's been adapting extremely well."

"Thank you." Rose nods, her gaze falls to my stomach, something that looks a lot like longing appearing on her face. "How far along are you?"

"Twenty-three weeks, so more than halfway there."

It still felt surreal. The time was flying fast, and there was still so much to do. So much to figure out.

My gaze goes to the man on the field, the one who changed my life, not once, but twice now.

Blake was crouching down and explaining something to one of the kids. He looked all serious and focused and seeing him like this did something to me.

He was good with the kids.

A good dad.

The thought fills my chest with warmth, and something inside me eases a bit. It didn't matter what happened between us; Blake would be a good dad to my baby, and that's the only thing that mattered.

"Ugh, how can one man be so gorgeous?" The groan coming from one of the moms sitting in front of us breaks me out of my thoughts. "It shouldn't be allowed."

There is a chorus of agreements coming from the women sitting around her.

"What do you think the chances are he'll take off his shirt?"

I didn't need to look to know who said that. Lucy Donovan had no filter, but she clearly had a thing for Blake.

"I'd pay some serious money to see all that glorious skin and abs on display."

Rose rolls her eyes and leans in, her voice dropping so only I can hear it. "Some things around here never change."

I swallow back my snort. No, it didn't seem like they did.

"What do you think? Does he have a six-pack or an eight-pack?" Lucy continues, her tongue darting over her lower lip as she blatantly stares at Blake.

I grind my teeth, feeling a pang of irritation at her ogling.

Is she for real?

We're at a peewee practice, for God's sake! Their children were right there, and they were objectifying their coach so openly?

"Lucy!" somebody chastises playfully before they all burst into giggles.

"What? It's a legit question. It's a hot day, after all. You can't tell me you haven't imagined Blake Walker without a shirt on."

Her statement is accompanied by more giggling.

"Are we five?" I mutter to myself, but apparently not quietly enough because Rose chuckles.

"Sometimes it seems like it."

Lucy fans herself. "That man is a piece of art, and I could lick every delicious inch of him."

Just then, Blake blows the whistle. "Practice is over, guys."

Before the words even leave his mouth, parents are jumping from their seats and rushing down to the field, some of the women tripping in their high heels. Why somebody would wear heels to a peewee practice, I'll never understand.

Of course, Lucy is the first one to reach Blake and all but throws herself at him. My fingers curl into a fist as I watch her flirt with him.

There was this stupid part of me that wanted to go down there, pull her back, and tell her to get her hands off my man.

Only Blake wasn't mine.

Not really.

Just because I was pregnant with his baby didn't mean I had any claim on him. That I wanted to have any claim on him.

Not at all.

Rose descends the bleachers, so I follow after her.

Blake might have stolen my coaching position, but there were some traditions he couldn't steal from me.

"Guys, I brought cookies."

Kids cheer as I pull out a container with chocolate chip cookies I baked last night based on my Grams' recipe. They didn't taste exactly the same, but they were similar enough to bring back the memories of after-school snacks and baking with Grams.

Rose glances at me. "Cookies?"

"It's a tradition I started when I took over the coaching position," I explain as I open the container and offer it to kids so they can take a snack.

"Miss Parker, did you see how I caught that ball?" Levi flashes me a smile as he comes to a stop next to me. His cheeks are red, hair plastered to his forehead from sweat, making my fingers itch to brush it away.

"I did. You were pretty amazing out there today. You all were; good job."

Levi's little chest puffs out. "I did it just like Dad."

"What did you do just like your dad?" The low voice sends a shiver running down my spine. I can feel the heat of his body radiating off of him as Blake stops behind me and looks over my shoulder. "Whatcha got here?"

"Miss Parker made cookies, Coach!" one of the kids explains.

"I can see that. The better question is, why haven't I been invited?"

Blake grabs one of the cookies and pops it into his mouth, his eyes falling shut as he chews and lets out a soft groan.

My stomach clenches as I watch him, and I bite the inside of my cheek. There was just something about seeing a man enjoy your cooking that did it for me.

His eyes open, and he stares straight at me. "*Damn*, that's so good."

His praise fills my chest with warmth, but I try to brush it off. "It's just a cookie."

"One damn good cookie," he says, his voice coming out low, almost like a caress. I suck in a breath, the air between us sizzling with pent-up tension. A soft rumbling sound comes from Blake's chest. "I actually had a destination in mind before you distracted me with your cookies." Blake's fingers skim over my back. "Wait a second."

"Wh-what?" I tuck a strand of my hair behind my ear and look up, noticing all eyes are on me. Rose is smiling at me, while Lucy is downright glaring.

Shit.

This was the last thing I wanted. If he didn't stop with all the touching, people would notice something was going on.

"Guys, I have a surprise for you!" Blake calls out as he goes to the bleachers and grabs bags that are lying on the side. I saw them earlier and thought it was extra balls or something, but apparently, I was wrong. Kids gather around him, their excitement matching his as he slowly opens the bag. "Wanna know what's inside?"

"Yes!"

"Okay, so, I've reached out to a few people I know, and they've agreed to make us team jerseys!"

"What?"

My mouth falls open as Blake pulls a dark purple jersey with a bear paw—our team's logo—on the front etched in gold.

"What do you think? Do we like them?"

Kids cheer happily around him as he hands them each one, along with a little duffel bag that contains God knows what.

As if he can feel my gaze on him, Blake looks up. "I cleared it with the principal."

The corner of my mouth twitches upward. "I didn't say anything."

Blake gives me a knowing look. "I know you."

I shake my head as he shifts his attention to the kids and continues handing out the stuff.

"That was very nice of him," Rose comments from next to me, a bag and jersey in her hand.

"It was," I agree.

Nice and mindful. Football stuff was expensive, and I knew a handful of kids who'd struggle to afford it. But that was who Blake was, wasn't it?

After the kids grab their bags, most parents gather their children, and they leave for the parking lot.

Not Lucy though.

Rolling my eyes, I turn my back to them, put away the now empty container and gather around the few balls that were still left lying around.

"I could have done that, you know," Blake comments as he joins me, picking up one ball and tossing it into a bag.

"It's fine, I don't mind doing it." Straightening, I notice we're alone. "No fans anymore?"

Blake just watches me for a second, until a smile flashes on his face. "Jealous, Blondie?"

"Wh-what?" I stutter, feeling the heat rise up my neck. "Of course not."

His irises twinkle in amusement. "Mm-hmm..."

"I just can't believe she's acting that way. In front of the children, no less. You should have heard her during the practice, she was insufferable, saying all..."

The words die on my lips when I see his smug expression.

Dang it.

I should have kept my mouth shut. My tongue darts out, sliding over my lower lip as I try to get out of this mess I've made, when Levi joins us, saving me from further discussion. "Do you have any more of those cookies, Miss Parker?"

"No, but I'll bake some more for our next practice."

His face lights up. "Yes, please!"

"Levi," Blake warns, but the boy ignores him. Instead, he beckons me closer. I crouch down so we're at the same level, and he whispers in my ear, "Don't tell Mrs. M., but your cookies are way better."

I chuckle softly. "I can't really believe that."

"They are!" he insists.

"C'mon, Cookie Monster. Time to go."

Levi goes to grab his backpack, and Blake uses this moment to lean down, his scent surrounds me, his lips brushing against my earlobe as he whispers so only I can hear him. "I think I like you jealous, Miss Parker."

I close my eyes for a second as tingles run down my spine at his words, and when I look at him, I find him watching me with a self-satisfied smirk.

Damn this man.

Glaring at him, I walk toward the parking lot, the Walker boys at my heels.

Blake's words ring in my mind all the way back home, his headlights following behind me as a silent companion.

Pulling up in front of my house, I get out of my car and glance over my shoulder, expecting to see Blake go into his house, but he murmurs something to Levi, who disappears inside, and he crosses the street, his long steps eating the distance between us.

I stop in my tracks. "Blake?"

"I have something for you."

Have something? For me?

Blake lifts his hand, a bag dangling from his fingers.

I shake my head. "I don't understand."

"It's a present. Open it," Blake urges. "It won't bite you."

Tucking a strand of hair behind my ear, I feel my heart kick up a notch as I slowly reach for the bag. Our fingers brush, electricity coursing through me. "What's inside?"

Blake shifts his weight from one foot to the other.

Is he... nervous?

I don't know why, but something about that realization calms me.

"It won't be a surprise if I tell you."

Holding his gaze, I slip my fingers into a bag, a soft material brushing against my fingertips as I pull the contents out.

"What—"

My voice trails off as I pull out the material and unfold it, my mouth falling open as I stare at the tiniest onesie I've ever seen.

"Blake, I—"

Just like the rest of the jerseys Blake got for the kids, this one has a golden bear paw logo on the front, and when I turn it around, I find Walker written across the back in big bold letters with the number 93 underneath it.

Blake's number.

My lip trembles as I let my fingers go over the soft material.

"When I had the others done, I got this idea that I should have one made for our baby. We could dress him or her in it when you guys come to the game, but if you don't like it, you don't have to use it. It was just—"

Before he can finish, I wrap my arms around him.

"This is..." My throat feels tight, and tears gather in my eyes.

He got a jersey.

His jersey with his name.

For our baby.

Shaking my head, I push down the knot lodged in my throat before croaking out, "Thank you."

Blake just stands still for a moment, but before long, his arms wrap around me, holding me tightly against him.

"No thanks needed, Blondie," he whispers, his palm sliding up and down my back.

That was where he was wrong.

To him, this might be normal, but for me, it meant everything.

Slowly, I take a step back. "I'll see you tomorrow for the appointment?"

Blake nods. "Tomorrow."

I start to turn around when a flicker of movement in one of the windows on Blake's house catches my attention.

Daniel.

I can feel his glare on me for a second longer before he lets the curtain drop back in place, and this time, when my stomach clenches, there is nothing warm or fuzzy about the feeling.

Chapter 16

BLAKE

"You know, this wasn't what I had in mind when you called and asked if I could stop by and help you around," I mutter as I grab a bale of hay and toss it into the tractor-trailer that's parked not too far from us.

Thank God because that shit's heavy, and we were nowhere near done.

"What did you think I needed help with?" Aaron asks, dusting his hands. "I'm a rancher."

A fair point, I guess. "I don't fucking know, dude. I guess I should be happy you didn't put me on a horse. Because I'm not doing that shit." Just the thought of it had me shuddering.

Moving farther down the pasture, I grab the next bale. The sun is up in the sky burning my skin as the sweat drips down my back, making my shirt plaster to my body as we work.

My muscles were aching in places I didn't even know they could. How Aaron was doing this every day and still managed to walk, I had no fucking clue, and I wasn't a stranger to physical work.

Still, it was better than sitting at home all day and waiting for Savannah's appointment to roll around so I could see her again.

And I wanted to see her.

Badly.

It's like the more time I spent with her, the more I wanted her. Some days, I wondered what would be enough because she was constantly on my mind. And not just because of the baby either. I wanted to know *her*. What did she do in her free time? Did she read more of those smutty books that made her blush, or did she prefer to kick back and watch TV? What did she like to eat? Did she have any cravings now that she was pregnant? Did she go to bed early or stay up late? There was so much I wanted to know, but, at the same time, I didn't want to scare her off.

And then there was Daniel. I was trying to give him a chance to come to terms with what was going on, which was harder than I anticipated. He completely shut me off and spent most of the time in his room, refusing to talk to me. I was willing to give him a little bit more time, but then we were getting to the bottom of it. Whether he liked it or not, Savannah and the baby were here to stay, and I wanted them all to get along because I knew if Daniel kept up with his attitude, Savannah would pull back. She wanted me to put my kids first, and she would never give us a chance if she knew it would upset Daniel.

Was it wrong of me that I didn't want that to happen? Was I selfish for wanting to have the best of both worlds? Daniel and Levi, but also Savannah and our unborn baby?

Giving my head a shake, I look up to find Aaron observing me quietly. "What?"

"Nothing."

"Bullshit. Something's definitely on your mind. Spill."

"What's with that scowl? I thought you figured things out with Savannah."

My eyes narrow at him. "How do you know?"

I didn't bring Savannah up once since we got here, which could only mean one thing.

"People have been talking."

The hair at my nape rises at his words. "What people?"

"Just people." Aaron shrugs.

I cross my arms over my chest, the muscle in my jaw twitching. "And what were those people saying?"

If somebody was talking bullshit about Savannah, I'll need to have a chat with them. Freaking small-town gossips.

"That the new coach is flirting with our favorite teacher during football practice."

Seriously?

"We're both coaching the peewee team."

Aaron raises his brow. "So, there was no touching during practice?"

I could still feel the silkiness of Savannah's skin under my fingertips as my hand found that little patch of flesh on the small of her back. I could see the way her teeth sunk into her lower lip and that heated look in her eyes as they met mine. I could feel the shudder that rocked her body.

My fingers curl into a fist as I try to keep my cool.

Okay, so there had been a little bit of touching, completely unintentionally and innocently.

"You're making it seem like I was groping her in public or some shit."

"Hey, I'm not saying anything." Aaron lifts his palms. "I'm just telling you what people have been saying in town."

"Who?"

"Lucy Donovan."

"Shit." I lift my hat and run my fingers through my hair.

I guess she didn't like that I brushed her off yesterday like I did. The woman's been trying to get my attention since that first day. I knew her type. I avoided it in a wide circle. Even if Savannah wasn't in the picture, I'd do the same. She reminded me too much of my ex. Somebody who's only focused on what I did and what I could give them instead of who I am.

"Apparently, she's been drinking with some girlfriends at The Hut and started to mouth off. At least, that's what some of the guys said today."

"I don't need this shit in my life. I'm trying to figure things out with Savannah and my kids, and this isn't helping."

"I get it, I really do. Do the boys know?"

"Yeah, Daniel saw me and Savannah, and he put two and two together." I run my hand over my jaw. "To say it didn't go well would be an understatement."

"Shit, I'm sorry, man."

"Yeah, well. I should have come clean as soon as I figured it out, but now it is what it is."

Dropping my hand, I make my way to the next bale of hay with Aaron on my heels. "I just don't know what to do with him, you know? I made a mistake. I get it. I should have done so many things differently when it came to my boys, Daniel especially, but damn it, some days I just want to shake some sense into him."

"Things will work out; just give it time. Give *him* time. He's sixteen. You know how fucked up that age is. His emotions are all over the place. I know I did a lot of dumb shit at sixteen that I regret now."

"I know, and I keep telling myself that. I'm trying to protect them, and I'm trying to do right by Savannah, and in turn, it feels like I'm messing things up even more on all fronts."

Aaron lets out a low grunt. "She's giving you a hard time because of the kids?"

"No, she's so fucking understanding. Daniel was all but yelling in her face and throwing accusations, and she didn't say a word. She keeps telling me I should put them first, which I do. That was the whole point of coming here, dammit, but it feels like I'm failing her. Like no matter what I do, it'll never be enough." My breathing is ragged as another bale of hay ends up in the trailer, and I turn to Aaron. "What the hell do I do?"

"Your best." Aaron shrugs. "You can only do your best and hope it's enough."

But what if my best isn't enough? What if I keep fucking things up across the board and then make not only irreparable damage to my relationship with Daniel but also Savannah and our baby?

The bile rises up my throat as more questions start to surface in my mind, but before I can do anything about it, my phone rings.

Sliding my hand in my pocket, I pull it out, noticing the unfamiliar number on the screen. I raise the phone to my ear and press the answer button. "Hello?"

"Mr. Walker?" an older feminine voice says.

"That's me. How can I help you?" I ask slowly. The voice sounds slightly familiar, but I'm not sure where to place it.

Aaron lifts his brow in a silent question, but I just shake my head. I wasn't sure what was going on, but for some reason, I could feel the trepidation rising inside of me.

"My name is Mrs. Dawn. I'm calling from Bluebonnet High. I'm afraid there's been an incident."

My fingers tighten around the phone as I feel my blood run cold. "What kind of incident?"

Did something happen to Daniel? Did he get hurt? Did—

"Daniel got into a fight with another student."

Cursing softly, I run my hand over my face, as I mutter, "Of course he did."

"Mr. Walker?" the woman asks.

"I'm sorry, I'm still here."

"Both boys have been suspended, so we need you to come to school to pick him up."

I let my hand drop to my side. "I'm on my way."

"What the hell were you thinking?" I ask the moment we step into the house.

It takes everything in me not to slam the front door behind me and yell at my oldest son, but somehow, I manage to keep myself in check. Yelling at Daniel rarely solved anything. On the contrary, really.

"I don't want to talk about it," Daniel grumbles, his gaze fixed on the floor. He starts to turn around, but I grab his shoulder and tug him back.

"Oh, no you don't. What the fuck, Daniel? Fighting in school? Not just that, getting *suspended* barely a few weeks in? Are you trying to set a new record of how quickly they can kick you out?"

"Well maybe then we can go back home." Daniel lifts his gaze and glares at me. His lip is busted and slightly puffy. A dark bruise has already formed around his left eye, closing it shut. The other kid, on the other hand, looked worse. Much worse.

"This is *home,* Daniel. If you get kicked out, you're out. The next closest school is a few towns over. But I guess you could always go and get a job."

Anger shines in his gray irises. Anger and something that looks a lot like shame. Not that he'd ever admit it out loud. No, he was too stubborn, too proud, to admit it out loud.

"This is not my home," he spits out, his cheeks flaming hot. "Just because you have a new girlfriend and a kid on the way doesn't make this place my home."

This time, when he spins on his heels and starts toward the stairs, I don't try to stop him.

"*Fucking hell*," I curse once he's out of earshot and run my hand over my face.

This was so messed up. I knew it would be; I didn't expect Levi and Daniel to jump at this all enthusiastically and accept Savannah into our family, but... I didn't expect this level of hatred at the idea either.

"Did I hear Daniel?" I turn around to find Mrs. Maxwell standing in the doorway of the laundry room, a basket with folded clothes in her arms. She gives me one look before asking, "What happened now?"

I pinch the bridge of my nose, feeling the headache building behind my temples. "Daniel got into a fight at school. He's suspended for a full week."

Her gray brows shoot up over the rim of her metal glasses. "So fast? You've barely been here for a few weeks."

"What can I say; the kid is talented."

Mrs. Maxwell tsks. "What that boy is is troubled. The divorce messed him up."

"Among other things." I let out a long sigh. "Am I doing the right thing?"

The question that's been bugging me ever since we came to Bluebonnet comes to the surface. It feels like I've asked myself this very thing a hundred times already, and I still don't have an answer. Will I ever have an answer?

Mrs. Maxwell gives me a soft smile. "Only time will tell; what I know is that you're doing the best that you can."

"The best that I can," I scoff. "What if that's not enough?"

What if the only thing that happens is I mess my kids up even more?

Mrs. Maxwell moves closer, shifting the basket to one side, her other hand patting my back. "You have to give it time.

Change won't happen overnight. Things are just... intense now."

I snort. "That's one way of putting it."

Between the move and Savannah...

"Shit." I pull out my phone checking the time. "Shit, shit, shit."

Savannah.

I was screwed.

Completely and utterly screwed.

Mrs. Maxwell presses her lips together. "You really should watch your tongue, you know that?"

"I'm sorry, but I have to go. I'm already late."

"Late to what?" Her brows furrow in confusion. "I picked up Levi from school; he went upstairs to change."

"Savannah has a doctor's appointment. I promised her I'd be there." I look up the stairs. I still had to talk to Daniel about what happened, and I haven't seen Levi—

Mrs. Maxwell presses her hand against my shoulder. I told her about Savannah after the whole debacle with Daniel. If she had any thoughts about the situation I got myself into, she didn't voice them out loud. "Go. I have everything handled here."

But that was the problem, wasn't it? I should have been the one who had it all handled. Not her.

"Are you sure?"

The older woman rolls her eyes at me. "When was I not sure?" She lets her hand drop. "Off with you. Make sure your baby momma is okay. You already have one person mad at you; you don't need two."

Leaning down, I press my mouth against the top of her head. "You're the best, Mrs. Maxwell," I say as I dash for the door, pulling the keys out of my pocket. "I'll see you later."

Chapter 17

SAVANNAH

"Savannah Parker?"

My head snaps up at the sound of my name. A pretty young nurse is standing in the doorway and watching me with a kind smile on her lips.

Is it my turn already?

My gaze goes to the clock on the wall, and my stomach sinks.

He wasn't coming.

The realization slams into me like a wave, knocking all the air out of my lungs.

Blake wasn't coming.

The disappointment leaves a bitter taste on my tongue. I swallow the lump in my throat, pushing it down.

So, what if he didn't come? This wasn't the first time I did this on my own. I've been coming here by myself since I found out I was pregnant. I was used to the curious stares from other couples sitting in the waiting room. For the pity that came when they realized I didn't have somebody with me.

It was fine.

I was going to be fine.

I told him he didn't have to come.

So, what if he took me up on it?

Maybe something came up, or maybe he changed his mind and decided this was too much trouble.

That I was too much trouble.

He wouldn't be the first person to come to that conclusion. I've learned early on that I couldn't rely on anybody but myself, so why should Blake Walker be any different?

We're in this together.

A shudder goes through me as his words ring in my head. The determined set of his jaw, his unyielding gaze as vivid as it was the day he said those words. He seemed so sure to prove me wrong. And for a second, I believed him. I believed that he could be different. That maybe, just maybe we could do this, and I wouldn't have to be alone.

You know better than to rely on others.

"Miss Parker?" I blink, the nurse's face coming into focus as she opens the door wider. "We're ready for you."

"Sorry." I jump to my feet, running my hand through my hair. "I spaced out."

Making sure to keep my gaze fixed in front of me, I pass by the other couples as I make my way toward the office.

"It's not a problem." The nurse shoots me a kind smile. "No company today?"

My stomach rolls uncomfortably at her question.

God, I hate this.

I know she was trying to be kind, but the question only made me feel worse than before.

Still, I force a smile out as I shake my head. "No, it's just me today."

Guilt flashes on her face. She tries to mask it, but it's already too late. "C'mon, let's get you..."

A loud *bang* echoes in the room before she can finish, followed by rushed footsteps. I turn around just in time to see no one other than Blake running into the waiting room. His chest is heaving like he ran all the way here. He's dressed in a pair of loose basketball shorts and a Lonestars tee, his hair a mess of curls as if he ran his fingers through it countless times.

"Is it our turn?" he asks, looking between the nurse and me.

"I..." My mouth falls open in surprise as I just stare at him, completely at a loss for words.

He was here.

Blake... was here.

"You came."

Those gray eyes fix on me. "I told you I'd be here."

He did, didn't he? But then he didn't show up, and...

"I thought..." I shake my head, pressing my lips in a tight line.

He came.

Blake just stares at me for a moment. I'm not sure what he sees on my face, but the next thing I know, his long steps are eating the distance between the two of us until we're standing toe to toe, his large palms cradling my face as he tilts my head back so I can look at him.

"I'll always come for you."

A knot forms in my throat. It's like all the feelings that I'm not sure how to voice out loud have gathered there, making it hard to breathe.

Blake's thumbs skim over my cheeks, his voice turning gentler. "I'm sorry I'm late. I would have been here earlier, but something came up."

His jaw clenches, and something that looks a lot like anger shines in his irises.

Was he mad at me or at what happened that made him late?

I wasn't sure.

I take a step back, putting so much needed distance between

us. "You didn't have to come if you were busy. It's just one appointment; it's not a big deal. I could have done it on my own."

His eyes narrow, but before he can say anything, the nurse clears her throat, reminding me that we aren't alone. "You guys ready?"

I force out a smile. "Yes."

Moving past her, I slip into the office and go straight for the chair. Tense silence fills the room as I go through the initial assessment—checking my weight and blood pressure as the nurse goes over her questions. Once that's done, she points us to the doctor's office.

"Lay down on the bed and get comfortable. The doctor will be with you shortly."

Thanking her, I slip into the office, Blake at my heels.

That tension only grows stronger now that we're alone in the room. Turning my back to the bed, I start to lift myself up when Blake appears in front of me. His strong hands land on my hips as he helps hoist me up.

I suck in a sharp breath as Blake gently rubs at my sides, his palms almost cradling my bump before letting his hands drop. "I'm sorry for being late. There was..." He tilts his head, his expression growing distant as he weighs his words carefully. "An incident earlier that I needed to take care of."

His jaw clenches as if he's holding back his irritation.

"It's fine. I told you; I can do this alone."

"Savannah."

My name comes out as a low growl, but I ignore him and continue, "Besides, you already have two boys, I'm pretty sure you're more familiar with this office than I am."

Something dark passes over his face. "You'd be wrong. I—"

Whatever he wanted to say was cut off by the entrance of Dr. Gonzales. "Savannah, it's so nice to see you today." She shifts her gaze to Blake, one of her gray brows quirks upward in a silent question. "And I see we have company today."

When I first came to her office, I told her the dad wasn't in the picture, so I guess it wasn't strange she was surprised.

"Dr. Gonzales, this is Blake Walker." I glance at him, and explain, "He's the dad."

"It's so nice to meet you, Mr. Walker." Like the true professional she is, Dr. Gonzales brightly smiles as she shakes his hand before her attention shifts to me. "How are you feeling, Savannah?"

"Good, a little tired." I lift my shirt all the way up, revealing my belly. "It also feels like I'm always hot and thirsty these days, but I guess that's to be expected since it's still crazy hot."

The doctor grabs the gel bottle and squirts some of it on my belly. "Are you drinking enough water?"

"I am."

"Good. Your blood work looks normal, so you keep that up, and we can discuss it some more in a few weeks. Then we'll also do a few extra tests."

"Extra tests?" My brows pull together. "Why? Do you think something's wrong?"

"No, they're all part of a regular checkup, so there is nothing to worry about. We're just making sure everything is going well with you two." She gives me a reassuring smile. "Ready to see that baby of yours?"

I nod silently as my teeth sink into my lower lip. Dr. Gonzales presses her wand against the goo on my stomach and spreads it around as she shifts her attention to the screen where an image flickers to life.

My heart does a little flip like it always does when I see it.

My baby.

The image is a blurry mix of blacks and whites adorning the screen, but there was no mistaking that the outline seemed more like an actual person with each visit than a speck of cells.

"*Holy shit,*" Blake mutters softly as he moves closer, his hand clasping around mine. I tilt my head back to look at him, but his gaze is firmly fixed on the screen, his lips slightly parted as he stares in wonder.

While he looks at the screen, I look at him.

It almost seemed like he was seeing it for the very first time, which was impossible. He had not one but two kids of his own.

Maybe this whole thing made it seem more real to him?

Blake's gaze falls to me, and a smile slowly spreads over his lips. "That's our baby."

"That's our baby," I echo, my teeth sinking into my lower lip as warmth spreads through my chest at the look of pure love on Blake's face.

My baby was loved, not just by me, but also by Blake.

Our baby.

"The baby seems to be doing well," Dr. Gonzales comments, her attention still on the screen as she takes some measures. "There you can see it." She points at the image. "Nice and steady heartbeat. All ten fingers and toes." The woman turns to us, glancing tentatively between Blake and me. "You still don't want to know the gender of the baby?"

I open my mouth, but before I can say anything, Blake shakes his head. "We're good."

I turn to him, surprised by his easy agreement. "Are *you* sure? Dr. Gonzales could tell you if you want to know."

"No, I don't care about the gender of the baby. I just want you two to be okay. That's the only thing I care about." The corner of his mouth tips upward slightly. "I will warn you, Levi is determined to have a brother, so..."

I let out a strangled laugh, tears welling inside my eyes.

"Shit, don't cry, Blondie. It was a joke. Okay, he really does want a brother, but he'll love the baby regardless. I don't remember the last time when he was so excited."

I brush my cheek with the back of my hand. "That's not why I'm crying. I just can't believe that my baby will have a family. An actual *family*."

He couldn't know how much it meant to me. Not really. A girl who only ever had a grandmother. She did a good job—an amazing job, really—raising me, and she loved me to pieces, just like I loved her. But there were some things she couldn't give me, no matter how hard she tried to be both my mother and my father.

"It does," he promises, his hand sliding to the back of my neck as he pulls me closer, his mouth pressing against my forehead. "You *both* have a family now, and that'll never change."

Chapter 18

BLAKE

"What do you think?" I tilt my head to the side as I look at Levi. "Do you like it?"

He grabs the loops of his jeans and pulls them up a little. "Yeah, I think they're okay. The last ones were squeezing me."

"Okay, then we'll get this one. You have to try on a few shirts."

Levi groans. "Do I really have to?"

"Yes. C'mon, it's a few shirts. Mrs. Maxwell said you've outgrown most of your clothes, and we need to get you new ones because you'll go to school in your boxers soon. You want that?"

"No," he pouts. "But once I try all of those, I wanna go grab a milkshake." He points his finger at me. "And fries."

Chuckling, I shake my head. "Fine. But you have to try on all of those, *and* if those don't fit, you're trying the correct size. And no complaining."

"Deal." He extends his hand, his face serious as I take it in mine for a handshake.

True to his words, he doesn't protest as he tries on every shirt from the rack I give him. After we settle on a few new ones, I collect everything we'll buy while he puts his clothes back on.

"Is that it?" The young attendant smiles at me as she folds everything and puts it into a bag.

"That's all. Thank you." Handing her my card, I look over my shoulder to search for Levi, who disappeared only God knows where. "This freaking kid."

"I think he went outside," the attendant supplies.

"Why am I not surprised?" Shaking my head, I grab my card and bag. "Thanks."

"I think it's really brave that you took him shopping yourself. You're such a good dad."

Brave? It takes all that's in me not to snort out loud. I all but lost my kid in a span of a few seconds. I was sure that would win me the award for Father of the Year. *Not.*

I force out a smile. "Have a nice day."

Turning around, I scan the space, searching for Levi, but he's nowhere in sight.

Seriously, when I find him, I'm going to strangle—

"Miss Parker!"

My head snaps up at the sound of Levi's voice. I turn to my left, just in time to spot a flash of gold as it disappears between the people.

Savannah turns around, her honey hair standing out in the crowd like a beacon. A smile spreads over her lips as she watches Levi running toward her. She bends down to listen to him while his mouth moves a mile a minute. Whatever he said has her laughing and fuck it if she doesn't look like the most beautiful woman in the world.

I lift my hand and rub at my chest, feeling an ache building behind my sternum.

Savannah shakes her head and ruffles Levi's hair as she straightens, her eyes scanning the space until they land on mine, and that smile grows softer, knocking all the air out of my lungs.

Fuck it.

It did something to me when she looked at me like that. And I liked it. I liked it a lot.

She lowers her gaze and says something to Levi. His hand slips into hers as they make their way toward me.

"I think you lost something, Mr. Walker," she teases, the corner of her mouth twitching in amusement as she tries to keep a serious face. My gaze zeroes in on those lush lips, wishing I could lean in and kiss that smirk off of her face.

Levi giggles. "He didn't lose me. I left."

"Which is something we'll talk about later. You can't just disappear like that without saying a word."

"I was just outside. And I wasn't alone. I saw Miss Parker, and I wanted to say hi." He tilts his head back. "What are you doing here, Miss Parker?"

"Shopping."

"Duh, we're at the mall. But you're not carrying any bags."

"That's because I just got here, and I'm still looking."

"What are you looking for? Maybe we can help you find it."

I don't bother pointing out that only a few minutes ago he was done with shopping and only wanted to get his milkshake and go home.

"Umm..." Savannah shifts her weight from one foot to the other and tucks a strand of her hair behind her ear. "I need to buy some things." There is a short pause as her gaze darts to me for a second before it returns to Levi. "For the baby."

She is baby shopping? On her own?

Before I get a chance to process her words, Levi's whole face lights up in excitement. "I wanna come. Can I come? I wanna buy something for my baby brother. Please?" He turns to me and clasps his hands. "Can we come, Dad?"

I watch Savannah as she presses her lips in a tight line, fighting to keep her composure. Those bright blue eyes meet mine, and I can see all the different emotions and worries shining in their depths as if she still quite doesn't believe that this is real.

"If Savannah doesn't mind our company."

Levi turns his pleading gaze to her. "Please, Miss Parker, can we come with you?"

"Umm... Oka—"

"Yes!" Levi fist bumps excitedly before she can even finish.

"Let's go." Levi grabs her hand and starts pulling her away. "I saw this one store..."

Savannah glances over her shoulder, her gaze meeting mine as Levi drags her in the opposite direction. Shaking my head, I hurry up to catch up to them.

"You should slow down, Levi. You don't want to fall, do you?"

"I'm not going to fall," he protests as he suddenly comes to a stop in front of a store. "Here. We can buy him Lego bricks—"

He's about to enter, but I place my hand on his shoulder. "Slow down, buddy, okay?"

"Fine."

I crouch down, so we're at the same level. "You remember what I said about the baby?"

He huffs out a long breath. "But I have a feeling, Dad! It's going to be a boy."

"Well, let's just play it on the safe side and get something for the baby regardless of whether it's a boy or a girl. Besides, the baby can't play with Lego bricks until they're a bit older, so why don't you pick out a toy they can play with when they get here?"

"Okay, I guess. What can we get him?" He purses his lips, his brows pulling together as he thinks.

Savannah's gaze darts to me, her teeth sinking into her lower lip as she tries to hold back her smile, and I can feel the corner of my mouth lift.

"I know!" Levi yells suddenly and bolts away.

"No running around, Levi," I call after him, pushing to my feet.

"Okay!"

Shaking my head, I turn toward Savannah to find that her face has turned serious. I move closer, my finger slipping under her chin and gently turn her to me.

"You okay there, Blondie?"

"Yeah. He's just being so sweet, and I..." She lets out a self-deprecating chuckle as she lowers her gaze. "It's silly, but I'm just emotional. These hormones are getting to me."

I slide my finger over her chin. "Or maybe you're just one big softy," I rasp out, my voice coming out tight.

I still couldn't get out of my head what she said the other day.

Family.

That's what she wants for her baby—*our* baby. While all the other women would have dozens of demands, this was the only thing she asked for.

A family.

Such a simple request from such a complicated woman.

A woman who I barely knew bits and pieces of. I wanted to know more. I wanted to know everything there was to know about her, but I was afraid if I pushed too hard too fast, she'd close off, and I didn't want that. I didn't want to scare her away.

I slide my thumb over the underside of her lip.

What is your story, Savannah Parker?

Her lips part, cheeks turning rosy under my watchful gaze. "Maybe."

"There is no maybe about it. You're a softy." I tilt my head to the side. "What did you want to buy?"

"I was planning to window shop, really. Trying to see what I'll need for when the baby comes. I've been pushing it off so far, but now that we're already halfway there..." She shrugs, her free hand going to her bump. "It feels more real, I guess. Or maybe I'm in the early stages of nesting."

"Nesting?" My throat grows tight as I watch her rub at the swell that's grown bigger in the last few weeks. Her stomach popped, and now there was no longer mistaking her for anything but pregnant.

With my baby.

A possessiveness unlike anything I've felt in a long time rises inside of me. There is this need to wrap her into my arms and make sure that she's happy and safe. To see her smile like this.

"You know when women prepare for the arrival of the baby? Buying clothes, putting together the nursery, cleaning, things like that..."

I could see it. Watching Savannah go through all the tiny clothes that barely cover my palm. Fighting with her over who'll put up the furniture because there is no way she'd just let me do it. Savannah, sitting in a chair, a small bundle in her arms.

I could see it so clearly in my head.

Her. Me. Us.

She looks up, those crystal blue eyes fixing on mine. She must see something on my face because her lips part, "Blake..."

I lean down, my hand going to the back of her neck.

I needed to kiss her.

I didn't care who saw us or what they said.

I would go crazy if I didn't kiss her.

It's been the only thing on my mind since that day in the hospital.

My fingers tighten on her neck.

The blue of Savannah's irises goes darker as I pull her closer, with only inches separating us...

"Dad! Miss Parker!"

Cursing silently, I close my eyes and press my forehead

against Savannah's. The sound of pounding feet coming closer matches the pounding of blood echoing in my eardrums. Savannah chuckles, her body leaning into mine.

"Later," I breathe out, a silent promise.

Blinking my eyes open, I grip her neck in warning. Her eyes flare, and I can see heat flash in her irises as I pull back, just as Levi comes to a stop and lifts a toy in the air. "Look! I got this for my baby brother." I open my mouth, but he's faster. "Or sister." He turns to Savannah, and I can see a little bit of uncertainty flash on his face. "Do you like it, Miss Parker?"

Savannah takes the stuffed elephant from Levi. I'm pretty sure I can see her lip wobble before she presses them together and inhales deeply.

I wrap my arm around her middle, pulling her to me. "Softy," I whisper into her ear, as I lean down and press my mouth against the top of her head, rubbing her arm.

She nudges me with her elbow, her attention on my son. "It's beautiful, Levi. I love it, and I'm sure the baby will love it, too."

Levi's smile grows bigger. "You think?"

"Yes." She ruffles his hair. "Thank you."

I watch as my son tilts his head. The movement is almost imperceptible, but I've been observing him intently for the last few months, trying to figure out how much of this whole thing with the divorce and move screwed him up, so I don't miss it. Levi was craving a woman's attention. Not just that, he craved a *mother's* attention. Something Reina so rarely gave him, but not Savannah. She loved and cared for her students like they were her own.

Was it because she didn't have the same when she was younger?

I guess it would make sense.

Pushing down the knot in my throat, I slide my hand on

Levi's back. "C'mon, you two, let's go and see what else they have."

Levi doesn't need to be told twice; he grabs Savannah's hand and pulls her toward the shelves. "C'mon, Miss Parker, you have to see this!"

Savannah laughs but doesn't protest or try to shake him off. Instead, she lets Levi drag her through the store and listens intently as he points out all the things he thinks the baby might need, which are mainly toys.

"You know, Levi, the baby needs other things." I fight my laughter as he tilts his head to the side, a frown appearing between his brows.

"What other things?"

"Lots of things," Savannah explains as she points at the selection. "A crib, stroller, one of these bouncy seats."

She looks them over, her attention fixing on one that's a light gray color.

I move closer, testing how compactly built it is. "This looks nice."

"It does," Savannah comments absentmindedly as she turns over the price tag. "*A hundred and fifty dollars?*" Her jaw all but hits the floor. "Are they nuts? For a bouncy seat?"

"It's not that bad—"

Her head whips in my direction as she shoots me a death glare. "Not bad? This is stealing! No way. There are way more important things I need to get. Like clothes and diapers and a stroller." She shakes her head. "Freaking bouncy seat. C'mon, Levi, let's go look at the strollers."

Taking his hand in hers, the two of them scurry off, but I make a note of the bouncy seat she was looking at before following after them.

If she wanted the damn bouncy seat, I could get her one. It wasn't about the money.

But I bite my tongue and watch her take in the store and all the things. I knew exactly when she found something she liked because her whole face would light up, only for some of the light to disappear when she saw the price tag. And yet, not once did she ask for anything.

Stubborn woman.

"*Oh my gosh.*" She lifts up a little blanket in the air and looks at it. "Look at how cute this is. It matches the elephant."

It really did. The blanket was white, with little gray elephants on it that indeed matched the one Levi found earlier.

But it wasn't the blanket that held my attention. It was her. The tears shone in her eyes. The bright smile. The pure happiness at such a simple thing.

"I think I'll get it. We can bring the baby home from the hospital in it. Maybe find a cute matching outfit."

We.

That one word echoes in my head as she and Levi continue chatting.

She said we. Not I.

It was the first time she did it on her own and warmth filled my stomach. She was starting to open up to me. To this idea of us. Of our family.

"What do you think, Blake?"

"I think it's perfect."

She's perfect.

"Then it's settled. I'll be getting this. Do you think we have time to check out cribs? I really need one of those."

As if I could ever tell her no.

"Lead the way."

Chapter 19

SAVANNAH

Blake doesn't say one word as I look at the cribs and discuss the pros and cons of each of my favorites with the salesclerk until I finally settle on one of those beautiful, old school, white wooden cribs. It was a classic that could fit a boy or a girl and go with whatever I chose to do for decorations of the room. Maybe dove gray? That could look cute, and it went with the elephant theme we had going on.

Which reminds me, I should really clear out my old room and make a nursery out of it.

And that meant I'd also need to finally move my own stuff into an actual room.

My grandmother's old room.

Her frail body lying still on the bed flashes in front of my eyes, and I can feel my throat go dry as a cold sweat washes over me.

"Will that be all?"

The question snaps me out of my thoughts. I give the man an apologetic smile, but before I can open my mouth, Blake's already extending his hand, a black card tucked between his fingers.

"Ye— Actually, no, wait. Levi, give the clerk the elephant so I can pay for it."

I turn to him, grateful for the distraction. "What are you doing?"

"What does it look like I'm doing?" Blake frowns, all innocent. "We can't very well leave without paying, can we?"

Seriously? That was the story he was going with? He knew exactly what I was talking about.

"I mean, what are you doing paying for my things?"

I have him, and he knows it.

He opens his mouth, and I expect a fight, but instead, he just shrugs. "It's *our* baby."

"It is, but these things will be in *my* house." I turn to the clerk, pulling out my wallet. "Just this, please. *Then* you can assist him."

The clerk's gaze darts over my shoulder. "Umm... I already ran the elephant."

"See?" Blake extends his hand. "Put that away, Blondie."

I turn around, cross my arms over my chest, and glare at him. "You can't keep buying things for me, Blake."

"Of course I can."

"Blake!" I protest, but he just grabs his card and thanks the clerk as another one brings the box with the crib. "Grab the elephant, Levi, and let's go to the car."

He takes the box and nods at the guy before starting for the door, Levi behind him. I grab the bag with my blanket and follow after them.

"You're driving me crazy; you know that?"

"The feeling is mutual." He glances over his shoulder. "Where did you park?"

Sighing, I point in the direction of my car. "This way."

Hurrying my step, I pull out my keys and unlock the car.

Opening the trunk, I eye it carefully before shifting my attention to the box in Blake's arms. "I don't think this will fit."

"That's what she said," Blake chuckles.

"Seriously?" I hiss, tilting my head toward Levi, who seems way more interested in the toy than us. "There is a child here."

This has him laughing even harder. "He's not paying us any attention, and even if he was, he wouldn't understand." He wiggles his brows. "So what do you say, Blondie? Too big for your trunk?"

"Stop it." I jab him in the shoulder. "You really are incorrigible, you know that?"

"I'm just asking." His gaze zeroes in on my mouth before locking with mine, his voice dropping lower. "You know, if you ask really nicely, I'll drive it back home for you since my truck's way bigger and all that."

I blink a few times, unsure if he's serious. "Are you for real?"

Blake just smirks, "What can I say? I need proper motivation."

Shaking my head, I let out a sigh. "Can you please drive the crib back home for me, Mr. Walker?" I ask sweetly, batting my lashes.

"You have to say pretty please," Levi corrects.

I shoot Blake a knowing smirk. So much for Levi not listening. "My bad, pretty please, Mr. Walker, can you help and drive the crib back home for me?"

"Fine," Blake grumbles. I expect him to pull back, but instead he leans closer, his warm breath making the goosebumps rise on my skin as his voice drops an octave so only I can hear him. "But next time, I won't be so easily swayed."

My throat bobs as he takes a step back, his gaze not missing anything. "C'mon, Levi. We'll meet Miss Parker back home."

I let out a long breath as I watch him call out to Levi, and the two of them leave. Shaking my head, I slide into the driver's seat, my body still buzzing from Blake's nearness. I trace my fingers over my lower lip, my stomach clenching.

What will happen once he actually touches me again?

Not that he tried it. Not after the hospital.

Will he do it?

Will I let him?

I shouldn't. It would only complicate things way more than they already are, and yet, I couldn't help myself, a part of me wanted to feel those full lips on mine. Hear that low groan as he devoured my mouth with his, my body coming alive under his touch.

I grip my fingers tighter around the steering wheel, pushing the thoughts of kissing Blake to the back of my head.

Although the A/C is on, the heat inside my car is excruciating, making my shirt stick to my skin. My stomach grumbles, reminding me I haven't eaten much today.

Thankfully, traffic is light, so it doesn't take me too long to get back home.

Blake's nowhere to be found when I park in front of my house and get out. I take in the house, noticing all the little details that have changed in the last few weeks.

Mostly thanks to him.

It started to look like the home I remembered from my childhood.

That familiar ache spreads inside my chest, my mouth going dry as I make my way to the house and unlock the door, leaving it open so Blake can enter once he gets here.

My gaze fixes on the stairs, the lump in my throat growing thicker. Swallowing it down, I force myself to place a foot on the step.

"You can do this, Savannah."

The photo frames hung on the wall, taking me back down

the memory lane I tried so hard to push back as I made my way up the stairs.

It hurt so much. Remembering Grams. Hearing her raspy laughter. The crinkles that would appear around her eyes every time she'd smile. The way her southern accent would grow thicker when she got annoyed with something.

There was a photo of the two of us in front of Bluebonnet High from my graduation. Grams was beaming that day. Birthdays and Christmases and holidays. It's always been Grams and me against the world.

I'm winded by the time I climb to the second floor, my vision turning blurry. I curl my fingers around the railing to steady myself, blinking my eyes a few times until my focus clears, and I'm facing the door to my grandmother's room. I try to swallow the knot in my throat, but my mouth is dry.

I swear, some days, I could still see her frail body as I found it that day.

Pale and lifeless.

People used to tell me that at least she went fast and wasn't in pain. I hated that statement with every fiber of my being. There was no solace in knowing that her death was fast. I didn't want her to go. She was my only family, and I wanted her to live for many more years. Because I might be a grown-ass woman, but I needed my grandmother. I needed her support and love in my life.

Pushing open the door, I linger in the doorway as I watch her room.

How many times had I snuck in here when I was a little girl just after Mom left, and I was too scared Grams would be gone once I woke up? Too many to count. But Grams never complained. Not once.

Moving inside, I look around the room. I'll have to go

through all of her things carefully, but I knew most of the furniture would have to go since it's too old.

My gaze falls on the dresser pushed against the wall. It was covered in dust, but I remember the color being worn down from years of use. Still, it looked sturdy enough. Maybe if I could repaint it, I could use it as a dresser in the nursery. I wanted Munchkin to know the woman who gave everything up so she could raise me.

A photo of Grams and me taken shortly after I moved here is sitting on the dresser. She looked so happy and proud.

"I miss you," I whisper softly, voicing the words out loud that I've been holding in since she died as I watch her smiling face. "I think now more than ever. I wish you could tell me what to do. I wish you could meet my baby. You'd have loved to be a great-grandmother."

That vise grip squeezes around my chest, making it hard to breathe.

I press my palm against my heart, rubbing at the spot.

I could see it. All the little things, all the moments, that we could have had but never will.

"Blondie?" Blake calls out, his loud footsteps echoing downstairs.

Wiping at my cheeks, I turn over my shoulder. "Upstairs. I'll be down in a second."

I give the room one last glance, allowing myself to mourn the woman that was my whole world for many years.

It was strange how things worked out. Just when I lost Grams, I got to meet Blake who gave me a chance for a family of my own. Our baby. Maybe it was a coincidence, but a part of me couldn't help but wonder if Grams had her fingers in it in some way. She must have known losing her would destroy me. And she knew better than anybody how much I wanted somebody to call my own.

"You'd love him, I think." I slide my tongue over my dry lips. "I wish you were here. But I think... I think we'll be okay."

Sucking in a long breath, I leave the room and descend the stairs where Blake is about to go up.

"There you are. I was just coming up to look for you."

I come to a stop, a couple of steps putting me on the same level as Blake. "I was just trying to figure out where I'll put the crib."

A frown appears between his brows as he looks at me. He lifts his hand and cups my face, his finger skimming over my cheek. "Are you okay?"

"Yeah. Do you mind taking the crib up for me?"

"Of course." His gaze shifts up the stairs before it returns to me. "Are you sure you're okay?"

"Yes." I nod slowly. "I think I will be."

If he finds my answer weird, he doesn't say anything.

"Okay, I'll take the crib up."

"Thank you."

Blake's thumb skims over my jaw, my lips parting slightly. His gaze lowers, but just then, my stomach decides to growl—*loudly*.

"When was the last time you ate?"

"It's been a while."

Blake shakes his head, clearly not happy with my answer. "I guess it's good I stopped to grab something to eat then." His hands drop on my waist, and he puts me down on the ground and gives me a gentle push toward the door. "Out. Now."

"I'm going, I'm going." I shake my head at his bossy tone as I make my way to the porch, where Levi is sitting on the floor next to the coffee table and slurping his drink.

"Hungry?" I ask as I sit on the swing next to him.

"Yes. We got you one too! It's"—he grabs one of the bags and peeks inside before handing it to me—"this one."

The smell of the burger and fries reaches my nostrils, and I can feel my stomach grumble once again. I pop one fry into my mouth, my eyes falling shut as the salty taste reaches my tongue.

"This is so good," I groan loudly, covering my mouth.

Blinking my eyes open I find Levi watching me, a contemplative expression on his face. I take a napkin to wipe my mouth. "Is everything okay?"

"Yes." Levi nods, his gaze falling to his food. He picks one fry and plays with it for a moment. "Miss Parker?"

"Yes?"

"What should I call you?"

I choke slightly, grateful that I finished my bite. "Umm... I don't think I understand. Do you mind explaining it to me?"

"Well, I call you Miss Parker." He glances at me, so I nod. "But Dad calls you Blondie or Savannah."

"Oh..."

I tuck a strand of my hair behind my ear. I guess I could see where he was coming from. This whole situation has to be confusing to a six-year-old. Blake and I were having a child together, but I was also his teacher, which only made the whole situation that more complicated.

Still, he brought it up because, for one reason or another, this was troubling him.

"What would you like to call me?"

He shrugs and lowers his gaze. "I don't know."

"Hmm... How about this?" I place my hand on his shoulder, giving him a gentle squeeze. Levi tilts his head back so he can watch me. "Since I'm still your teacher, when we're in school, you have to call me Miss Parker."

His face falls a little in disappointment, and I can feel my heart break for this little boy. He was so sweet; there was no way I could ever say no to him.

"*However*," I continue, those big gray eyes fixing on me, "when we're out of school, you can call me Sav."

"Sav?" he repeats as if he's testing the word, but I don't miss the skepticism in his tone.

"Yes, it's short for Savannah. It's what all my friends call me."

Levi's whole face lights up. "Really? Does that mean I'm your friend, too?"

A strand of hair falls into his face as he flashes me a smile.

"Yes, we're friends."

"Yes." Before I know it, he jumps to his feet and wraps his arms around me. "You're my best friend, Sav. After Kyle." He tilts his head back. "He's my best, *best* friend."

I chuckle softly. "I think I can live with that."

I extend my hand and gently brush his hair back. He tilts his head into my touch, a longing expression flashing on his face.

And that damn ache is back inside my chest, making it hard to breathe.

I knew how he was feeling. After all, I used to be him when I was his age. So desperate for somebody of my own, somebody who'd love me. At least he had a father who adored him and was there for him.

"Levi!"

My head snaps up at the sound of the harsh tone. Levi's hands loosen, and he pulls back to look at his brother, who's storming across the street and based on the expression on his face, he's livid.

I push to my feet, my heart thundering wildly inside my chest, the sudden movement making me sway slightly. My hand grabs for something to steady myself, only to land on Levi's shoulder.

"Let's go," Daniel says to his brother, his jaw set in a hard line.

"No, I'm talking to Sav!" Levi protests. "You should be in your room anyway. You were grounded."

Grounded?

Blinking a few times, I see Daniel's angry gaze land on me, and for the first time, I notice his disarrayed looks. There is a dark bruise under his eye, and his lip has been busted.

Holy shit.

"What happened to you?"

Instinctively, I lift my hand, but he slaps it away. "Don't touch me."

I curl my fingers into a fist, feeling the sting in my palm. "I'm sorry."

"If you were actually sorry, you'd stay the fuck away," Daniel yells.

Levi turns to his brother. "Why are you so mean to her? She didn't do anything to you."

I bite the inside of my cheek. My stomach rolls with unease at the anger shining from Daniel, but then my gaze falls on Levi —sweet, kind-hearted Levi. I didn't want to be the reason for two brothers fighting. They both had the right to process everything that had happened in their own way, and I didn't blame Daniel one bit for reacting the way he did.

I gently squeeze Levi's shoulder. "Levi, it's fine. You—"

"You're not our mother!" Daniel's loud shout intensifies the ringing in my ears.

He grabs Levi's hand and tugs him away, making me lose my balance. I try to reach for something else to hold onto, as black spots appear in front of my eyes.

Shit. I blink furiously, but even that doesn't help clear my vision, which makes the anxiety rise inside my chest. *What the hell is going on with me?*

"Just because Dad fucked you doesn't make you anything to

us, so don't you dare act like you are our mother. Because you're not. If I were yo—"

His mouth keeps moving, but I can't hear a word of what he says. A droplet of sweat falls in my eye. I blink it away, but my vision still stays blurry, my lungs tightening. I open my mouth to suck in the much-needed air, but it only makes things worse.

A hand touches my arm.

I blink, Levi's worried face coming into view.

My tongue darts out, sliding over my dry lips. I open my mouth to reassure him, but no words come out.

My throat bobs as I swallow, looking up to find Daniel watching me.

And is there a trace of uncertainty on his face?

I must look really bad if that's the case.

I'm fine. I take a step forward, that frown between his brows deepening. That boy, so much like his father. *I'm going to be just fi—*

The words don't get a chance to form before the ground tilts on its axis, my hands flying to my belly as the world goes completely black.

Chapter 20

BLAKE

Putting the box with the crib on the floor inside the room Savannah left open for me, I dust my hands just when my phone rings inside my pocket. I pull it out, the corner of my mouth lifting when I notice the name on the screen.

"Andrew Hill, to what do I owe this pleasure?"

The low rumble of my agent's chuckle—my *ex*-agent, I suppose—greets me from the other side of the line. "Hello to you too, old man. What? Can't a guy check in on his friend?"

"I would assume you have your hands full with your much younger clients. *Working* clients."

Andrew groans. "Don't remind me. Between some of those little fuckers and my own kids at home, I do have my hands full. That's why I'm calling. I need somebody normal and grounded to remind me why I'm doing this in the first place because I'll tell you some of the shit I deal with... It definitely tests my sanity."

I burst out into laughter. "Wait until they reach their teenage years, and then you get to talk. The idea that I have to go through the teenage years two more times after Daniel..." A legit shudder goes through me. "At least I don't have to do it at the same time."

Andrew and his wife, Jeanette, had twins. Not just that, twin *girls*. How he was staying sane, I had no idea.

"Don't even remind me. I love those girls, but damn, they'll take me to an early grave." There is a short pause. "Wait, scroll back, did you say *two* more times?"

"Shit," I pinch the bridge of my nose.

"What the hell, Walker?" The chair screeches in the background. "I thought we were better than that."

"We are, it's..." I let out a long sigh. "There has just been a lot going on."

"Clearly. Spill."

I tell him about Savannah and everything else that has happened since we moved here, including the whole mess with Daniel.

"Holy shit, man. I don't envy you one bit. And you've just made me feel way better about my situation; at least I don't have to worry about how I'll spin this to the press. Give me blurry images of drunk players any day of the week."

"You're welcome," I mutter dryly.

"It's a tough situation to be in, that's for sure." There is a short pause, and I can hear a clicking of a pen. It was Andrew's tick, a sign that he was mulling things over. "You need legal advice?"

Legal advice? Why would I—

"God, no. Blondie and I... Well, I'm not gonna lie and say we're perfect, but we're working things out. No need to involve lawyers."

"Okay. I figured I'd put it out there. If you need help, you let me know."

"Thanks, I appreciate it, man."

I doubted I'd need it, but it was good to know I had my long-time friend guarding my back.

"Good. Now, there was actually a reason why I called you. I

talked to one of your sponsors, and they want you to come up for a photoshoot. I'll forward you the e-mail with the details."

I groan loudly. "I knew you didn't call just for kicks and giggles."

"Yeah, well, we can't all be retired by thirty-five. Some of us have to work."

"Oh, please, what would you do otherwise? You'd get bored within the first twenty-four hours."

I was pretty sure that if Andrew wanted, he could easily retire. But the jackass liked bossing people around too much to do that. That being said, he did expand the business, taking in a few other agents in the last few years to help lighten his case load so he could spend more time with his family. These days, he was extremely picky when it came to selecting his new clients.

"Probably, and then my wife would kick me out of the house, and I love my wife, so... Anyway, there is also another thing. I've been getting calls about your plans now that you're retired."

"Okay, so? You know my plans."

Andrew grunts. "Stay in your perfect little town and be a rancher? Those plans?"

"Now, I wouldn't take it that far..."

My words trail off as I hear loud shouting.

"Walker?"

"Wait..."

I listen intently as the yelling continues—a voice that sounds a lot like Daniel's.

What the—

"I have to go, Hill. Send me the details, and we'll talk later."

"Fine. This isn't o—"

I hit the end button before he can finish. Sliding the phone in my pocket, I leave the room and run down the stairs, just in time to hear Daniel shout, "Just because Dad fucked you doesn't make you anything to us, so don't you dare act like you are our mother. Because you're not. If I were you, I wouldn't get cozy because he'll get sick of you and dump you before you know it. He's—"

My heart is beating wildly inside my chest as I get to the front door. The color drains from Savannah's face, and she sways on her feet.

From the corner of my eye, I see the look of surprise and shock on my sons' faces, but right now, all my attention is on the woman in front of me. Her hands are on her belly as if she's trying to protect our baby even now as her body is swaying.

"Savannah!" I yell as I start running like my life depends on it. In a way, it does. Only a few steps separate us, but it feels like she's miles away.

My heart is stuck in my throat until my arms finally wrap around her at the very last second. As gently as possible, I lower her body to the ground and push her hair out of her face. Her skin is impossibly pale, and sweat coats her face, making her hair stick to it.

"Blondie, open your eyes," I urge, my thumb skimming over her cheek. Her chest is rising and falling slowly. Wrapping my palms around her wrist, I press the tips of my fingers against her pulse, only to be greeted with an erratic heartbeat. *Fuck.* "C'mon, baby, don't do this to me. Open those pretty blue eyes for me, Blondie."

This can't be happening.

She has to be okay.

They both have to.

"D-daddy, wh-what is going on?" Levi's stuttering voice breaks through the ringing in my ears. I look up and find him standing next to me, his face pale, eyes wide. "Is Sav okay? Why is she not waking up?"

"I don't know, buddy," I admit honestly, returning my attention to Savannah, who's still not moving. I scan her body, looking for any obvious injury or bleeding, but there is none. That has to be good, right?

"It's all your fault!" Levi yells at Daniel.

"I didn't do anything!" Daniel defends.

"She was worried about you, and you pushed her away!"

"I-I..." I turn around just to see fear creep on my older son's face as he glances at the woman on the floor. His Adam's apple bobs as he swallows, those gray eyes turning to me. "I didn't mean to. I just wanted her to leave us alone. I never wanted for any of this to happen. Dad, I..." With each word, the panic in his voice becomes more evident.

"Hey, it's fine. It was an accident. She's going to be fine."

She has to be fine.

Sliding my hands under Savannah's body, I lift her into my arms as I start for my truck.

"Open the door. I'm taking her to the hospital."

Daniel runs in front of me and opens the passenger's side door before giving me space to put Savannah onto the seat. I slide her body down as gently as possible, doing my best to strap her in place as I adjust the seat so she's lying down. Once secure, I skim my palm over her cheek, the knot in my throat growing tighter with each second her eyes stay firmly shut. "You're going to be okay. You hear me? You're going to be okay."

I didn't accept anything else as an option.

Savannah and our baby had to be fine.

Reluctantly, I pull back. Closing the door, I jog to the driver's side and slip inside.

The boys are already sitting in the back, neither of them saying anything as we drive to the hospital. My fingers clench around the steering wheel as my gaze darts to Savannah every few seconds.

We're almost there when Savannah stirs next to me. I all but jump out of my seat.

"Blondie?" I glance at her, feeling my heartbeat speed up as I shift my attention between the road and her. The last thing I needed was to get us all killed.

She groans softly.

"C'mon baby, open those pretty blue eyes for me," I urge, my palm falling to her knee and giving her a gentle squeeze.

"B-Blake?" she croaks out, and it's the most beautiful sound I've ever heard.

She blinks a few times, her eyes slowly opening.

"Savannah!" Levi cries out from the back, the relief I'm feeling evident in his voice. "You're awake. I was so scared."

Savannah tries to push up, but the seat belt holds her in place. "What happened?"

I tighten my hold on her. "Don't try to move, we're almost there."

"Where? What's going on?"

"You fainted."

Her eyes widen, making her skin seem even paler as she places her hand against her stomach. "B-baby?"

"There was no bleeding." I rub my thumb over the inside of her knee. I could feel her anxiety, and I knew it wasn't helping at all. "At least not from what I could see, but I want the doctors to check you out. Just so we're sure."

Savannah swallows audibly and nods. "Okay." Those big blue eyes meet mine. "Blake, what if—"

"No." I shake my head before she can even finish. "You're okay. You *both* are okay."

Nothing else is an option.

SAVANNAH

"The heartbeat is nice and strong." The young technician smiles. With a press of a few buttons, a strong *whooshing* sound fills the room.

A soft whimper escapes me. I cover my mouth and tilt my head back to find the same relief I'm feeling written all over Blake's face. His shoulders relax visibly, and he closes his eyes for a second as his fingers grip mine tightly.

Our baby is fine.

That one thought echoes inside my head. I didn't care about anything else except for that.

She nods absentmindedly as she continues looking at the screen. "Everything seems to be in perfect order and progressing as it should based on how far along you are."

"You're fine," Blake echoes as if he needed to reassure himself. "After she fell... I just needed to make sure they were okay."

"It's completely understandable." The technician removes the wand from my stomach and hands me a paper towel which I gratefully take. Or I would if Blake wasn't faster. He gently pushes my hand away and cleans all the goo from my stomach. "Based on the scan, the baby looks fine. We're still waiting for the lab results to see what might have caused this." She takes off her gloves and tosses them to the garbage. "The doctor should be with you shortly with more info."

We thank her as she leaves the room. Blake tosses the tissues away and tugs my shirt in place.

"You know, I could have done that, right?" I try to force out a smile, but it falls flat.

Blake just stares at me silently, his hand cupping my cheek. And then his eyes meet mine, and I can see all the emotions that he's been pushing back until now reflected in his irises.

"I was so fucking scared, Savannah," he croaks out. "I heard the commotion, so I rushed downstairs. Daniel was yelling, and you were pale as a ghost, and then you fell…" He shakes his head. "I was so fucking scared that something had happened to you or the baby."

"Hey," I cover his hand with mine. Turning my head, I brush my lips against his palm. "We're fine. The baby is fine."

"You *fainted*," he points out. "You fainted, and there is nothing that I could have done to help you."

"Blake…"

He seemed so calm and collected this whole time, my rock through the whole admission's process. He was holding my hand while they drew my blood and while we waited for the technician to make sure the baby was okay, not once moving an inch from my side. And up until now, I didn't even realize how much this whole thing upset him.

He leans down, his forehead pressing against mine. "After we're done here, I'm taking you home, and you're not leaving my sight."

My heart does a little flip inside my chest at his words, the wild intensity in his gaze. There would be no negotiating with him. Not on this. Not now.

Before I can say anything, the door opens. Blake's lips press against my forehead before he pulls back, and I can see the older woman standing in the doorway.

"Dr. Gonzales, hi!" I sit upright quickly, which is a mistake. The sudden movement makes the IV dig deeper into my hand. I wince softly, falling back against the pillow.

Blake turns to me immediately. "What's wrong?"

"Moved too fast." I look at the doctor. "What are you doing here?"

"I just came in for my shift when I heard somebody mention you were admitted. How are you feeling?"

"I'm feeling like I'm ready to go home," I answer without missing a beat. I was so done with staying in the hospital. "Please? I'm not below begging."

The woman chuckles softly. "As soon as you finish your IV. But first, I wanted to talk to you about your blood work. We just got it back."

I knew that look. The tone of that voice. And it meant nothing good. My throat bobs as I swallow.

"What's wrong with her blood work?" Blake asks, his hand taking mine and rubbing gently over my knuckles.

Dr. Gonzales glances between the two of us until her gaze finally settles on me. "The blood work showed that your blood sugar was through the roof."

Her words echo in my head as I try to wrap my head around it.

"Wh-what..."

"What does that mean?" Blake asks, and I've never been more grateful to have somebody by my side.

"How have you been feeling lately?" Dr. Gonzales asks instead.

"Okay, I guess?" My tongue darts out to slide over my dry lips. "A little bit tired, but I figured that's normal since the last few weeks have been crazy between moving and the beginning of the school year."

Add to it everything that happened with Blake, and yeah...

"Nothing else?" The doctor persists. "No blurred eyesight, dizziness, thirst, dry mouth, sweating, increased need to go to the bathroom?"

"I..." I glance at Blake, feeling the bile rise in my throat. "Some. But it's still pretty hot, so I thought..." I swallow hard. "Did I do something wrong?"

Were there signs that something was going on, and I completely ignored them? Put my baby at risk? Should I have taken this more seriously and mentioned it during my last visit?

So many questions swirl inside my head, my lungs closing up.

"No." Dr. Gonzales shakes her head. "There is no way you'd have known. The testing for gestational diabetes isn't usually done for another few weeks. However, in some women, it appears before that."

My brows pull together as her words register in my mind. "Gestational diabetes? What is that?"

"Gestational diabetes occurs when your body can't make enough insulin during your pregnancy, which can be dangerous for mom and the baby, but it usually goes away after the birth."

I have diabetes?

Blake's hold on me tightens.

My lifeline.

"But... I'm trying my best to eat healthy, and to avoid everything you've said. Maybe I sho—"

"You did nothing wrong, Savannah," Dr. Gonzales says gently. "This is something that's completely out of your control. Gestational diabetes isn't like regular diabetes. I've treated many women who were top athletes, made sure they ate healthy, and still, they had gestational diabetes. The good thing is, we caught it early, so we can treat it accordingly."

"What can we do to help her?" Blake asks. "Will she have to start taking medication, or what's the process here?"

"To begin with, I would like you to try managing your blood sugar levels with a diet. This basically means that you'll keep a diary of your blood sugar levels after every meal and jot down what you ate. It's also important to drink a lot of fluids and move as much as possible. Ideally, your fasting blood sugar will be under 100 mg/dL, and just after a meal, it shouldn't go higher than 200 mg/dL. If that doesn't work, and your levels stay up, we'll have to put you on insulin."

My mind spins as I try to process all of this information and not freak out. "I can do that."

At least, I think I could.

"I'll prepare you a few brochures to look at when you get home, and I'd like to see you in my office in a couple of days so I can check you out and you can ask any additional questions you might have."

"Thank you, doctor," Blake says. "We appreciate that."

Dr. Gonzales glances at the IV. "Your IV is almost done. I'll tell the nurse to prepare your discharge papers and to come and unhook you." She starts for the door, only to look over her shoulder. "Also? Try to keep your stress to a minimum, Savannah."

I let out a strangled laugh. "I think that's easier said than done, doctor."

Dr. Gonzales nods in understanding and leaves the room, the silence settling over the two of us.

I pinch the bridge of my nose, feeling the weight of this revelation settle over me.

Gestational diabetes.

I have gestational diabetes.

It was still hard to wrap my head around it.

I've heard the term before, but I never looked into it much. I never thought I'd need it. What a freaking joke that was. But what if Dr. Gonzales was wrong? What if I did something that caused all of this? Maybe if I were more careful, none of this would have happened. Maybe…

"Hey." Blake crouches down so we're at the same level.

Determination shines in his gray eyes as he forces me to look at him. That calloused hand cups my cheek, sending shivers through my body. I bite into my lower lip, tears blurring my vision. "I know this is scary, but you're not alone in this, okay? You heard the doctor, this shit happens, and there is nothing that you could have done to stop it. The most important thing is that we caught it in time, and that you both are doing well. We'll figure out the rest together. I've gotcha, Blondie."

A lump forms in my throat, and I force it down, my voice coming out raspy, "Blake, I..."

My words are cut off when the door bursts open, and Levi appears in the doorway. "Sav! Are you okay?"

Blake stands, his shadow falling over me, so I use this moment to look away and brush my cheeks, wiping the tears away.

Blake wraps his hand around Levi before he can jump onto me. "Easy there, buddy. Savannah isn't feeling well."

"You're not going to faint, are you? That was scary."

"I'm not going to faint." I shake my head, forcing out a smile. "I'm sorry I scared you. I'll be better soon."

"Good." Levi nods. He slips out of Blake's grasp, and before either of us can react, he comes to me. He hugs my legs and presses a kiss against my belly. "There, all better."

He flashes that toothless grin at me, proud of himself, and my heart melts.

This little boy will be my undoing.

"What was that for?" I ask, trying to keep my cool, which isn't easy when he's being so freaking sweet.

"Daddy usually kisses me when I'm sick, and it makes me feel better, so maybe you and my baby brother will feel better too."

Tears threaten to come out once again. God, I was such a mess. I squeeze my fingers into a fist, my nails digging into my skin to stop the tears from coming. "Thank you, Levi," I rasp out, cupping his cheek. "You are right, I already feel better."

If possible, his smile grows even bigger, and a lock of hair falls into his eyes. "See? I told you it helps!"

"It sure does." Reaching out, I push the lock of hair out of his face. He leans his head into my touch, his smile falling a little.

"You're really going to be okay?"

"Savannah and the baby had a health scare, buddy, but we'll take care of her, and she'll be better in no time," Blake explains.

The movement over Levi's shoulder catches my attention, and when I look up, I find Daniel standing in the doorway. He narrows his eyes on my hand, and my fingers itch to pull back. I can still hear the loud *slap* as he pushed my hand away earlier today, and see those angry eyes zeroed in on me.

But there was no anger on his face now. No, he's pale, which only makes the bruises on his face stand out more.

He opens his mouth as if he wants to say something, but just then, the nurse appears from behind him, so he lets her through. The next time I look at the door, he's already gone.

Chapter 21

BLAKE

"Dad?" Levi whispers softly. "Are you taking Sav home?"

Savannah wiggles in my arms before her head settles against my shoulder, still firmly asleep. She must have been exhausted because of everything that had happened, since she crashed before I even managed to get out of the parking lot.

"No, she'll stay with us tonight."

There was no fucking way I could leave her in her house all alone. Not after what happened today.

"Like a sleepover?" Levi asks excitedly, holding the door open for me.

"Yes, like a sleepover. Brush your teeth and get into your PJs," I whisper to the boys as I move further down the hallway. "I'll come and check in on you in a minute."

Pushing open the door to my room with my shoulder, I slip inside and walk to my bed. As gently as possible so as not to startle her, I lay her on my bed.

Pulling back, I sit on the mattress next to Savannah and brush her hair out of her face.

She is okay.

Safe and sound in my bed.

She is okay.

Maybe if I repeat it enough times, I'd believe it.

Savannah blinks, and sleepy blue irises meet mine. "Blake?" She looks around, clearly confused. "Where am I?"

"In my bed. You fell asleep."

"Gosh, I'm so—" she starts to push upright, but I place my hand on her shoulder to keep her in place.

"No, stay here."

Her lips part in surprise. "Blake I—"

I knew what she would say, but I couldn't let her go. It wasn't rational, this need to make sure that she's all right, but it was there, and there was nothing I could do to stop it. Today was a clusterfuck of epic proportions, and it made me realize just how fragile this whole thing is. How fragile she is and how quickly I could lose her. Lose *them*.

"Stay here, and let me take care of you," I croak out, taking her hand in mine. "Please, Blondie. I'll go crazy worrying about you. What if you start feeling bad or something happens, and—"

"Okay," she whispers, her fingers wrapping around mine. "I'll stay."

I let out a long breath, feeling my shoulders relax. I grip her fingers, my other hand going to her hair. Neither of us says anything as I brush her hair away in gentle strokes until her eyes grow heavy, and she dozes off once again, her breathing evening out.

"Dad?"

I look up at the softly spoken question and find Levi standing in the doorway dressed in his PJs. Pressing my finger against my lips, I get up and exit the room, closing the door behind me.

"You done?"

"Yes." Levi glances toward the door. "Is Sav really going to be okay?"

"Miss Parker," I correct, "will be fine. She's just tired."

Levi crosses his arms over his chest and lifts his chin. "Sav told me I have to call her Miss Parker when we're in school, but I can call her Sav when we're home. That's what her friends call her." He gives me a pointed look. "Because I'm her friend."

Chuckling softly, I drop my hand to his shoulders and steer him toward his bedroom. "Okay, then. *Sav* is going to stay here so I can keep an eye on her. Now off to bed with you."

Levi climbs into his bed, and I pull the covers over him.

"Sav is really nice, Dad. I like her. I don't want anything to happen to her or my baby brother."

"It won't. We'll take care of her."

Levi nods. "Yes, we'll take care of her."

I brush his hair away before leaning down to kiss the top of his head. "Sleep tight. I'll see you in the morning."

With a "Goodnight," I slip out of the room, closing the door behind me. I can hear the water running in the bathroom, so I make my way downstairs and into the kitchen. Grabbing a glass from the cupboard, I open the highest shelf and pull down the whiskey I stashed there behind some of the rice crackers I knew the boys didn't like. Pouring two fingers of amber liquid, I make my way out on the porch and sit down on the stairs.

I pull out my phone and type in gestational diabetes. Now that everybody was asleep, I could finally do what I wanted to since the doctor told us Savannah's diagnosis—research. I couldn't help her if I didn't know what we were dealing with.

Dozens of different results pop up on the screen immediately. I start reading each article, making my anxiety grow stronger. So many things could go wrong, and there was only so much Savannah or I could do to help her.

Squeezing my glass, I lift it and down the drink in one go. The whiskey slides down my throat, and I embrace the burn.

What if something goes wrong? What if she can't manage it

with diet? What if something happens to the baby? What if something happens to Savannah?

"Is she really okay?"

Glancing over my shoulder, I find Daniel standing in the doorway watching me.

"Let's hope so."

Daniel nods, his gaze turning distant as he bites the inside of his cheek.

Placing the glass on the floor next to me, I face forward and look up at the dark sky. I knew we should probably talk about what had happened this afternoon, but I didn't have it in me to get in another screaming match with him.

I expect Daniel to leave, but instead, he sits on the step next to me. For a while, we stay in silence, neither of us saying anything.

"Did I..." He clears his throat. "Was I the reason she ended up in a hospital?"

My head whips in his direction. "What?"

His body is stiff, fingers curling into fists in his lap so tightly his knuckles have turned white. The panic is written all over his face as he rushes out in one breath, "I swear I didn't mean to hurt her. I didn't even realize I pushed her that hard or that she would fall. I didn't want to h-hurt her, Dad." His tear-stained eyes meet mine, and hearing his voice break is like a kick to my gut. "I s-swear... I didn't want to hurt her."

"Hey." I place my hand on his knee and give it a firm squeeze. I couldn't remember the last time I saw him cry. Or show any sign of fragility. Lately he's been full of rage that's been brewing under the surface for the last few years. "You didn't hurt her."

"B-but she fell. And I—"

"Breathe," I whisper, gripping his knee tightly. "C'mon."

I watch his chest shake as he sucks in a long breath and lets it out, repeating the motion a few times. Once he's calm enough, I explain, "Savannah has gestational diabetes."

Daniel blinks, his brows pulling together. "What is that?"

"High blood sugar in pregnancy. Her blood sugar spiked suddenly, and her body couldn't deal with it, so she fainted. It's not your fault, Daniel."

He blinks a few times as if he's trying to wrap his mind around it. Daniel lets out a long breath, his whole body shuddering as if the weight has fallen off his shoulders.

I pull him to me and repeat, "It's not your fault."

He nods and buries his head in the crook of my neck. I didn't realize this whole situation hit him as hard as it did, so I just held him, rubbing his back, until I could feel that he's calmed down enough.

"But Daniel?"

Pulling back, he bows his head and rubs at his eyes. "Yeah?"

"This shit has to stop," I say slowly and wait for him to lift his gaze before I continue. "I know that this situation is far from ideal. I know this isn't what you would have wanted. I understand that you're angry, but the only person you should be angry at is me. Savannah? She didn't do anything to you. She's just trying to be nice and do the best that she can with the cards that she's been dealt. What you said to her today crossed every line. You had no right to act that way or to call her those names."

Red creeps up his cheeks in embarrassment, but he doesn't try to deny it.

"She didn't choose this. Do you think anybody sane would willingly choose the mess that's our family? Because if I was in her place, I sure as hell wouldn't."

"I guess not," Daniel mumbles.

"This wasn't some elaborate plot on her or my side, but she's pregnant, and there is no changing that. That baby? It's your brother or sister." His throat bobs as he swallows, but he doesn't say anything. I run my hand over my face, letting it fall into my lap. "You'll apologize to her for what you said today."

Daniel opens his mouth, and I can see one of those testy comments is on the tip of his tongue, but he bites the words back and nods. "Okay."

"And you'll be nice to her. No snarky comments and no glaring. She's dealing with a lot as it is, and gestational diabetes isn't something to joke about. She doesn't need any more stress than she's already under. And not because she's trying to be your mother." I give him a pointed look. "But because she doesn't want my relationship with you boys to suffer because of her."

Daniel pushes to his feet. "We didn't need her for that."

"No, we didn't," I agree. "That's the mess I made all on my own, but I want to make this right. I love you, Daniel. Despite the fact that some days you drive me crazy, and I contemplate strangling you, you're my son, and I love you. I'll always love you."

Daniel's Adam's apple bobs as he swallows. He shifts his weight and runs his fingers through his hair. "I said I'll apologize, geez." His hand drops. "I'm going to bed."

He shakes his head and goes toward the door. I watch him for a moment longer, and just as I start to turn, I spot him lingering in the doorway.

"Dad?"

"Yes?"

I'm not quite sure what's going on in his head. I haven't known for a while now. The little boy he used to be, who'd run into my arms every time he'd see me, was long gone. Mostly thanks to my actions. Now he was a young man full of resentment at me and the world, and I was trying my best to get through to him.

Today felt like the beginning, though. To what, I wasn't exactly sure. Only time will be able to tell.

Daniel opens his mouth, but no words come out. "Nothing." He shakes his head before slipping into the house.

Running my hand over my face, I pinch the bridge of my nose and just sit there in silence. I could feel a headache brewing behind my temples as everything that happened today played on a loop in my mind.

Sighing, I pick up the glass and enter the quiet house. I make sure everything is locked before I go upstairs to check on Savannah. All the information I read about gestational diabetes was still going through my head, and I couldn't stop thinking about all the bad things that could happen.

I push the door open, the light peeking through the crack in the door, making Savannah's hair shine brightly.

Staying as quiet as possible, I go to my dresser and pull a pair of loose basketball pants on. I'm just about to head out when I hear Savannah's soft voice. "Blake?"

It's slightly raspy from sleep, or maybe she needs some water. The doctor said she should drink more fluids. And now that thought has sneaked into my head, I couldn't stop more dark thoughts from entering my mind.

"Yeah?" I close the distance between us. "You okay? Need me to bring you any—"

"No, I'm fine. I just heard you moving around the room."

"Sorry, I needed to change, I'll lea—"

"Don't..." She shakes her head and extends her hand. "I—Can you hold me? Every time I close my eyes, I feel like something bad is going to happen, and..."

She visibly shudders at the thought.

"I'm here."

Sliding my hand from hers, I go to close the door and

navigate through the darkness back to the bed. The mattress dips under my weight as I slide under the covers.

"What if something goes wrong?" Savannah asks softly.

"It won't." I extend my hand blindly, my fingers settling on her midriff. "We'll figure it out together."

Savannah moves closer, her body nestling against mine as if it were made for me.

As if *she* were made for me.

I slide my palm over her hard stomach, my fingers sprawling protectively over the bump. I brush my nose against her neck and inhale her sweet, flowery scent.

"I've gotcha, Blondie." I brush my lips against her nape, her body shivering in my arms. "Go to sleep. I won't let anything bad happen to you or our baby."

Chapter 22

SAVANNAH

The first thing I notice when I wake up is the warmth. It's like I'm cocooned in the softest blanket next to a fireplace. I try to push away the covers, only for them to tighten harder around me.

No, not covers.

A person.

My eyes fly open as the events of last night play in my mind.

Shopping with Blake and Levi.

Coming home.

Daniel storming over, anger blazing in those gray irises that are so much like his father's.

You're not our mother!

The blackness.

ER.

Can you hold me?

The bright early morning sun entering through the curtains makes me wince softly. My eyes fall shut.

Blake's bed.

I'm in Blake's bed.

This time, I blink my eyes open slowly, letting them adjust

before I take in the simple bedroom. Plain white walls. No photos or memorabilia of any kind. Simple and efficient.

I shift slowly, but there is no space to move because Blake's body is plastered to mine; his chest is pressed into my back, arm wrapped around me, hand resting over my middle, as if he's trying to protect me and our baby.

A warm feeling spreads through my chest.

Let me take care of you.

There was so much desperation and fear in his voice last night I couldn't say no. It was like all his walls had fallen, and he let me see the man hiding underneath. A man who was desperately worried something might happen to me.

Not just our baby.

But *me*.

I couldn't remember the last time that was the case. I was usually the caretaker, and it felt nice to be the one somebody was taking care of.

The one *Blake* is taking care of.

I peek over my shoulder to look at him. His eyes are closed, his long, dark lashes fanning over his cheeks. The light scruff on his chin has turned darker overnight, making him look rugged in the most delicious way and reminding me just how good feeling that stubble against my skin felt like.

"You really have to stop wiggling that ass, Blondie."

I jump in surprise at the sound of Blake's gruff voice, the motion pressing me harder against him.

And I mean every. Single. Inch. Of. Him.

Holy gods.

I press my thighs together instinctively, trying to alleviate some of the ache that's building inside of me. Which is a mistake because his hard cock only presses harder into my ass, making us both groan softly at the touch.

Blake opens his eyes, sleepiness still clinging to his face as his arms tighten around me.

"Keep. Still," he growls into my ear.

"I thought you were asleep."

"I was until you started rubbing against me."

"What?" I glare at him. "I wasn't rubbing against you! I was trying to pull away."

The corner of his mouth tips upward just slightly, amusement dancing in his irises. "The way you're pressed against me suggests otherwise."

I open my mouth, but before I get a chance to say anything, the door bursts open.

"Hey, Dad, it's—" Levi comes to an abrupt stop, surprise flashing on his face for a split second before a grin breaks across his mouth. "Sav! You're still here."

Heat rises up my neck as the panic slams into me.

Blake's son just caught us in bed together.

The silence stretches in the room for what feels like forever. A knot forms in my throat, making it hard to breathe as the strong beat of my heart echoes in my eardrums. I open my mouth, but no words come out.

Dear God, make the ground open up and swallow me whole.

"Levi," Blake shifts behind me as he leans against his forearm. "What did we say about knocking?"

"That I have to knock before entering the room."

"More like bulldozing," Blake mutters into my hair, so only I can hear him, his warm breath making my skin tingle as he fixes his gaze on Levi. "Then why aren't you knocking?"

"I forgot." He shrugs, his attention moving to me. "Does that mean you'll move in with us?"

"Wh-what?"

Move in with them? Where did he get that idea?

I glance over my shoulder at Blake who doesn't seem the least bit fazed by the question.

Levi runs toward us and jumps on the bed. "That way, I can be with my baby brother or sister *all* the time."

"Levi, why don't you go downstairs, and we'll join you in a few so we can make breakfast?"

Levi lets out an exaggerated sigh. "Fine. But it's a good idea!" He jumps to his feet and dashes away, yelling loudly, "Hurry up, I'm *starving*."

My mouth is still open as I stare at the door, trying to wrap my head around what just happened.

Groaning, Blake falls on the mattress behind me. "Fuck, this kid will be the death of me."

Death of him? He almost gave me a heart attack.

"Moving in?" I turn over my shoulder to look at him. "Did you—"

"What? No. I didn't tell him anything, but he's right, you know." Blake gives me a pointed look. "It's a good idea."

"Blake..." I bite the inside of my cheek, unsure of what to say.

He couldn't be serious.

"You know we have to figure this thing out," he says gently. "I want you to give us a chance. A real chance, Savannah."

He was serious about it. About us. About the idea of there being something... more. And if I said yes to moving in, he'd be hauling the stuff in a second, no questions asked.

My gaze falls to his mouth, and my tongue darts out to slide over my dry lips. I could still taste him on my tongue. Feel those lush lips pressed against mine. Feel *him* pressed against me.

"We should get up. Levi is waiting." Pushing the covers back, I all but jump to my feet, a mistake because the sudden change makes the white dots play in front of my eyes. I sway on my feet as a rush of warmth washes over me, making my shirt plastered to my body.

I extend my hand, looking for something to steady myself, only to connect with a hard chest.

"I've gotcha." Blake's fingers wrap around my forearm as he pulls me to him.

I let out a shaky breath. "I'm fin—"

I don't get a chance to finish before Blake picks me up into his arms.

"What are you doing? I just got dizzy there for a second."

"Exactly, I want to check your blood sugar."

"It's because I got up too fast," I protest, but he isn't listening. "Blake! Put me down. Levi is downstairs."

"So what?"

"So you can't carry me like that. You'll scare him."

Blake comes to an abrupt stop, his jaw clenching. "Fucking hell, Blondie. Fine." He gently puts me down, his arm going around my middle. "But we're checking your blood sugar."

I don't even try to protest as he steers me down the stairs, toward the kitchen, where I can hear Levi's carefree voice chatting away, clearly not the least bit fazed by what he saw.

"And then Daniel came and yelled at Sav, so she fainted, and we had to take her to the hospital." Levi looks toward the door. "They're here. See? I told you Sav had a sleepover in Dad's bed."

If I thought Levi catching us in bed was bad, it has nothing on him blurting it out in front of Blake's housekeeper.

The older woman glances toward us over the rim of her glasses. "A sleepover, huh?"

If I don't die of mortification today, nobody will.

I tuck a strand of my hair behind my ear. "It wasn't like that."

Gray brows shoot up. "Daniel didn't yell at you, and you didn't faint?"

"I mean, I did, but..."

"Can we try not to chase Savannah away?" Blake appears in front of me and places a small black bag on the counter. In one swift movement, he unzips it and starts pulling things out.

A glucose monitor?

"Where did that come from?"

"I bought it yesterday."

He grabs one of the small needle thingies and puts it into a device that looks like a pen, making sure it's all secured properly before he extends his palm toward me. "Hand."

"But I put it into my bag." At least, I was pretty sure I did. Everything after the hospital was a bit blurry. I look over his shoulder. "Where did you put it? I should check my phone—"

"This isn't the one from your bag. Hand," Blake repeats.

Rolling my eyes, I place my hand into his just as Levi joins us. He's still in his PJs, his head mussed from sleep as he climbs into the chair next to mine.

"There is one in the car too. Dad said not to touch it because there are needles inside." Levi looks at me, his eyes wide. "Why is he sticking it in your finger?"

"So he can test my blood sugar," I explain absentmindedly as I glance at Blake, my brows furrowing. "You have one in your house and another in your car?"

"Umm..." Blake clears his throat and looks down, all of his attention fixed on my finger like it's the most interesting thing in the world. And is that a blush that's creeping up on his cheeks? "It's just for precaution. You know? In case you don't feel well."

It was definitely a blush.

Was Blake Walker embarrassed?

"In case—" I suck in a breath as the needle pinches my

finger. A drop of blood appears on my fingertip, and he scoops it onto the test strip that's already connected to the little monitor.

Levi moves closer, his gaze is fixed on my finger for a moment before he looks at me. "Does it hurt?"

"No, it's just a little pinch."

"You made a face like it hurts."

Shit, this kid was too observant for his own good.

"I just got surprised there for a second." I grab a towel from the counter and clean my hand before showing it to him. "See? No blood."

Levi makes a small huffing noise as if he doesn't trust me completely. I gently ruffle his hair. "I'm fine."

Blake grunts. "Your blood sugar is up."

My stomach sinks at his words. Blake turns the monitor so I can see it.

137, and I didn't even eat anything yet.

"The doctor said it should be a hundred tops." He gives me a pointed look.

"Does that mean Sav has to go to the doctor again?" Levi asks, moving closer to me.

A dark expression passes over Blake's face, but he quickly schools his features and gives Levi a reassuring smile. "No, buddy. We'll make Savannah something nice and healthy for breakfast, have her drink a lot of water, and see how she feels in a little bit."

"Oh, you don't have to—"

"I know I don't *have* to, but I want to." Those serious eyes bore into me as his thumb rubs over my wrist. "Let me take care of you, Blondie."

There were those words again.

A shiver runs down my spine at his intense gaze, warmth rising up my neck. My chest tightens, making it hard to breathe.

Seconds tick by as we just stare at one another. It seems

like his gaze is sucking me in, and I'm falling deeper under his spell, unable to resist him. Not when he's looking at me that way.

"Does that mean I have to eat healthy too?" Levi asks, breaking the tension between us. "Because I don't like that."

Blake and I exchange a look, and I have to bite the inside of my cheek to prevent myself from laughing.

I wrap my arm around his shoulders. "No, you can eat whatever you want."

"Good, because I want waffles."

"Waffles coming right up." Mrs. Maxwell winks at him.

"With chocolate syrup!" Levi adds.

"Is there any other kind?" Amusement dances in the older woman's eyes. Her gaze lingers on us for a moment longer, her face softening before she starts preparing food, and Blake joins her, the two of them working in silent unison.

I feel slightly guilty for just sitting there, but Levi is chatting away telling me about his favorite character from a cartoon that he dreamt about, when plates appear in front of us, and my stomach rumbles in protest.

I gaze longingly at the waffle covered in chocolate before switching my attention to yogurt with fruit and some kind of seeds.

"You don't like it."

Blake starts to pull the plate away, but I place my hand over his. "No, it looks great."

"But waffles look better."

"What can I say, Munchkin knows what it wants. But this will be perfect. Thank you." I sink the spoon into the bowl and take a bite, a small moan coming out. I cover my mouth as I look up to find Blake watching me, his irises dark. "This is really good."

The corner of his mouth tips up. "Good. Eat."

Instead of joining us, Blake goes to the coffee machine and grabs a cup, leaning against the counter as he watches us.

"Sav?" I turn to Levi, who's enjoying his waffles, a little bit of chocolate smeared over his cheeks. "Why do you call the baby Munchkin?"

"Because I don't have a name for the baby just yet. And I have to call it something."

Levi thinks about it for a second, his face serious. "I guess you're right." Levi nods, and his face lights up. "I could help you pick it up!"

"You could help me pick it *out*," I correct. "Any suggestions?"

"Hmm..." He purses his lips, his brows furrowing in concentration. "I have to think about it."

"How about you think about it as you get dressed?" Blake interjects. "We'll be late for school, so finish your breakfast and go change."

Shit.

"Okay, I'm going."

From the corner of my eye, I can see Levi stuff the rest of his food into his mouth before he jumps out of his seat and leaves the room, just as my gaze lands on the clock on the stove.

"I should go also." I push to my feet. "I have to get rea—"

"You're not going to work today."

My shoulders stiffen at Blake's firm tone. Slowly, I turn to face him. "What are you talking about? Of course I'm going to work."

"Blondie..." Blake growls, clearly annoyed.

"What?" I cross my arms over my chest. "I have to work, Blake. Not all of us get the luxury to retire at thirty."

"Thirty-five."

I wave him off. "That's beside the point."

Blake lets out an annoyed groan. In a few short steps, he

closes the distance between us, his hands landing on my shoulders. "Your sugar was high," Blake whispers, some of that fear I saw on his face slipping past his steady exterior. "You were in the ER just last night. Stay home. Please? Just a few days, that's all I'm asking of you."

Dammit.

How was I supposed to say no when he was looking at me like he wanted to wrap me up into his arms and never let me go?

I couldn't, that's how.

"*Please.*"

That tone.

It was my undoing.

He was my undoing, and I wasn't sure what to do about it.

There was something about this big, strong man showing me that he cares that melted any reservations I had.

"Fine. I'll call the school and let them know I won't be coming in."

Blake blinks as if he wasn't expecting me to agree so quickly. "Yeah?"

I poke him gently in the chest so he doesn't get any ideas. "But just for a day or so."

He chuckles softly, a small smile curling his lips as his fingers wrap around mine. "I wouldn't dare think otherwise."

My body tingles at the contact, my heart thumping faster against my rib cage.

I toy with my lip, my teeth grazing over the sensitive flesh. Blake's gaze lowers, zeroing in on my movement, and I can feel my mouth go dry under his watchful stare.

"Dad!" Levi's loud yell echoes in the house. "Where is my shirt? The one with the Spider-Man?"

"It's in the closet. The first drawer," Blake yells back, his eyes never leaving mine.

"I can't find it."

Blake groans, his fingers tightening around mine.

"You've been summoned," I chuckle softly, just as Levi calls him once again.

"Coming!"

I bite the inside of my cheek as he rubs at the back of my hand before reluctantly letting go.

My gaze lingers on his retreating back. Okay, and maybe it drops a bit lower. After all, I'm just a mere human, and that is one *fine* ass.

"He really likes you, you know?"

Shit.

She's been so quiet that I totally forgot that Mrs. Maxwell was still here, and now she caught me staring at her employer's ass.

Great. Just great.

"Oh, you have it wro—"

"Nonsense. I've been with these boys for years, all the way back when Daniel was in diapers." Mrs. Maxwell starts piling dishes into a stack. "I've seen Blake when he was happy, and I've been with him when everything fell apart. And things have been falling apart for him for a while."

She glances at me over the rim of her glasses. I press my lips together. I wanted to ask her what she meant, but at the same time, I didn't think it was my place to probe into Blake's private life. If he wanted to tell me about his ex, he could do it himself. Did I even want to know about the woman he spent the better part of his life with? A woman he had two children with? Just thinking about it made the bile rise up my throat.

"You're good for him." Mrs. Maxwell smiles softly. "For *them*."

"I don't know about that. All I've been doing is causing trouble for Blake with his kids."

"Do you mean Daniel?" She waves me off. "The issues Blake and Daniel have had started way before they moved here. Were you the catalyst? Sure. Your whole situation is quite unusual, and I can see how upsetting it might be for Daniel and Levi, but you aren't the root of the problem between the two of them. They go deeper than you can imagine." Mrs. Maxwell lets out a sigh and picks up the plates, continuing as she makes her way to the sink. "In his core, Daniel is a good kid. He's just been dealing with a lot in the last few years. However, that doesn't excuse what he said. I raised that boy better, and he'll get a piece of my mind later, but... Don't give up on him. Don't give up on *them*. I don't remember the last time I've seen Blake so happy. And Levi? That boy's been apprehensive about others ever since his mom walked away, but not with you. They need you, Savannah." She looks over her shoulder and gives me a pointed look. "And I think the feeling is mutual."

My throat bobs as I swallow, her words ringing in my head.

She was wrong though.

Wasn't she?

Nobody ever needed me, and I didn't think the Walker boys were any different.

Mrs. Maxwell's gaze shifts over my shoulder, and I can see a scowl appear on her face as she crosses her arms over her chest. "Look who finally decided to wake up."

I turn around and find no one other than Daniel standing behind me.

Shit. How much did he hear?

"Do you have to yell at me so early?" Daniel grumbles, glancing at me.

The bruises on his face were even more vibrant than yesterday, different shades of purples and blues coloring his skin and making his gray irises stand out even more.

"I should go." I turn toward Mrs. Maxwell. "Thank you so much for breakfast."

Before either of them can say anything, I get to my feet and slip past Daniel and toward the door.

Staying there was a bad idea.

Mrs. Maxwell didn't know what she was talking about because Daniel most certainly did *not* want me here.

I spot my bag on the little table by the door. I grab it quickly and get out, my hand diving inside as I try to find the key to my place.

"Miss Parker... Savannah, wait!"

I stop in my tracks at the sound of Daniel's voice behind me. Slowly, I turn around and find Blake's son standing in the doorway, his chest rising and falling like he was running after me.

"I'm sorry."

I blink, unsure if I heard him correctly. "Daniel, you don't have to..."

"No, I do." He shakes his head. "I really am sorry. I shouldn't have yelled at you, and I shouldn't have said those things. Maybe if I didn't..."

Daniel's throat bobs as he swallows, and although he's trying to keep a straight face, I can see the whole thing upset him. My fingers itch to touch him and give him some reassurance, but I don't think it's what he wants, so I keep them in place.

"Daniel, what happened wasn't your faul—"

"I looked it up," he interrupts before I can finish. "Last night. I have internet; I'm not dumb. It says stress can be the cause of all of this. I never wanted to hurt you, or the kid, I just..." His eyes meet mine. "I never wanted to hurt you."

"I know that. I never thought you wanted to hurt me either." The silence settles over us. My teeth sink into my lower lip as I contemplate my next words carefully. We couldn't go on like this. I knew it, and he knew it. But the least I could offer him was the truth. Because he was right. He wasn't Levi. Daniel was a teenager, almost an adult, really. Letting my lip pop, I move closer to him. "Can I be completely honest with you?"

Daniel shifts from one foot to the other, clearly uncomfortable. "I guess so?"

"I don't want to be your mother." Although the words are said gently, I can see that I have his attention. Good. I needed him to understand this. "I would never dream of taking her spot. The idea hasn't even crossed my mind. However, I will not push Levi away just because. Not only because I'm his teacher, and it's not in my nature to do so, but I genuinely like him. I think he's a great kid.

"More than that, this baby is coming. Both Blake and Levi want to be in his or her life, and honestly? I want it, too. I was prepared for it to be just Munchkin and me, but I'm glad my baby will have a real family. That's all I ever wanted."

It was like saying it out loud lifted some of the weight off my shoulders.

I wanted Blake and whatever this thing between us was.

I wanted to give it a shot.

"I don't know what will happen in the next few months, but I can promise you two things right now. First, I'll never get in the way of you and your dad," I say softly, observing his silent reaction. "And secondly, if you ever need me, no matter what or when my door will always be open to both of you. The only thing I ask of you in return is not to judge my baby on my actions. That's the only thing I need."

"That's all?" Those sharp gray eyes meet mine. "You want me to be... kind to the kid?"

"Yes, that's all." I extend my hand to him. "Do we have a deal?"

His gaze falls to my hand. A few heartbeats pass in silence

as he just stares at me, and I have a feeling that he'll push me away once again, but then his warm palm envelops mine.

"Yeah, we have a deal."

Chapter 23

BLAKE

> HILL:
> They want you in Austin tomorrow.

I snort out loud. This was typical of Andrew. No "hello," no "how ya doin'," just straight to the point.

> BLAKE:
> Can't.
>
> Savannah ended up in a hospital.

> HILL:
> Is everything okay?

> BLAKE:
> It is now, but she's still recovering so I don't want to leave her alone just yet.

> HILL:
> I'll see what I can do, but I'm not making any promises.

> BLAKE:
> If they want me, they can damn well wait.

Hitting the send button, I drop my phone on the floor next to me before grabbing the dumbbells and continuing with my reverse lunges.

Savannah's been quiet, and I've been trying to give her space, not that I liked it. No, I didn't like it one bit, so I did the only thing I knew—I exercised.

My legs are burning by the time I'm done with my work out for today when my phone buzzes again. I expect it's Andrew with some kind of an update, but it's not him.

> **BLONDIE:**
> There are packages on my front porch.

Grabbing a towel, I wipe the sweat off my face as a grin spreads over my mouth just as another message pops up.

> **BLONDIE:**
> Why are there a gazillion packages on my front porch?

> **BLAKE:**
> You went shopping?

> **BLONDIE:**
> You know damn well I didn't.

Yes, I knew she wouldn't. Hell, I was pretty sure that if somebody pointed a gun at Savannah's head and told her to spend my money, she wouldn't do it. That's why I decided to take things into my own hands.

> **BLONDIE:**
> Blake?

> **BLAKE:**
> Yes, Blondie?

BLONDIE:

> What the hell did you do?

I push to my feet and make my way out of the gym.

Some of the stuff that I ordered was heavy, and I didn't want Savannah to get any ideas in her head about carrying those on her own. Or, knowing her, she'll probably try to return them.

"Hey, I'll be—" I stop in my tracks when I come to the living room just in time to see a book fall on Daniel's face. "What the hell are you doing?"

He pulls the book back, his face coming into view. The bruises have started to heal, which means that instead of intense purples, his skin was colored in different shades of yellows, blues, and greens.

"Studying."

"Mm-hmm, I can see that."

He sits up, closing the book without a backward glance. So much for studying.

"Where are you going?"

"Over to Savannah's. She got some packages, so I'm going to carry them inside."

"I can help."

His words make me pause for a moment, surprised by his offer. "You want to help?"

"I mean, if you don't want me there..." Daniel shrugs, trying to play it cool, but I can see him already retreating into himself.

Shit.

"No." I shake my head immediately. "I could use your help. Some of the stuff is heavy, so it'll be easier if we carry it together."

"I can do that." Daniel nods, pushing to his feet, his gaze darting toward the window. "You sure she won't mind?"

And there it was again.

That uncertainty.

I hated to see it.

I hated that I didn't know what to do to mend the relationship with my son.

"She won't mind." Just then, my phone buzzes again. "I'm pretty sure she's pissed at me."

Daniel gives me a side glance. "What did you do?"

"She was looking at all that baby stuff the other day but barely got anything, so I ordered it for her."

"Oh..."

I watch him as he mulls over the information, an unreadable expression on his face. After everything that had happened, I wasn't sure how he was going to react to this news, but I didn't want to tiptoe around it. Whether he wanted it or not, this baby —his brother or sister—was coming. And Savannah? She deserved better than for me to keep her like a dirty little secret.

"You coming?" I ask gently.

This was his out if he wanted to take one. As much as I wanted him to get along with Savannah, I knew that pushing him too soon into something he wasn't ready for would result in a disaster.

Daniel bobs his head. "Yeah, sure."

Together we make our way toward the door, and sure enough, Savannah is standing on her front porch, her arms propped on her hips as she talks to the mailman about the packages.

Daniel whistles softly. "You weren't joking."

"No, I wasn't."

I hurry my pace to save the poor guy.

"I didn't order any of these." Savannah shakes her head. "You probably have the wrong address."

"This is the right address, ma'am. See?" He shows her his phone. "It says right here."

"Well, I didn't order any of these, so you can take them back be—"

"I'll take it from here," I say to the guy, who gives me a grateful smile.

Savannah, on the other hand? She looks like she's contemplating strangling me.

"Look who finally decided to show up." She crosses her arms over her chest and lifts her chin, determination shining on her face. "What the hell, Walker? Did you write the wrong address when you were ordering your stuff? I really hope that you're planning to take those because I don't want them sitting on my porch."

I take a step closer, my eyes scanning her face. All that blonde hair was piled in a messy knot on top of her head, and some of the color had finally returned to her face after taking it easy for a few days. Or maybe it was just because she was pissed at me. The jury was still out. Regardless, I liked seeing her like this. I could deal with her temper; I'd take it any day of the week over seeing her pale, lifeless body lying on the ground.

The corner of my mouth twitches upward. "You look cute all pissed off like that."

She disentangles her hands and jabs her finger into my chest. "Don't you try and change the subject. Are these your packages, and what are they doing at my house?"

"I ordered them for you."

"You..." Her lips part as she just stares at me for a long moment, some of the color draining from her face.

"Blondie..."

"No." She shakes her head. "No, I can't accept that. You have to take them back. I can't pay you back for all of this."

Pay me back? My brows pull together. "I don't expect you to pay me back, Savannah. It's for *our* baby."

"I know, but—" Her throat bobs as she swallows, her gaze darting to all the boxes. "I can't. It's too much, and I—"

I cup her cheeks and turn her attention back on me. "Blondie, what is this about?"

"I—" she sucks in a sharp breath. "I just can't."

Daniel clears his throat. "I'll give you guys a few."

Thankful for some privacy, I skim my fingers over Savannah's cheeks. "Come here."

Letting my hand fall, I grab her palm in mine and pull her toward the swing on the porch. Savannah wants to sit down, but I'm faster, pulling her into my lap. "What is going on, baby?"

She's biting her lower lip, her fingers clasping in her lap. I place my palm over hers but don't say anything. I wanted her to come to me in her own time. I wanted her to know that no matter what, I'd be there for her, ready to listen.

"You must think I'm crazy," she says after a while, letting her lip pop as she glances away. "Here you are trying to do something nice, and I—"

Gently, I slip my finger under her chin and turn her to face me. "You're not crazy, but I want to know why this is such a big deal. It's just a few things."

"A few things," she snorts. "Things have a price, Blake. And this is a lot of things."

"They do." I nod slowly in acknowledgment and assess her silently for a second. This went deeper than her simply not wanting to accept the gift; only I couldn't quite pinpoint why, so I changed the subject. "You wanna know why I got them?"

Savannah nods silently.

"Because I saw you liked them the other day. You had this little half-smile on your face when you spotted something you loved, so I made a note of it."

Her eyes widen in surprise, making me chuckle. "I see you, Savannah."

"Blake..." She shakes her head, one strand slipping from her bun.

"I *see* you," I repeat, needing her to know it. Maybe if I said it enough times, she would believe me. "And sue me for wanting to make you happy and see that smile on your face. Be the one who *puts* that smile on your face. Besides, spoiling people I care about makes me happy." I brush away the runaway lock gently, my fingers grazing the soft skin of her neck. "It was only my mom and me growing up, and she worked her ass off to make sure I had everything, but before I got a chance to give her back all she did for me, she died. So now that I can, I'm not waiting a moment to spoil the people I care about."

Her fingers tighten around mine. "I'm so sorry, Blakc."

"Me too." My gaze grows distant, the memories of the past coming back to the surface. It's been a while since I thought about my mom. "She was a good woman. I saw what it did to her when my dad left. She had to quit college and get a low-paying job to support us. I promised myself I'd never be like him."

Understanding flashes on Savannah's face, some of that tension leaving her body.

"I..." Her tongue darts out to slide over her lips. "My mom wasn't like that. She used her pregnancy to blackmail my father, but he didn't take the bait, and by then, it was too late for an abortion, and she never let me live it down. Everything that happened was somehow my fault, everything she did came with a price tag. So yeah, I'm not really the best when it comes to stuff like this."

What the actual fuck?

For a moment, I thought she was lying. She *had* to be lying because I couldn't believe anybody would act that way, but the empty, hopeless expression on her face told me otherwise.

Dammit.

"Savannah, baby, I'm so sorry."

She forces out a smile. "It's fine. It happened years ago."

"No, it's not fine."

Not in the slightest.

My jaw clenches as I try to hold back my anger toward a woman I've never even met.

However, it did explain a lot about the woman sitting in front of me. Her reservations when it came to our baby, her constant stubbornness, and the independence she was clinging to with both hands. For a good reason, since she had to learn from an early age how to take care of herself.

She lifts her hand, her fingers tracing over my scruff as her gaze meets mine. "We make quite a pair, don't we?"

My stomach tightens at her gentle touch. Those blue eyes turn dark, lips parting as she just stares at me. Pink spreads over her cheeks, and she sinks her teeth into her lower lip, drawing my gaze to that lush mouth that's been tempting me ever since I kissed her. Hell, ever since I first saw her.

"We sure do," I croak out, my voice coming out tight.

Savannah's nails graze over my jaw, sending a zap of electricity down my spine. A low groan comes from deep inside my chest, and it takes everything in me to hold back.

She was vulnerable right now. Hell, she was still recovering from her ER visit, and her blood sugar had been all over the place. She didn't need me groping her.

I let out a long breath and focus back on the topic at hand. "If you don't want the baby stuff, I understand. I'll tell Daniel, and we'll take—"

A finger presses against my lips.

"I..." Her tongue darts out, sliding over her lower lip. I can see her mind work, fighting with herself, with her demons. "I can keep it."

"Are you sure?"

Savannah nods. "You're right. Munchkin is our baby, and you bought these things for his room."

The corner of my mouth twitches in amusement, my brow rising. "His? Did Levi get to you?"

Savannah pokes me playfully. "You know what I me—"

Suddenly, she sucks in a breath, her brows furrowing.

"What's wrong?" My smile falls as I take her in, trying to figure out what just happened.

"Nothing," she says quickly, but I don't miss how she moved her palm to her side.

"Blondie," I growl in warning. "I'm calling bullshit on that one."

Something was definitely wrong.

"Blake, I'm fine. Really."

"Well, something isn't right," I insist, my scowl growing deeper. "I can see it on your face. Do we need to go to the ER—"

"No." She shakes her head quickly. "It's just a kick. We're fine."

A kick?

I blink, unsure if I heard her correctly.

"Munchkin is kicking," she whispers, almost like she's afraid she'll scare the baby. A smile slowly spreads over Savannah's face, her gaze meeting mine, wonder and love shining on her face.

Before I can say anything, she takes my hand and places it on her stomach.

I suck in a breath when my fingers press against her bump. I don't know what I expected, but it feels harder than it looks.

"I don't—"

The words die on my lips when I feel a strong jab against my palm. My head snaps up to find Savannah watching me, a big smile on her lips. "See?"

Dammit, she looks beautiful when she smiles.

"This is just..." I shake my head, still unable to wrap my mind around it. "Wow."

Our baby.

Kicking.

"It's amazing, right? I've been feeling Munchkin move for a while, but this one was really strong. At first, I didn't even know if it was a kick. I was talking to Becky, complaining about the flutters in my stomach, thinking it was indigestion or something, and she told me it was the baby. Wasn't it like that with the boys?"

My lips press in a tight line. "No."

"Oh."

Savannah's smile falls, some of that previous insecurity coming back, and I immediately feel like a jackass for snapping like that.

"I'm sorry, I..." I run the fingers of my free hand through my hair, trying to come up with the right words. "I never had this before. The doctor's appointments. The kicks. All the little moments? I've never had it."

Savannah's brows pull together in confusion. "But you have Daniel and Levi, how..."

"My ex didn't want me there," I admit, that old disappointment laced with a touch of resentment toward my ex-wife coming back to the surface.

But hell, we were already rehashing other parts of our past; I might as well tell her this too.

"At first, I thought that she was simply anxious about the whole thing. We were just two kids who got pregnant a few months into our relationship. God knows I was scared shitless. We talked about it, and we agreed to continue with the pregnancy, but after a while, I understood that it wasn't anxiety. She hated being pregnant. She hated all the changes she was going through. Hated her body. I tried my best to reassure that I loved her and found her attractive, but she slowly started to pull away until she didn't even let me touch her, and I could only respect her wishes. It actually surprised me when she was the one who suggested we try for a second baby when I knew how unhappy she was the first time around. I thought she changed her mind, but it was just more of the same. Looking back, I think it was her way of trying to save our marriage, the little good that did. So yeah, this is a first for me, too."

Silence settles over us, my words still ringing in the air. I feel raw after telling her all of that, sharing a part of my past I never admitted to out loud. Not to anybody. But I wanted Savannah to know. I wanted her to understand just how much this meant to me.

"Blake, I..."

"Don't look at me like that."

"Like what?"

"Like you feel sorry for me."

Savannah shakes her head. "I feel sorry for *her* because she'll never get this back." She takes my other hand, placing it on her stomach just in time to feel another, softer kick. Those blue-sky eyes full of wonder meet mine, a gentle smile on her mouth. "It's pretty amazing, right?"

"Sure is." I rub my thumb over the hard swell, waiting, hoping really, to feel our baby kick again. "Thank you for letting me experience this, Savannah."

"Anytime. I—" She sucks in a breath when another kick connects to her side. "This one was the strongest one yet. You think we have a football player on our hands?"

There it was again—we.

"You really do think it's a boy," I tease her.

"I do not!" She shoves me back. "Girls can play football, too."

The motion does nothing to push me, but it makes her rock against my lap. I bite back my groan. "They sure can."

Savannah's expression softens, and my gaze falls to her mouth once again. She was sitting so close that I would only need to lean forward to clear the distance between us and claim it.

Claim her.

Dammit, down, boy.

"How about we get those packages off your porch?" I ask, changing the subject before I did something I shouldn't.

Savannah blinks, her cheeks turning a deeper shade of pink. "Umm, yes, sure." She scoots off my lap, and I have to bite back another groan. "They should go upstairs to the nursery. Or I guess what's going to be a nursery since I have yet to touch it."

Savannah goes for one of the packages, but I jump to my feet and gently move her out of the way. "You're not carrying it."

"But—"

"No, Blondie," I give her a stern look that has her rolling her eyes.

"Fine, be my guest." She lifts her hands in resignation and goes toward the door.

"I will." Chuckling, I grab the boxes and follow after her, only to run into Daniel, who's sitting on the stairs. He lifts his gaze and looks between the two of us tentatively.

"Can you grab some of the boxes?"

Daniel shifts his attention between the two of us before getting up. "Sure thing."

We climb the steps, and Savannah opens one of the doors. "It's not much just yet, but this is where I'm planning to have the nursery for Munchkin. You know, once I throw all the furniture out and whatnot."

Placing the boxes by the wall, I straighten and take in the room. The old wallpaper was peeling at the corners, and dark, rusty furniture was taking up a lot of space. The furniture she shouldn't be trying to move even if she weren't pregnant.

"Where do I put this?" Daniel asks, a stack of boxes that's taller than him in his hands.

"By the door," I answer, my brain spinning. Daniel straightens and dusts his hands to find me watching him.

"What?"

I shift my gaze to Savannah. "We can help with that."

Chapter 24

SAVANNAH

"Savannah Jane Parker!"

I turn around to find my very pissed-off best friend marching across Main Street toward me, a car seat in her hand.

"Becky, wha—"

"A hospital? Really?"

I wince softly at her accusing tone. "It wasn't like that."

Becky raises her brow. "So, you didn't end up in a hospital?"

"No." I tuck a strand of hair behind my ear. "It was the ER."

"Oh, well, now that makes me feel so much better!" Becky bites out sarcastically. She lifts her free hand and lets it fall, only to wince at the loud slap. Her gaze falls to the car seat, and she lets out a long sigh when she finds Jackson is still firmly asleep. "I guess you only don't like sleeping at night, huh? You're lucky I love you so much."

Jackson purses his lips in sleep, and it's the cutest thing I've ever seen. "He's so big already."

"He's not shy when it comes to eating, that's for damn sure. He's his father's son, through and through." She turns her attention to me. "But don't you go changing the subject on me, missy. Why didn't you say something? I would have been there!"

So much for distracting her.

"I didn't say something because you have your hands full with Jackson; you don't need to worry about me. How did you find out anyway?"

"I ran into Mrs. Miller at the store this morning while I was buying a few things for my mom, and she asked me how you were doing. And when I looked at her blankly, she informed me of what happened." Becky gives me a knowing look. "Apparently, your neighbor saw Blake carrying you to his truck, so she got worried."

I snort. "So she went around and blabbed it to half the town?"

Seriously, sometimes I wished I just stayed in the city. Then I wouldn't need to deal with all the nosy neighbors and all the gossip.

"You know how people around here are." Becky waves it off, her face turning serious. "What happened? Are you okay? Like really okay?"

"I'm fine. I just fainted."

Becky's mouth falls open. "You fainted?!"

Sighing, I tell her everything that played out that day, the diagnosis I got from Dr. Gonzales in the ER, and my checkup appointment a few days later.

"So let me get this straight." Becky shakes her head once I'm done. "You had a fight with Daniel, and you fainted, so Blake took you to the ER, only to find out that you have gestational diabetes, but you're *fine*?"

There is no missing the skepticism in her tone.

"I'm doing better," I reassure her. "My sugar levels have been in the normal range for the last few days, and now I know what I'm dealing with and the reason I felt so shitty for a while now. So, while no, it's not ideal, I'll take it as a silver lining."

"I guess when you put it like that..." Becky sighs and looks around. "What were you up to anyway?"

I tilt my head toward the hardware store behind me. "I really need to start working on the nursery." The corner of my mouth lifts in a tentative smile. "Wanna help me pick out the colors?"

Becky rolls her eyes. "How is that even a question? What are we looking for?"

I pulled the door open for Becky and let her pass in front of me. The bell rings, and when I look up, I find Malcom Jamison glancing up from behind the counter, where he's serving the old Mr. Timms. His smile grows bigger when he sees us, "Becky, Savannah, how are you ladies doing?" His attention shifts to me, his smile falling as he takes me in. "I heard about the ER. Are you okay?"

Freaking small towns.

Becky coughs and gives me an I-told-you-so look, which I pointedly ignore.

"I'm doing better." I force out a smile. "I'm actually here to look at the paint colors you have."

"Oh, sure." He rubs the back of his neck. "They're on the back wall, so you can check it out, and I'll join you ladies in a bit."

"Perfect, thank you."

Shooting him a grateful smile, Becky and I make our way to the back of the shop, where the smell of the paint is the most intense.

"Do you know what you want? I'm guessing something neutral?"

I hum non-committedly as I take one of the sample sheets and flip through the colors. "I think so. I'm considering gray, maybe like this one?" I show her the color I have in mind. "Levi bought this adorable stuffed elephant for Munchkin, so now I'm kind of thinking of running with the theme since it's pretty gender-neutral."

"That's so cute. Levi will be an amazing big brother."

"I know, right?" A smile spreads over my lips. "He's so excited about the baby."

"Can't say I'm surprised. That boy is born to be a big brother. He's a caretaker just like his daddy."

The image of Blake's serious face inches away from mine as he held me in his arms while I had a panic attack the other day flashes in my mind. He was a caretaker, all right. He made me feel safe, unlike anybody else. He made me want to let go and lean on him, although I knew better than to rely on others because, like it or not, people left, and yet...

I bite the inside of my cheek. I could see him, clear as day, the determination written all over his face, but then his eyes turned that stormy gray color, and I could have sworn that he was going to kiss me. And I wanted it. I wanted it so badly.

"So... How are things going with your baby daddy?"

"Umm..." I blink, pushing the thoughts of kissing Blake out of my mind. "Fine."

"Just fine?" Becky arches her brow, her grin growing wider. "Because a moment ago, you had that look that would suggest something's going on."

Shit, I was so caught.

"You're imagining things." Color starts rising up my cheeks, so I turn my back to her and shift my focus on the samples once again. "We're just two friends trying to figure out how to navigate this mess we've created. What about this one? Maybe the first one was a bit too dark."

"Savannah..." Becky starts but is quickly interrupted by Malcom.

Thank God.

"Did you ladies find what you wanted?" he asks, glancing between the two of us.

"I think so." Becky's eyes narrow, letting me know this is far from done, but I'll take any reprieve I can get. "I'm debating between these two shades of gray. I worry the darker one could be a bit too dark for the nursery, then again, the furniture is white so..."

"Did you think about adding wallpaper, maybe?" Malcom waves us over. "We don't have many options for children's rooms, but I can show you what our supplier has available online, and we could order some for you."

We follow him to the front of the store. He turns his laptop and opens a browser, pulling up a page, so I move closer.

"They have some really amazing options," Malcom explains, his shoulder brushing against mine as he points at the screen. "Do you know what you want? They have stuff for both girls and boys so—"

I tuck a strand of hair behind my ear. "I actually don't know what I'm having."

Malcom glances at me, his brows raised. "Really?" He winces and shakes his head. "Sorry, I didn't mean to probe. My sister was pregnant a couple of years ago, and she had this big ass party to find out with all of our family. I didn't understand what all the fuss was about, but hey, she was happy so..."

"No fussing over here." I rest my hand on my bump. Munchkin was quiet, then again, this baby was a night owl. "I just want Munchkin to be healthy; that's the only thing that matters."

"Munchkin, huh?" He grins at me. "That's a cute nickname."

"Thanks." I glance at the laptop. "Do you think we can find something neutral? Maybe with elephants?"

Malcom blinks and quickly nods. "Elephants, sure, let's see... How about this?"

The bell rings as I lean down to look at the small details on the image. Elephants were scattered around in the sky in different poses, some were sleeping, others playing, and one even had a balloon tucked in its trunk.

"This one is adorable," Becky says, just when I feel a hand slip around my waist.

"What is?"

The familiar, deep voice has the hair at my nape prickling at attention.

"Blake!" I look over my shoulder, and my heart does a somersault when I find Blake's face only inches from mine. "Wh-what are you doing here?"

Blake's eyes take me in quietly, an unreadable expression on his face. His palm slides over my bump, and almost immediately, I can feel a soft kick. And I'm not the only one.

The corner of Blake's mouth tips up as he rubs his thumb over the spot, almost in a greeting. "I guess somebody missed me."

His excitement is palpable, and I can feel the warmth spread inside my chest. How could anybody take this away from him? I still couldn't wrap my mind around it.

"We went to get ice cream, but then—" Levi chimes in happily, but Blake interrupts him quickly. "Then I saw the store, and I figured I'd grab some sandpaper and check out what colors they have for that dresser you wanted repainted for the nursery."

My lips part in surprise. "Oh, that's..."

"No." Levi shakes his head before I can finish, drawing my attention. "We saw Sav through the window, and you—"

"Wanted to say hi," Blake finishes once again. "Which is good because look at this, she found elephant wallpaper."

Becky snorts loudly. My attention darts to her to find an amused expression on her face at Blake's clear attempt at distraction. But what did Levi have to say that Blake wanted to hide? It didn't make any sense.

"I wanna see!" Levi exclaims as he rushes for the counter.

Before I get a chance to move, Blake's hand around me tightens, my back plastering to his strong chest as he pulls me out of the way.

Just friends? Becky mouths, her smirk growing bigger.

I press my lips together, feeling the heat rise up my neck, but I don't say anything. What was there to say? We *were* friends. We certainly weren't a couple. It didn't matter that my body got all tingly at even the smallest of touches and that I dreamed of him kissing me again. It was these damn pregnancy hormones. That's all.

Besides, starting something more would only make this whole situation even more complicated, and we have enough complications as it is.

"They look like the one I got for Liam!" Levi's whole face lights up.

"Liam?" I repeat, my brows pulling together as I glance to Blake, who just shrugs, clearly as clueless as me.

"My baby brother, duh." Levi rolls his eyes exaggeratedly, making us all burst into laughter. Levi blinks. "What? You said I can pick up the name."

"You get to help pick *out* the name," Blake corrects.

Levi crosses his arms over his chest. "Liam is a nice name. Like Levi."

"Don't listen to them." Becky ruffles his hair. "Liam is a kickass name."

"You said ass, Aunt Becs!" Levi giggles.

Becky leans down and whispers conspiratorially. "Don't tell your dad."

Levi makes the motion of zipping his lips, still grinning as Becky lifts her hand for a high-five.

"Corrupting my kids," Blake huffs and shakes his head.

Becky rolls her eyes. "As if that's necessary when they were surrounded by football players."

"Do I need to put you two in time-out?" I raise my brow at the two of them. They were worse than a group of first graders.

Levi's eyes widen. "Uh-oh, you're in trouble."

The corner of my mouth twitches at his serious expression, but before I can say anything, a throat clears, reminding me that we're still in the store.

"You want me to order the wallpaper?" Malcom asks. "It might be a couple of weeks, though."

"Sorry, yes, that should be fine. And I'll get some of that gray paint we talked about."

"Sure, you want me to deliver it to your place?"

"We can grab that now," Blake interjects. "And I'll need some of that sandpaper, primer, and some paint for wood." He glances down at me. "Do you want to keep the original color?"

"Umm... Yes."

Blake nods. His hand lingers on my stomach for a second longer before he pulls it back. "I'll go and grab it. Where is the paint?"

Malcom takes Blake to the back of the store, Levi at their heels. Which leaves me alone with Becky, who's grinning knowingly.

I shoot her a warning glare. "Don't you start."

Becky's smile grows wider. "I didn't say anything."

I roll my eyes at her because we both know that's bullshit if I ever heard one. There was no stopping my friend when she set her mind on something.

"I've gotta go now. Miguel's in Austin, and I still have to stop to check in on Chase before this little one wakes up." She pulls me in for a hug. "Tell yourself what you want, but there is nothing *friendly* about the way that man holds you, Sav. And he sure as hell didn't come to pick out the colors. He came because he was jealous."

Of course she couldn't let it go.

I swallow hard as Becky pulls back and gives me one last knowing look before waving goodbye just as the footsteps come closer.

I turn around in time for Levi to come running back, his arms wrapping around my legs. "Daddy let me pick the color."

"Did he?" I ruffle his hair and look up just as Blake and Malcom come from behind the shelves.

Blake's eyes land on me, his brows pulling together. "No Becky?"

"She had to leave. Did you get everything?" I reach for my bag, but Blake's eyes narrow, a soft growl coming from deep in his lungs.

"Blondie, I think I'll need to put you in time-out."

I open my mouth to protest, but the look he shoots my way has me reconsidering. Sighing, I let my hands drop. "Okay, okay. I'm not even going to look at it."

Blake just stares at me for a moment longer as if he's waiting to fight me, but when he realizes I'm serious, he walks around me, his body brushing against mine as he leans down and whispers, "Good girl."

His husky voice has a shudder run down my spine.

If the man knows the effect he has on me, he doesn't show it. Instead, he walks to the counter, where Malcom runs our order.

"Where is your car?" Blake asks as we leave the store.

"I took a walk."

My doctor suggested that I should consider doing some light exercise since it helps with gestational diabetes, so I've been trying to go on a walk at least once a day.

Blake nods in understanding, his hand slipping to the small of my back. "Let's get you home?"

His warm palm burns through the layers of clothes separating us as he guides me across the street where he parked his truck. He drops the paint in the bed, and we huddle inside.

The drive back home passes quickly, Levi's cheerful chatter filling the space all the way back home.

"You go inside, and I'll be back in a few. I'm just gonna drop these off at Savannah's, okay, buddy?"

"But I wanna go with you," Levi pouts.

"Well, you need to go home and take a shower since tomorrow is a school day."

He huffs and stomps his foot. "I don't wanna go to school if Sav's not there. It's boring." Those innocent gray eyes turn toward me. "When are you coming back?"

"I'm actually returning tomorrow."

"For real?"

A smile spreads on my lips. "For real. So I'll see you then?"

"Yes!" Levi fist pumps excitedly. Before I get to react, his arms wrap around me in a quick hug, and he dashes into his house, yelling over his shoulder, "I'll see you tomorrow."

Blake shakes his head. "I swear that kid likes you more than he likes me."

"He does not," I protest as we go to my house. I pull out the keys and let him inside. "You can just drop them somewhere here. And once again, thank you so much for buying them."

"You don't have to keep thanking me, you know that?" Blake walks past me. "I'm doing it because it's for us. Munchkin is our baby. Besides, remodeling keeps me busy."

My gaze darts down his muscled back, watching the way his bicep flexes while he holds onto the can of paint—the way those gray sweatpants molded to his thighs and ass.

He shouldn't look that hot doing something so mundane, right?

"I actually wanted to talk to you about something."

Blake turns around to face me. My cheeks heat under his watchful gaze at being caught staring.

"Umm, y-yes. Sure." I tuck a strand of hair behind my ear. "What's up?"

Something about the way he was looking at me had the hair on my neck prickling at attention.

"I'm leaving—"

I blink, unsure if I heard him correctly.

He's leaving?

My pulse speeds up as I just stare at him, his mouth is moving, but I can't hear a word he says from the buzzing in my ears. There is only the loud echo of my frantic heartbeat in my eardrums.

Where?

Thump-thump-thump.

When?

Thump-thump-thump.

He couldn't be leaving.

Thump-thump-thump.

He said he'll be here for me and the baby.

He promised.

People lie.

"Blondie." Calloused palms cradle my face, snapping me out of my thoughts. Blake tilts my head back, his serious eyes fixing on mine. "What's going through that pretty head of yours?"

"Nothing." I look away, or at least I try to, but Blake's not budging. "It's fine. You can go. I was determined to do this on my own any—"

"On your own?" His brows pull together. "What are you talking about?"

What am I talking about?

"You leaving. It's fine." I nod decisively, pressing my lips together. I will *not* break. Not yet, anyway. So what if he was nice this whole time? Trying to convince me that we'd find a way to make this work, and I started to believe him. I shake my head. "I'll be fine. You can leave."

"I hope so, but if something happens, I want you to call me. I've been pushing this trip off, but they've been riding my ass trying to get me to come. I don't like the idea of leaving you after the hospital scare from last week, but it's just a couple of days, and I'll be barely two hours away, so if something is wrong, *call me*."

"Two hours—" I blink, my cheeks flaming hot in mortification as his words settle in. "*Oh.*"

He was leaving.

To Austin.

Because of work.

Can the earth open up just about now and swallow me whole?

"Blondie?" Blake's eyes narrow. "What did you think I was saying?"

"Nothing," I mutter, trying to pull back, but Blake's hold on me tightens.

I can see the realization slowly dawn on him. His lips press into a tight line, a muscle in his jaw ticking. He's clearly unhappy, and there is no escaping the twinge of guilt inside my stomach.

I was the one responsible for putting that expression on his face, and I didn't like it. The last few weeks he's been trying so hard to make this thing between us work, to help me overcome my fears, and reassure me he is here for me and our baby. And what did I do the first chance I got? Let my past take over and jump to the conclusion.

Tears burn my eyes, so I bite the corner of my mouth.

Blake's calloused fingertips slide over my cheek, snapping me out of my thoughts. His expression turns gentler. "I'm here for good, but I have to do this."

"Of course. You didn't have to push it back on my part. I'm fi—"

"Hell, yes, I did," Blake grits, some of that temper rising to the surface. "Dammit, Savannah. You're more important to me than work, don't you see that? I'm falling for you."

My heart skips a beat, my lips parting as his words echo in the quiet.

He didn't say what I think he just said...

But he did.

I could see it. It was written in the determined set of his brows and the taut line of his mouth. He meant every word.

"Blake, I..."

I'm falling for you.

"Fuck, I didn't want to say it like that." Sucking in a long breath, he shakes his head and leans down. For a second, I wonder if he'll kiss me, but he just presses his forehead against mine. "You don't have to say anything back. Just... Just listen, okay? I'm not going to leave you alone after you've been in a hospital. Not simply because you're the mother of my child but also because the thought of leaving you makes me physically ill. The idea that something could happen to you, and I'm not there... I get that you're afraid, and that people disappointed you in the past, and it's something that you won't get over so quickly, but I need you to give me the benefit of the doubt. Okay, baby?"

"I know."

Rationally, I knew it.

I believed him.

But my mind, my heart...

Maybe I've just been burned one too many times.

I'm falling for you.

Would he mean it if I couldn't get over this fear? Would he stay if I unintentionally pushed him back one too many times because I've been hurt by other people?

"I don't think you do." He pulls back, his lips brushing against my forehead. "But it's okay. I'll repeat it as many times as I need until you actually believe me. Better yet, I'm going to show it to you."

I swallow hard. "A couple of days?"

"Yeah. I have to do this commercial stuff and check in with my accountant and real estate agent. I'll probably stop by the facilities to see the team since it's been a while."

"What about the boys? Are they—"

"The boys are staying here. Mrs. Maxwell will be with them until I come back, which will be in no time."

No time, right. Because it's just a couple of days.

Two days.

And then he'll be back.

"Two days, Blondie."

"Two days."

Chapter 25

BLAKE

BLAKE:
Ready for your first day back?

BLONDIE:
I think so. I almost overslept because the baby kept me up all night.

Are you still here?

BLAKE:
No, I left early. I wanted to beat the traffic. I actually just got here, but have no desire to go in.

Why did I agree to this again?

BLONDIE:
You're asking me?

BLAKE:
Yes.

BLONDIE:
Time to put on your big girl panties, Walker.

BLAKE:
I'd rather take off yours.

NEED YOU TO CHOOSE ME

BLONDIE:
Thank you so much for the lunch box, you didn't have to do that.

BLAKE:
Texting during school hours? I didn't take you for a rulebreaker, Miss Parker.

And, I know I didn't have to, but I wanted to.

BLONDIE:
Well, thank you. I really appreciate it.

And it's my lunch break so I'm technically not breaking any rules, Mr. Walker.

BLAKE:
Were you a good girl in school too? Always in class on time? Following all the rules?

BLONDIE:
Yes.

BLAKE:
I figured.

BLONDIE:
And let me guess, you were the playboy jock who broke all the rules.

BLAKE:
Jock yes, playboy not really.

And I might have broken a rule here or there.

BLONDIE:
You can't tell me you didn't have girls falling at your feet.

BLAKE:

I didn't say that, but I never paid them too much attention, I was too focused on playing the game.

I bet I would have noticed you.

BLONDIE:

You wouldn't. Nobody ever noticed me.

BLAKE:

Idiots, all of them. But their loss is my gain.

So about our previous conversation...

Don't you go thinking I forgot about that, Miss Parker.

BLONDIE:

Look at that, the warning bell just went off...

BLAKE:

You're no fun, Miss Parker.

BLONDIE:

I'm lots of fun!

I didn't miss this at all.

Instead of being home with my kids or helping Savannah with the nursery, I was stuck in freaking traffic, trying to make my way to the Lonestars' facilities during rush hour.

The day had been dragging on between working on the commercial, doing a few photoshoots, and interviews; I was beat. The only reason why I pushed through had been because I was texting with Savannah during the day. I wasn't a big texter, but it was fun talking to her. *Flirting*. Getting to know her.

After everything that happened yesterday and the way she

reacted, I wondered if leaving was a good thing and if maybe I should postpone it. I fucking hated seeing her like that, so small and insecure. Granted, I could have probably phrased it better, which was my own freaking fault. She was hurt too many times, so it wasn't really surprising she was guarded now, always expecting people to leave.

Well, I wasn't going anywhere, and I was determined to show it to her no matter what.

Then there was the other little tidbit.

I'm falling for you.

I didn't plan on telling her that. Not just yet. She wasn't ready to hear those words, but now they were out, and there was no taking them back. Not that I wanted to take them back. I meant every single word I said. I was in love with Savannah. It was completely unexpected, but now that she was in our lives, I couldn't imagine it without her.

The music on the radio dies down when my phone connects with a call. I glance toward the screen, my brows pulling together when I see Mrs. Maxwell's name. Levi generally used her phone to call me, but not until later in the evening before going to bed, and they've barely finished with school.

I press the answer button. "Hey, Mrs. M., how are things going?"

"Hey, Blake, I'm so sorry to bother you."

Something about the tone of her voice has me sitting straighter in my seat. "It's no bother. Is everything okay? Are you all fine?"

"The boys are good," Mrs. Maxwell answers immediately, and some of the worry eases off my chest, but before I can say anything, she continues, "but there actually is a reason I'm calling. My daughter-in-law just went into labor. I know I was supposed to watch the boys until you got back…"

"You know I'm old enough to stay home alone, right?" Daniel yells from the background. "Tell her she can go, Dad."

Shit.

I run my hand over my face, glancing at the clock. If I left now, it'll probably take me double the time to get back since the traffic is still insane due to rush hour. And then there were the appointments I already had scheduled for tomorrow. I could probably do them over the phone, and if I go now, I could make it home by dinner. Possibly.

"I can stay. I shouldn't have—"

"No," I interrupt before she can finish. "You absolutely should *not* stay. You should be with your family in case they need you."

"But the boys—"

"—will be fine. Can you give me Daniel for a moment?"

"Thank you, Blake." Mrs. Maxwell swallows audibly before collecting herself. "Daniel, your dad wants to talk to you."

There is some rustling before Daniel picks up the phone. "You told her she can leave, right? I'm almost seventeen, Dad. I don't need a babysitter. No offense, Mrs. M."

"Well, your recent behavior would suggest otherwise, don't you think?"

Daniel grits his teeth. "The other guy started i—"

"I don't care who started it. You shouldn't be fighting with your classmates. How can I trust you that you can be left home alone and take care of yourself and your brother while I'm gone when you're acting this way?"

"We'll be fine. I can do this. It's just one night."

I press my lips together as I think over his suggestion, unsure of what to do. Daniel was sixteen. Hell, I was home alone and taking care of myself overnight when I was much younger than him. Then again, Daniel hasn't really been the best example of a responsible teenager.

Am I playing with fire here if I let them stay alone tonight? What if something happens to either of them? Miguel was in Austin this weekend, Aaron left for some cattle fair or something, and Becky had her hands full with her own baby. I couldn't ask her to look after my own kids.

And Savannah... Yeah, I wasn't going there, not after what just happened in the last few weeks.

I run my hand over my face.

"Everything will be fine," Daniel repeats. "I promise, Dad."

"Okay," I let out a long breath, praying I don't regret this. "But no going anywhere. You two stay at home. There is a number to the pizza place in the junk drawer, along with some cash. Order food when you boys are hungry. No parties or any other kinds of shenanigans. And be nice to your brother."

"Deal."

"I mean it, Daniel. I trust you can take care of yourself and your brother for one night. This is a trial run, understand?"

Daniel groans, "I know, Dad."

"Keep your phone close and call me if you boys need anything. I have my phone on me. If anything happens, I'll get in the car and come home."

"Okay, but nothing will happen."

I really hoped so.

"Can you put Mrs. Maxwell on the phone? And Daniel—"

"Call you, yeah, yeah, I know."

I pinch the bridge of my nose; this boy will be the death of me. "Don't get sassy with me. I mean it."

"I know you do. Here."

There is some ruffling as Daniel hands the phone to Mrs. Maxwell. "Are you coming home? You really shouldn't cancel your appo—"

"I'm not coming home. I'll stay as planned, and Daniel will be home with Levi."

"Oh." There is a beat of silence as Mrs. Maxwell processes the words. "Are you sure about that? I can stay—"

"Go, be with your family."

"You boys are also my family."

"We know. You're our family too, and we're so lucky to have you." I take a turn into the Lonestars' parking lot.

"You sure are. Okay, I'll let you go."

"Let me know how things turn out and if there is anything you need. And Mrs. Maxwell? Congratulations, Grandma."

We say our goodbyes just as I pull my truck into the parking lot and kill the engine. Running my fingers through my hair, I just stare at my phone, hoping I did the right thing.

BLONDIE:
Done with work?

The corner of my mouth lifts when I read Savannah's message.

BLAKE:
Worried about me, Blondie?

I slip out of the truck and go toward the door, my gaze glued to the phone. The little dots appear on the screen before they disappear once again. It happens a few more times as she writes, only to delete whatever she wants to say.

BLONDIE:
More for the people you had to work with.

You can have an attitude.

BLAKE:
Attitude?

I don't have an attitude.

BLONDIE:
Mm-hmm...

BLAKE:
I don't.

BLONDIE:
Keep telling yourself that, Walker.

"Yeah, right," I scoff. "I don't have an attitude."

"Mr. Walker?"

My head snaps up to find the security guards looking at me.

"Sorry." I shake my head and put away my phone. "How are you doing, Freddy? How's that granddaughter of yours?"

The guard smiles at me at the mention of his family. "Good. She grew so much in the last few months."

We chat a little bit more before he lets me through to the back. The practice must have just ended because the locker room is buzzing with activity. The players closest to the door notice me first.

"Look who remembered we existed," Joshua Mitchell, one of the running backs, jokes as we fist bump.

"What can I say, retirement keeps me busy."

Big J visibly shudders. "Don't say the r-word. It's bad luck. Besides, busy with what? Didn't you buy that house in a small town? I didn't take you for a rancher."

Miguel elbows him in the gut. "People have lives outside of football, asshole." Miguel tilts his head to the side. "Okay, *kind of*... Our boy here is coaching peewee football these days." He wiggles his brows. "Although I think it mostly has to do with the teacher, but..."

Surprise flashes on my ex-teammates' faces.

"Seriously?"

"Peewee football? Are you shitting me?"

"Forget about the football. I wanna know about the teacher. Is she hot?"

I glare at my best friend, soon to be my *ex*-best friend.

"Now I remember why I didn't come here sooner; you assholes are worse than a bunch of gossiping old ladies."

Miguel throws his arms around my shoulder. "And yet, you still love us."

"As much as I like a pest," I mutter dryly, shoving him away.

"Walker!" Coach's head pops into the locker room. "I thought I heard your voice."

"Hey, Coach." I extend my hand toward the older man, who squeezes my fingers tightly. "How are you doing?"

"Good." His bushy gray brows are pulled together, set in a permanent scowl. Considering he has to deal with a group of fifty grown-ass men who have a tendency to act like children, I can't really say I blame him. "Busy, trying to keep these boys in line," he grumbles, scanning over the players before his gaze lands on me. "You in town long?"

"Until tomorrow, gotta get home to my boys."

Coach nods. "How are they doing?"

"Good. The move has been... an adjustment."

"Understandable. You have a moment to stop by my office tomorrow before you leave? I want to talk to you about something, but I promised my wife I'd be home on time for once, so..."

My brows raise in surprise. "Umm, yeah, sure."

"I'll see you tomorrow then." He slaps me on the back before turning his attention to the rest of the locker room. "Don't go wild tonight because I'll kick your asses tomorrow at practice."

"Yes, Coach!" they say in unison, the words echoing in the locker room as the door closes behind the man.

I glance at Miguel. "You know what this is about?"

"No idea." He grabs his bag. "Wanna go grab dinner?"

Before I get a chance to answer, Big J wraps his arms around our shoulders, his duffel bag slamming into my bag, "Screw dinner. We're grabbing drinks, and Blakey here will tell us all about his hot teacher."

Chapter 26

SAVANNAH

Slipping my hoodie on, I run my fingers through my hair before descending the stairs. A hot bath has helped relax my tense muscles, but my feet were still killing me from standing all day long.

Some tea, a book, and my feet lifted on the coffee table, that's what I need.

After a quick stop in the kitchen, I go to the living room. Taking a long sip of tea, I place my mug on the coffee table before grabbing the book and sitting down. I let out a long sigh of relief as I curl and uncurl my toes, feeling the ache in the soles of my feet.

What I would give for a massage right about now.

The loud buzzing sound snaps me out of my thoughts. Letting the book drop in my lap, I lean forward and grab my phone.

BLAKE:
You still up?

BLONDIE:
Yeah, why?

BLAKE:
Just checking.

What are you doing?

BLONDIE:
I've been reading.

BLAKE:
Is it one of those smutty books of yours?

BLONDIE:
Blake...

BLAKE:
What?

You can pretend all you want, but I've seen what you're reading.

BLONDIE:
Romance novels. I'm reading romance novels.

And resting my feet. I think my ankles are starting to get swollen. At least I won't see how ugly they are because soon enough I won't be able to see my legs at all.

BLAKE:
Your feet aren't ugly.

And I can give you a massage when I get back.

I sink my teeth into my lower lip as the image of Blake's calloused fingers digging into my feet appears in my mind, which brings other things, other memories, to the forefront of my mind. Blake's hands on other parts of my body, roaming my skin, and making the goosebumps appear on my flesh.

BLAKE:
Are you the hot teacher?

What the—

I blink, staring at the message thinking I read it wrong, but nope.

> **BLAKE:**
> Our buddy's been awfully tight lipped about you, but he's been grinning like a fool while looking at the phone, so...

What the—

I start to type back, when another message pops on my screen.

> **BLAKE:**
> Sorry, the assholes stole my phone.

> **BLONDIE:**
> Assholes?

> **BLAKE:**
> My ex-teammates.
>
> They're annoying the crap out of me.

I bite the corner of my lip, fighting back a laugh as I try to imagine Blake fighting his former teammates for his phone.

Thump-thump-thump-thump.

The loud banging coming from the front of my house makes my head snap up. My smile falls, brows pulling together.

Who the hell is knocking on my door this late?

My gaze shifts to the time on my screen; it was almost ten in the evening. A new message from Blake appears, but before I get a chance to look at it, there is another, more frantic knock.

Putting the phone on the coffee table, I push to my feet, my back protesting the sudden change. I place my hand against my lower back as I make my way toward the door, just when there is another knock.

"I'm coming!" I yell, hurrying my pace. "Where is the fi—"

I pull open the door and come to a halt when I see Daniel standing on my front porch. Those eyes that are so much like his father's are wide, hair disheveled as if he ran his hand through it a dozen times. His breathing is ragged, his chest rising and falling rapidly as he tries to catch his breath.

"Daniel?" I glance over his shoulder to find the front door to his house left wide open. No trace of Levi or Mrs. Maxwell anywhere in sight. "What's wrong? Did something happen?"

"I messed up," he says, his voice laced with panic and guilt as he spills the words out in a blur. "I didn't mean to. I really, really didn't mean to. He was fine... He—"

He?

"Hey, hey, hey..." I place my hands over his shoulders and give him a little shake to get his attention. "Take a deep breath for me, okay?"

I watch as he sucks in a shaky gulp of air, his eyes filling with tears.

What the hell happened?

But I couldn't ask him that. Not while he was this upset.

"Now let it out slowly." I release a breath along with him. "Just like that. Again."

He does as asked, taking deep breaths until his breathing calms down a little.

"Can you tell me now what's going on?" I ask softly.

He nods, and his Adam's apple bobs as he swallows. "I messed up, and I don't know what to do. Levi... He's sick."

Sick? My fingers dig into his shoulders harder as my mind starts coming up with all the different scenarios. *What did he mean by sick? I saw Levi this morning in class, and he was fine.*

"Where is Mrs. Maxwell? Is she at the house with him?"

Daniel shakes his head. "She's not here. Her son called that his wife went into labor and asked her to come, so I said I'd take care of Levi. I assured Dad that I could do it. Levi started complaining shortly after Mrs. Maxwell left that he wasn't feeling well, but I thought he was faking it because a few guys stopped by, and we were playing video games and wouldn't let him join us." His cheeks turn red in embarrassment. "Only he wasn't lying. He has a fever, and he's throwing up, and I don't know what to do." He swallows hard, looking away. "Dad said to call him, but he's away, so it's not like he can do anything, and I didn't know who else to call. And you said..."

He didn't have to finish because I remembered the promise I made him not that long ago vividly.

If you ever need me, no matter what or when my door will always be open to both of you.

Daniel presses his lips together, his fists flexing and relaxing by his sides. I can see he's fighting with himself. He wanted to be brave and keep the promise he'd made to his father, but he was in over his head. This couldn't have been easy for him. To come here and ask me, of all people, for help. Yet he did it. Because he knew it was the right thing to do.

"You did well in coming here," I reassure him, loosening my grip on him and rubbing over his arms. "Where is Levi now?"

"Home."

"Okay." I nod, letting my hand drop. "C'mon, let's go check in on your brother."

The relief that flashes on his face is almost palpable. "You'll come?"

"Yeah." Closing the door behind me, I start toward the house across the street. "Does he have a fever? Or just throwing up? Maybe he ate something bad?"

"He was hot when I checked, and I didn't see him eat anything." We enter the house and slowly start climbing up the stairs. "He suddenly started to throw up. I tried to give him some Tylenol, but he couldn't keep it down."

Just then, as if he were waiting for us, a loud retching sound comes from one of the rooms.

"Shit!"

I don't bother reprimanding Daniel as I hurry my pace.

The first thing that hits me when I step into the bathroom is the smell of puke. My stomach rolls uncomfortably, and I have to bite the inside of my cheek to stop myself from gagging.

Levi's small body is lying on the floor, his back pressed against the edge of the bathtub. His clothes are rumpled, and there is a puke stain on his shirt, like he couldn't make it in time to the toilet.

Daniel is already sitting on the floor next to his brother, shaking his shoulders. "Levi? Wake up."

Levi murmurs something groggily, turning his head. His cheeks are bright red, lips slightly parted. Moving closer, I crouch down and press my hand against his forehead. *Shit*, he didn't just have a fever, he was burning up.

"Do you have a thermometer? I want to check his temp before we try to give him any medicine."

"Yeah, it should be here somewhere." Daniel looks at his brother for a moment longer before he finally gets up and disappears out of the room.

I gently brush Levi's hair out of his face. His locks are sweaty, curling at the ends. "You'll be okay," I whisper softly.

"S-Sav?" Levi blinks his eyes open. His gaze is blurry as he watches me, a frown appearing between his brows.

"Hey, buddy." I shoot him an encouraging smile. "I'm here. How are you feeling?"

Levi's tongue darts out, sliding over his chipped lips. "My t-tummy is hurting."

"I know, baby, but we'll have you feeling better in no time. You'll see."

"I w-want D-Daddy," he hiccups, his eyes filling with tears.

I wanted Blake here too. He'd know what to do. How to make his son feel better. But he wasn't here.

I slide my thumb over his cheek, brushing away the tears. "I know, but Daddy is away for work. I'll be here with you until he comes back. How does that sound?"

Before he can say anything, Daniel comes back into the bathroom. "I found it."

"Thank you." I take the thermometer from him and turn back to Levi. "Let's check that temp for a second, okay? And then we'll get you out of these dirty clothes and into some fresh PJs."

Levi nods weakly, and I slide the thermometer under his arm. His eyelids start to flutter close almost immediately, and I can see him fighting sleep. It doesn't take long before the thermometer starts to beep. I pull it out, checking the screen. 102.4°F.

"Okay, here is what we'll do..."

Daniel helps Levi onto his feet, and between the two of us, we manage to get him out of his dirty clothes and give him a lukewarm shower. The poor kid throws up two more times—some of it landing on my shirt.

"I'm s-sorry," Levi says immediately, his lip wobbling. "I didn't mean t-to."

"Hey, it's fine. It's just a shirt. Don't you worry about it. C'mon, time to get out."

I gently dry him with a towel, before we help him into a clean pair of PJs. "Let's put you to bed."

Levi wraps his arms around my legs and buries his head into my side. "When will Daddy be home?"

"Sometime tomorrow, I think." I wrap my arm around his shoulders, rubbing at his arm. "But in the meantime, we get to have a slumber party. How does that sound? I can read you a story or we can watch cartoons?"

Levi peeks up at me. "Can we go to Daddy's bed?"

"Umm..." Seriously? What was I supposed to do now? It didn't feel right going into Blake's room—his private space—especially since he wasn't here. Not that I wanted to be in his bed when he was here. Not at all.

Levi's lip wobbles slightly. "He lets me sleep in his bed when I'm sick."

"Go." Daniel tilts his head to the dirty bathroom and puke on the floor. "I'll clean this up."

Sighing, I tighten my hold on him. "Okay, then let's go to his bed. Can you walk?"

Levi nods silently, so I grab the syrup from the counter, and together we make our way to Blake's room. The last—and only, really—time I was in his room, I didn't get a chance to really look at the space.

I don't know what I was expecting to find, but the room is pretty neat. A big, king-size bed dominates the space. An emerald green blanket is covering the pristine white sheets. There is a shirt tossed at the bottom of the mattress, like Blake took it off in a hurry and couldn't bother throwing it into the laundry basket. A big TV is hanging on the wall across from the bed, with a chest of drawers underneath it and a few trinkets scattered on the surface.

Going to the bed, I pull the blanket back so Levi can slide inside before tucking him in.

"Do you want me to put on some cartoons?" I turn around to look for the remote, but he grabs my hand. For a kid who spent the afternoon throwing up, he sure had some strength left in him. "Don't leave me."

9 years old

"Where did Mom go?" I whisper, my fingers gripping the edge of the comforter.

Grams brushes my hair back, a distant expression on her face.

It wasn't the first time I'd seen that look on her face. It was always there when she was talking to Mom.

She shakes her head slightly. "I don't know, bug."

My throat becomes tight at her words.

Mom said she'd be back, but it's been over a week now. It's the longest she's been away.

She left.

For good this time.

I could see it on her face the day she left—she wasn't coming back.

"Try to get some rest now, okay?"

The loud creaking of the bed echoes in the room as she pushes to her feet. I extend my hand, my sweaty fingers wrapping around Grams' wrist. My ears are buzzing, my heart beating wildly against my rib cage as I tighten my hold on her, those crystal blue eyes crinkled at the corners shifting to me.

"Don't leave me."

Although his words are barely a whisper, there is no missing the fear and desperation in his voice. I know all too well how it feels to be left behind and cling to every last bit of the familiarity, and a little bit of my heart breaks for the boy in front of me.

Pushing the memory back, I gently brush his hair out of his face. "I'm here. I'm not going anywhere."

Levi's forehead still feels warm, but not as much as it was when I just got here. Maybe he did manage to get down some of the medicine after all.

"Promise?"

"I promise. I'm not going anywhere." I sit on the bed, and he slides closer to me almost instantly. "Can you try to drink a little bit more of that medicine for me?" Levi nods, so I grab the syrup and pour it for him. "Sleep."

Levi nuzzles his face into my side. He looks so young when he sleeps, so vulnerable, that it breaks my heart.

So much has happened in his short life, so many changes, it's not even strange he's so scared of being left alone.

"I wish you were my mom."

I suck in a sharp breath, stunned by his words.

They're said so softly that, at first, I think I've imagined them. I knew Levi liked me. He was an affectionate kid who wasn't afraid to show his emotions, but this? I didn't know what to do with this. How to feel about it.

"He fell asleep?"

I jump a little bit in surprise at the sound of Daniel's voice. Looking up, I find him standing in the doorway.

Did he hear what Levi said?

I watch him carefully but can't find an answer on his face.

You're not our mother!

Daniel's words were still echoing in my head, even now. I didn't blame him for saying it. Not one bit. He was right. I wasn't their mother. I would never be their mother. I didn't want that. But was it so wrong of me to want them in Munchkin's life? For wanting my baby to have a family, siblings, I so desperately wanted but never had?

"Yeah, I think he's wiped out." My gaze falls to the little boy sleeping soundly in bed, still holding onto me. I brush one curl out of his face. "Let's just hope he keeps down the medicine and doesn't throw up again."

Daniel moves closer, his attention on his brother. "Dad's going to kill me."

There is no fear on his face anymore, just resignation. And tiredness.

"He's not going to kill you."

"I promised him that I would take care of Levi. He's been gone for less than twenty-four hours, and Levi is sick. I messed it all up."

"You didn't mess it all up, Daniel." He looks at me, biting at his lip. "Things don't always go how we expect or plan them. What matters is what you do with that. You saw you were over your head, and you came to ask for help. Levi is clean, he had his medicine and is resting. You did everything you were supposed to."

"But if I watched over him like I said I would..."

I shake my head. "He would still have gotten sick. There was no avoiding that."

Munchkin's foot connects with my ribs, kicking the air out of my lungs. I press my hand against the spot, rubbing at it.

Daniel notices it too, his eyes narrowing. "Are you okay?"

"Fine. Baby is kicking. I think I have a future football player on my hands." The corner of my mouth lifts up, but Daniel stays silent, his attention still on my stomach. I wonder what's going through his head, but I fear that if I ask, this temporary truce might be over, and I don't want to risk it.

"You should go and get some rest. I'll stay here with him."

Daniel shakes his head. "No, it's... I want to stay here. Do you mind if I turn on the TV?"

I look down at sleeping Levi. He's out, and I don't think he'll be waking up anytime soon. "It's fine."

Daniel grabs the remote and turns on the TV, lowering the volume. "You watching Criminal Minds?"

"You know it?" Daniel asks as he sits down on the other side of the bed, propping the pillow against the headboard.

"Know it?" I scoff. Curling my hand under the pillow, I turn my attention to the screen. "I grew up watching it."

From the corner of my eye, I can see Daniel roll his eyes. "You know you're not that much older than me, right?"

"Yeah, yeah. I'm still older."

A companionable silence settles over us as we watch the show. One episode turns into two, and before long, sleep claims me too.

Chapter 27

BLAKE

Killing the engine, I pick up my phone to check for any messages, although I knew there weren't any. After Savannah hadn't responded to my texts last night, I tried calling her, but she hadn't picked up her phone. And neither did Daniel. The latter didn't surprise me, although I did specifically tell him to keep his phone on him at all times.

How was it that teenagers spend all their time glued to their phones, but that *one* time you call them because you need them, they don't pick up, I'll never understand.

I glance toward Savannah's house but don't see any movement there.

The need to go over and see her is almost overwhelming, but I have to check in on my kids first.

At least the house is standing, so I guess there is that.

Eerie silence greets me as I step inside. I close the door behind me and listen intently, but nothing.

"Daniel?" I look down the hallway. "Levi?"

They didn't go out, did they?

I walk toward the back of the house, checking the rooms, but the whole first floor is empty, just like the backyard. An uneasy feeling rises inside of me, but I push it back as I turn around and climb the stairs, taking two steps at a time.

I start to open Daniel's door when I see that the door to my bedroom is cracked open.

The door I know I left shut.

Weird.

With one final look at Daniel's bedroom, I go toward the end of the hallway. Even before I push open the door, I can see the bedsheets on the floor in the corner of the room.

What the—

I enter the room and stop in my tracks at the scene in front of me. My heart does a little flip inside my chest at the sight of Savannah sleeping in my bed next to my sons.

Levi is curled against her, his fingers gripping Savannah's as if, even in his sleep, he's afraid that she'll leave him if he doesn't hold onto her. His lips are slightly parted as he breathes soundly. Daniel, on the other hand, is on the other side of the bed, sleeping in an upright position against the headboard, his head is tilted to the side, and my own neck prickles in solidarity with his at the pain he'll be in once he wakes up.

What the hell happened here?

I move closer, other little details catching my attention—the thermometer sitting on my nightstand next to the bottle of kid's Tylenol—the new bedsheets. An almost stale smell fills the room—and things finally start to make sense.

Levi must have gotten sick. That's why she was here taking care of my boys.

Something I should have been doing, but once again, I was away when they needed me.

That familiar guilt spreads through my stomach, making the bile burn my throat.

My jaw clenches, but before I get a chance to go down the road of self-loathing, Savannah groans softly, the covers rustling as she shifts in bed. Those crystal blue eyes open, blurry with sleep, cheeks flushed.

Fuck, she looks gorgeous, all sleepy and ruffled like that. Her hair is sprawled over my pillow, a large shirt swallowing her whole.

My shirt.

Mine.

Savannah might not be ready to admit it just yet, but she was mine.

Ours.

This here, it just further proved it.

A sudden surge of possessiveness slams into me, leaving me breathless in its intensity.

Her eyes fix on me, and she blinks a few times. I can see the exact moment it finally hits her. Her eyes widen, lips parting slightly. "You're home." Her voice is groggy, a lock of honey hair falling in her face.

Home.

There it is again.

I suck in a breath, my lungs feeling tight as I just stare at her. "I'm home."

Not this house or even this town, but her.

She was my home.

Savannah, my two boys, and our unborn baby.

Unable to resist it, I reach forward and brush it away, my fingers skimming over her soft skin. I trace the underside of her mouth. "I'll always come back home to you."

My palm slips to her nape, fingers tangling between those unbound strands.

Savannah sucks in a shaky breath. "Blake, I—"

"Sav?"

My body goes still, and Savannah's eyes widen at the sound of Levi's voice.

Reluctantly, I pull back and shift my attention to my son, who's rubbing at his eyes.

"Hey, buddy. How are you doing?"

Levi's hand drops, his mouth falling open when he sees me. "Dad!" He sits upright, and in his haste, he kicks Daniel, who jolts from sleep. "What— Dad?"

"You're back!" Levi yells, and before I get a chance to react, he jumps out of bed and toward me. I manage to wrap my arms around him at the very last second.

"Somebody's happy to see me," I chuckle softly, rubbing at his back.

He squeezes me tightly for a moment before pulling back. His face was still a bit pale, and there were bags under his eyes, but for the most part, he seemed like his usual self. "When did you get home?"

"Just now, and imagine my surprise when I find you all in bed at noon!"

"It's noon already?" Savannah asks, pushing upright.

Levi looks over his shoulder, a smile lighting up his whole face. "Sav, you're still here!"

The genuine surprise on Levi's face makes my throat go tight.

Levi doesn't notice it because he squirms out of my hold and goes to Savannah, wrapping his arms around her middle. Instead of protesting or being annoyed by him, Savannah smiles at my boy, her hand resting on his back. "I promised I'd be here until your dad came, didn't I?"

"You did, but I didn't think you'd stay."

Savannah's lips part in surprise at Levi's words, at the nonchalance with which he said them.

He, too, was used to people leaving. His mother sure didn't think twice before packing her shit and fleeing without a backward glance.

Just like Savannah's.

Daniel shifts, drawing my attention. He's quietly observing the duo, an unreadable expression on his face.

"I'd never do that."

No, she wouldn't. Because she knew exactly what it felt like to be left behind.

Savannah leans down, her lips pressing against Levi's forehead. The gesture is instinctual and maternal, and Levi is drinking in every second of her attention. "No fever." She ruffles his hair. "How is your tummy?"

Levi tilts his head, "Better, I think."

Just at that moment, Levi's stomach growls loudly, and he giggles.

The corner of my mouth tips upward. "Hungry?"

He lets go of Savannah and turns to me. "I'm starving!"

"How about I go and make us that soup you like?"

"Can we have pancakes?"

This kid. I shake my head. "How about soup first, and then we'll see how you feel?"

"Fine, I guess. Can we at least watch movies?"

"Sure, we can watch movies."

Savannah slides from the bed, and I slowly take her in. The bright red toes, her long creamy legs, my shirt falling to mid-thigh and hiding her bump, her teeth nibbling at her lower lip, the flushed cheeks...

"Umm..." She shifts slightly. "Can I just use your bathroom, and I'll leave you guys to it?"

She wants to leave?

Before I get to say anything, Levi's already at her side, his fingers wrapped around her wrists, shaking his head. "You can't leave." He glances at me, a determined expression on his face. "Sav can stay with us and watch a movie, right, Dad?"

"Of course, she can stay if she wants to," I say slowly,

weighing my words. Did I want her to stay? Hell, yes. But on the other hand, she has her own life, and she just spent the night taking care of my kids; it wouldn't be fair to ask her for more. "Maybe she's busy, buddy."

Levi presses his lips together, not one to take no easily. "Are you busy?"

Savannah looks between us and tucks a strand of hair behind her ear. "Well, no."

"Stay." Levi purses his lips. "Pretty please? I don't want you to leave."

"Might as well give up now," Daniel says. "He'll become more annoying than ever if you don't agree."

Those crystal blue eyes glance from one person to the other until they finally land on me. I want to be a good guy and tell her she can go, and we'll be fine, but I don't want to be a good guy. Not when it comes to her.

"What do you say, Blondie? Wanna hang out with us?"

She grazes her teeth over her lower lip, letting it pop. "Okay," she whispers, her words barely audible. "I'll stay."

"Yes!" Levi throws himself at her, making her sway on her feet. "We'll have so much fun. I'll pick out the movie, and—"

"Why don't you go and do that?" I let my hands land on Levi's shoulders. "Savannah will come down in a little bit."

Savannah shoots me a grateful smile, and I push Levi toward the door, Daniel at our heels.

We descend the stairs, and Levi goes to the living room. He grabs the remote and jumps on the couch, coughing slightly.

"Are you sure you're okay?" I press my palm against his forehead, but no fever, just like Savannah said. "Want me to get you some tea?"

He shakes his head, his attention on the TV. "I'm good."

"Okay, then. I'll go and heat that soup up."

Slipping into the kitchen, I pull open the fridge and grab the pot with some soup Mrs. M. made for the boys before she left. When I close the fridge, I find Daniel standing in the doorway.

"Did you want something different to eat?" I ask as I turn on the stove.

"No, this is fine." From the corner of my eyes, I can see him shift his weight from one foot to the other. "You won't ask me what happened? Why didn't I call?"

My brows quirked up as I lean against the counter. "Do you want to tell me?"

Daniel's throat bobs as he swallows. "Levi told me he didn't feel good a little after Mrs. M. left, but I didn't believe him." His head drops down, and he rubs at the back of his neck. "Some guys from school came by. We were playing video games, and I thought he was making things up, so I told him to go and play. He did, and I forgot about it until I went to grab a drink and heard him vomiting. I tried to give him some medicine, but he kept throwing up. I was thinking of calling you, but you were in Austin, and he wasn't feeling well, so I went to Savannah's."

Pushing from the counter, I cross the distance between us and place my palms on his shoulders. "You did good. I wouldn't be able to get here in time anyway, so you did what you had to in order to help your brother."

Daniel nods slowly. "She came. She didn't even blink when I asked her, she just... came."

I wasn't surprised. Not in the slightest. That was the kind of woman she was. I didn't know what I did to deserve her in my life, but I was one lucky bastard to have her.

"She's a good woman."

I glance up when I see a flash of blonde on the staircase, my lungs suddenly feeling tight.

Savannah.

Lifting my hand, I rub at my chest as I watch her go to the living room and smile at Levi as she sits next to him, letting him scoot into her side. That pressure grows sharper, more intense, leaving me breathless as the realization sets in.

I might have lied to her after all.

I wasn't *falling* for her.

No, it was too late for that.

I was *in love* with her.

Now, I just had to convince her to give me a chance.

Chapter 28

SAVANNAH

This was a bad idea.

　I wasn't thinking.

　Not when all three of the Walker boys were looking at me with those big gray eyes full of hope that tugged at my chest. There was no way I could say no to them.

　But now I was paying the price.

　Blake's fingers run up and down my arm absentmindedly, making goosebumps appear on my flesh.

　I peek at him, but his gaze is fixed on the screen, the light and shadow playing on the strong lines of his face and accentuating the dark stubble covering his strong jawline.

　I could still feel the sharp bristles under my fingertips.

　It reminded me of *that* night.

　The way his lips skimmed over my skin raising the prickles in their wake as he made me feel more alive than any man before him.

　I bite the inside of my cheek, my thighs pressing together.

　I was grateful for the darkness because I was pretty sure my face was beet red.

　Here we were, having a movie night with his kids, no less,

and I was thinking about sex with Blake? What the hell was wrong with me?

I shift in my seat, trying to alleviate the ache between my thighs, only to bump into a hard body behind me.

Shit.

"Sorr—" I start to pull back, but Blake's faster. His free arm sneaks around my middle, and he pulls me flush against him. "Better."

How was this better?

My heart skips a beat as my gaze darts to the kids, expecting some kind of reaction, but their attention is on the movie playing on TV, the loud sound muffling their voices.

"I don't think I thanked you."

Blake's quiet words have me pulling my brows together. "Thanked me for what?"

"For jumping in yesterday. Daniel told me what happened. Thank you for being there for them."

"You don't have to thank me. It wasn't a problem. I'm just glad Levi's feeling better."

The little guy managed to finish his soup, but in the end, he decided not to have pancakes. And there were no new trips to the bathroom, so I hoped that the worst was behind him, and he'd be back to his normal self in another day or so.

"Me too."

Blake's large fingers rest on my side. My shirt skims up, and his thumb slides over my naked ribs, and of course, Munchkin chooses this exact moment to kick against his palm.

"I swear that baby knows when you're near."

Blake hums happily, his palm sprawling over my bump. "You think?"

Another kick.

"Yup."

"I like that." He skims his thumb over my stomach. "Don't worry, baby; Daddy's here."

The softly spoken words make my chest ache. There was so much love and affection in them.

For a while, they continue playing the game. Munchkin would kick, and Blake would rub the spot, leaving goosebumps on my skin. He seemed oblivious to the effect he had on me, and here I was, completely wired up at the slightest of touches.

Up and down, down and up.

Over and over and over again.

Then Blake kisses my neck.

My eyes fall shut, my mouth going dry.

He's taunting me.

He must be.

There is no other explanation.

Didn't he see the effect he was having on me? That every time he touched me, my body would come alive under his attention?

"Levi's asleep," Blake whispers, breaking me out of my thoughts.

I glance toward the other side of the couch, and sure enough, Levi's head was on the armrest, eyes closed, lips parted. The little dude was completely out of it as the closing credits started to roll, making me realize I didn't see much of the movie.

"I think he's still recovering from last night. We were up half the night because he was throwing up."

"Probably." Blake gets up, and my body misses his nearness almost immediately.

Pushing back the feeling, I follow suit, my gaze falling on the sleeping boy. A lock of hair is in his face. Instinctively, I extend my hand and brush it away, my heart swelling when he leans into my touch.

"Daniel's also out."

Pulling my hand back, I look toward the bean bag. Daniel's eyes are closed; his body is relaxed now that his father is home. He looked so much younger when he was asleep. He was still just a boy, really. A boy who's had his world turned upside down one too many times in the short sixteen years he's been here.

"I should get going. It's late, and you need to put them to bed."

Blake's hand slides to the small of my back, sending shivers running down my spine. "Let me walk you out."

I shake my head, taking a step back. I needed to get out of here before I did something stupid. Like kiss him. Or tell him to ask me to stay. "Go and take care of your family, Blake."

His lips pressed into a tight line are the last thing I see before I turn my back and walk out of Blake's house and to my own.

My heart is thumping hard against my rib cage as I close the door behind me and run my palm over my face. My skin was burning, the ghost of Blake's touch still lingering on my flesh.

Pushing from the door, I tug my shirt off as I make my way to the bathroom. I needed a shower. A cold one.

But even the cool water couldn't erase Blake's touch, and I felt equally frustrated and tense when I got out. Rubbing at my skin, my gaze falls to the discarded shirt.

Blake's shirt.

After Levi threw up for the second time sometime in the middle of the night, there was no saving my PJs, and since I didn't want to leave them alone, I decided to just take one of Blake's while mine was washing. Something I completely forgot about when Blake came back home.

My fingers wrap around the soft material, and I bring it to

my face. Blake's masculine scent still lingers on the fabric, and I can't help but inhale it in. Sandalwood, pine, and ginger fill my lungs, and for a moment, it's like he's sitting behind me, his arms wrapped around me, those calloused fingers tracing my skin...

I should toss it into the laundry so I can wash it and return it, but do I do that?

No, I slip it on, letting the soft cotton brush against my skin.

Knowing there is no way I'll fall asleep keyed up like this, I pad into the kitchen barefoot and put on the kettle for tea before settling in the living room and grabbing my book.

I start reading, but the images of Blake keep popping into my mind. The look on his face when I woke up. The way those gray eyes zeroed in on my mouth. The feel of his hard chest behind me, his hand slipping around my waist.

Shaking my head, I look at the page, but when I don't know where I left off, I start from the beginning, only to realize the main characters are about to get it on, which doesn't help at all.

I shift in my seat, trying to find a comfortable position, but the only thing it does is make my tee rub against my hard nipples. I press my thighs together, feeling this need simmering inside me, ready to burst at any minute.

Groaning, I close the book and put it next to me.

I needed a release.

And there was only one thing that would help with that.

Biting the inside of my cheek, I let my hand slide down my body. My skin tingles at the smallest of touches. My breasts feel heavy, my nipples are rock-hard, and my panties are so damp it's embarrassing.

I was hot for my baby daddy, and he didn't even notice the effect he had on me.

I play with the hem of my shirt, my fingers brushing the place Blake had touched only moments ago. The way those rough fingertips played over my skin was engraved into my memory.

I slide my hand over my stomach, my fingers squeezing my aching breast. My breath hitches as I tweak my hard nipple, the sensation going straight to my core and making my pussy clench.

In my mind, it was Blake's hands on my body, not mine. Those rough fingertips skimming my sides, cupping my breasts. Those long, talented fingers tweaking my nipples.

My eyes fall shut, a moan ripping from my lungs.

I shouldn't be doing this, but there was no way I'd be able to fall asleep if I didn't get some kind of release, even if it was by my own hands.

I uncurl my fingers and let my hand move lower, over the swell of my stomach and between my thighs. The first brush of my fingers over my clit makes my whole-body quake.

Bracing my feet against the coffee table for better leverage, I move my hand lower. The slickness between my thighs makes it easy for my finger to slip inside my pussy.

"*Fuck.*"

My legs fall open wider as I pull my hand back, and this time, I slide two fingers inside. There is a soft ache as my fingers fill me, stretching me.

Damn, I missed this.

This feeling of fullness and ecstasy.

I continue thrusting them deeper, the heel of my palm rubbing against my clit, and making my toes curl.

I was close.

So damn close.

"Blake..."

"*Holy fuck, Blondie.*"

I bite the inside of my cheek as I find my G-spot. I swear I could hear him like he was here in the ro—

My eyes shoot open, and there he is.

My whole body freezes as I try to process what's happening.

Blake.

Standing in my freaking living room.

His hands are pressed against the doorway as if he's holding himself back, those gray eyes the color of the stormy sky fixed on me as I suck in a sharp breath.

"Wha—"

I start to pull my hand back, my cheeks red.

Holy hell, Blake was actually he—

"Don't."

My fingers freeze just at my entrance. Blake's tongue darts out, sliding over his lower lip, his fingers clenching around the doorway as he growls softly, "Don't you dare stop now."

"You can't be serious."

"Oh, I'm serious. If you're going to use me to get off, I want to watch. Show me. Show me how you make yourself come."

I should probably feel embarrassed, but I couldn't. Not when I was this close to the edge. Not when Blake was watching me like that. He made me feel like the most beautiful woman on the planet.

I lift my chin a notch because two could play this game. "I wouldn't need to make myself come if you did it yourself, you know."

"You..." Surprise flashes on his face for a split second as he processes my words, but then he runs his hand over his jaw, and there is only hot, burning desire left. "My mistake. One that won't happen again. I can't have my girl unsatisfied, now, can I?" The muscle in his jaw ticks, and I can feel my heart start racing faster. "Did you do it often?"

"Blake..."

"Did you?" he repeats, and there is no mistaking the commanding tone of his voice.

I shake my head no.

"I thought so. C'mon, Blondie, show me how you do it. I can see how much you need it. Even from here, I can see you're dripping for me. Rub that tight pussy and show me how you make yourself come."

He's right.

I need it.

Desperately so.

I pull my fingers out and slide them back inside, my gaze locked on his as he watches my every move, approval shining on his face.

"Good girl." His voice is a low rasp that has goosebumps prickling my skin. I quicken my pace, each time my fingers slip deeper until I finally hit the right spot, and my mouth falls open. My toes press into the table as I arch my back, needing more.

So close.

I was so damn close.

"Look at you. So fucking beautiful. So fucking sweet. I swear I can still taste you on my tongue. That's the image I get off on late at night when I can't sleep. I wrap my hand around my cock and make myself come thinking of how perfect you were that night, like a fucking goddess. I think about that tight pussy and how much I want to feel it wrapped—"

"Blake, *fuck.*"

My legs squeeze my hand tightly as wave after wave of pleasure courses through me, my whole body shaking with the intensity of my orgasm.

My breathing is ragged as I collapse against the couch, trying to regain some sense of composure.

"Fuck, you're stunning."

I blink my eyes open, just in time to see Blake push from the doorway. His long steps eat the distance between us, and before I know it, he's shoving the coffee table away, and he's in front of me. His large hands cup my face as his mouth crashes against mine.

Finally.

I rake my fingers over his back and grab the hem of his shirt, tugging it upward. Breaking the kiss, Blake takes off his shirt and tosses it to the side before doing the same to mine. He finds my nipple and sucks it into his mouth. My back arches, fingers digging into his hair as I pull him closer. Too soon he lets go, and grabs my hand into his, his lips wrapping around my fingers.

A low groan comes from deep in his lungs as he licks my fingers clean before letting them go with a pop.

"You taste so fucking good. Even better than I remember."

His eyes hold me hostage as his fingers tug my panties down, and he grabs my ankles.

"Blake, wha—"

I don't get to finish before he slides my legs over his shoulders and settles between my spread thighs, his tongue dipping into my soaked pussy.

"Holy gods."

Blake murmurs something unintelligible as he licks me from bottom to top. His stubble scratches me in the most delicious way as his tongue sinks into me. He's like a starved man, and I'm his dinner.

He flicks his tongue over my clit, the friction sending a jolt of electricity straight to my core.

"Blake," I all but plead softly with him.

My hips arc upward.

I needed more.

Not just that, I needed him inside me.

"Not before you come on my tongue, baby."

I shake my head and let out a groan in protest that soon turns into a loud moan when his lips wrap around my clit and pull it into his mouth, and his fingers sink inside of me.

The second orgasm catches me completely off guard.

Blake continues fucking me with his finger, his tongue swirling over my nub of nerves as my whole body quivers.

His teeth scrape gently over my clit, sending a shudder through me as he pulls back, licking his lips.

I take in his body. The way that powerful, tattooed chest rises and falls with each quick intake of breath. The large bulge that his shorts can barely contain. He leans down, his mouth brushing against mine, letting me taste myself on his tongue. One of his brows raises in question. "Good?"

His chest brushes against my hard nipples, and I can feel my belly tighten.

I should be spent by now, but after these past few weeks of him teasing me with his kisses and touches, I didn't think anything would satisfy me.

"More." I curl my leg around his waist, pulling him to me. "I need more."

Blake doesn't need to be told twice as he pushes his pants down, his hard cock springing free. My thighs clench around him at the sight of him.

"I'm clean," he murmurs as he wraps his hand around his length. "There hasn't been anybody since you."

I don't know why, but that revelation lifts the weight I didn't even realize I've been carrying this whole time.

"Me neither."

His eyes darken as he moves closer.

"Good."

Blake slides his cock through my wet folds before he sinks into me in one long thrust.

"Holy..."

His mouth captures mine, swallowing my moan as he kisses me.

It was stupid. I was only lying to myself when I thought

taking the edge off with my fingers would be enough. Nothing will ever feel as good as Blake. His dick is stretching me in the best way possible as he braces his hands next to me so as not to squish me, our bodies brushing together.

"Blondie," he growls, breaking the kiss. "Look at me."

I blink my eyes open, his face coming into view—every hard line, every prickle of hair, and age mark. He's beautiful. And he's mine.

"You're mine, you get that? No more playing around. No more bullshit. Mine." His fingers grab my chin, forcing my lips apart as his mouth hovers over mine. "Say it, Savannah. Say who you belong to."

My pussy clenches around him. *Fuck, I was so close. So freaking close.* "Blake..."

"Say it." He pulls back, his tip teasing my entrance, taunting me. And he knows it. "This gorgeous body." He slides that calloused hand over my side. "This tight pussy. This ass. This stubborn mouth. Who does it belong to?"

"You," I breathe. My nails dig into his back as he shoves into me in one long thrust, kickstarting my orgasm.

"Damn right it does," he grits as his thrusts become stronger, harder, more erratic until his whole body goes rigid in my arms, and he comes inside me with a low growl.

He rolls to his back, pulling me with him, and we just lie like that, both of us catching our breaths. I lean against his chest, listening to the hard beat of his heart, for once completely spent as his fingers run up and down my back.

I'm not sure how long we stay like that, but I must have dozed off because the next thing I know, I'm in Blake's arms.

"What—"

"I had to go and turn off the stove. I've gotcha now."

Shit, I was so tired I completely forgot about the tea, not that I needed it.

Blake's arms tighten around me as he carries me up the stairs and into my room where he puts me to bed. I expect him to leave, but he lays next to me, brushing my hair back.

"Blake?"

"Hmm?"

"I'm not complaining, but... What are you doing here?"

Those silvery eyes meet mine, his expression turning serious. "I didn't like how you left." He shakes his head and corrects, "I didn't like that you left, period. Tonight showed me just how good it could be." His fingers interlock with mine, giving them a squeeze. "How good *we* could be."

"Blake..."

He presses his finger against my lips. "No, let me finish. What I said earlier. It wasn't just empty words said in the moment. I meant every single thing. You're mine, Savannah. I don't want to play any more games or hide around. I want us to be together. I choose you, but I need you to choose me back."

My heart does a little flip inside my chest, his words ringing in my head.

I need you to choose me.

Wasn't that what I said just weeks ago? That I wouldn't settle for less than somebody who's going to choose me for me? And now here he was, asking me that exact thing.

I swallow the knot in my throat, my words coming out raspy, "I'm scared."

"That makes two of us. Because I'm scared shitless, Savannah. You. This baby. The boys. I don't want to mess it up."

"You won't. If somebody will mess it up, it's me." I lift my hand, tracing his jaw, and admit softly, "But I want to try. I want to try so badly. You make me feel, Blake. You make me wish for things I have no right wishing."

"Good." Leaning down, he presses his mouth against mine. I

moan softly, my hand going to the back of his neck and deepening the kiss. Blake's palms cradle my cheeks. Breaking the kiss, he presses his forehead against mine. "Because I plan to make every single wish come true."

Chapter 29

SAVANNAH

"No, I'm telling you. That man was only an asshat on the outside, but it's clear as day that he had a soft spot for her since the very beginning." Mrs. Santiago gives a decisive nod.

Jessica rolls her eyes. "He was a grouch of epic proportions, you mean."

"He wasn't a grouch," Mrs. Santiago protests, just as Becky refills her glass with wine. "Thanks, honey." She offers her a smile before continuing, "He's just dealing with a lot. They both are, really. And he was so sweet to her. Like when her car broke down, and he fixed it for her? It was such a swoony moment."

"Not before grumbling about her driving a piece of shit car and how unsafe it was."

"That's true."

My phone buzzes, drawing my attention away from the discussion at hand. I pull it out, the corner of my mouth lifting when I see the name on the screen.

BLAKE:
Done with the smut club?

BLONDIE:
In a little bit.

> **BLAKE:**
> And it's not a smut club. It's a book club.

BLAKE:

> Blondie, I've seen the books you've been reading.

> And they would suggest otherwise.

"I don't see what's the problem." Mrs. Tyson points her bony finger at Jessica. "I'll let you know, young lady, the quiet, grouchy men are the best in the sack."

Jessica's mouth falls open, her cheeks turning pink, and I struggle to swallow back the snort at her words. Because what were the odds, really?

"Mrs. Tyson!"

The older woman harrumphs. "What? No need to act all demure now. We've all had sex around here."

"Only in my dreams," Becky mutters as she sits next to me, making the whole group chuckle, just as another message pops on my screen, and I can feel the heat rise up my neck.

BLAKE:

> Not that I'm complaining.

> As a matter of fact, I wouldn't mind recreating a few of those scenes. Just saying. You know in case you wanna see how accurate they are and all that.

> **BLONDIE:**
> I'm sure that'll be such a hardship for you.

BLAKE:

> What can I say? It's a sacrifice I'm willing to make for the greater good.

> I can't have you going around all needy after all.

> BLONDIE:
> Does that mean you'll come over tonight?

I worry at my lip as I wait for his response.

I knew it was selfish of me to ask that of him because what if one of the boys woke up in the middle of the night and went to him, but he wasn't there? And yet, the words were out before I could think them through. I couldn't help myself. I liked spending time with Blake. And it wasn't just the sex either. I liked the feel of his arms around my body. I liked to just talk to him as we cuddled on the couch. I liked him, plain and simple. And it scared me shitless.

"What are you reading?" Becky nudges me playfully. "It has to be good if you're all flushed like—" I lock my phone and lift my gaze, but based on her smug smile, she's already read my messages. *"Oh my God, finally!"*

Shit.

I shoot her a pleading look, but it's already too late.

"What finally?" Mrs. Tyson interjects, the discussion forgotten, and now all the attention is on me.

"Umm..." I squirm in my seat, my ears buzzing as I try to come up with some answer.

"We were just talking about something," Becky offers.

"Are you talking about the fact that the new Coach is sneaking out of Savannah's house in the middle of the night these days?" Mrs. Miller raises her thin brows as she grabs her wine glass and nonchalantly takes a sip. "As if that's something new."

What the— My mouth falls open, making the older woman snort.

"What? We all knew it was just a matter of time before you two got together." Mrs. Miller waves her hand dismissively. "The man's had a thing for you since the first time he stepped into this town, and who could blame him? So when Charlotte told me she saw him sneaking out the other day, I can't say I was surprised."

"You and *Coach*?" Jessica points her finger at me accusingly as she glares at me. "I knew something was going on between you two during the town fair!"

"Town fair?" Mrs. Tyson snorts. "Try football practice. I've never seen a man run faster in my life when that kid threw a ball and almost hit Savannah. It was quite epic, if I might say so myself."

My ears are buzzing as they continue fighting over who was the one who figured out first there was something going on between Blake and me. My mouth feels dry, making it hard to swallow.

I hated this. I've been the center of gossip so many times growing up. When I was five, my teacher was giving me a pitying look when I was the last one at school because my mom couldn't find the time to come and pick me up. Or when I was six and some of my classmates were laughing at me because I came to school in dirty clothes. At eight, when we finally moved to Bluebonnet, everywhere I went, I could hear soft whispers about that Parker girl causing trouble. And, finally, at nine, once my mom was gone, and everybody talked about how she left me behind and wondered if she would ever come back.

But Blake wasn't my mother.

You're mine, Savannah. I don't want to play any more games or hide around. I want us to be together. I choose you, but I need you to choose me back.

No, Blake most definitely wasn't my mother.

It wasn't fair for me to expect him to put everything on the line if I wasn't determined to do the same for him. He deserved better, and so did I.

We deserved better.

"They're like the freaking FBI," Becky mutters next to me.

There was no "like" about it. The two of them would give the FBI a run for their money.

"It's true."

The group stops their discussion, and once again, I'm the center of attention, their curious glances making my stomach roil.

You can do this, Sav. It's not like they don't know it. At least part of it. Might as well get it all out.

"Blake and I, we're together. I know it's not really professional since I'm his son's teacher and all, but we met before..." I curl my fingers, my nails digging into my skin as I tilt my chin up, bracing myself for whatever's coming next. "I know you all thought that my ex is my baby's father, but that's not true. It's Blake. He's the father."

I hold my breath, my shoulders tense as I wait for their reaction for what feels like forever, and for once, they actually seem surprised.

"You've gotta be shitting me!" Jessica's mouth falls open, her eyes wide.

"Oh, thank God!" Mrs. Miller raises her glass. "I was worried you'd be connected to that tool for the rest of your life. I guess that explains a lot of things."

"That's good, honey." Mrs. Tyson nods and pats me on the leg. "Blake's so good for you. I don't think I've seen you smiling so much before he came here."

"Didn't I tell you something's going on between them?" Mrs. Miller smirks. "I have a nose for those things. Charlotte will be so jealous when I tell her I was right. That woman has them right under her nose but is too blind to see anything."

I blink as they shift their conversation while my heart still thunders in my chest.

Just like that, my secrets were out, and now they were

already discussing Charlotte, and their upcoming town meeting and the bake sale.

"They didn't say anything," I whisper softly, still not quite able to wrap my mind around it.

"What would they say?" Becky shrugs and gives me a pointed look. "They already knew about your little rendezvous. But why am I only finding out about it just now? You and Blake finally get together, and you've been quiet this whole time? I swear these days, I'm the last one who finds out what's going on in my own town. If Miguel weren't home today, I'd make you go out for drinks so you can tell me everything."

"Miguel is home? And you're here?"

A smile spreads over my friend's face. "He insisted he'd be with Jackson so I could go to the book club, but he's leaving early in the morning because they're flying out for a game, so you can bet I'll use every second we have left since he won't be back until Thanksgiving."

The mention of the upcoming holiday makes my smile fall. Last year, I spent Thanksgiving with Grams, but this year it'll be just me all alone in that house. A strong kick against my ribs makes me suck in a breath.

Okay, maybe not *completely* alone.

"You should come." I look up to find Becky watching me. "The Fernandezes host the Thanksgiving party at their place. It's family and friends. You should come." Becky winks at me. "Bring your baby daddy with you. If you guys aren't planning to celebrate alone?"

Alone? As in Blake, the boys, and me all together?

"No." I shake my head. "We didn't discuss it."

"Think about it."

Wasn't it too early for something like that? Celebrating a holiday seemed so... big. That's what families did. But we weren't one. Not really. Right?

The image of the boys and Blake from the other day pops into my mind. All of us in PJs, cuddled in the living room, watching movies. It felt homey. It felt *real*.

Could this really be our life, or was I just fooling myself?

"What are we reading next?" Mrs. Miller asks suddenly, snapping me out of my thoughts. "I hope this one has more spice in it. Some of us appreciate creativity."

Becky and I exchanged a look, and I'm not sure if we were more amused or disturbed by her comment.

After deciding on our next read, a steamy billionaire romance this time around, people start to gather their things and leave. I stay with Becky to help her clean up before closing the café.

"Do you need a ride home?" Becky asks as she locks the door.

"No, I'll just wal—"

The words die on my lips as I look up and see the tall figure leaning against the black truck on the other side of the street.

"Blake." My heart is hammering against my rib cage, the loud echo dulling the noises around me.

He looks up, a big smile spreading over his face when he spots me. "Blondie."

Fine lines crinkle around those intense gray eyes as they take me in from head to toe, making my skin burn.

"I guess not," Becky chuckles. "I'll talk to you later."

Blake pushes from the truck and walks toward me, his gaze locked on mine.

"What are you doing here? Is everything okay? Are the boys—"

Blake's hands cup my cheeks, and his mouth lands on mine before I can finish. My fingers wrap around his wrists as his mouth sweeps over mine in gentle, teasing strokes before he breaks the kiss. I let out a soft moan in protest, not ready to let go, that has him chuckling.

"Hi."

"Hey."

"The boys are fine." He skims his thumb over my lower lip, sending a shudder down my spine. "Mrs. Maxwell is with them. I saw your car in the driveway, and I didn't want you to walk back home when it was dark. Did you have fun?"

"I—" I let out a shaky breath. "Yeah."

"Good. Ready to leave?"

I nod silently, my tongue sliding over my lower lip. Blake lets his hand fall, those long fingers intertwining with mine as he leads me to his truck. He holds the door open for me and helps me inside before walking around and sliding into the driver's seat.

"Tired?" Blake asks as he pulls the truck onto the road, the soft country music playing on the radio.

"A little bit."

He glances toward me, excitement shining on his face as the corner of his mouth tips upward. "Too tired to spend some time together?"

I eye him carefully, unsure of where he's going with this. "Not that tired."

What was he up to?

If possible, his smile grows even bigger. "Good."

Blake returns his attention to the road as he turns his blinker on and changes direction.

The direction that's most definitely *not* going toward our neighborhood.

I expect him to elaborate, but he stays silent as he navigates the dark streets of our little town.

I turn my attention to him. "Care to share where we're going?"

Amusement dances in his irises. "You'll see soon enough."

I open my mouth to protest, but his hand falls on my leg, giving me a soft squeeze. I press my thighs together, the desire pooling in my belly.

"Needy much?" Blake teases, his thumb moving in gentle strokes just above my knee.

It was strange how well he knew me. It's like he had a radar or something that told him just what I needed. And one thing about Blake: he didn't shy away from giving me what I wanted. No, quite the contrary, he made it his mission to do so.

"You're not playing fair."

"I never said I'd play fair, Blondie." That smirk only grows bigger. "We're here."

Killing the engine, he opens the door. I look around, my brows pull together as I stare at the darkness.

A parking lot.

And not just any parking lot.

Blake opens my door and helps me out. "You brought me to school?"

"Yeah, I figured we could have a date."

My brows pull together in confusion. "A date?"

At school?

My skepticism must be obvious because Blake explains, "At first, I thought we could go to dinner, but I know you don't like to eat late because of your blood sugar, and I know you've been struggling with that."

I open my mouth to protest, but he just gives me a pointed look. "That little frown appears between your brows every time you see somebody eat something you like but know you can't have because it'll be bad for you and our baby. And I'm not putting you through that."

"How—" I just stare at him, dumbstruck. I didn't realize anybody noticed. It sucked royally because I'd see something or smell something or just get a craving, but I always had to weigh my options, and more often than not, the answer was no.

The corner of Blake's mouth lifts upward, as he moves closer. His palms gently cup my cheeks and tilt my head back. "When will you realize it? I see you, Blondie."

His words make the warmth spread through my belly, and my heart does that little flip inside my chest.

"I see you, baby," Blake repeats, skimming his thumb over my jaw before he lets his hand drop.

He slides his arm around my waist, his palm settling on the small of my back as he leads me toward the field.

The space is quiet, the smell of grass and the faint scent of smoke filling the air.

"This is my favorite time to be on the field."

Surprised, I tilt my head to look at him, but his attention is fixed on the fifty-yard line. "Really? Not game day?"

"Game days are crazy, but there is something about the calm that settles over the field once the game is done, and you can drink everything in."

I guess I could see it. There was peacefulness in the quiet like this.

"Is that why you brought me here?"

"Kind of." Coming to a stop, Blake lets go of my hand, opens a blanket over the grass, and kneels down, extending his hand toward me. "Come 'ere."

I bite the inside of my cheek and look around. "Should we even be here? What if somebody—"

"Damn, woman." Before I can finish, Blake's hand snakes around my waist, and he tugs me to him. I let out a loud yelp in surprise as I'm pulled to the blanket, Blake's body hovering over mine. "Blake! What are you doing?"

"Nobody will come." He brushes my hair away and smirks.

"We're in a small town, Texas, where all the respectable people are already home and in bed."

"I'm respectable," I counter, jabbing my finger into his chest playfully. Blake's fingers wrap around my wrist, and he presses them against his chest.

"Oh, I know that," he whispers, his warm breath tickling my skin. Blake leans down; his nose traces the column of my neck. "My good girl."

I suck in a breath, my fingers fisting his shirt. The warmth of his body seeps into my skin. His heartbeat thunders against my palm, strong and steady, just like him. "But I like getting you down and dirty."

"That's so cheesy."

"I'll give you cheesy."

A soft chuckle turns into a moan when Blake nips at my neck playfully before kissing the sensitive skin. I slide my hand over his pecs and to the back of his neck. My fingers sink between his silky strands, and I pull him to me, those stormy eyes the last thing I see before my mouth presses against his—once, twice, three times—before my tongue slides past his lips and into his mouth. His velvet tongue tangles with mine in a sensual dance.

Blake rolls to his back, pulling me with him. My shirt skims up, the cool night air teasing my skin, a complete contrast to Blake's burning touch.

A shudder runs through my body, making goosebumps appear on my skin.

"You're cold," Blake whispers, breaking the kiss.

"It's fi—"

Before I get to finish, Blake's already pulling back and sliding his jacket off.

"Arms."

I don't protest as he helps me put the jacket on, pulling it tightly around me. The material falls over my shoulders, Blake's spicy scent wrapping me into a cocoon of warmth. Even with my bump, the jacket swallows me whole. It almost feels as good as being wrapped in Blake's arms. *Almost.*

Once he's done, Blake lets his hands fall to my waist, resting them on my bump as he takes me in. There is undeniable heat burning in his eyes as he looks at me. Desire unlike anything I've experienced except with him.

"I like this."

"What? This jacket?" I glance down, noticing the team colors. It was his coach's jacket. "I always wondered why I never got one since I'm still part of the team, even though you stole my position."

Blake smirks. "There was a reason for that."

"Oh, yeah?" I quirk my brow at him. "And what's that reason, Coach?"

"So once you're cold, I get to give you mine. See my name on your back. Let everybody know who you belong with."

This time when a shiver runs down my spine, it has nothing to do with the cold and everything with the possessiveness in his tone.

"That's so high school."

"Maybe," he whispers, his nose tracing the column of my neck before he places a kiss to the hollow of my shoulder. "But you like it."

Yes, I did.

I liked it a lot.

Chapter 30

BLAKE

> **BLONDIE:**
> Do you have a ladder?

I blink a few times as I reread the message, but the damn thing doesn't change.

A ladder? Why would she—

My gaze drops to the timestamp.

Cursing loudly, I slip my phone into my pocket and go to the kitchen, where I can hear the radio softly playing as Mrs. Maxwell works.

"Hey, Mrs. M., I'm going over to Savannah's. She messaged me something about a ladder." The image of Savannah trying to balance her weight on a ladder sends a chill through my bones. Her bump has really grown in the last few weeks, and she shouldn't be climbing anywhere. It has a "bad idea" written all over it. I shake my head, pushing those thoughts back. "Can you keep an eye on the kids?"

Mrs. Maxwell snorts. "What kind of question is that? Off with you." She grabs a towel to dry her hands. "I'll go check in with the boys and see if they want to go to the movies this afternoon. Levi's been talking about it for days."

I open my mouth to protest, that familiar pang of guilt eating at me. Levi heard in school that they were premiering the new Spider-Man movie in the small Bluebonnet theater, and he's been talking on and on about how he wanted to go. I was planning to take him, but with all the other stuff, it just didn't come up.

"Hey," Mrs. Maxwell places her hand on my shoulder. "You both need to learn how to let people help you."

I guess she had me there. I was constantly telling Savannah that she doesn't have to do everything on her own, and yet, here I was trying to do just the same.

"I have the kids; you go and help your girl." The corner of her mouth curls up. "You and Savannah deserve some alone time too."

I run my fingers through my hair, not bothering to tell her we've been sneaking our alone time in the middle of the night for weeks now. "Okay, but if you need anything, just call. And you still have your card—"

She rolls her eyes and pushes me toward the door. "I've been doing this for years, mister. I think I can manage. I'd tell you to be careful, but she's already pregnant so..." She winks at me. "Have fun."

Before I can say anything, she closes the door in my face, and I can hear her calling Levi and Daniel from the other side of the door.

Shaking my head, I make my way across the street, scanning the space for any sign of Savannah, but there is none.

What is she doing?

Knocking on the door, I wait for a moment, but when there is no answer, I press the door handle.

"Seriously, this woman—"

Yes, this was a small town, but she should take her safety more seriously.

"Blondie?" I call out, looking down the hallway, but there is no answer.

I peek into the living room, hoping to find her curled on the couch reading one of those smutty books, but once again, it's empty. Turning on my heels, I glance at the kitchen before making my way up the stairs. "Sav? You in here?"

Did something happen? She didn't fall, did she?

My hand grips the railing harder as my heart kicks up a notch, dread spreading through me as my mind starts playing different scenarios in my mind, each one worse than the other. My palms turn sweaty as I take two steps at a time, my voice more frantic.

"Savannah?"

The door to her bedroom is open, but there is nobody inside.

Where the hell is she?

I move down the hallway.

"Savannah, where the hell—"

I stop in my tracks when I reach the doorway of the nursery.

"Blondie." Her name comes out shaky as I grip the doorway.

Savannah's back is turned to me, and headphones are covering her ears. The music is so loud, I can hear it all the way here.

Taylor Swift.

She was listening to music; that's why she hadn't heard me.

But she's fine.

Nothing happened to her.

I close my eyes for a moment and suck in a long breath.

She's fine.

I lean against the doorway, my body sagging in relief as I just watch her. Savannah's singing along to the music softly, her body moving to the beat as she *shakes it off*, making her ponytail sway. She's dressed in overalls that have the tiniest pair of shorts I've ever seen, along with a gray sports bra underneath it.

Fuck, she's stunning.

My mouth goes dry, muscles taut with the need to go to her, pull her to me, and claim her in the most basic way possible.

Just then, she turns around, holding the paintbrush as a microphone. Her eyes widen, her mouth falling open as she lets out a surprised yelp.

"Blake! You scared the crap out of me," she mutters as she lowers her headphones. "What are you doing here?"

"I got your message, so I came to check in on you. And it's a good thing I did." I tilt my head toward the chair that's standing on the side. "You weren't climbing on that thing, were you?"

"Nope," she answers quickly.

Too quickly.

My eyes narrow at her. "Blondie."

Her cheeks heat, and she ducks her head, a strand of her hair falling out of her ponytail.

I push from the door and cross the room, my finger slipping under her chin and tilting her head back. My thumb skims over her lower lip, and she lets out a soft breath, lips parting.

"What?" She shrugs and mutters softly, "The chair is pretty sturdy."

This woman.

"I'll give you sturdy. Why are you even painting? The fumes can't be good for you or the baby."

"I got the wallpaper and decided to put it up, hence, asking for the ladder, but you didn't answer, so I just figured I'd do it myself." She shrugs nonchalantly. "Besides, the window is open."

This stubborn, stubborn woman.

"Twenty minutes. I didn't get back to you for twenty minutes."

She points at the wall. "And see how much I got done already?"

I shake my head; there was no winning with her. "You're driving me crazy, you know that?"

She pokes her tongue at me. "The feeling is mutual."

The corner of her mouth tilts upward, and I can't help but lean down and press my mouth against hers in a hard kiss. "I'm going to grab the ladder and a paint roller." I swipe my thumb over her lower lip and take a step back, giving her a warning look. "Stay. Put."

"Yessir!"

My cock twitches at her words, my mind coming up with all the other scenarios in which I want her so agreeable. She notices it too because her teeth sink into her lower lip, cheeks turning pink.

Focus on the job.

Shaking my head, I hurry back to my house. It doesn't take me long to find everything I need in my garage and make my way back to find Savannah still in the nursery, humming softly as she works.

She glances over her shoulder at me. "The boys are back home?"

I shake my head as I place the ladder by the wall and get to work. I dip my roller into the bucket with paint, squeezing the excess out. "No. Mrs. Maxwell offered to take the boys out to the movies. Which means I'm all yours."

We chat about our day as I paint the room. The space isn't that big, so it doesn't take us long to put on the first coat of color. While I focus on the big surfaces, Savannah puts on the fine touches around the door and windows.

Running the back of my hand over my forehead to wipe off the sweat, I drop the roller into the bucket and turn to find Savannah taking in the room, a soft expression on her face.

Crossing the room, I slide my arms around her middle, letting my hands rest against her bump. "What do you think?"

Savannah sighs, leaning into me. "It's perfect. The wallpaper is such a nice touch; it really makes the room special. I can't wait to put—" Her gaze meets mine over her shoulder, and she lets out a soft chuckle before biting at the inside of her cheek.

I narrow my eyes at her. "What?"

"You have paint on your cheek," she teases, pointing at her jaw. "Just about here..."

I rub at the place where she indicated, but it only causes her to giggle harder.

"You're only making it worse."

"How am I making it worse? I'm trying to wipe it off."

"You are." She turns around to face me and lifts her arm, her finger rubbing at the scruff on my jaw. Those blue eyes take me in, amusement dancing in her irises. "As a matter of fact, you're all splotchy."

"I'll give you splotchy."

Before she can react, I take the paintbrush from her hand and gently swipe it against her cheek.

Her mouth falls open, eyes widening. "Blake!"

Unable to resist it, I swipe the brush over her nose and wiggle my brows. "You were saying?"

She lifts her hand and swipes at her cheek, staring at the paint covering her fingertips. "Oh, now you've done it."

For a second, I think I might have gone overboard, but then a wicked smile spreads over her mouth. "Game on."

I don't even have a chance to move before she dips her hand in the bucket with paint and smears it over my face and chest, giggling the whole time as she takes a step back.

I glance down at my shirt, where her palm print is plastered in the middle of my chest, before slowly lifting my gaze to her retreating body.

"Oh, it's on, baby."

Slipping my hands into the paint, I lunge after her. Savannah lets out a loud shriek as my hand smears paint over her side, and in turn she does the same to my shoulder.

We're both laughing as we paint each other. I grab her ass, pulling her closer to me, my knee slipping between her thighs. Her fingers slide under my shirt, leaving a trace of paint over my abs. I suck in a breath, my laughter dying as her nails scratch at my skin, sending tingles down my spine. My cock jerks in response to her touch.

"Blondie..."

Her name is a soft rasp coming from deep in my lungs.

She tilts her head back, heat blazing in those blue irises. I cup her cheek, my finger running over her chin before I slip my hand to her neck and pull her to me, my mouth crashing over hers.

My fingers dig into her skin, loose strands tickling my wrist as I pull her to me, my tongue swiping into her mouth. There is nothing gentle about the kiss. Just this raw, aching need that's building inside of me to have her, *claim* her, in the most basic way possible. I fuck her mouth with my tongue as she grinds herself against my hard length, and a low moan bubbles out of her.

"We're all dirty," she pants, breaking the kiss.

"We are." I move my hands to her cheeks, smearing the paint over the soft skin. "Very, very dirty."

It was silly. We were acting like two kids, but damn it, if it wasn't the most fun I had in ages. And it was all because of her.

"What are we gonna do about it, Blondie?" I ask, my voice coming out rough.

"I think we need a shower."

Her teeth sink into her lower lip, her fingers curling around the hem of my shirt and tugging me after her as she starts walking backward.

My eyes are locked on hers, the space between us sizzling with pent-up tension as she pulls me to the bathroom.

The moment the door closes behind us, I tug her to me, my mouth crashing over hers. The kiss is hectic as we rip into each other's clothes, tossing them aside until there is nothing between us, only skin on naked skin.

I lift her into my arms, my lips tracing her neck as I carry her into the shower and turn on the water. The icy blast cascades over my burning skin, but neither of us minds as we explore each other's bodies.

I nip at her lower lip as she pulls back and runs her hands down my chest and abs, her fingers curling around my thick length.

"Savannah…" I hiss and watch her lower to her knees in front of me.

"Yes?" She bats her eyelashes innocently. Her tongue peeks out, sliding over her lower lip, giving me a few slow pumps before she takes me into her mouth.

"Fucking hell, woman," I curse as she swipes her tongue over the underside of me and slowly pulls back until my tip is the only thing left between those pretty pink lips. "You're killing me."

She hums happily, the corner of her mouth tipping slightly as she licks the precum from my tip.

"Good," she murmurs and takes me into her mouth.

"*Fuuuuck.*"

My eyes fall shut for a second. I slip my fingers into her hair, fisting the silky strands as she slowly takes me deeper into her mouth, her hand pumping at my base.

I tighten my grip on the back of her head. "I'm going to fuck that smart mouth of yours, and you'll take it like a good girl," I whisper, my voice coming out rough.

She hums her agreement, desire burning in her irises. The

sound sends vibrations over my sensitive dick as her tongue swirls around me.

Groaning, I pull back and fuck her mouth. My fingers are fisting her hair, controlling the movement as she takes me deeper.

"Fuck, you're glorious, Savannah." I untangle one of my hands and slip it under her chin, my thumb rubbing over the underside of her lip. "So fucking stunning."

She might be the one on her knees in front of me, but I was hers.

She had all the power, and she didn't even realize it.

"So fucking mine."

There is no mistaking the possessiveness in my voice as I say the words out loud.

Savannah's eyes widen, her cheeks are flushed, her grip around my cock tightening as her hand falls between her thighs.

"Fuck that pussy with your fingers, Blondie. I want you wet and ready for me once I sink inside you because I won't be leaving anytime soon."

Dropping my hand, I cup her tit, tweaking her hard nipple.

She moans as I fuck her mouth, each time slipping a little bit deeper. The pressure builds inside my spine, and my abs flex. Her eyes were watering when I hit the back of her throat, barely holding onto control. Cursing loudly, I pull her back. Her teeth graze over my length, making me shudder as my cock pops out of her mouth, and I tug her to her feet.

"Blake, wha—"

"Hands on the wall."

Turning her away from me, I press my front against her back. One of my hands slides just under her stomach, while with the other I interlock my fingers with hers and place our hands against the tiles.

In one swift movement, I enter her from behind.

Savannah sucks in a breath, her sweet cunt squeezing around my length like a vise grip.

"Blake," she moans softly, her eyes falling shut as she trembles in my arms. "I need..."

"I know exactly what you need, baby," I whisper and nip at the hollow of her neck as I fuck her, each time sinking deeper into her.

Rubbing at the swell of her belly, I slide my hand lower, cupping her sex and teasing her clit. The small bundle of nerves pulses against my thumb.

I nuzzle the side of her face. Savannah glances at me, her eyes heavy with need. I watch them darken, her lips parting as I hit just the right spot. Her body shakes as she comes.

"You're so fucking beautiful." The words are more like a growl as I speed up my movements, chasing my own release.

I capture her lips, swallowing her moan as my tongue sinks into her mouth. The kiss is messy as I slam into her—over and over again. Wild and needy.

Savannah's hand wraps around me, pulling me closer, her nails digging into my skin as she comes again, just as I let out a roar and explode inside of her.

Savannah goes limp, so I wrap my arms around her body and pull her to my chest, kissing her shoulder. "I've gotcha, Blondie."

"Mm-hmm..." She blinks her eyes open and glances at me over her shoulder, her hand cupping my cheek. Her hair is wet, cheeks flushed, and there are still remnants of paint on her face, but I don't think she's ever been more beautiful to me. "I know."

The trust shining in those blue irises makes my throat tight. The words I wanted to tell her so badly are on the tip of my tongue, but I swallow them back and press my mouth against her forehead in a gentle kiss as I pull out of her.

"We're still dirty," she says, pressing her thighs together.

"I like when you're dirty," I chuckle, the corner of my mouth lifting in a self-satisfied smirk. "Tell you what, I'll help you wash off, and then I'll take you to bed and get you dirty all over again."

"Promises, promises," she singsongs.

"You should know by now that I'm very good at keeping my promises."

Chapter 31

BLAKE

"You do realize it's weird that you sneak into the house every morning, right?"

I jump in surprise, the door slamming behind me and making me wince. "Fucking hell, Daniel."

Turning around, I find my son leaning against the kitchen doorway, a cup of coffee in his hand. He watches me silently, making me feel like I'm the teenager here and not him.

Talk about turning the tables.

I run my hand through my hair. "I'm not sneaking in." The lie slips from my lips easily, which only makes him arch his brow. "I... I went out for a run."

"Yeah," he deadpans, rolling his eyes. "Because you have a tendency to go out running in last night's clothes"—his gaze lowers, taking me in—"and flip-flops."

Shit.

I guess he had me there.

"Seriously, it's a legit question. It's not like we don't know you and Savannah are together." He stops for a moment, his eyes narrowing at me. "You were with Savannah, right?"

My mouth falls open at his question.

"What—" I shake my head. "Of course I was with Savannah! Who else would I be with?"

"Don't ask me." He shrugs. "I just don't get why you're sneaking around then."

Great, and now I was being reprimanded by my sixteen-year-old. It's too fucking early for this.

"I need coffee," I mutter, going straight for the machine and pouring myself a large mug before taking a long sip.

"Is it because of us?" Daniel asks, finally breaking the quiet. "Because of me? I apologized—"

"No," I say quickly before he can finish. "Not in the way you think, at least." Sighing, I lean against the counter. "Savannah doesn't want to make you boys uncomfortable by sleeping over."

Daniel frowns. "What's the difference? It's not like we don't know about you guys."

"True, but the difference is that this is your home, and we both are trying to respect that. It's one thing to know that Savannah and I are dating and a completely different thing to have her sleep over."

Just because I was all in didn't mean everybody else was on the same page. I wanted Savannah, more than that, I was in love with her.

Did I hate the fact that I couldn't have her in my bed? Fuck, yes. I wanted to have her in my arms and not have to worry about setting an alarm so I could sneak into my own house before the boys woke up, or God forbid, what would happen if one of them was looking for me or needed my help, and I wasn't there. It was tiring as hell, but she was right. Levi and Daniel both deserved time to process this on their own terms. They deserved to get to know her and figure out what they wanted out of all of this.

"These last few months... They've been challenging for everybody, and we're all just trying to do our best. Trying to figure out how this is going to work, and that also includes you boys. Okay?"

"Yeah, I guess." Daniel nods, but the line between his brows grows deeper.

I decided to let it go and change the subject. "What are you doing up anyway?"

It wasn't even five in the morning yet, and he didn't have to go to school for a few more hours.

Daniel shrugs his shoulders. "I have a project due today."

My brows shoot up. I don't know what was happening with Daniel suddenly, but he was taking school way more seriously than he ever did before. Not that you'll hear me complain about it. The end of the semester was coming quickly, and for once, he wasn't failing, and I didn't have to yell at him constantly that he should be studying.

"That's good."

"I don't know. We'll see what my teacher says."

"You need help?"

"Nah." Daniel shakes his head. "I'm good."

"Okay, but if you need anything, I'm here."

"Thanks." Daniel starts toward the door. "I think I'll go up and check if everything's okay."

"Sure thing. And Daniel?" He stops in the doorway and looks over his shoulder at me. "I'm proud of you."

Surprise flashes on his face, making me realize it's been way too long since I've said those words to him.

"I mean it. I know this last year has been rough for you, between the divorce, moving here, Savannah, and the baby..." I shake my head. "Don't think I don't see that you're trying because I do, and I really appreciate it."

Daniel tilts his head, his expression distant. "You like her. Savannah, I mean."

It wasn't a question, but I still answered him honestly. It's the least he deserved.

"I do. I like her a lot."

Another nod.

He starts to turn around. I expect him to leave, but he holds back for a heartbeat longer.

"Maybe you should ask her to stay."

SAVANNAH

"You can do this! Go, Bears!" I yell loudly as the kids get into positions.

Between the huge ass helmets on their heads and the shoulder pads tucked under their purple jerseys, they seem even smaller than usual. If I weren't nervous, I'd find it adorable. As it was, I was happy I didn't pass out.

Just then, Munchkin kicks against my bladder. *Again.*

Cursing under my breath, I glance at the clock. The second half barely started, which should leave me more than enough time to get to the bathroom and back.

Pushing to my feet, I hurry to do exactly that, but when I open the door, I find Rose O'Neil standing inside, a phone to her ear.

"John, where are you?" Her back is to me, her fingers gripping the phone tightly as she listens to whatever he's saying. "You promised! You promised him that you would come."

"This is more important, Rose!" John's muffled voice comes through the speakers.

"I'd imagine keeping a promise to your son would be more important."

"I don't have time for this bullshit, Rose. We'll talk about this later."

"Of course," Rose mutters to herself, letting her hand drop as she pinches the bridge of her nose. "Everything is always more important than your family."

I start to pull back to give her a moment, but the door slips from my fingers and closes with a bang that has her turning around.

"Sorry." I wince. "I didn't want to interrupt you."

"No worries." She slides her phone into her bag and tucks a strand of dark hair behind her ear. "I should get back out there anyway."

With a forced smile, she leaves. I watch after her for a moment longer before shaking my head and slipping into the stall. I do my business and wash my hands, hurrying back outside.

My gaze goes to the clock as the kids line up, and I take my seat. It was the final minute, and the opposing team was at four and twenty. If the Bears wanted a chance to win, they needed to intercept this play before the clock ran out or their opponents scored, which would put them in the lead.

I wanted them to win so badly.

For the kids.

For Blake.

All of them have been working so hard since the beginning of the season and have come a long way.

My gaze darts to the sidelines where Blake is standing. His shoulders are relaxed, the bill of his ball cap throwing shadows over his face, his clipboard tucked under his arm as he stares at the field, seemingly completely at ease.

The whistle blows, and the kids get into action as the clock ticks down. My teeth sink into my lower lip as the ball flies through the air, and one of the receivers catches it.

He tries to go for the end zone, but one of our boys gets in front of him.

And not any boy.

Number 93 is written in big, gold letters on his back.

Blake's old jersey number, the one Levi insisted on wearing because he wanted to be like his father.

They shuffle, going left and right as the receiver tries to pass him, but Levi's faster, his hand tugging the flag from his waist and lifting it in the air in victory.

The bleachers erupt into cheers, and the team rushes toward Levi. Kyle is the first one to get to him, pulling him into a big hug before the rest of the team joins them in celebration.

A smile spreads over my lips. I push to my feet, my palm resting on my stomach. It was mid-November, and these days I could swear that my stomach was getting bigger by the day, but Munchkin seemed to be doing well, and on our last checkup, the doctor assured me everything was okay and on track, which is the only thing that was important.

Blake nods at something the other coach says, shaking his hand before he turns around, and his eyes land on mine.

My teeth sink into my lower lip as that heated gaze takes me in, stopping on my mouth as I let my lip pop. The corner of my mouth lifts. "Congrats, Coach."

A low rumble comes from deep in his chest. His fingers intertwine with mine, and he pulls me to him, his lips brushing against my forehead as he whispers into my ear, "How fucked up is it that I want to hear you call me that when it's just the two of us, *Miss Parker?*"

His deep voice sends a shiver running down my spine.

Damn this man and the effect he has on me.

But I couldn't resist it.

Couldn't resist him.

"I don't know... I guess we can discuss this later, *Coach*."

Heat flashes in those stormy eyes, his fingers tightening around mine. For a second, I wonder if he'll say fuck it all and drag me away, but before Blake can do or say anything, a little body slams into my legs. "Sav!"

Blake's hands land on my forearms, steadying me. "Easy there, bud."

"Sorry, but I'm just so excited. We won!"

Levi pulls back and flashes me a bright smile. He took off his helmet, his sweaty hair curling at the ends and a mud stain on his cheek. I lift my hand and swipe at it, chuckling softly. "You guys played so well."

"Right?" He bounces on the balls of his feet excitedly. "Did you see how quickly I got his flag? One second, he was standing there, and the next, I had it, and we won."

"I saw that; you were amazing." I lift my hand, and he gives me a high-five before turning to his dad. "I played good, right, Dad? As good as you?"

Blake ruffles his hair and leans down, extending his curled fingers for a fist bump. "You played way better than I ever did."

Levi's whole face lights up like a Christmas tree. "Really?"

Movement over Levi's shoulder draws my attention. Kyle is standing there scanning the crowd, holding his helmet. His gaze lands on Levi and Blake, and there is no missing the sadness in his eyes as he watches them. It was an expression I was familiar with. Rose comes behind him, her arm resting on his shoulder. He looks up, a smile spreads over his face, but it dims slightly as Rose signs to him; probably telling him that his father didn't make it.

Small fingers wrap around my free hand and give it a tug. "Do we get cookies?"

"What kind of question is that? Of course there are cookies. Help me give them to your teammates?"

"Yes!"

Levi starts pulling me toward the bleachers when somebody calls Blake's name. I look over my shoulder, but he waves me away, promising he'll join us soon.

I grab the containers, handing one to Levi, who immediately grabs the cookie and pops it into his mouth. "So good!" he mumbles around the mouthful, and I can't help but chuckle. "I'm going to take these to my friends."

Straightening, I watch him run off when a flash of gold behind him catches my attention. My brows pull together as I look toward the exit, just in time to see the retreating back of a person—a woman—before a couple leaves the field. My heart is beating wildly inside my chest as I stare at them, but once they turn left the other person is gone.

It's impossible.

I press my shaky hand against my stomach, still staring at that empty exit when a low snarl makes my shoulders tense.

"This is completely inappropriate! She's his son's teacher."

I didn't have to turn around to know who said that. I would recognize that voice anywhere.

Lucy Donovan.

Then again, should I even be surprised? I knew it was just a matter of time before somebody brought it up. This was a small town filled with conservative people, most of whom went to church every Sunday, and they still frowned at women having children out of wedlock. I was surprised I didn't get more nasty comments up until now. Or maybe I was just too stuck in my own world to notice.

The bile rises in my throat, my palms turning sweaty.

"How did anybody allow this? It—"

"Allow what?" A loud snort snaps me out of my thoughts. "I didn't see the same energy when y'all threw yourself at him earlier today. Or do you think it's more appropriate for *Coach* to date the mother of one of his players?"

Mrs. Miller stops next to me, her bony hand wrapping around the handle of her walking stick, and for a second, I wonder if she'll do something with it.

Lucy must think the same thing because her gaze glances toward the stick, frowning before she shifts her attention to Mrs. Miller. "That's not the same thing."

Mrs. Miller arches her brow. "No? Because it looks pretty much the same from where I'm standing."

Lucy's mouth opens and closes and opens again, but no words come out. Somebody chuckles. Lucy snarls, her cheeks are bright red in embarrassment, but she flips her hair back and lifts her chin. "It's *not* the same. I was just trying to give him a proper southern welcome, that's all. Coach just moved to Bluebonnet recently, after all."

Mrs. Miller pointedly looks at Lucy's cleavage. "Yeah, I can see just how nice and inviting y'all can be."

Her snarky comment has me pressing my lips together to stop a snort from coming out, something Lucy doesn't miss. But before she can say anything, a hand sneaks to the small of my back. "Ladies."

My body relaxes into Blake's touch, at least, until Lucy notices it and glares at Blake's hand on me.

"Coach, good game." Mrs. Miller smiles at him.

"Thank you, it was all the kids." Blake's silvery eyes meet mine. "Ready to go home?"

Lucy scoffs, but before she can say anything, Mrs. Miller pats Blake on the arm. "Yes, you guys should do that. Savannah should get some rest."

Blake's head whips in my direction, his palm sliding to my bump. "Is everything okay? Is the baby—"

"The baby is fine," I reassure him, placing my hand over his.

"And you? How are you feeling?" Blake lifts one hand, tucking a strand of hair behind my ear. "You look a little pale. Maybe—"

"I'm fine. Really." I give his hand a squeeze. "Let's just go home."

Blake watches me for a second longer before nodding. He takes my hand into his, and we say goodbye to Mrs. Miller as we walk away. I swear I can still feel Lucy's glare fixed on my back.

Blake keeps giving me curious glances as we grab our stuff. Levi joins us, and we make our way to the parking lot and Blake's truck.

"Do you wanna stay for dinner?" Blake asks once we get to his house.

I open my mouth; however, Levi is faster. "Yes, you should stay. Please, Sav?" he begs, clasping his palms together.

Knowing there is no point in fighting, I don't even try. Levi goes to take a shower, and I join Blake in the kitchen, where he starts working on dinner. Washing my hands, I start working on the salad. At some point, the boys come too. They set the table while we finish the meal, and we all sit together to eat. Levi chats about the game, and even Daniel talks about his day, and the school project he was working on.

"I didn't realize you were such a good cook." I place the plates into the sink once we're done with dinner, pushing up my sleeves. It only seemed fair to clean up since Blake was the one who did most of the cooking.

"There are a lot of things you have yet to learn about me, Blondie," Blake whispers, his arms wrapping around my waist from behind as his lips brush against the side of my neck. "Besides, I like feeding you."

My eyes fall shut as warmth spreads through me, my whole body relaxing against Blake's strong chest. He sways us from side to side in a slow dance.

"I should go home. It's getting late."

Blake's arms tighten around me. "Or you could stay."

"Blake..." Sighing, I turn around in his arms.

He gives me a pointed look. "Daniel caught me sneaking into my own house this morning, and I got scolded by my teenager."

My mouth falls open. "What?!"

He couldn't be serious.

But based on his expression, he was.

"And he was right."

"A-about what?"

Those calloused fingers cup my cheeks, his forehead pressing against mine. "The boys know about us. We're having a baby together. There is no reason for me to wake up in the middle of the night and sneak into my own home." He watches me for a moment as I process his words. "It's just sleeping, Blondie. I'm not asking you to move in." My eyes widen. "Yet." He slides his thumb over my lower lip. "We'll have to talk about it soon, though. You know that. But for tonight, I want to share a bed with you. Stay with us, Savannah."

The determination written on his face knocks all the air out of my lungs as Blake stares at me.

"I want you to stay. Sleep in my bed. Let me wake up with you in my arms. *Stay*."

"I..."

How many times did I wish for that exact thing? For somebody to just stay and choose me. Too many to count. But nobody ever did. That's why I closed myself off. If I didn't expect people to stay, then I couldn't be hurt. But Blake wasn't like them. No. He was putting himself on the line for me. And over the course of the last few months, little by little, he was sneaking under my skin, he wasn't just lowering my walls, he was shattering through them, and I couldn't stop it. Even scarier, though, I didn't want to stop it.

"Okay." I nod. "I'll stay."

A smile slowly spreads over his lips. "Yeah?"

"Yes. I'll stay."

Chapter 32

SAVANNAH

A soft creak wakes me up, and before I manage to figure out what's going on, a pair of big hands wrap around me and pull me into a hard body as Blake buries his head in the crook of my neck.

Big *cold* hands.

"Blake!" I hiss softly, a visible shudder going through me, which only makes him chuckle as he tightens his grip on me. "Good morning to you too, Blondie."

"What— Why are you so cold?"

"I was outside."

Outside? Why would he—

His palms sneak under my shirt—*his shirt,* really—pressing against my warm skin. "Holy—"

"You're so warm."

I squeeze my thighs together as I glare at him over my shoulder. "And I'd prefer to stay that way."

"Don't worry, baby, I can get you warm in no time."

Chuckling, I squirm in my seat. "Not before I pee my pants."

Blake groans but lets me go. "I'll go make us some coffee."

"Sounds perfect."

I push to my feet as fast as I can and make my way to the bathroom that's attached to Blake's bedroom, where I quickly do my thing before splashing some water on my face and brushing my teeth.

After the second night at Blake's place, I woke up and found a few of my things in the bathroom. At first, I thought that he had taken them from my house, but nope. He bought them. For me. It made this whole thing that much more real. My shampoos were lined up next to his in the shower, and there was a pink toothbrush along with his blue one. He wanted me here, in his space. They all did.

Once I'm done in the bathroom, I slip into the quiet hallway. Both of the boys' rooms were closed, so they still must be sleeping. As I make it downstairs, I'm greeted by the scent of coffee coming from the kitchen.

Blake must hear me because he turns around, two coffee cups in hand. "Just in time."

"God, I need this."

Blake smirks, placing them on the coffee counter. "Did somebody keep you up last night?"

"You know damn well who kept me up." I jab my finger into Blake's chest. "Not that your baby is any better."

"Now it's *my* baby, huh?" Blake chuckles. He pulls me to him and hoists me onto the counter effortlessly, something he does every morning, so I'm not even surprised. "Hear that, Munchkin? You're my baby now."

"Yes, *your* baby. If you're not keeping me awake, the constant kicking against my ribs and bladder is. I swear I had to get up like five times."

"Poor baby." Blake leans down and kisses my bump gently. His eyes twinkle in amusement, and I don't even have it in me to be angry at him. "You need to give your mommy a breather, or she gets cranky."

"I'm not cranky," I mutter, my fingers sliding through his mussed curls.

"Of course not," Blake fights a smile as he pushes to his feet.

"I'm not. Just sleep deprived."

"We can take a nap later."

He grabs my diabetes kit from the drawer and sets everything up, taking my hand in his so he can test my fasting sugar. He turns the monitor so I can see the results.

"You're good to go. How about I make us some breakfast? Veggie omelet?"

"I can help."

I start to push off the counter, but Blake's hands land on my hips. "Or you can stay right where you are and let me cook for you." He leans down and presses his mouth against mine in a quick kiss. "Drink your coffee."

Not leaving me room for discussion, he pulls back and gets to work, chopping veggies and mixing eggs before he pulls out the pancake batter out of the pantry. Sipping on my coffee, I watch his bicep flex with every movement he makes, and suddenly, I'm hungry for something other than food.

Blake must feel me staring at him because he glances over his shoulder, his eyes darkening. "Blondie..."

My tongue darts out, sliding over my lower lip when the sound of pounding feet against the stairs snaps me out of my thoughts.

"Are those pancakes?" Daniel asks as he enters the room, rubbing at his eyes.

"I can't bake a cake for shit, but I can make some mean pancakes for the birthday boy." Blake flips the last of the pancakes onto the plate before wiping his hands and turning around so he can pull Daniel into a hug. "Happy birthday."

Wait... what?

"What about me?" Levi whines. "I want pancakes."

Blake chuckles as he pulls back. "You can have pancakes too."

I glance between the three Walker boys, who're still discussing the pancakes, as I try to wrap my head around it.

"It's Daniel's birthday?"

All three heads turn in my direction, making me realize I said the words out loud.

"Seriously?" I glare at Blake, who winces. "Sorry, I spaced out."

"It's really not a big deal," Daniel says quickly. "I told Dad not to make a fuss about it."

"That's not the point." I bite the inside of my cheek and shift in my seat, unsure of what to do. Should I hug him? I didn't think he would be comfortable with the gesture. But a handshake seemed so... cold. In the end, I settle for a simple, "Happy birthday, Daniel."

"Thanks." He shifts his weight from one foot to the other and rubs at the back of his neck as he glances from me to Blake and back. "It's really fine. It's just another day."

But it wasn't.

That was something I didn't realize until I moved in with Grams, who made a fuss about every holiday, every birthday, every milestone. It wasn't big or elaborate, but she made it special for me. She made *me* feel special.

"C'mon, let's eat before the food gets cold." Blake grabs the plates and puts them on the table. I start to slide off the counter to join them, but he's there, his hands landing on my hips to steady me.

"You good?" Blake asks softly, tilting my chin back so I have to look at him. "With everything else going on, I spaced out and forgot to tell you."

I give him a small smile. "Yeah, we're good."

Blake watches me for a moment longer before leaning down and pressing his mouth against mine.

"Are you gonna kiss *all* the time now?" Levi groans, making us break apart. Blake's finger slides over my lower lip as he just stares at me.

"Any chance I have."

Pulling back, he takes my hand in his, and we join them at the table, where we dig into our food.

"Any plans for today?" I glance at Daniel, who's all but shoveling the food into his mouth. I swear, between him and Blake, they could eat a whole horse together.

"Not really." He shrugs. "I'll probably just stay home."

"Well, I wanna party for my birthday with balloons and chocolate cake. Oh, and a bouncy house. And I'll invite my *whole* class," Levi interjects and nods. He's so serious I have to bite the inside of my cheek to stop from giggling.

Daniel just rolls his eyes at him and pushes to his feet, plate in hand. "He'll change his mind like ten times—" He stops in front of the sink, his brows pulling together as he squints out the window. "Is somebody coming over?"

"Not that I know of," Blake answers nonchalantly.

A little too nonchalantly.

I raise my brow, but he just winks at me.

"There is a truck in our driveway," Daniel points out, glancing at Blake, who's fighting a smile.

"Is there?"

If possible, Daniel's frown becomes even bigger. "Yeah, is it Mrs. Maxwell?" Daniel turns to the window and tugs back the curtain. "It's her day off— *Holy shit!*"

Daniel drops the curtain as if it burned him and spins on his heels, his mouth falling open as he stares at his father, unblinking. "Holy shit."

"He said a bad word," Levi points out. "*Twice.*"

Blake ruffles his hair. "We'll let it slide this time around, buddy."

"Is this..." He points at the window, his hand shaking slightly.

"It is." Blake gets up and pulls out a set of keys from his back pocket. *Car keys.* "You wanna go and check it out?"

"Hell, yes!" Daniel takes a step toward Blake but then suddenly stops as if he remembered something. "Is this for real? This isn't a joke? It's mine? Like really mine?"

I watch as different emotions play on Blake's face for a second before he nods. "It's yours." He tilts his head toward the door. "C'mon, let's go check it out."

The two of them leave the kitchen, Levi at their heels.

"I wanna see!" he yells loudly, not one to be left behind.

Rising from my seat, I follow after them. I lean against the doorway, letting them have their moment together. Daniel walks around the car, his eyes big as saucers, as Blake points out a few things to him.

"It's a secondhand one, and it needs some work done, but it should be good for what you need." Blake points his finger at Daniel. "I expect you to keep good grades and find a job to pay for the gas, but..."

Before he gets to finish, Daniel throws himself at Blake and hugs him. "I don't care. Thanks, Dad."

For a heartbeat, Blake just stands there, frozen, his arms hanging by his sides. It's obvious he's completely blindsided by the gesture.

I guess it's to be expected. Although they both clearly love each other, they've just been butting heads for way too long. Way too similar for their own good, these two. But somewhere along the line, they've started to heal and mend their relationship.

A deep ache spreads behind my sternum. I raise my hand,

rubbing at my chest as I watch Blake hug Daniel, his eyes falling shut as he just holds on for a long moment, taking it all in.

"Can we go test it out?" Daniel asks, bouncing on the balls of his feet once he pulls back, his excitement obvious.

"Sure thing."

Blake hands him the keys, and Daniel just stares at them before shaking his head and unlocking the truck. When Daniel looks up, his eyes meet mine. "You wanna come with us?"

I rest my hand against my stomach. "I have some work to do, but you boys have fun."

"I'm going!" Levi rushes toward the back seat and jumps inside.

"You sure?" Blake asks over the roof of the car.

"Yeah, papers won't get graded on their own, unfortunately, but I wanna hear all about it once you get home."

Daniel nods and slides into the driver's seat, but not Blake. He walks to me, his palms cupping my cheeks as he brings his mouth to mine in a hard kiss. "I'll see you later."

With that, he joins his boys, and soon enough, the car pulls from the driveway. I stay in the doorway until I can't see them any longer before slipping inside. I tidy up the space, cleaning after breakfast before I lock and leave for my own house.

I grab my work bag and drop it in the living room before going to the kitchen to get a glass of water. As I turn the faucet off, my gaze falls on Grams' cookbook I left on the counter the other day. Wiping my hands, I flip through the pages until I find the one I want and get to work.

"Sav! Daniel sucks at driving," Levi says as he runs into my living room and comes straight to me. I move the papers I've been grading at the very last second before they can scatter to the ground as he jumps on the couch next to me. "Like a lot."

"I don't suck at driving." This comes from Daniel, who's glaring at his younger brother.

"You do." Levi pokes his tongue at him and turns to me. "The truck was making these weird noises, and he was tugging us back and forth, back and forth, and one time it was so strong, I almost flew out of the car, but the seat belt tugged me back, and now my chest is hurting."

"It was an accident," Daniel protests, his cheeks slightly pink as Levi rubs at his chest. "It's different from Dad's truck. It's not like I did it on purpose. I just forgot about it for a second."

"His truck is diesel," Blake explains as he joins us, two big pizza boxes in hand. "You'll get the hang of it soon. Now, let's eat before the food gets cold."

I sit straighter in my seat as he places the boxes on the coffee table. "Where did you guys go?"

"Uncle Miguel's." Daniel grabs a slice of pizza and shoves it into his mouth. "He called Dad when we were driving, so we stopped at his house to show him and Becky the truck."

Blake hands me a smaller pizza box as Daniel describes the whole drive in the smallest of details and how excited the Fernandezes were when he showed it to them as I nibble at my pizza. It was a thin, whole-grain crust with some cheese and veggies.

"Do you think..." Daniel starts, rubbing the back of his head. "Can I take a few friends to the mall tomorrow after school and treat them to burgers?"

"Yeah, that sounds good."

Daniel looks up, that smile still on his face. "Thanks, Dad. Today was the best." He pushes upright. "I'll go and text the—"

"Actually..." I brace my hands against the cushion and slowly get to my feet. "There is one more thing."

Before they can say anything, I make my way to the kitchen to grab my surprise. For a moment, the nerves get the better of me, but I push them back as I return to the living room to find the Walker boys talking amongst each other with matching confused expressions on their faces. They must hear me approach because their heads turn in my direction, and I watch as different emotions play on their faces.

"I know it's not much but..." I shrug, placing the tray on the table in front of Daniel. "Happy birthday, Daniel."

He just blinks and stares at the cake, silent for what feels like forever.

"You made this?" Daniel finally breaks the quiet, his voice coming out gruff.

I shift my weight from one foot to the other, my palms turning sweaty under his watchful gaze.

Shit. I shouldn't have done it.

The cake has blue frosting with something that should look like a black car on it. Since I finished it barely an hour ago, it didn't have the time to properly cool off. And while my baking skills weren't shabby, I sucked at decorating. It was a silly idea to begin with.

"Yeah." I run my fingers through my hair. "It's fine. I know it's not that fancy since I'm not really skilled but—"

The words are cut short when Daniel gets to his feet and hugs me. I suck in a breath, my gaze meeting Blake's over his son's shoulder as he squeezes me tightly.

Daniel is... hugging me?

"Thank you," Daniel croaks out, his words coming out muffled as he buries his head into the crook of my shoulder.

Blake's face softens. I let out a shaky breath and wrap my

arms around him. "It's just a cake. I wish I knew earlier so I could have bought you a real present."

Daniel shakes his head. "No, it's not."

He lets his hands drop and takes a step back. I want to ask him what he meant but don't get a chance to.

"Not fair! I wanna cake for my birthday too!" Levi interjects, clearly feeling left out. "You'll make it for me, right, Sav?"

I chuckle and ruffle his hair. "I can do that, sure. Do you wanna try it?"

They all nod in agreement, so I cut them each a slice before sitting down. The boys moan loudly as they dig in, and I can feel my smile growing bigger as I take a small piece of cake myself, the first taste bringing back all the memories with my Grams.

The first birthday cake I ever got was when I was nine. Grams taught me how to bake it. I remember her raspy laughter when we made a mess of the kitchen and sitting on the porch and sharing a slice.

"Damn, this is good."

Daniel nods in agreement. "What cake is that? It's vanilla, but there is something else."

"It's a secret." Yearning spreads through my chest, that familiar ache back in place. My gaze drops to the cake, my throat feeling tight, so I swallow down, fighting the wave of emotions. "It's my Grams' recipe. She made it for my birthday every year."

Understanding shines in Blake's eyes. He wraps his arm around my shoulders, his lips brushing against my temple. "It's an amazing cake."

"I know. I couldn't believe my luck when I found the recipe in her cookbook. It was our thing." The corner of my mouth lifts up as I remember all the happy times with Grams. And there were many of them. She made me feel special. More than that, she made me realize that I matter, and I'm loved. "Every birthday, every celebration. She never missed a thing. Never let me feel less than. I always said one day I would make it for my kids."

I lean my head against Blake's arm as tears blur my vision. God, how I missed her. I missed her every day, but in moments like this, it was worse than before. It was like the reality hit me all over again, the realization that she was gone. But not forgotten. Never forgotten.

"That's a great tradition to keep, Blondie," Blake's soft whisper breaks me out of my thoughts. He slicks back a strand of hair behind my ear.

I blink the tears away, my voice coming out raspy, "Yeah, it is."

"I changed my mind," Levi pouts, driving my attention. "I want this cake for my birthday."

"You sure? I can make you a chocolate one."

Levi shakes his head. "I want this exact one. On May 15th. That's when it's my birthday."

My mouth twitches upward in amusement at his serious face. "May 15th, got it."

Levi slides another piece of cake into his mouth, his voice coming out muffled. "When is your birthday, Sav?"

"July 2nd."

"We should bake you a cake too. We can do that, right, Dad?" Levi turns to Blake, his expression hopeful. "That way Sav can also have her tradition."

"Only if she shares her recipe with us." Blake winks at me. "Whatcha say, Blondie?"

"Hmm..." I purse my lips and tilt my head back. "It's a really old recipe. I guess I'll have to think about it."

"Brat."

I giggle softly, but the sound is swallowed by Blake's mouth pressed against mine. The kiss is too damn short and so freaking tempting, but the boys start making gagging sounds, so we pull apart. Later. We'll get back to this later.

All of them request another slice of cake before we go back to their house.

Blake's fingers tighten around mine as we walk slowly behind the boys, his arm wrapped around me.

"Daniel will never forget today," Blake says softly, so only I can hear him.

"Of course not. He got his first car. Did you see how giddy he was?"

"Fuck the car. He'll never forget what *you* did for him today, Sav." Tugging at my hand, he pulls me to a stop, his palm cupping my cheek. "Today you gave my boys something much more precious than a car."

"It's just a cake and a very poorly done one."

"You're so wrong." Blake shakes his head. "You shared yourself with them in a way they'll never forget, Savannah. You gave them a memory to cherish. Your kids. That's what you said. *Your* kids."

"I..." My mouth falls open as the realization hits me. "I'm sor—"

Blake presses his finger against my lips. "Don't you dare apologize."

"I know they have a mother, and I'd never try to get in between that, but..." I bite the inside of my cheek. "I tried so hard to resist it."

"It's okay, baby." He rubs his thumb over my lower lip. "I know."

"No, it's not okay." I shake my head, needing him to understand. "Every time I'd care for somebody, I'd end up losing them. And I can't lose another person. I can't lose *you*, Blake.

Any of you, really. Because losing you? It would kill me. That's how much I love you, and it scares the living crap out of me."

Something dark and primal shines on Blake's face. "Say it again."

I blink as Blake moves closer, his other hand rising to frame my face and hold me in place.

"Wha—"

"Say it again, Savannah. I've been waiting to hear those words for way too long."

"I love you, Blake Walker," I whisper, my voice coming out shaky as I voice the words out loud. "I'm completely and utterly in love with you and those boys."

"About fucking time you admit it."

A low growl that comes out of Blake's lungs is stifled when his mouth crashes over mine. He devours my lips, our bodies brushing together.

My fingers slide into his hair, tugging at the strands. "Blake..."

"Again," he murmurs, his teeth grazing down my neck and making my skin prickle under his touch.

"How many times will you make me repeat it?" I breathe, feeling a shudder go down my spine.

"Forever." Placing a kiss on the hollow of my neck, he glances up at me. "I want you to repeat it to me forever."

"That's an awfully long time."

"I don't know about that. To me, it doesn't seem like long enough."

Letting out a soft breath, I press my forehead against his. "I love you, Blake Walker."

"I love you too." He tilts his head to the side, his mouth brushing against mine. "And when the kids go to bed, I'll show you just how much."

Chapter 33

BLAKE

"Why did I think this was a good idea?" Savannah mutters as I hold the door open for Levi to get out.

"Is Gage here yet?"

"I think so, buddy. Go and look for him."

Levi doesn't need to be told twice before he runs toward the house, Daniel at his heels. I walk around the car to find Savannah tugging at the hem of her dress.

"What's wrong?"

"This stupid dress. I look like a whale." Savannah mutters as she once again pulls the stretchy material down. "I should go back ho—"

"Stop this," I mutter as my hand lands on her hip before she can slip back into the car. I pull her to me, my finger slipping under her chin and tilting her head back. "You look sexy as hell, Blondie."

Leaning down, I press my mouth against hers in a long kiss.

I wasn't even joking. My dick got so hard when I saw her coming down the stairs in that dress, it was embarrassing. The soft wool material hugged her every curve, accentuating her bump. Savannah was always gorgeous, but there was something extra sexy and almost primal about seeing her pregnant with my baby like this. I couldn't get enough of her.

"You should go inside." She starts to turn around. "I'll just drive back home for a few minutes—"

Closing the door, I pull her toward me, her back to my chest as my hand slides to her huge belly. And if it's to be believed by the way her lips part and her cheeks turn a rosy color, she doesn't miss the massive bulge inside my pants that's pressing into her ass.

"Does this seem like I don't find you sexy?" I brush a lock of hair behind her ear and spin her to face me. "Because if you need more reassurance, we could go hide in the barn or something, and I could show you just what I think of that dress." I wiggle my brows suggestively.

She presses her palm against my chest and pushes me back. Or at least she tries to. "You're crazy, you do realize that?"

"Crazy about you, most likely." Leaning down, I press my lips against the hollow of her neck.

Savannah sucks in a sharp breath, her fingers digging into my shirt at the gentle touch. She's been extra sensitive lately, and I couldn't help myself but tease her every chance I got. I loved seeing her react to the smallest of touches.

"B-Blake, we shouldn't—"

"Yo, you two coming inside, or do you plan to play nookie out there the whole day?" Miguel yells loudly.

Groaning, I press my forehead against her shoulder and inhale deeply, letting her sweet scent fill my lungs.

Savannah chuckles, her hand rubbing over my back. "You sound like you're being tortured."

"That's because I am." I straighten to my full height. "One day, Blondie. One day it'll be just you and me, and nobody will stop me from doing some very dirty things to you."

She sinks her teeth into her lower lip, and there is no mistaking the effect my words have on her.

The corner of my mouth tilts upward as I intertwine my fingers with hers and pull her toward the house. "C'mon, let's go inside."

"And here I thought you'd ditch us." Miguel smirks knowingly when we climb onto the porch. Jackson is leaning against his chest, his big eyes taking everything in as he sucks on his pacifier.

"Don't tempt me." I lift my free hand and brush my finger over the tiny hand. "Hey there, little guy."

"Look how cute he is," Savannah coos, her voice turning soft. "He's growing way too fast."

I glance down at her, giving her hand a squeeze. "You're not going to start crying, are you?"

"Of course not," she protests, but there is no missing the loud sniff.

Shaking my head, I wrap my arm around her. "I know you, Blondie, you're one big softy."

"Am not. It's these damn hormones." She brushes at her cheeks. "And he's adorable. Just look at him. I can't believe that in a month, we'll have one of our own."

"One month," I murmur softly, rubbing my thumb over the back of her hand.

Savannah shifts her gaze to me, happiness and excitement radiating off of her. God, I loved to see her like this. Loved that I was the one who put that expression on her face. I loved her, and every day I was falling in love with her a little bit more.

"C'mon, you two; let's go inside. I don't need to see you tear your clothes off each other."

Savannah's cheeks turn red in embarrassment.

"You're imagining things." Chuckling, I place my hand

against Savannah's back and steer her toward the door. "Where's your better half?"

"Becky is out there in the kitchen, helping around and keeping an eye on her mom."

"Her mom's here?"

A cacophony of voices is coming from the house as we step inside. The Fernandezes were a lively bunch, and they opened the door of their home to their workers and friends for the holidays.

"Yeah, she's been having a good day, so we decided to bring her over. I think being around Jackson calms her a little bit. I was actually just bringing him down from his nap when I saw you guys outside. Can't have you traumatizing the little kids."

I shove him back. "You're an asshole, Fernandez."

Miguel laughs at my remark when a loud whistle pierces the air. "Well, hello there."

The hair at the back of my neck prickles at the sound of the familiar voice. I turn to glare at Miguel. "You invited them?"

Miguel rolls his eyes. "They invited themselves, per usual."

Three tall figures fill the doorway.

"Don't act so happy to see us, Walker." Franco smirks.

Big J nods. "It's hard to believe, but he got even grumpier in his old age."

"I'll give you old age. I can still wipe the floor with both of you."

"Only in your dreams." Big J shifts his gaze to Savannah, a grin spreading over his lips. "And who do we have here? If I realized small towns hide so many pretty ladies, I'd have come here sooner. I don't think we've had the pleasure of meeting. I'm James, but people call me Big J."

He winks at her as he extends his hand toward Savannah. The corner of her mouth tips in amusement as she slips her free hand into his. "Is there a reason for that?"

"'Cause I'm big." Big J wiggles his brows at her, still not letting go. "*All over.*"

Fucker.

"Get your dirty paws off my girl, Callahan," I growl as I pull Savannah back, my arms wrapping around her.

Shocked expressions flash on my teammates' faces. Maybe if I weren't so annoyed, I would have actually been able to enjoy it.

"That's the hot teacher?" Big J asks, his jaw on the floor.

"Walker has a girl?" Luke Stone, one of the linebackers for the Lonestars, asks. "Since when?"

"You need to keep better track of what's going on, Stone." Franco shakes his head and whistles softly. "Damn, dude, you work fast. A girl and a kid?"

"Yes, Blondie's my girl." I give them a pointed look. "The mother of my child, so I better not see you trying to flirt with her."

Savannah rolls her eyes. "He's joking."

"No fucking way."

"Dad! You said a bad word," Levi yells from the living room, where I can see him playing with Gage.

"Yeah, Dad." Savannah smirks at me, mischief playing in her irises. "You should be careful how you're talking because there are little ears all around us."

There was something about the way she called me dad that sent a shiver running down my spine.

Leaning down, I press my mouth against her earlobe. "There will be nobody around later on, Blondie, so I'll get to talk to you as dirty as I want."

Color blooms on her cheeks as she bites at her lip, trying to keep a straight face. "I'm going to find Becky and leave you boys to catch up."

"Wanna take Jackson with you?" Miguel offers.

"Sure thing. C'mere little dude."

I watch as he switches the little guy from his arms to Savannah's. Her face softens as she cradles the baby to her chest and whispers something to him, her lips brushing against the top of his head.

"How did that conversation with Coach go?" Luke asks just as Savannah turns around, his question making me freeze for a moment. "Did you guys meet up?"

Savannah smooths her hand over Jackson's back, peeking up, a curious look on her face.

"Umm, yeah. He just wanted to catch up while I was in the city."

"Really? He made such a fuss about it."

Big J laughs. "You know Coach, he's one big drama queen."

Savannah rolls her eyes. "Let's go, Jackson. Let the boys talk about more important stuff, like football."

"Is she trolling us?" Big J asks as we watch her leave. "Damn, she has a nice ass."

"She sure is." I slap him over the head. "And eyes up."

My teammate smirks. "You're so jealous."

"Damn right."

"Blake Walker. Dad." Big J shakes his head as he takes a pull from his beer. "I didn't see that one coming."

"He already has kids; you do realize that, right?" Miguel points out.

"I'm referring to his old age, asshole." He shoots me a smug smile. "You sure you're ready for it, Walker?"

"I'm ready. You laugh at me all you want, Callahan. If I

were you, I'd be worried about myself. Pushing thirty, man. By the time you have kids, you'll be a grandpa."

Big J chokes, his eyes going wide at my words. "Oh, hell no. I'm not having kids. Like ever. See all this?" He points at his body. "It's too good to settle for only one woman."

"You're a pig, J," Luke mutters, his gaze locked on the screen where the game's playing out. The guy's been sticking to water the whole night, and his eyes were sharp as he was observing every move they made since the Lonestars will be playing against them in a couple of weeks.

"An honest pig."

I guess nobody could fault him for that.

Savannah's laughter comes from outside, drawing my attention toward the window.

Once everybody gathered, we all sat down for lunch that Mrs. Fernandez prepared. I swear that woman's cooking was from another planet. It was that good. I ate so much I don't know how the hell I managed to get out of my chair. I'll need to put in some serious workouts if I plan to get rid of all the extra calories.

"You're so smitten."

I don't even try to deny it as I push to my feet. "You'll see one day; you just wait."

"Thanks, but no thanks."

Chuckling, I leave the room and go to the car before I walk around the house and to the back porch.

Eyes the color of the sky meet mine, and a smile spreads over her face as she shifts in her chair.

"You didn't check your sugar."

She glances at her watch, her mouth falling open. "Shit, I totally forgot." Savannah pushes from the chair. "I'll just go and grab—"

I wrap one arm around her and slide into her seat, pulling her into my lap.

"I've gotcha, Blondie."

"Is that your emergency kit?"

The corner of my mouth lifts as I open the bag and prepare the glucose meter. "Sure is. I told you it'd come in handy."

Taking her hand in mine, I go through the motions of testing her blood sugar.

"Is she okay?" Becky asks as she joins us.

"*She* is sitting right here, you know?" Savannah gives her a pointed look.

"But he has the monitor. You're feeling fine, though?"

"If by fine, you mean completely stuffed, then sure, I'm fine."

My brows pull together when the reading appears on the screen. "It's 168."

"That's not too bad." I quirk my brow, which has her rolling her eyes. "What? It's not. It's Thanksgiving, and Mrs. Fernandez made such amazing food I could barely contain myself."

"I know." I brush a strand of her hair behind her ear. "I just don't want to see you get sick again."

Just the thought of something happening to Savannah made me paralyzed with fear.

"I'll drink more water, and if I don't feel well, I'll let you know."

"Here you go," Becky says, immediately handing her the bottle, which Savannah takes without protest.

"You need to take care of yourself and your little one, young lady," Mrs. Fernandez chimes in, her gaze landing on me. "Let that strong man of yours take care of you."

"That's what I've been telling her, Mrs. F."

"You should listen to him."

"Hear that, Blondie?" I wiggle my brows at her. "You should listen to me."

Savannah elbows me playfully. "In your dreams."

I tighten my hold on her as I lean in to whisper into her ear. "Oh, baby, in my dreams, you're always a good girl for me, doing exactly what I tell you."

She glares at me, her cheeks pink. The women exchange amused expressions before they change the topic to nursery and baby stuff.

The fire crackles in the pit, the sound of kids' laughter echoing in the late night as they play.

At some point, the guys join us outside, dissecting the game before switching to planning their strategy for their next opponent.

Savannah's eyes close for a moment before she blinks them away, trying to stay up. I tighten my arms around her and pull her into me, my lips pressing against the side of her neck. "Ready to go home?"

"Yeah, I'm beat. Let me just go to the bathroom real quick."

Levi's head snaps up. "We're leaving?"

"In a little bit, buddy." I help Savannah get to her feet, my palm rubbing at her lower back. "Take your time."

She shoots me a grateful smile as she walks toward the house while Levi joins me.

"Sav is moving like a penguin," Levi whispers, making me choke on laughter. Not that he was wrong.

"A cute penguin."

Levi nods. "She's walking funny, though."

"I know, buddy, but don't tell her that. We don't want to hurt her feelings."

Levi nods, making a zipping motion over his mouth. I spot Daniel and wave him over, and after a few minutes, Savannah comes out of the house.

Saying goodbye to people, we start toward the car. Levi slides in next to Savannah, and she rests her hand against his back, rubbing at his shoulders as she listens to him chat away about some game they were playing.

The moment we slip into the truck, I place my hand over hers, my thumb rubbing over the back of her hand.

This.

This was what I've always wanted.

What my soul has craved.

And it's all connected to the woman sitting next to me.

I've never felt this content, this at peace sitting with anybody else.

The drive home doesn't last too long. Walking around the truck, I help Savannah out, but instead of going to my house, she starts walking away.

I wrap my arm around her waist and pull her to me. "Where do you think you are going, Blondie?"

"I just need to grab a few things. I'll come back quickly."

"I don't mind sharing," I call out after her.

She rolls those pretty blue eyes at me, fighting back a smile. "It'll just be a few minutes."

"You're having another sleepover at our place?" Levi asks, clearly excited about the prospect.

"Yes, buddy. Savannah will have a sleepover at our house. She's just going to grab a few things first."

We'll seriously need to talk about the elephant in the room. I didn't want her going back and forth, not when we've been spending most of the time together. Especially not after the baby was born. Mine or hers, I didn't care which house we settled on, but we'd be moving in together. And soon.

"I wanna help."

Before I get to stop him, Levi runs after her. Cursing

silently, I turn toward Daniel, who's already at the front porch, and toss him the key. "We'll be back in a few minutes."

"Sounds good."

Spinning on my heels, I rush after the two daredevils.

"Do you wanna sleep in my bed tonight?" Levi asks as they climb the steps to Savannah's porch. "That would be so much fun."

"I don't think we'd both fit in your bed."

The automatic light I installed not too long ago turns on, and Savannah looks up from her bag, key in hand, only to come to a sudden stop. Even from a distance, I can see her body go completely still, her shoulders squaring.

The hair at my nape rises as Savannah steps in front of Levi, shielding him.

Something was wrong.

Very, very wrong.

I hurry my pace, my footsteps eating the distance between us.

Her voice is cold and completely devoid of emotions as she grits, "What are you doing here?"

"Sav?" Levi asks, a trace of fear lacing his voice as he clings to her.

Savannah's hand lands on his side in reassurance. "It's fine. Why don't you go home?"

Before Levi can answer her, the swing creaks, and a low voice asks, "Not gonna say hello to your mother, Savvy?"

Savannah's mother?

I climb on the porch, my gaze going over Savannah's shoulder to the woman standing in front of her and taking her in.

The resemblance between the two is staggering. Savannah looked like a carbon copy of her mother, only there was gentleness and compassion in her that the older woman didn't share.

Her gaze meets mine, the shadows making her eyes seem darker and her smirk turns knowing.

My jaw clenches as I remember what Savannah told me about her childhood and this woman who made it hell for the little girl she brought into this world. I step closer, my hand landing on Savannah's back.

"I can see the gossip is true, after all."

Savannah flinches visibly at the words, and her mother's eyes crinkle in amusement.

"My baby girl is pregnant. I'm going to be a grandmother, how—"

She tries to move closer as if she's going to hug her. I'm about to step in between them when Savannah pulls back. "You'll be nothing." She tilts her chin up. "I think you should leave."

Her mother's smile falls. "We have to talk."

"No, Clara. We don't." She points to the street. "It's time for you to go."

"You can't—"

"She said you should leave." I step in front of Savannah, my tone leaving no room for argument.

If she wasn't going to leave, I had no problem removing her.

Clara presses her lips together and tries to look around me. "This isn't done."

With one final glare, she spins on her heels and disappears down the street.

I turn my attention to Savannah. All the color has drained from her face. Her gaze is distant, her hand resting on her belly as if she wanted to protect our baby from her mother at all costs.

"Sav, baby?" I ask tentatively, moving closer. "Are you okay?"

She blinks and looks up, but that emptiness is still clinging to her gaze. It's like she turned off a switch inside her, and only a shell of a woman was left. "Yeah. I'm just tired."

"Okay. Let's get you—"

Savannah shakes her head. "I think I'll sleep in my bed tonight."

What?

Hell to the no.

I slide my finger under her chin and lift her head to face me. "Savannah..."

Her lip trembles, some of that vulnerability peeking through the cracks of the fortress she built around herself, but she presses them together. "Not tonight. I can't deal with this tonight, Blake."

Her words are like a punch to my gut. She takes a step back, breaking the contact between us, and before I can come up with a way to change her mind, she's already slipping into her house and locking the door.

"Fucking hell," I mutter quietly, running my fingers through my hair.

"Dad?" I glance down at Levi, who's watching me with wide eyes.

"Sorry, buddy. You okay?"

He nods, nibbling at his lip. "Was that really Sav's mom?"

"I think so, yes."

"She made Sav sad. I don't think I like her."

That made two of us.

"Is Sav going to be okay?"

Looking down at my son, there is no missing the worried expression on his face, so I rest my hand on his shoulder and pull him into my side. "I don't know, buddy."

Chapter 34

SAVANNAH

The loud bang has me jumping in surprise. I look up from my book only to see Mom rushing down the stairs in a frenzy.

Dread settles inside my belly as I close the book, not even bothering to check where I left off before I get up.

"Mom?" I slide into the hallway to find her slipping into her shoes. My gaze darts to the bag tossed over her shoulder. "What's going on?"

She looks up, surprise evident on her face as she straightens and shoves her blonde hair out of the way. "Savvy, you're home from school."

"Yes."

I don't bother pointing out that it's Saturday, and there was no school today. She was a mess. Her cheeks were red, her eyes bloodshot. She's been drinking. Again. She hasn't been drinking since we got here a couple of months ago when we moved in with Grams after Mom's boyfriend kicked us out of his house. Then again, I heard her and Grams shouting last night when I was supposed to be asleep. Grams was mad because Mom didn't show up for my school play. Not that I expected her to since she didn't come to any of my other school stuff. But Grams was there, sitting in the first row and clapping excitedly the whole time. She even gave me flowers after.

"Where are you going?"

"Just have something to take care of." Mom plasters a smile as she opens the door. "I'll be back before you know it."

What?

I didn't want to leave. In the last few weeks, Bluebonnet has turned into my home.

But she said I. Not we.

She was leaving.

Without me.

My heart starts beating faster as I just stare at the empty doorway. Something wasn't right here. What would she have to take care of?

I follow after her, my anxiety growing deeper. "Mom! You can't le—"

She opens the car door and shoves the bag inside before looking up. "I'll be back, Savvy."

With that, she slips into the seat, the door to our beat-up car slams shut with a loud groan. I watch as she looks over her shoulder, reverses out of the driveway, and speeds away.

Never once glancing in my direction.

"You look like a mess." Becky's eyes narrow as the door closes behind me, and for a moment, I wonder if coming here was a good idea after all.

"I bet *Coach* kept her up all night long." Jessica wiggles her brows suggestively. "I wish somebody kept me up for something more fun than studying for my finals."

The bile rises in my throat when I remember the hurt

expression in Blake's eyes as I slammed the door in his face last night. The expression I put there when I pushed him away, but seeing my mother for the first time in the last fifteen years messed me up.

Why the hell was she here after all this time? What did she want?

Different questions were popping into my mind as I tossed and turned the whole night, mixing with the memories of the past I worked so hard to forget, only for them to come up to the surface in a blink of an eye.

Fifteen years, and she still had the power to hurt me.

It was like I was that nine-year-old girl all over again, just wishing for her mother to notice me, to love me, to choose me.

But she never did.

I can see the gossip is true after all.

A shudder runs through me just as a hand lands over mine, snapping me out of my thoughts. I blink to find Becky watching me with a worried expression. "Are you okay?"

"I— Yeah. I just need that coffee. I slept like crap."

"I've gotcha," Jessica chimes in and grabs a to-go cup.

Becky's eyes narrow at me. I shift my weight from one foot to the other, feeling uncomfortable under her watchful gaze.

"What's really going on?"

Shit.

"Nothing, I'm just tired." I look away, a strand of hair falling into my face and shielding me from view.

"Here you go."

"Thanks." Pulling out my wallet, I place the bill on the counter and grab my cup. "I'll see you guys later."

Before they can say anything, I turn on the balls of my feet and go for the door, only to crash into somebody as I step outside.

"Oh, I'm so…"

"Savvy."

My muscles tense, my body locking up as the memories of the past slam into me.

One word.

How can one word hold so much power over me after all this time?

"Don't call me that," I bite out, my fingers curling into a fist, nails digging into my skin as I push back the memories that wanted to come out.

"Fine." The muscle in her jaw twitches. "But we have to talk."

Talk?

"It's been fifteen years, *Mom*. There is nothing to talk about."

I walk past her, needing to get away from her, but she follows after me. "I heard about your grandmother."

"Is that why you came back?" I turn around to face her. "Because let me tell you, you're only, oh, I don't know, eight months too late. Then again, I can't say I'm surprised."

In the light of day, I can see Clara Parker better than I could last night. These days her light hair is more gray than blonde. The alcohol and cigarettes have taken their toll. Her skin looks washed out, frown wrinkles are more prominent, making her seem much older than her fifty years.

"I recently found out."

I snort out loud. "And that makes it better how exactly?"

Mom glances at me. "You always were difficult, even as a child."

Red, hot anger boils in the pit of my stomach at her words. "Me? I'm the difficult one here? If I remember correctly, you were the one who left without a backward glance and hasn't cared to get in contact in the last fifteen years, so I'm sorry that I didn't welcome you with open arms. I'll try to remember that for when you decide to pop back into my life in another decade or so." I shake my head and turn around. "I'm done here."

"You think you're so much better than me?" Mom calls after me. "But let's be real, you and I? We're the same, Savvy."

I spin on my heels and point my finger at her. "I'm nothing like you!"

"No?" Mom's smirk becomes bigger as her gaze falls to my stomach. "Because I'd beg to differ."

Instinctively, I let my hand drop and cover my bump. I didn't want her anywhere near my child. She destroyed my life. I wouldn't let her do the same to my baby.

Why? Just why did she have to come back? Why now?

"Hey, who's that with Savannah Parker?"

"Who... Oh, that's her mother. She basically dropped her daughter with her grandmother and left the town years ago. I didn't realize she came back."

The soft whispering makes my head snap up. Mrs. Timothy was standing in front of her shop with another lady, both of them glancing in our direction. They duck their heads when they see me watching them, but I can see their mouths move as they continue whispering.

And they weren't the only ones.

There were people walking on the street, all of their curious gazes fixed on us, making the bile rise up my throat. My cheeks are burning and sweat coats my skin.

Mom steps in front of me, a smile plastered on her face. "People talk Savannah, and I've heard some very interesting stories since I've been back. About you." That smirk grows bigger. "About your baby daddy." She moves closer. "How you've been playing house." Another step. Her head tilts to the side as her eyes meet mine, her pupils are dilated, swallowing the blue irises. "Do you seriously think it'll last? That he could love you? That he will stay?" She shakes her head. "You know how men are, Savvy. You've seen it firsthand. They leave. And your baby daddy is no different. You just wait and see."

She lifts her arm, the back of her hand skimming over my cheek, but I push it back.

"You don't know anything about me or Blake. But regardless, I'm nothing, *nothing*, like you. I'd never do to my kid what you've done to me."

I hurry past her.

I need to get out of here.

"Savannah!" she yells after me, but I ignore her as I continue walking down the street. I curse myself for not taking the car. "I'm not leaving."

No, I didn't think she would leave.

I didn't know what her plan was, but she wouldn't leave until she got what she came for.

Whatever that might be.

Clara Parker was like a tornado.

There was no stopping her once she set her mind on something. It didn't matter what destruction she caused in her wake or the lives she destroyed.

Chapter 35

BLAKE

"Levi, it's time for bed."

"But Daaaaad," Levi groans, clearly unhappy.

"Dad nothing. Go up and brush your teeth. I'll be there in five to check on you."

"Fine," he huffs, crossing his arms over his chest as he marches up the stairs.

Running my hand over my face, I grab the glass he left on the table and take it to the kitchen, my gaze darting toward the window and the house across the street that's completely in the dark.

Fucking hell. Where is she?

Just then, my phone buzzes, and my heart kicks up a notch.

Savannah.

It had to be—

"Hey, have you heard from Sav today? I've tried calling her, but she hasn't been picking up her phone," Becky says, a trace of worry clear in her voice.

My fingers grip the phone tighter, my jaw clenching.

"No, I haven't seen her today."

Where the hell are you, Savannah?

"Dammit. I really needed to talk to her after—" The words die on her lips before she finishes, an icy chill running down my spine.

"After what?"

"I..."

"After what, Rebecca? Does it have to do something with her mom?"

"How—" Becky curses loudly. "Shit, she was there, wasn't she?"

"Waiting for us on the porch when we got back."

My statement is followed by more cursing coming from the other side of the line. "I knew something was off when she came to grab coffee, but she didn't say a word. But then I saw her talking to somebody in front of Reading Nook, but by the time I realized what was going on, Sav had already run away. I hoped she went home."

"Fucking hell." I run my hand over my jaw, feeling the tension growing behind my temples. "No, she's not home. And last night, she kicked me out before we could talk about it." No matter how hard I tried, I couldn't erase Savannah's empty face from my mind. "I've never seen her so... detached."

The woman with the biggest heart I knew, the one who had a smile and a kind word for everybody, was completely devoid of emotion.

Knowing what I knew about her mother, I couldn't really blame her, but dammit, I wanted to be there for her.

"I'll go over there and see if she came back home in a little bit."

"If you see her, tell her to call me."

"Will do."

"Take care of her, Blake."

I wanted to. I wanted to so badly. Now if only she'd realize that she wasn't in this all alone and actually let me be there for her.

"I will try."

We say our goodbyes, and I go upstairs to check in on Levi, who's thankfully already completely out of it. That boy loved protesting bedtime but always crashed before his head hit the pillow.

Closing the door to his room, I walk down the hall and softly knock on Daniel's door before pushing it open. He looks up from his laptop and slips off his headphones. "What's up?"

"Levi's in bed, but can you keep an eye on him anyway?"

"Yeah, sure." Daniel sits upright. "Are you going to Savannah's?"

"Yeah, I want to see if she's home." I start to turn around, but Daniel's next words stop me. "Did you and Savannah get into a fight or something?"

"No, why do you think that?"

Daniel shrugs. "You've been sulking all day, and last night she didn't sleep at our place so…"

Dammit.

He's way too observant for his own good.

"No, we didn't get into a fight." I run my fingers through my hair. "Savannah… Her mom came back and upset her. She just needs some time."

Daniel nods, his brows furrowing. He opens his mouth as if he wants to say something else but changes his mind at the very last second. "Yeah, sure. Go, I'll be here if he wakes up."

"Thanks, Daniel."

Turning around, I slip out of his room and descend the stairs two at a time, trying to come up with a plan.

What if she didn't come home? Where do I look for her? Where could she have gone? I had no clue. No fucking clue. None of the places that I would generally expect to find her were open, so where was she? What if something happened to her?

The dread spreads through my body, making my steps falter.

Maybe her sugar spiked, and she fainted again, and there was nobody to help her.

That thought has me running faster. I pull open the door, determined to find her, even if I have to turn this whole damn town upside dow—

"Blondie."

Her name falls from my lips, a prayer and a plea.

She's standing at the bottom of my porch. Her hair is a wild mess of curls, and her eyes are bloodshot, tears streaming down her cheeks.

She was coming here.

She was coming to *me*.

"B-Blake."

The wobble in her voice breaks something in me.

I take a step forward, but she's faster.

Savannah runs to me, and I can barely open my arms before her body slams into mine. Her fingers dig into my shirt as she buries her head into my chest and sobs.

"Shhh... I've gotcha, baby," I whisper, my arms curling around her and squeezing her to me as best as I can with her bump in the way. But neither of us cares much as I hold her tightly and press my lips against the top of her head. Inhaling her sweet scent, I can feel my body relax.

She is here.

Safe.

"I've gotcha."

Savannah's body shakes uncontrollably as she cries. My throat feels tight. I hated feeling helpless, and that's exactly what I was. I would do anything to take away her pain, but the only thing I could do was hold her. So that's exactly what I do. My palm gently rubs up and down her back, as I whisper into her ear, not once letting go.

At one point, I hear a soft creak, and when I glance back, I find Daniel standing in the doorway. His serious gaze shifts from Savannah to me, a frown appearing between his brows. I shake my head silently, and he nods, slipping inside without a word.

"Why did she have to come back?" Savannah croaks out, her voice coming out muffled. "After all this time, why is she here now?"

My jaw clenches tightly, and it takes everything in me to keep my body relaxed. "I don't know, baby. But she won't come near you again."

Savannah pulls back, sniffling softly. I lift my hand and cup her cheek. Her eyes are puffy from crying, her nose red, and her lashes glued together, and yet, she's the most beautiful woman I've ever laid my eyes on. Fuck her mother for coming back and making her cry like this.

"You can't stop her. She's told me she isn't going to leave until she gets whatever she's here for." Those wide blue eyes meet mine. "She knows about you. About the boys."

"Good."

"It's not good!" she protests, her fingers digging into my shirt. "What if she comes again? Tries to talk to Levi, to Daniel?"

"I wanna see her try." Savannah starts to shake her head, but I slide my hand to the back of her neck and hold her still, my forehead pressing against hers. "I mean it, Savannah. Let her try and see what happens when you touch the people I love."

Savannah sinks her teeth into her lower lip to stop it from trembling.

I caress her cheek, wiping away the tears. "I won't let her

hurt you. If she wants to talk to you, she can try and get through to me."

"I'm more worried about the boys."

I just stare at her for a moment before shaking my head. "Of course you are."

Leaning down, I press my mouth gently against hers. Savannah kisses me back without reservation, her lips sliding against mine when a shiver runs through her.

Breaking the kiss, I pull back. "You're freezing. Let's get you inside."

My hand slides to the small of her back as I guide her into the house, and for once, she doesn't try to protest as we climb up the steps and into my room, where I help her get out of her clothes and into one of my shirts before we slip into bed.

I curl around her, my palm resting over her belly, content just to hold her.

"She told me we're the same," Savannah says after a while. "What if she's right? What if—"

"The hell you are," I say immediately, not even allowing her to finish that sentence.

"You can't know that."

"I can. I *do*." My fingers slide under her chin, and I turn her to face me. "You're more of a mother than she could even dream of being, Blondie. And she knows it."

Savannah blinks, a tear slipping down her cheek. "I'm not a mother. Not yet, anyway."

"I think Levi and Daniel would beg to differ," I counter gently. "I see the way you're with them. I've watched them fall in love with you as much as I did over the last few months. You might not have given birth to them, but you've shown them more love and affection in the last few months than their mother ever did. Don't let her, of all people, tell you otherwise."

Savannah's eyes mist, and she presses her lips together,

trying to hold back her tears. I brush away her hair and lean down, my mouth skimming against hers in a soft kiss before I press my lips against the top of her head. "I love you, Savannah."

"I love you too." Her fingers interlock with mine, holding on for dear life. "Don't leave."

"Never."

Chapter 36

BLAKE

"You're up early." I slide my arms around Savannah, pulling her into my chest, my hands resting just underneath her bump, and I gently lift it up.

"Damn, that feels so good," she moans softly, her body relaxing against mine.

"I thought we established I have very talented hands," I tease, my lips brushing against the top of her head.

"Mm-hmm…" She tilts her head back. A small smile plays on her lips, but it's not reaching her eyes. "*Very* talented."

It's been a few days since Savannah disappeared on me. She hadn't brought that day or her mother up since, but I could see it was still bothering her. She was pale, and the circles under her eyes were growing darker by the day because she couldn't sleep, and what little sleep she did get was interrupted by nightmares. I tried asking her about it, but she brushed me off, so I dropped it. I knew her mother's reappearance was the cause of it, and the only way things would go back to normal was when Savannah knew her mother was gone for good, unable to reach our kids.

Turning her around, I place a kiss on her lips. "I'm going to check in on the boys, or we'll be late." I wiggle my brows at her playfully. "I wouldn't want my son's teacher to rip me a new one."

Savannah chuckles. "You better hurry up. I heard she's very strict."

Laughing, I let my hands drop and go toward the stairs. "Boys, if you don't hurry up, we'll be late!"

There is some commotion, but soon enough, Levi appears at the top of the stairs, his backpack on his shoulders. "I'm here. I'm here."

"Daniel ready?"

"He said he's coming now."

"Okay." I slide my hand to his back. "Want some cereal before we go?"

"Yes." His whole face lights up when he spots Savannah in the kitchen. "Good morning, Sav!"

Savannah's head snaps up, a guilty expression crossing her face as she looks at us. "Morning. Umm... your phone's been ringing."

My gaze falls to the counter, where I left my phone charging last night. "Who's calling—" I take my phone off the charger and look down, the name on the caller ID making me pause.

Coach Higgins.

Shit.

"Dad, can I have Lucky Charms today?" Levi asks, drawing my attention.

"Yeah, sure. Gimme a sec, buddy." Silencing the phone, I turn it face down to find Savannah still watching me. She nibbles at her lip, her brows set in a deep frown. "I'll call him later."

Before Savannah can say anything, Daniel runs down the stairs, and we get pulled into the craziness of the morning routine with the boys grabbing breakfast and searching for their things as we finally get on the road. Daniel drives on his own since he's picking up one of his friends, and I drive Savannah and Levi to school.

"The doctor's appointment is today, right?" I ask as I pull in front of the school and put the car in park.

Savannah unbuckles her seat belt. "Yes, at one."

"Okay. I'll see you at twelve-thirty then." I lean forward, pressing my lips against hers. "Have a good day." I glance over my shoulder, extending my fist for Levi to bump. "You, too, buddy. Be good to your teacher."

"Sav is my teacher," Levi giggles. "And I'm always good, right, Sav?"

"Most of the time."

Saying their goodbyes, the two of them exit the truck, and I wait for them to be safely inside before I continue on my way.

I stop at the store and grab a few things we need before making my way back home. Just the other day, I'd finally started working on the dresser for the nursery, so I hoped I would get that finished before I had to pick up Savannah for our appointment.

Slipping out of the truck, I pull out my phone to call Coach as I start to go toward my house to put the groceries away when I spot movement across the street that has me stopping in my tracks.

I do a double-take when I see familiar blonde hair, but while Savannah's hair is rich and glossy, this one is streaked with gray and tangled.

"Fuck."

My jaw clenches as I watch her from a distance, my fingers balling into fists when I see her crouch down and lift one of the plants.

Cursing silently, I march across the street, my voice coming out icy when I stop at the bottom of the stairs. "Looking for something?"

Savannah's mother freezes at the sound of my voice. Time seems to slow down as she weighs her options. Finally, after what feels like forever, she squares her shoulders and pushes to her feet, facing me.

In the light of the day, the resemblance between the two women is uncanny. The same sky-blue eyes that I stare into every day are narrowed at me now. But while Savannah is all good and kindness, her mother is the polar opposite—cold, calculating, mean.

Her jaw works as she observes me for a moment, the corner of her mouth lifting in a mocking smile. "Who do we have here? I don't believe my daughter introduced us the last time." She extends her hand toward me. "That girl has never had the best manners. I'm—"

"I know exactly who you are. What I want to know is, what the fuck are you doing snooping around here?"

Her smile falls, all pretense of kindness gone. "I don't see how that's your business, this is my hou—"

"It's Savannah's house," I bite back, not in the mood to play whatever game she has on her mind. "And you're not welcome here."

The vein in her forehead twitches in annoyance at my words but ask me if I care.

"I mean it, if you don't get the hell off this property, I'll gladly toss you out."

"You wouldn't do that."

"Do you wanna try me? Because let me tell you, there isn't much I wouldn't do to protect the people I love."

My words ring in the air as we just stare at one another.

"Anything?" Savannah's mother quirks her brow as she moves closer, her calculating smirk making the hair at my nape rise. "Because there is an easy way to get rid of me, Blake Walker."

I try to school my features, but she must see the surprise on my face because her smile only grows bigger.

"I've asked around about you." She tilts her head, her eyes taking me in slowly. "Gotta know who my daughter's baby daddy is, after all. And I've learned some very interesting things. What can I say? Small towns. People *love* to talk. Get into other people's business."

"What do you want?" I grit, although I have a feeling I know where this is going.

She glances down, her fingers tracing over the railing. "I've found myself in an unfortunate... predicament, shall we call it? And you could help me out of it. Give your mother-in-law some cash to help her out, and I promise I'll get out of your hair before you can blink."

"Hell, no."

Her head snaps up at my harsh words, eyes narrowing at me. "You sure you wanna do that?"

I move closer so we're standing eye to eye. "I'm not giving you shit. Now get off this property before I throw you out."

Her eyes throw daggers at me as she grinds her teeth. "You're going to regret this."

Icy chills run down my spine. "Is that a threat?"

"No, it's a promise."

With that, she pushes past me and walks away, not once looking back.

Chapter 37

SAVANNAH

"PJs. *Check*. Wipes. *Check*. Baby clothes. *Check*. Diapers. *Check*. Pads. *Check*. Little makeup bag. *Check*. Going home clothes. *Check*."

With each item I check off, I place it into the open suitcase on my bed.

"What else am I missing?" I nibble at my lip, tapping my pen against my jaw, as I glance down at the list. "May—"

"Are you talking to yourself now?"

I jump in surprise and turn around to find Blake leaning against the doorway of my bedroom; fingers casually looped around the hoops of his jeans and a teasing smile playing on his mouth.

"Blake! You scared the crap out of me."

He just raises his brow. "Next time, you might try locking the door." He pushes from the doorway and enters the room. "What are you doing?"

"Packing my hospital bag. You heard Dr. Gonzales, the baby could come any day now, and we don't have anything ready. My bag isn't packed. I didn't wash any of the baby clothes. The nursery isn't put together." I shake my head, the panic rising inside my belly and making it hard to breathe the longer I think about it. "Munchkin could be here, and we're not ready—"

"Hey..." Blake's hands land on my shoulders, and turn me to face him, his palms cradling my cheeks as he looks at me. "*Breathe.*"

Those intense gray eyes bore into mine. A shudder goes through my body as I suck in a long breath, and the vise grip around my lungs loosens a bit.

"Dr. Gonzales also said your blood pressure and sugar are higher than she'd like, and you should take it easy. No stress."

He's right, dammit. I hate it when he's right.

But it was easier said than done when all I could think about was that my stuff was scattered between two houses, and there were a bunch of things we had yet to do.

Before I can stress any more about it, my phone rings from somewhere on the bed. Blake lets his hands drop, and I go in search of the device, which is conveniently at the bottom of the mess I've made.

"Hello?" I ask, my voice coming out breathless.

There is a pause, and for a moment, I think the call was disconnected when Becky's voice comes through the line, "Please tell me you're not having sex to induce the labor."

I'm pretty sure my eyes turn into saucers. "Wh-what? No. I was trying to find my phone in the mess that's my bed."

Becky sighs dramatically. "That's not fun. Oh, well, in case you need it, it does help."

"Becky!" I chastise, feeling my cheeks heat.

Blake just arcs his brows, an amused expression on his face as he mouths, "I'd be down for it."

Why was I not surprised?

I glare at him as Becky continues, "What? It's true. Try it, and you can thank me later."

These two... "Was there a point to this phone call?"

"As a matter of fact, there was. Can you come to the Reading Nook? I'm thinking of making some improvements, and I need another set of eyes."

"I don't know, Becky." My gaze falls to the mountain of stuff on my bed. "Can you send me a photo? I have to finish packing the hospital bag, and—"

"She'll come," Blake says loudly, his arms wrapping around my middle.

"Blake, we just talked about it—"

"Yes, we did." He gives me a pointed look. "And we agreed that all this stress isn't good for you or the baby. A couple of hours won't change anything."

I bite the inside of my cheek as I think his words through. I guess he was right, and I could always ask Becky what she took with her. It was a win-win.

"I'll get that tea you like going," Becky offers, and my mouth waters immediately at the suggestion.

"Fine." I let out a sigh. "I'll come. But just for a fe—"

"Perfect!" Becky chimes happily. "I'll see you soon."

Putting Blake's truck in park, I unbuckle my seat belt. He insisted that if I wanted to drive on my own, I better take his truck because it was safer. And since it was higher and easier for me to get in and out of, who was I to fight him on it?

Locking the door, I go toward the café, the warm air and scent of coffee hitting me in the face when I open the door.

"I really hope my te—"

"Surprise!"

My heart flips inside my chest. I come to a stop, my mouth falling open as I take in the space. "Wha—"

The room has been completely transformed. There are silvery-white balloons filling the space, and an "Oh, baby!" sign is hanging from the wall. Somebody moved around the furniture. A few tables were pushed together on one side of the room, and there was food, desserts, and drinks next to a bunch of gift bags sitting on another table.

I look at the expectant faces of the women in the room, all smiling widely at me. "Wh-what's going on here?"

"We threw you a surprise baby shower, of course!" Mrs. Miller chimes excitedly.

"I'd say she's surprised, all right, Trish." Mrs. Tyson nudges her friend.

I shake my head, still unable to wrap my mind around it. "But Becky said..."

"I had to get you out of the house somehow." A smug grin flashes on Becky's lips. "What do you think? Do you like it?"

Like it?

"It's..." I shake my head, my throat feeling tight from all the emotions swelling inside my chest.

They did this. For *me*.

As I try to compose myself, I notice more details.

An elephant pattern on the napkins, just like the wallpaper I chose for Munchkin's nursery.

And flowers.

And not just any flowers.

The bouquets of wildflowers had poppies scattered in between whites, yellows, and greens.

"It's stunning." Tears fill my eyes, blurring my vision, but I blink them away. "You didn't have to go through all the trouble to do this. It's way too much. We have every—"

"Nonsense!" Mrs. Miller answers immediately. "Every upcoming mother deserves to be pampered a little bit."

"Mrs. Miller is right, honey." Mrs. Santiago smiles at me.

"We've already organized the party, so you might as well just enjoy it." Becky grins at me.

"She's right." Mrs. Fernandez nods. "Besides, you deserve every bit of it."

Mrs. Tyson lifts one of the cupcakes. "You should try some of the desserts Becky made. They're divine."

I clear my throat, but before I can say anything, Becky sneaks an arm around my waist and pushes me to the chair. "Don't worry; they're all low sugar and gluten-free."

"Try the peanut butter cookies." Jessica winks. "I don't know what she put in them, but they're addicting."

I grab the cookie and take a tentative bite, the rich flavor exploding on my tongue and making me moan.

Shit, that's good.

"What did I tell you? I've been begging Becky to add it to the menu. People will fight over them."

"She isn't wrong."

"We'll see. But enough about me; today is all about Sav and her baby." Becky claps her hands excitedly. "You should open your presents!"

Everybody sits down with their desserts while Becky hands me bag after bag for me to open. There were picture books, diapers, toys, and clothes—so many tiny, adorable clothes—along with some stuff for me—face masks, perfume, and books, as well as one set of silky PJs.

Becky bursts into laughter when she sees it and turns to Mrs. Miller. "That's a good one."

"I know." The older woman smirks. "Somebody's gotta get her something fun around here."

I glance at the sheer material. "More like scandalous."

"Hey, you've gotta do what you've gotta do. Babies don't make themselves; you youngsters should know that better than anybody.

Coach can thank me later." Mrs. Miller wiggles her brows, and I can feel my cheeks heat, which causes more laughing. "You've found a good one there. He's a good dad. A good *man*."

"He is," I whisper softly, the corner of my mouth lifting. "Although, I'm not really sure I can take credit for that."

I never planned on meeting Blake. He just came into my life when I least expected him and turned it upside down.

One year.

It's been less than a year, and everything was so different than it was before.

I was different.

A hand lands on my shoulder, giving it a soft squeeze. I look up to find Mrs. Miller watching me with a serious expression. "Are you ready?"

I rub at the swell of my stomach, feeling Munchkin move. "I hope so."

"Your Grams would be proud."

My eyes turn misty at the compliment. "You think so?"

Mrs. Miller huffs out a laugh and pulls me into a hug. "I know so."

Slipping out of the truck, I go to the bed and grab as many bags as I can. Not an easy task since there were so many. I still couldn't believe they did all of that for me.

Once people left, I offered to help Becky clean up the mess, but she just shooed me out of the café before I could even finish the question.

My gaze darts to the house across the street. My back was killing me, and all I could think about was Blake's enormous bed, and his arms wrapped around me as I told him what just happened.

But first, I had to drop all these things at my place. Because that's where the nursery was. Or what is going to be the nursery. If I ever got around to finishing it.

I guess in order to do that, I should spend some time at my house.

Something that was happening less and less these days because I was at Blake's place more often than not.

Turning around, I climb to the porch and slide the bags into one hand and pull out the key to my place. Unlocking the door, I close it with my hip as I climb up the stairs.

Muffled voices coming from down the hallway have me stopping in my tracks.

What the hell—

"Hand me a screwdriver?"

The question is followed by clinking and cursing coming from the nursery. Letting my hand drop, I follow the sounds. The door to the nursery is left ajar, just enough so I can see a tall figure hunched on the floor, muscles flexing as he works on tightening the screw.

"Seriously, I don't know who the idiot is who wrote those damn instructions, but he should be fired," Blake mutters as he gets up and dusts his hands on his sweatpants.

"You said a bad word, Dad," Levi chimes in from somewhere in the background.

"Tell you what, when you're older and you're putting together furniture, you have my blessing to say as many bad words as you'd like. Deal?"

Levi's giggles fill the room. "Deal."

Blake pushes to his feet. "C'mon, help me get this up."

Daniel joins him, and together, they lift whatever they've been working on off the ground.

Daniel hands him another piece that Blake puts inside it and tests the stability before he moves to the side, and I can finally see what they've been up to.

The crib.

I suck in a sharp breath and cover my mouth, but not quickly enough because Blake turns around, a weary expression on his face.

"Blondie, you're home."

"You put together the crib," I whisper, my lip wobbling slightly as I look up just as Blake crosses the room, his tall frame filling the doorway of the nursery.

"You said the nursery wasn't finished." Blake shrugs.

As if that's all it takes.

I shake my head. "You put together the crib."

"Actually..." Blake's eyes twinkle with excitement. "Promise you won't freak out?"

"What—"

He pulls back and pushes the door so I can get a good look at the nursery.

"We wanted to surprise you, and if these damn instructions were correct, we would have finished by now..."

The dark gray nursing chair was sitting in the corner, next to the space where the crib would go. On the other side of the chair was a small bookshelf filled with books and a small light on top of it. They put in the new curtain rod and hung the striped—white and gray curtains. Grams' old dresser, freshly repainted, was placed underneath the window. On the opposite side, there was another shelf filled with more toys and books.

"Blake, this is..." I shake my head, tears filling my eyes all over again as I turn to face them.

Levi's smile falls, his face turning serious. "You're sad again. Don't you like it?"

The worry on his face makes my heart melt. This little boy will be my undoing.

Wiping at my cheeks, I smile at him. "I love it. This is perfect."

"Really?"

"Yeah, really."

I open my arms, and Levi runs to me, wrapping his hands around my middle. "I don't like seeing you sad, Sav."

"These are happy tears. Thank you for doing this for me." I look over Levi's head at the two older Walker boys. "All of you."

"Of course." Blake tips his chin at me. "What's with the bags? Did Becky convince you to go rogue and shop?"

"No. I got all of this. Ladies from the book club organized a surprise baby shower for me."

Levi pulls back, his brows furrowing. "What's a baby shower? The baby's in your belly; it can't take a shower."

Blake and I exchange a look, both of us trying to hold back our laughter but unsuccessfully.

"That's not what she meant," Daniel chuckles.

"That's what she said!" Levi purses his lips, clearly unhappy to be left out. "I'm right. Baby can't have a shower."

"You're absolutely right. This is a different kind of shower. It means they threw me a party and gave me a gift. Well, they gave me gifts for Munchkin."

Levi's eyes grow big. "I want that kind of shower."

"It's the best," I chuckle softly at his comment. "Wanna help me open them?"

"Yes." He stands taller. "I already put books on the shelf, and Dad said I can put toys in the bed once they're done."

"I can see that. You did a great job."

I sit down on the chair and let the bags fall on the floor. Together, we unpack all of the stuff for Munchkin, and I pile together all the clothes so I can wash them while Blake and Daniel finish with the crib.

I'm putting away the final things in the dresser when Blake's arms wrap around me from the back. "Done?"

"Yeah." Closing the drawer, I turn around and wrap my arms around Blake's shoulders. "I can't believe this is it. Thank you for putting this together."

"Anytime." Blake leans down, his mouth pressing against mine. "Let's go home?"

Home.

Only this was my home.

Mine and Munchkin's.

Some of the excitement I felt only moments ago dissipates, doubt creeping in.

Because he was referring to his house.

What would happen once Munchkin was here? Blake didn't bring the topic of living together up again, but I couldn't very well go back and forth with a little baby, now could I? Should I bring it up? Were we ready for something like this? Were the boys ready?

That familiar feeling of unease rises in the pit of my stomach as more and more questions pop to the surface, but I push them down. "Yeah, sure."

Chapter 30

BLAKE

"Ha! I win!" Levi jumps to his feet and does a victory dance, his smile growing bigger when he spots me. "Dad, Sav is so bad at UNO."

My brow quirks up as I join the two of them in the living room. "Is she?"

Levi nods. "This is my third win."

I turn my gaze to Savannah, an amused smile playing on my lips.

"I'm just warming up. I'm going to win a game," she huffs, grabbing the cards, and mutters, "Eventually."

"Of course." Chuckling, I stand behind her and place a kiss to the side of her neck. Her eyes fall shut for a second as she fights a shudder going through her body. She's always so freaking responsive to me. "Are you sure you're okay doing this? I can stay home."

Savannah overheard me talking to Aaron and insisted I should go and meet him for drinks while she was home with the kids. And while I knew she was more than capable of doing it, I didn't want her to think she *had* to do it.

Savannah's face turns serious for a moment, but she quickly schools her features and forces out a smile. "We're fine. Go."

She wasn't fine. Yes, she's become more like herself lately, but there were still these moments where she'd get a distant look on her face as if she was expecting something bad to happen.

"I hate leaving you now that we're so close to the due date." I rest my hand on top of her stomach, just in time to feel a strong kick against my palm. "Hello to you too, little one."

I let my palm slip under the hem of her shirt and rub at the hard swell of her stomach; those blue eyes darken as they meet mine over her shoulder. "I promise to call you if I go into labor."

"It's not funny. I plan to be there." I press my mouth against hers. "Every." Kiss. "Single." Kiss. "Second." Kiss. "Of." Kiss. "It." Kiss.

Savannah lets out a shaky breath. Her cheeks are flushed, pupils dilated. And I'm seriously considering ditching Aaron so I can stay home and have my way with Savannah.

"Dad, go!" Levi grabs my hand and pulls me away. "Sav promised to play with me tonight."

Savannah chuckles softly, biting the inside of her cheek. I give her a warning look as I glance down at my son. "You stealing my girl, buddy?"

Levi puffs out his chest. "Yes. Sav's my girl tonight." He pushes me toward the door. "Go."

I shake my head, amused by his response. "Okay, you two have fun then." I glance at Savannah. "And call me if you need me."

"We'll be fine."

I'm still chuckling as I slide into my truck and drive to The Hut. The local bar is relatively full, although it's the middle of the week. I scan the dimly lit space until I spot Aaron and Miguel sitting in one of the booths, their heads huddled together as they talk. I glance at the bartender and point at the guys, signaling for another round of whatever they're having before I join them.

"Both Fernandez boys? To what do I owe this pleasure?" I slide into the open seat next to Aaron.

"Becky threatened she'll kick his ass if he didn't get out of the house, so I felt it was in everybody's best interest for him to come with me."

Miguel's scowl grows darker at his brother's words, not that I can blame him. "Tough loss, man."

"Yeah, it sucks," Miguel mutters, taking a pull from his beer.

If he was drinking this close to the end of the season, I knew things were bad. Miguel followed the meal and workout regimen the Lonestars staff provided us to a T.

"You guys still have a chance of winning the conference."

Did the loss suck? Sure, it did. I've had my fair share of losses, and some hurt more than others, but you couldn't allow yourself to wallow in self-pity. Instead, you had to focus on figuring out where things had gone wrong and find a way to fix them. No great team got to the top without a loss here or there.

"Maybe." His eyes meet mine. "That last tackle in the fourth? Bryan got a concussion. He's out for the time being. And Mike's still not at one hundred percent after his injury from last season."

"Shit. That sucks."

Bryan was the starting QB. If he was out so close to the playoffs, the team was screwed, especially considering Lonestars traded their backup quarterback just recently and had to rely on the kid that was straight out of college to take the lead.

"It does, and then there is the whole thing with Higgins."

Something about the way he says it has me pausing. "What with Higgins?"

Higgins has been Lonestars defensive coach for as long as I've been there. Even longer. He was cunning and took no bullshit, which was part of the reason why he was considered one of the best in the league.

"He's been off this whole season. He's there, but he isn't there, ya know? And just the other day, I heard a rumor from some of the ladies in the admin office." Miguel's expression darkens even more, if possible. "Cancer."

"Shit." I run my fingers through my hair thinking back at the interaction I had with the man a few weeks ago when I was in Austin. I'd noticed that he lost some weight, and the circles under his eyes were darker, but I wrote it off as the stress that comes with the job. There is always a lot on the line, especially if you're trying to win a back-to-back championship, and everybody wants to see you fail. "I guess some things make more sense now."

"What?"

"They offered me a job."

Miguel's mouth falls open in surprise. However, before either of them can say anything, the server stops by our table with the drinks.

"They want you to play again?" Aaron asks the moment the server is gone.

"No." I grab my beer, running my thumb over the label. "They offered me a coaching position."

"No shit." Miguel's eyes widen. "They want you to take Coach Higgins' place?"

"They didn't specify. I assumed they meant the assistant position, but now..." I take a pull from the bottle, letting the cool liquid slide down my throat. "Even if I wanted the job, it would be stupid of them to put me as the main defense coach."

"Why the hell do you think that?"

"Because I don't have the experience?" I point out the obvious. "Coach Higgins has been doing this for the past twenty years. I haven't coached a day in my life."

"That's bullshit," Miguel bites out. "You know what's the first thing they told me when I got to Austin? Stick to Walker.

He knows his shit, and if you need anything or help practicing, he's your guy. And they weren't wrong. I wouldn't have been half as good of a player if you didn't help me with the transition that first year. Hell, even now, some days when the coach is showing us new plays, the first thing I do is turn around so I can ask you what you think. And I'm not the only one."

Miguel's words leave me speechless for a moment. I always had a good relationship with my teammates. When you work together as much as we do, you become somewhat of a family. I still talked to some of them, even some guys from my previous teams, but this...

"You left a legacy, Walker. I'm sure guys would be ecstatic to have you back as a coach."

"I..." I open my mouth, unsure of what to say.

I love football, I really do, but I love my family more. The whole point of retiring and moving to Bluebonnet was so I could spend more time with my kids. To take this job would defeat the purpose of this whole move. It would mean long hours, going back on the road for half the year. It would mean time away from my boys, from my newborn baby, from Savannah...

"Does Savannah know?" Aaron asks quietly as if he can read my mind.

I blink, the room coming into focus. "No."

The flash of blonde over Miguel's shoulder draws my attention as the person in the booth next to ours gets to their feet.

My muscles tense as recognition sets in. "Fucking hell."

Savannah's mother spots me. Her light blue eyes hold nothing of the warmth her daughter expresses. No, they're empty, her pupils dilated, and her cheeks pink from drinking. The corner of her mouth lifts in a smirk, the calculating expression on her face sending a shiver of unease running down my spine.

Why the hell is she still here?

My fingers clench by my side. I never wanted to punish a woman more than I do her for hurting Savannah the way she did, and it took everything in me not to do exactly that.

I guess it was too much to expect her to disappear into the hole she crawled out of.

"What?"

"Savannah's mother is here."

"Seriously?" Miguel looks over his shoulder.

"When did she come back?"

"A few days ago," I mutter, glancing up, but the woman was gone.

Dammit.

"How is Savannah doing now that she's back?" Aaron asks, drawing my attention. "Somebody saw them having a fight on Main Street the other day."

The muscle in my jaw twitches in irritation. "She says she's fine, but I can see the whole thing has hit her hard. And her mother isn't making it easier on anybody, especially not Savannah."

Miguel curses. "Did she at least say what she wants?"

"Money," I grind my teeth, my brows pulling together as I remember the interaction with the woman.

"Okay, so just pay her off and be done with it."

Aaron snorts. "As if it's going to be that easy."

"That's why I refused to pay her when she asked. If I give in once, there is no guarantee that she won't come back and ask for more, and I can't have that. I want her out of our lives, and I want her out for good." I run my fingers through my hair. "Savannah doesn't need any more stress than she's already dealing with. I don't want her near Sav, or any of the kids for that matter." I glance toward the door, that uneasy feeling spreading inside my gut. She was sitting right behind us. Did she hear what we were talking about? "I think I'll go. I don't like this one bit. Savannah is home alone with the boys, and now that I know her mother is still here, I wouldn't put it past her to cause some trouble."

"You think she'd do something?" A dark scowl flashes on Aaron's face. "To Savannah? Or the kids?"

"Physically? No." I push to my feet, pull out my wallet, and toss a few bills on the table. "Then again, words are her weapon of choice."

The sound of glass shattering draws our attention.

"I told you to gimme a-another drink, Mick," the guy slurs loudly, his fist connecting with the bar.

He's a younger guy, probably around Miguel's age, but the dark beard covering his jaw makes him look way older. His slacks and dress shirt are wrinkled after a day of work, eyes bloodshot, and his hair a mess. He's obviously been here for a while.

"And I told you that you're done for tonight, O'Neil. Go back home before I call your old man to let him know you're shit-faced, and he needs to come and pick you up."

"F-f-fuck y-y-you," he mutters, jumping to his feet. The sudden movement makes the chair fall back with a loud *thud*. "I'm not shift-f-faced."

The guy sways on his heels, grabbing the bar at the very last second to steady himself. "You'll call nofbody. I'm a paying c-customer, Mmmick, and I wanna my d-d-drink."

Not drunk, my ass. "You know the guy?"

"Unfortunately," Miguel mutters. "We played ball in high school together."

The bartender just shakes his head, not fazed in the least. I guess working here, he's had to deal with his fair share of drunks.

"You're done, John. And if you don't want this to be the last time you step foot in my bar, you'll leave now."

The guy glares at the bartender, anger flashing in his eyes. "Wh-wh-whateverrr..."

He starts to turn around, but Mick grabs his hand. "Keys."

I can see legit fumes coming out of John's ears.

"You know the rules. Hand me the keys. You're not driving when you're drunk."

"S-Screw y-you, Mick," he spits but puts the keys into his hand before spinning on his heels and running into Miguel.

He looks up and blinks a few times before recognition flashes on his face. "F-F-Fernandez, fancy seeing you h-here."

"John." Miguel nods, steadying the man before he takes a step back. "You good?"

"Peachy," he bites out, his eyes narrowing. "What are you d-doing here? Sh-shouldn't you be out in Austin playing in the b-big leagues?"

There is bitterness in his tone that's hard to miss.

"I am. I'm just home for a few days before I have to go back."

"Home for a few d-days," the guy scoffs. "Only you'd get a chance to be on the roster and decide to commute. If I w-were you, I wouldn't get so co-o-ozy in your spot, Fernandez. The NFL is a b-bitch."

Miguel ignores his silent jab. "You going home? We can give you a ride."

"I'm f-f-fine." He turns to the bartender, shooting him an annoyed glare. "I'm going to find somewhere else to drink since Mick is being a p-p-prick." He shakes his head, chuckling at his own joke before stumbling toward the door.

We stay behind, Miguel's attention on John's retreating back before turning his gaze to the guy behind the bar. "He like this often?"

The bartender grunts his agreement, a scowl etched between his brows. "More often lately than before. He just talked to his agent, and the guy dropped him. Said no team wanted him, not even on the practice squad."

Miguel and I exchange a silent look. We were both aware of how the NFL worked. Even when you were on an active roster, there were no guarantees. The team could cut you at any moment. Nobody was safe. Not really.

"I just hope he gets his shit in order. I really don't want to call his old man, but I'll do it if I have to. Somebody needs to put this boy straight before he gets himself or somebody else into an accident."

Aaron goes still at the mention of the accident, his jaw tightening, and the guy notices it.

"Oh, I'm so sorry, Aaron, I didn't—"

"It's fine," he cuts him off and glances at Miguel. "I'll wait for you in the truck."

With a nod in my direction, he goes for the door. Mick curses softly. "I wasn't thinking straight."

"Don't stress about it. Aaron is..." Miguel shakes his head. "He changed after Cheryl's accident."

"Such a tragedy." Mick tsks.

"It was," Miguel agrees, his attention shifts to the door. "I'm going to check in on him. I'll see you later."

The older man grunts and nods.

Saying our goodbyes together, we make our way to the parking lot, my gaze going to Aaron's dark form sitting in his truck, fingers curled around the steering wheel. "Will he be okay?"

"I hope so." Miguel runs his fingers through his hair. "He hasn't been the same after the accident, and since the anniversary was just the other day, he's even more wound up than usual." He turns to me and pats me on the back. "I'll see you soon?"

"Sure thing." I start walking toward my truck when Miguel calls after me.

"And think about what we talked about."

Shaking my head, I pull open my door, and slide into my car, Miguel's words still ringing in my head all the way back home.

The light is still on in the living room when I enter, the TV softly playing in the background. I follow the sound, peeking into the room, only to come to a stop when I see Savannah and Levi sleeping together on the couch, my son's head resting on her lap, not a care in the world.

The corner of my mouth lifts as I quietly enter the room and pull away the blanket so I can pick him up. It won't be too long now that he would be too big for me to carry, but I wanted to cherish these last moments I had.

"Wha—" Savannah croaks. She blinks a few times, a smile forming on her mouth as her gaze fixes on me. "Blake."

She pushes upright, and I can see her flinch slightly.

I move closer, taking her in from head to toe. "You okay?"

"Fine. Just uncomfortable. Your baby is sitting on my bladder."

I let out a soft chuckle. "I love how it's always my baby when they're doing something bad like it's my fault."

"Of course it is." Savannah smiles sleepily. "You were the one who got me pregnant. When did you get home?"

"Just now." I glance down at Levi. "How was everything?"

"Good. I don't even remember when we crashed."

"Can't say I'm surprised." Leaning down, I press my mouth against the top of her head. "Let's put you to bed, Blondie."

"Did you guys have fun?" Savannah asks as she walks past me and toward the stairs.

"Yeah, it was okay." Clara Parker's smirk pops into my mind, but I push it back, focusing on the woman in front of me. She didn't need to know her mother was still around. It would only upset her more than necessary.

"Just okay?"

"Yeah, there was this one guy who made a scene at the bar? Miguel knows him. John something."

"John O'Neil?"

"Yeah, I think that's the one."

"That's Rose's husband." I look at her blankly, so she explains, "Kyle's parents?"

"Oh, right."

"He got drunk?"

"Yes. Apparently, his agent gave him the boot." I tilt my head to the side. "I'll put Levi to bed."

Savannah nods, and I slip into the dark room, gently lying Levi down. He murmurs something in his sleep but doesn't wake up as I tuck him in.

Savannah's just exiting the bathroom when I get to the bedroom. "Did you have fun with Aaron?"

"It was okay." I grab the back of my shirt, pulling it off. "Miguel was there, too."

"He's back?"

"Yeah." Sliding my jeans off, I walk toward the bed and slip in next to Savannah. "He'll have to go back to Austin soon, but for now, he's here."

"I don't know how Becky can do that," Savannah hums pensively as I wrap my arms around her, pulling her to my chest.

"What?"

"The long distance. Not having Miguel around, while having an infant at home, all while running a business. She's handling it like a queen. It's just..."

The conversation I had with the guys earlier comes to the front of my mind.

Miguel's parting words.

Savannah snuggles closer to me, her voice soft. "I'm just glad it's not me. Does that make me selfish?"

And now I feel like a complete asshole; here she was opening up to me, something I wanted from the very beginning, while I've been keeping this from her.

"No." I brush her hair back to find her fast asleep. "Of course not."

Chapter 39

SAVANNAH

"You know you didn't have to come today, right?"

I shoot Blake an annoyed look. "It's the final game for the kids. Of course I had to come."

Sliding out of the truck, I feel a jab of pain in my lower back that leaves me breathless. I press my palm against my side, rubbing at the sore spot.

It wasn't necessarily a kick. I've become familiar with Munchkin's movements over the last few weeks. This felt different. More like a tightening?

A frown appears between Blake's brows as he watches me carefully. "What's wrong?"

"Nothing," I say quickly.

Too quickly.

Blake's lips press in a tight line, his eyes narrowing.

"It's just some back pain, that's all." Sliding my hand to the back of his neck, I pull him down and press my mouth at the corner of his lips. "I'm fine."

Blake grumbles, his hand slipping around my waist. "You should be home, *resting*."

"I will. Once this game's done."

"Dad!" Levi yells from the entrance to the field, Daniel behind him. "C'mon, we'll be late."

His excitement is palpable, and I can't help but chuckle. "Yes, Coach. You don't want to be late, now do you?"

A deep rumble comes from Blake's chest, his irises darkening with need as his lips claim mine in a hard kiss. "Can't leave without my good luck charm, can I?"

I shake my head. "Once a jock, always a jock."

"Exactly, you don't mess with what's working."

I bite the inside of my cheek, trying to hold back my laughter because, hey, who was I to complain?

"You head to the field. I need to use the bathroom."

Blake chuckles. "Again?"

I pinch him slightly. "Don't you tease me. Yes, again."

Blake lifts his arms in surrender. "Fine. I'll see you later."

With another quick kiss, he follows after Levi while I make my way to the bathroom as two ladies are exiting. We say hello as I slip inside and go into a stall where I do my business. I'm just finishing dressing when the door to the bathroom opens.

"Did you see who just showed up?" Lucy Donovan chuckles, clearly amused.

My hand pauses at the doorknob, not sure if I should go out or stay.

"I didn't think she'd come after what happened the other day," another voice joins in. Probably one of Lucy's friends.

What were they talking about? Who showed up?

"Rose was always good at pretending everything was perfect," Lucy snorts, which has a few other women giggling. "Oh, how the mighty have fallen."

"I heard John came to her parent's house and was yelling in front of it, demanding she come back. It's what everybody's been talking about," another mom chirps in, her voice slightly muffled by the running water. "Can you believe it? His agent just dropped him, and she does what? Leave the poor man?"

Rose left her husband?

I still remember that interaction I witnessed a few weeks ago between the two of them. That day, she asked him to come. Not for herself but for their son, and he turned his back on her. How many times did he do that? I don't remember seeing him once at any of the games or school activities. Hell, even when they were out in town, it was always Rose with Kyle.

Lucy smirks. "That just confirms she's been after one thing, and now that her husband doesn't have any chances of making it into the NFL, she's cutting her losses."

"At least I left him. You can't say the same thing, now can you? What was it? Husband number two? Or was it three?"

The silence that follows Rose's words is almost deafening.

"The next time you gossip about somebody, you should probably check that you're actually alone," Rose continues, her voice even.

There is some mumbling from the women as they scurry out of the bathroom, the door shutting firmly behind them.

Rose lets out a shaky breath, cursing softly.

Slowly, I unlock the door and peek out. She looks up immediately, her gaze meeting mine in the mirror. Her face is pale, and there are dark circles under her blue eyes.

"Are you okay?"

"Yeah." Rose runs her fingers through her hair. "We need to stop meeting like this."

I let out a nervous chuckle. "Tell me about it."

The corner of Rose's mouth lifts for a moment in a half-hearted smile before her face turns serious. "I shouldn't have said that, but my mouth was faster than my brain."

"Well, I think you were really kind, all things considered," I offer gently as I move to the sink and turn on the water.

"Yeah, well..." Sighing, she glances at the door, a distant expression on her face. "I should go to the field. The game's about to start."

She rubs at her arm but doesn't attempt to move.

Shutting the water off, I grab some towels to wipe my hands. "Wanna sit with me?"

Rose looks at me. "What? No, I couldn't—"

"It's fine, really. Trust me, you're helping me." I slip my hand through hers and start toward the door, but Rose's soft wince has me stopping and glancing at her. "Are you oka—"

The sleeve of her shirt is raised slightly, enough for me to spot a smidge of purple on her skin before she hides it.

Was that a bruise?

"Yeah. I just..." Her throat bobs as she swallows, those wide blue eyes avoiding my gaze. "You don't want to deal with my drama."

I press my lips together, trying to hold back the question that's on the tip of my tongue.

"It's fine. I know it doesn't help much today, but soon enough there will be something else they'll focus on."

Rose's shoulders relax, if only slightly. "Let's hope so."

Together we make our way to the field. Yes, there are glances, but Rose just lifts her chin higher as we walk to the bleachers and sit down to cheer our boys until the final whistle blows, signaling our victory.

People rush to the field to celebrate with the kids. I push to my feet, another jab of pain going through my middle. The pain had been present the whole day, but there wasn't a pattern to when it would happen, so I didn't know what to make of it. It couldn't be labor pains, could it? We still had a few weeks to go before Munchkin was here.

"You going?" Rose asks, realizing I'm not following her.

"Yeah, I—"

A flash of silvery-gold hair catches my attention and makes me stop in my tracks.

"Miss Parker?"

Mom smiles at me from a distance, and I can feel the hair at my nape prickle.

"No." I shake my head. "I'll join you in a bit."

Rose's brows shoot up, her gaze going toward my mother before it returns to me. "Okay."

Pushing through the people, I make my way to the side where she's standing, away from everybody else.

"What are you doing here?" I eye her carefully, unsure of what she's up to now. With Clara Parker, you could never be sure. But she seemed almost... normal.

"I'm leaving, so I came to say goodbye."

I blink, unsure if I heard her correctly. "You're..." *She's leaving?* "What?"

"Leaving." She quirks a brow. "Isn't that what you wanted?"

"I'm just surprised. You didn't bother saying goodbye the last time," I point out. I wasn't sure what game she was playing, but there was no way that she was leaving just like that. "What's with the sudden change?"

She glances around and snorts, the disgust evident on her face. "I've realized that coming here was a waste of my time."

Her words shouldn't hurt, but they did. Even after all this time, there was a part of me that hoped that one day my mother would care about me.

But she wouldn't.

Clara Parker only cared about one person—herself.

It was better this way.

"Okay." I rest my hand against my stomach. "I hope you find what you're looking for."

Those blue eyes that are so much like my own, narrow. "Such a goody-two-shoes. Just like your grandmother."

Tsking, she turns around and starts to walk away.

I watch her retreating back, sadness and relief mixing inside my chest. Sadness for the little girl who'd never get the mother she deserved, and relief because I can break the pattern. I can be different. For me. For my kids. They'll never know this pain.

I'm about to turn around when she suddenly stops.

"Oh, one more thing." Slowly, she turns around, an uneasy feeling crawling down my spine, as she smirks at me. "I heard congratulations are in order."

The nonchalant way she says it, has my stomach railing up.

"What are you talking about?"

"Your baby daddy." Her smile grows bigger. "Didn't he share the happy news with you?"

I press my lips into a tight line. I should have known she wouldn't leave just like that. This was another one of her games, a way for her to taunt me. "I'm not doing this with you."

Her lips part mockingly. "This isn't a game, Savvy."

My fingers curl into a fist. "Don't call me that."

"He didn't tell you, did he?" She shakes her head. "Of course he didn't. I told you; I tried to warn you, but you wouldn't listen. All men are the same. They all leave."

"Blake isn't leaving."

"Isn't he?" She tilts her head to the side. "His team called him. Did he tell you why?"

The rejected call from Blake's coach flashes in my mind.

How did she know about that?

It couldn't be.

Could it?

"Savannah!"

The sound of pounding feet moves closer, matching the erratic beat of my heart echoing in my eardrums.

Mom closes the distance between us, her hand brushing a strand of hair behind my ear as she leans in. "All these years, and history is repeating itself. I told you, baby. You and me? We're the same."

Her words still ring in my head when a hand wraps around my arm, and I'm tugged back. "Don't touch her," Blake hisses.

Mom lets her hand drop, her gaze on me. "Ask him."

With that, she turns around and walks away toward a waiting car.

Leaving.

Once again, without a backward glance.

"What did she want? I saw Rose, and she said you went to talk to a blonde woman. Are you—"

Blake tries to reach for my face, but I pull back and meet his gaze. "Is it true?"

Blake just stares at me for a moment, surprised by my reaction.

"You're leaving?"

Then I see it.

The recognition.

The *guilt*.

"Blondie..."

"Is. It. True?"

Chapter 40

BLAKE

"Is. It. True?"

Fuck, fuck, fuck.

I run my fingers through my hair as I watch tears glisten in Savannah's eyes. Different emotions play on her face—sadness, disbelief, and betrayal are reflected at me as she fights for composure.

I hate her mother for putting her through it.

But not as much as I hate myself for keeping this from her.

The woman I love more than anything.

The mother of my child.

I should have known something like this would happen.

Savannah's mother couldn't get what she wanted, so she decided to cause havoc before she left.

And I let her.

"Savannah, baby, it's not..."

Savannah's lip wobbles as she shakes her head. "I can't believe this."

One tear slips down her cheek, and it breaks something in me.

This was my fucking fault.

She turns on the balls of her feet and starts to walk away as fast as she can.

"Blondie!" I run after her. "Just wait, dammit. Let me exp—"

In her hurry to get away from me, she almost trips. My heart stops for a second, time slowing down, and I go into a sprint, my arms wrapping around her before she can fall.

"Fucking hell, Savannah! Talk to me."

"Let go of me."

She fights my hold, trying to slip away from me, but I'm not loosening my grip on her.

"It's not like that."

She turns in my arms, those tear-stained blue eyes throwing daggers at me.

"Then how is it, huh? How is it, Blake?" she yells, her curled fist connecting with my chest. "I saw the phone call! Here I was trying to come up with a way to ask you to move in together, all the while you were planning on leaving?"

Wait, what?

Savannah shakes her head, and continues, her breathing ragged, "I guess I should have known something was going on when you put together that nursery for me at my place, when we've all but been living together for the last few months, and you never said anything again. Not after—"

"Fucking hell, woman," I growl, my hands cupping her cheeks as I pull her in for a kiss, the only way I knew how to shut her up.

Savannah's eyes grow wide in surprise as I slide my fingers to the back of her neck, tangling them in her hair as I hold her in place.

For a moment, she tries to fight me, but it doesn't take long for me to coax her compliance. What starts off as a hard kiss soon turns into gentle caresses of my tongue against hers until her body relaxes against mine.

I can taste the saltiness of her tears on my tongue, so I disentangle my fingers and swipe my thumb over her cheek, wiping them away.

Breaking the kiss, I press my forehead against hers, my voice coming out rough. "You're driving me crazy, you know that? But it's my own damn fault for not telling you anything."

Savannah bites into her wobbling lip. "It's fine, just go, we'll be—"

Once again, I press my mouth against hers, biting into her lower lip in warning. "Will you let me finish?" I shake my head in exasperation. "Yes, my coach called me. And yes, they offered me to come back as a coach..." Savannah opens her mouth, so I hurry up. "I told them no."

"They... *What?*"

"I told them no. That day when I was in Austin, and my coach first brought it up, I told them no. That's why they've been calling me. They wanted to see if I changed my mind, but I haven't. I'm retired for good, and that's exactly what I told them."

Savannah just stares at me, her mouth open. "You told them... *no?*"

"I'm not going anywhere, Blondie. That's why I didn't tell you in the first place, a mistake I'm not planning to make again, by the way. In my head, there was nothing to tell. There was only one path for me. One choice. And that choice is you."

"Are you insane? You love football!"

I let out a humorless chuckle. Didn't she see it? Knowing Savannah, probably not. Only Savannah could get upset with me for hiding something, and then later try and convince me that my choice is a mistake.

"Not as much as I love you." I slide my finger under her chin. "Nothing will ever compare to you, Blondie. I want you. I want our kids and sleepless nights. I want to teach Daniel how to fix his truck and coach Levi's football team. I want to sit with you at the bonfire and take our kids to the town fair. I want all of those little moments, and I want them with you. Nothing will ever compare to that. Nothing will ever compare to *you*."

"Blake..." My name is a soft whisper. She bites the inside of her cheek, but there is no stopping the tears that slide down her face.

"I will always choose you, Blondie." I wipe the tears away, pressing my forehead against hers, and breathe her in. "Always."

"I choose you too, Blake," she murmurs as more tears spill down. "Gosh, I'm a mess. I hate these hormones."

"That's one of us." Tilting her head back, I press my mouth against hers in a gentle kiss. "I'll take all your mess"—kiss—"and emotions"—kiss—"and fears"—kiss—"and I'll crush them one by one until there is no doubt in your mind that this is real. That we're real, and I love you. That I will always love you."

Her fingers splay over my cheeks, and those crystal blue eyes stare into mine. "I love you, too, Blake, and it scares me. It scares me so much because the thought of losing you. Of losing those boys..."

"We're not going anywhere. Now, about that living situation you mentioned earlier..." I brush a strand of her hair behind her ear. "Did you mean it?"

Savannah bites the inside of her cheek. "I know the boys might not be open to the idea, and if that's the case, I completely understand and respect that. They've been through so much in the last year, I don't want to put them through more stress, however..."

Her throat bobs as she swallows.

"However?" I urge, needing her to say it.

"I want us to live together. All of us. I want our baby to grow up in a loving home with both parents and siblings."

"We'll talk to them." I nod in agreement. "See how they feel about us moving into your house."

"Blake, I can..."

"No." I shake my head. "You love that house. It's your grandmother's house, the house you grew up in." I brush my lips against her forehead. "We'll figure it out."

"Thank you."

Savannah tugs me down, her mouth sweeping over mine. Letting out a soft groan, I move closer, our bodies brushing together. Goosebumps prickle her skin as my fingers spread, my grip tightening as I tilt her head back and deepen the kiss.

My tongue slides over my lower lip, tasting the saltiness of her tears. Then she opens for me, letting out a soft moan as her tongue meets mine, teasing and swirling.

And fuck, I'm a goner for this woman. Completely and utterly gone.

"Blake," she moans softly, her warm breath brushing against my lips as she breaks the kiss. "I—"

"Yeah?"

I blink my eyes open, and her gorgeous face comes into focus. Her cheeks are pink, lips parted, as she tries to catch her breath.

"Let's go find the boys and—"

I take a step back, but she clenches her fingers around mine, squeezing them tightly. "I can't."

My brows pull together. "What?"

Then I notice that one of her hands is pressed against the side of her belly. Her brows furrow, but she forces out a smile. "I think I'm in labor."

Holy shit.

I run my fingers over my face. "It's too early. You still have a few weeks to go."

"I know that, but apparently, this little one doesn't care."

"What's going on?"

I look up to find Daniel and Levi watching us.

The corner of my mouth lifts up. "The baby's coming."

Chapter 41

SAVANNAH

"Where do you want this?" Blake asks as he and Daniel carry the tree into the living room, the smell of pine already filling the space.

"Can you put it over there?"

I watch as the two of them maneuver the tree into the corner of the room, cursing every time they get stuck or bump into something before they finally manage to place it on the floor.

"You know, they have fake trees, right?" Daniel asks, dusting his palms off.

"You did not!" I gasp loudly.

"What?" He shrugs. "They're the same, only they're way easier to manage, and they don't make such a mess."

"No way." I shake my head, not believing the words leaving his mouth. "They're most certainly not the same. Inhale."

Daniel's brows furrow as he glances between Blake and Levi. "What?"

"Inhale. Do you smell that?"

He rubs the back of his neck but does as asked. "I guess?"

"And what do you smell?"

His nose crinkles as if he's trying extra hard to think. "A tree?"

"Christmas!" I press my hand against my forehead and let out an exasperated sigh. Seriously, these kids will be the death of me. "It smells like Christmas. And no fake-ass tree will ever be able to replace that, so no, we'll not have a fake tree in our home."

A strong jab of pain spreads through my middle. Letting my hand drop, I rub at the side of my belly.

"No fake trees." Blake's hand slides to the small of my back as he looks at me. "You're frowning."

"I'm forty weeks pregnant, I'm big and uncomfortable, and I've been dealing with Braxton Hicks for the past two weeks. Your baby can't decide if it'd rather kick my ribs or bladder, so it's kicking both, and at this point, I think I'll never see my toes again. If that's not a reason to frown, I don't know what is. And, on top of that, Daniel just said we should get a fake Christmas tree."

All the words come out in a rush, and I can feel my lower lip wobble as I try to regain my composure.

What I thought were the first signs of labor a couple of weeks ago turned out to be a false alarm. Something that apparently happens more often than not and based on the words of Dr. Gonzales, is simply my body just preparing for the real thing. As if this wasn't the real thing. The constant pain felt very real to me.

Blake turns me to face him, his hands cupping my face. "Blondie..."

"I'm sorry, I'm just one big mess." I shake my head. "The last few weeks have been a lot."

After everything that played out with my mother—who was now gone, hopefully, for good—and with my due date approaching, Blake insisted we should sit the boys down as soon as possible and talk to them about this new change.

They took the idea of living under one roof way better than I hoped, and within a week, they were moved into my place, and Blake put his house on the market.

I won't lie, the shift wasn't the easiest, but I didn't expect it to be. We're all still adjusting to our new normal, but I hoped with time, things would get easier.

"Let's just decorate the tree, and then we can watch movies and drink hot chocolate. Or, well, you guys can drink it, and I'll just inhale the sweet scent."

"A little while longer," Blake whispers, leaning down and pressing his mouth against mine in a soft kiss. "Where are the lights?"

I hand him the box before grabbing one with the ornaments I pulled from the attic. "You boys wanna help me?"

Levi blinks, a confused expression crossing his face and matching his brother's.

What in the ever lo—

"We can help?" I watch as a smile flashes on Levi's face, "You mean it? Really?"

For a moment, I just stare at him, speechless.

"Of course! I can't do it all by myself, can I?"

"Mom usually brought people to decorate our tree, and we couldn't touch anything so we wouldn't break it," Levi says quietly, his smile falling.

I press my mouth in a tight line.

I should have known. The Walker boys didn't talk a lot about Blake's ex, but any time a little detail like this came out, I disliked the woman more and more. Who paid for professional decorators and told their kids they couldn't touch the Christmas tree?

Blake's ex, apparently.

A dark expression passes over Daniel's face before he looks away, almost like he's embarrassed, and I instantly feel bad for saying anything.

"I'm going to grab something to drink."

Dammit.

I opened my mouth, but no words came out, and even if they did, he was already gone.

"It's fine," Blake says softly so Levi can't hear him, his hand brushing against the small of my back. "Just give him a minute."

"I shouldn't have said anything."

"You didn't do anything wrong. You're different from anything they've been used to. It'll take some time for them to adapt."

"Can I put these on?" Levi asks, suddenly lifting the box.

Blake brushes his lips against the top of my head. "Go decorate the tree. I'll go check in on Daniel."

Nodding, I shift my attention to Levi. "What did you find?"

"Look." He looks up with one of Grams' vintage ornaments in his hand. "They're so shiny."

"They are. You wanna know a secret?"

Levi's eyes grow wide as he nods, and I lean down. "They were my favorite when I was a kid." I wink at him. "Where do you want to put them?"

He turns to the tree. "I can put them anywhere?"

"Anywhere you want."

Levi thinks for a moment before he places the first ornament. I hand him the next one, directing him every now and then a little until the box is empty. I start to crouch down to get the next one when Daniel appears at my side.

"Where do you want these?" he asks as he opens the box and pulls out an ornament.

"Why don't you do the high parts?"

Daniel stops for a moment, but he nods. "Okay, I can do that."

I can feel a slight jab in my side. Resting my hand against my belly, I rub at the spot, when from the corner of my eye, I spot Blake leaning against the doorway and watching us from a distance.

Our eyes meet, and the corner of his mouth tips up as he pushes from the door. "Have a place for one more?"

"Always."

Between all of us, we put all the decorations on in no time. Well, the boys put most of them on while I hand around the ornaments, trying my best to ignore the ever-present pain, which seems to be growing by the minute.

There was no more reservation on their faces. Even Daniel was smiling, and that's saying something.

"It looks so pretty!" Levi says as he takes in the tree.

"It's not done just yet." I look around the floor, until I spot the box I'm looking for and pull out a shiny gold star and hand it to him. "One final touch."

His smile turns blinding as he watches the star.

Blake crouches next to him. "Ready to put it up?"

Levi nods silently, so Blake lifts him up while Levi slides the star in place.

"I did it! This is the best tree ever."

"You guys did a great job."

"We did." Blake puts him back down, and Levi turns around. "Is it time for cookies and a movie now?"

I chuckle at his question, but the sound dies when the strongest contraction yet, makes me double down in pain.

Holy shit. Stupid Braxton Hicks.

"Blondie?" Large hands land on my waist. "Are you okay?"

I press my lips together and nod.

Blake's serious eyes watch me for a moment. "You're not okay. You've been rubbing your back this whole time."

"I probably overdid it. Just give me a few."

"There is no probably about it. Sit down."

I open my mouth to protest, but Blake shoots me a death glare, so I let out a sigh and do as he asks.

"Happy?"

"Yes. Now be a good girl and stay seated like that. I'll clean this up and bring the snacks."

I watch him put all the boxes on top of each other and pick them up. My stomach tightens again, stronger this time.

"Are you really okay?" Levi asks as he snuggles next to me.

I wrap my arm around him. "I'm really okay."

Levi nods, his attention on the TV. "Sav?"

"Yes?"

He tilts his head back. "Do you think Munchkin will come before Christmas?"

"I don't know. It depends on when Munchkin is ready to come."

"But when will he be ready?" He sits upright and turns to me. "How is Santa going to know if Munchkin is here so he can bring him a present? He needs to get a present."

I bite the inside of my cheek, trying to keep a straight face. "I'm sure Santa won't forget about Munchkin."

The pressure builds in my belly, making me squirm in my seat, but when nothing helps, I push to my feet. "I'm just going to—"

The words die on my lips as I feel something trickle down between my legs just as Blake enters the room, two cups of hot chocolate in his hands.

"Sav, did you just pee your pants?"

My cheeks turn bright red at Levi's question.

Holy shit.

"You did, didn't you?" Levi pats my hand. "It's fine, accidents happen. That's what Dad always used to tell me."

"Levi," Blake chastises as he puts the cups on the coffee table. "We don't point that stuff out. It—"

"Blake?" I grab him with my free hand as another wave of pain spreads through me, this one stronger. "My water broke. It's time."

It wasn't just back pain.

A contraction.

An actual contraction.

"It's fine, babe, let's go upstairs, and I'll help you clean up. It's not a big..." Blake trails off, and his brows furrow. "It's time?" I watch as the realization slowly dawns on him. His eyes fall to my stomach, and for a moment, I think he might actually freak out. But then his head snaps up, his eyes meeting mine. I watch as different emotions play on his face. Uncertainty. Fear. Surprise. Excitement. Joy. "It's time? You sure?"

I bite into my lower lip and nod, my throat feeling tight.

"Okay." In the blink of an eye, any doubts are gone, and there is only strong and steady Blake left. "It's going to be okay."

Levi glances between the two of us. "Time for what? What's going on?"

Blake pulls back, his hand falling to the small of my back as he looks at his youngest son. "Munchkin is coming."

Chapter 42

BLAKE

"I'm done," Savannah says as her back crashes against my chest, her fingers loosening their grip on mine. "I can't do this any longer."

Her voice is low, exhaustion evident in every softly spoken word. Not that I can blame her, she's been at this for hours.

"I need you to push, Savannah," the doctor says as she glances up at the woman sitting in my arms.

Savannah shakes her head. "I can't."

Her cheeks are flushed, beads of sweat coating her forehead and making the honey strands that slipped her braid plaster to her face.

"You can," I insist, tightening my hold on her.

I brush her hair out of her face. Savannah tilts her head back so she can look at me. "You're wrong," she protests, letting out a long exhale.

"I'm not wrong. I know you, baby. Besides, you're not alone in this. I've gotcha, Blondie." I rub my thumb over the back of her hand reassuringly. "A little bit more, and we'll meet our baby."

"Bl—"

Her words die down when another contraction hits her.

Savannah groans loudly; her grip on my fingers tightens to the point of pain, but I don't let go.

"That's it, babe," I murmur, my lips brushing against her ear. "You're doing so great. I've never been more amazed by you than I am right now."

I rub at her back with my free hand, as I continue whispering soft reassurances, until finally, *finally*, loud crying fills the room.

Savannah lets out a sob as her body rests against mine. Her chest is rising and falling rapidly as she sucks in long gulps of air.

"You did it, Blondie." My words come out raspy. My heart is in my throat as I brush her hair out of her face and press my forehead against hers. This stunning, amazing woman. "You're fucking incredible, you know that?"

Savannah blinks those pretty blue eyes open, the corner of her mouth lifting in a smile. "I did it."

"You did. Our little Christmas present."

Savannah's eyes fill with tears, and her throat bobs as she swallows.

"It's a girl," the doctor announces as she brings the small baby and places it on Savannah's chest.

Savannah places her hand against the baby's back as her gaze falls to our daughter, and I just stare at them, completely at a loss for words. It's like all the air is knocked out of my lungs as I watch the woman I love holding our baby.

My girls.

Holy fuck.

My chest tightens as I just stare at Savannah, completely in awe. Of her. Of the baby we created. Of this moment.

Tears stream down her face as she gently rubs her finger over the baby's exposed arm.

"A girl," Savannah whispers, her voice thick with emotion.

Those light blue eyes meet mine, and I can see tears glistening in them. "We have a girl."

"We do." I shake my head, still unable to wrap my mind around it. "A little girl."

I cover her hand with mine and just stare at the tiny body pressed against Savannah, taking her in.

The frown between her pale brows. A little patch of mussed hair. Those small, pursed lips. Her little hands with ten of the tiniest fingers.

Then she opens her eyes, and I'm a goner.

Completely and utterly gone for this little girl.

"She's perfect, Sav," I croak out, blinking the blurriness from my gaze. "So fucking perfect, just like her mom."

Savannah lets out a strangled laugh. "I'm far from perfect."

I shift my attention to her. "You're always perfect to me."

She bites into her lower lip, her throat bobbing. Before she can say anything, the nurse joins us.

"Let me get her so that we can clean her up."

My hand tightens around Savannah and the baby, and the nurse doesn't miss the motion. She gives me a reassuring smile. "Just for a little bit. I'll get her back to you in no time. Don't worry, Dad."

"Highly unlikely," I mutter under my breath.

Still, I force myself to pull my hand back, so she can take the baby, my gaze not leaving her as she maneuvers my daughter into her arms.

Savannah pokes me in the chest, drawing my attention. "You know she's been doing this for a while, right?"

I look down at her, amusement dancing in her irises. "Well, she's handling precious cargo." I cup her face, my thumb skimming over her cheek. "Thank you."

"What for?"

"For this. For bringing our little girl into this world. For allowing me to be here with you so we can share this moment. I honestly didn't think it was possible to love you more than I already did, but I was wrong. So fucking wrong. I love you, Savannah. I love you both so freaking much it hurts."

"Blake..." She shakes her head, tears streaming down her cheeks. "I love you too."

"I know, baby." I brush the tears away gently before I lean down and press my mouth against hers. "I know."

SAVANNAH

"She's so tiny," I whisper, my finger tracing over my daughter's small hand, all the way to the tips of her fingers. "How is it possible that she's so small, and yet it feels like my whole universe has been altered?"

It felt surreal.

I have a daughter.

For so long, I wanted somebody of my own, and now she was here.

A little baby girl with a patch of blonde curls on her head, hiding behind the tiniest pink hat and the darkest blue eyes imaginable. The nurse said they'll lighten with time. Would they be blue like mine or gray like all the Walker boys? Or maybe they would be some weird mix of both. I think I kind of liked that idea.

"She has your nose," Blake whispers into my ear, his lips pressing against the side of my neck. My eyes fall closed as a shiver runs down my spine. "You should be resting."

Blinking my eyes open, I glance at Blake. Those silvery eyes are fixed on me as he watches me intently.

"I am resting."

"Sleeping," Blake protests. "You should be sleeping."

"I'm just too nervous to sleep. What if something happens? What if she needs me? What if she cries and I don't wake up and—"

Blake cups my cheeks gently and presses his mouth against mine, effectively shushing me. "That's why I'm here. Let me take care of you two."

Before I get a chance to answer, there is a soft knock on the door. I shift in the bed, a jab of pain going through my stomach. Blake's brows furrow when I flinch.

"I'm fine," I say quickly, turning my attention to the door. "Come in."

Blake slips from the bed just as the door opens, and two dark heads peek inside.

"Is Munchkin here yet?" Levi asks immediately, as he slips into the room, Daniel at his heels.

He gives me an apologetic look. "I told him we should wait but..."

"I wanna meet—" Levi comes to a stop by my bed, his mouth falling open as he sees the baby in my arms. "Munchkin is a girl!"

"Yes, it's a girl," chuckling softly, I fix her hat so it's not slipping into her eyes. "What do you think?"

"She's so pretty." Levi extends his hand and touches her fist gently. "And so small."

"She is." Blake places his hands on Levi's shoulders and gives them a squeeze. "So you have to be very careful with her. Okay?"

"'Kay." Levi looks up at me. "Can I hold her?"

"Not now, buddy. Once she wakes up."

"Fine." Levi's smile falls a little, but he nods. "I brought her a toy so she doesn't have to sleep alone tonight."

"What's her name?"

I look to the foot of the bed, where Daniel is standing quietly, his gaze fixed on the baby.

I swallow the knot in my throat. "Poppy."

My gaze falls to my sleeping daughter, and I can't help thinking of the woman who raised me. I missed her today more than usual. She should have been here. She would have been so excited to meet her great-granddaughter. Although, knowing Grams, she would probably already embrace Levi and Daniel as her own and spoiled them rotten. That was the kind of woman she was. There wasn't a better way to honor the woman who showed me love unlike any other.

"Her name is Poppy Walker."

Poppy's brows furrow, and she lets out a wail in protest. I coo softly and rock her against me.

"Is she okay?" Daniel asks, moving closer.

"Why is she crying? Did we do something wrong?"

"No, buddy," Blake reassures Levi immediately. "Babies cry, that's all."

Poppy blinks a few times, her unfocused gaze darting toward the three boys hovering over her.

Warmth fills my chest as she stares at them with those big dark eyes. Their voices die down, their whole attention on her.

"Hey, there, pretty girl." Daniel gently brushes the back of his finger over her clasped hand. "No need to cry."

I bite my cheek to stop a sob from coming, but Blake doesn't miss it. He slides next to me and wraps his arm around me. "You okay, Blondie?"

I nod silently, my attention still on the boys who are staring at their sister.

"Can I hold my baby sister now?"

Blake pulls back, amusement dancing in his irises.

"C'mon, sit down in the armchair, and you can hold her for a few minutes."

Levi scurries off immediately, he's practically buzzing with excitement.

"Hello, there, Princess," Blake whispers as he gently scoops the baby into his arms. My heart melts as I watch him hold Poppy close to his chest, his large hand covering her small body protectively. "Wanna go and bug your big brother for a while, huh? He's so excited to meet you. Extend your arms, buddy," Blake instructs as he goes to Levi. "You need to watch her head, okay?"

"Okay." Levi nods. "I'll take good care of her. I promise, Daddy."

"I know you will." Blake crouches down and gently places Poppy in Levi's arms.

He sucks in a breath, his arms clutching around Poppy and holding her close. "I think she likes me. Look, she's smiling at me."

"She was just born, I don't think she knows how to smile." Daniel rolls his eyes as he goes to the armchair and sits down next to Levi.

"Poppy smiled at me." Levi pokes his tongue at his brother before his gaze drops to the bundle in his arms. "I guess that means she likes me better than she likes you. Right, Poppy? You like me better? That's good because I love you so, so much."

These boys.

"And it's good you came now," Levi continues chatting away while Daniel just sits and watches them. "Christmas is in a few days, so now Santa won't forget about you. We can share a stocking, and I'll add your name on it so Santa knows you're here."

My lip wobbles at his kind words.

This moment right here was everything I wanted but never dared to hope for.

Poppy will be okay. She will be loved and protected. Hell, she already had all three of the Walker boys wrapped around her little finger.

Blake glances over his shoulder, his face softening as he stands up, and comes to me, brushing his thumb over my cheek. "I don't like to see you crying, Blondie."

"They're happy tears." I tilt my head back. "You were wrong, Blake."

Blake quirks his brow, a confused expression on his face. "About what?"

"Thank *you*." I cover his hand with mine. "For being patient with me. For choosing me even when I was giving you a hard time. But more than that, thank you for giving me everything that I ever wanted and then some."

"Blondie..." Blake's hold on me tightens. "Anything you want is yours. I'm yours." He leans down, his mouth brushing against mine. "And I'll always choose you, baby. Always."

Epilogue

BLAKE

Spring

"Tighten this here." I point at the engine. "Yes, just like that."

"You boys almost done?"

I look up, a smile spreading over my face when I see Savannah coming out of the house, Poppy in her arms. My little girl's face lights up when she sees me, and my heart melts.

"Just a bit. You leaving?"

Savannah nibbles at her lip. "Maybe I should stay? You're busy, and I don't wanna leave Poppy alone…"

"I'll look after Poppy," Levi chimes in immediately, letting his bike drop.

We pulled Daniel's truck out of the garage to do some work on it while Levi was riding his bike in the driveway.

"Hear that? We've got her, right, Princess?" I extend my arms and gently pick her up, lifting her in the air. "You're gonna hang out with the boys, and we'll have so much fun."

Poppy lets out a bubbling sound. I chuckle, pressing a kiss onto her cheek before looking at Savannah. "Go." I lean down and kiss her. "Have fun with the girls; you deserve it."

Savannah nods slowly, that unsure expression still on her face. "Call me if she needs me?"

"Will do," I promise. "I love you."

Savannah smiles. "Love you too."

With another nod, Savannah goes toward her car, once again looking back at us. I lift Poppy's hand and wave at her as she pulls out of the driveway.

"Can I hold her now?" Levi begs.

"Why don't you go and grab a blanket, and you two can play together."

"Okay."

He runs toward the porch and grabs a blanket, bringing it to us. I help him spread it out and put Poppy down. Levi joins her, that stuffed elephant he got her in his hand, and she wiggles her arms to grab it. That plushy was one of her favorites, and Levi took great pride since he was the one who picked it out for her.

"You good, buddy?"

"Yeah, I've got her, Dad." He leans down and brushes his nose against hers. "Right, Pop-Tart?"

Poppy purses her lips and blabs something, which has Levi giggling.

With one last glance at the duo, I push to my feet and join Daniel. I show him how to change the oil before we call it quits for the day.

Grabbing a bottle of water, I hand it to him before taking a sip from mine.

"Are you planning to propose to Savannah?"

I choke at Daniel's question, some of the water spilling down my chin.

Shit.

Levi looks up from the blanket. "Dad and Sav are getting married?"

"I..." I glance between the two boys. "What are you talking about?"

Daniel rolls his eyes at me. "You can't tell me you haven't thought about it."

Only every moment of every day; I just didn't know the best way to bring it up. It was hard toeing this line between being a father to them and a man who was desperately in love with a woman. But my children came first, always, and I knew Savannah wouldn't have it any other way.

"How would you feel about it if I asked Savannah to marry me?" I ask tentatively, watching for their reaction.

"Fine." Daniel shrugs. "Savannah is cool. Maybe a bit too cool for your old ass."

"I'll give you old." I ruffle his hair, which only makes him laugh. It's a sound that'll never get old. "But seriously, would you be okay with that?"

"Does that mean Sav will be our mom?" Levi asks softly, his gaze falling down to Poppy, who's kicking her chubby legs.

Dammit.

I didn't see that one coming. Although, maybe I should have. Daniel and Savannah had a good, friendly relationship, but he was different. Older. Levi was a whole other story. He was just a boy who lost his mom and wanted to love somebody—wanted somebody to love him. And Savannah did exactly that. She filled the void Reina left when she disappeared without a backward glance. She loved and cared for them like they were her own. And in her heart, I knew they were.

Going to him, I sit down by his side. "If Savannah and I marry, that would make her your stepmom, yes."

"But she's Poppy's mom," Levi points out as Poppy grabs one of his fingers and brings it to her mouth.

"Yes, she is."

He purses his lips, a sad smile tugging at the corner of his mouth. "I want her to be my mom, too. Do you think she'd want that?"

My throat feels tight. I meet Daniel's gaze over Levi's head, a trace of that old anger on his face before he manages to school his features.

I open my mouth, unsure of what to say, but Daniel's faster, his voice coming out raspy. "You should ask her."

Levi's head snaps up, surprise evident on his face. "What if she says no?"

Daniel rolls his eyes. "She won't say no. Just ask her."

"He's right, you know." I ruffle his hair. "As a matter of fact, we could ask her together."

Pushing to my feet, I make my way to the tool closet. I open a drawer and pull out a little black box that I've been hiding inside for the last few months. It made the most sense since I knew that nobody would find it in there, and I'd been right. My throat feels tight, the weight of it feeling heavy on my palm.

And yet, it felt right.

That was the reason I bought it on impulse. I was in Austin for business, and I met with Andrew, who was in the city to meet with a few of his players. He was running late, so I was strolling downtown when I spotted the ring in the window, and I just knew I had to have it for when the time was right.

"Dad, what are you— *Shit,* is that...?"

I turn to face my son and flick open the box, the gems shining in the light. It felt perfect and so much like Savannah, so much like our family, and when I proposed to her, it would be to officially make her ours, and we'd become hers.

"An engagement ring. I had it for a while now, but..." I shrug. "What do you think?"

Levi peeks at the box. "It's pretty."

"She'll love it," Daniel agrees.

"I hope so." I let out a nervous chuckle, brushing my sweaty palm against the side of my leg. "It felt symbolic somehow."

Daniel nods slowly, his eyes still glued to the ring. "When will you do it?"

"I don't know. I didn't really think about it. I wanted to talk to you boys and see how you felt."

Understanding flashes in Daniel's eyes and a little bit of guilt, too. "Is this why you've been waiting? Because you thought it would upset us?"

I shake my head. "You're not the only ones who need time. All these changes are a lot for everybody to take, including Savannah."

"But you love her."

"I do. She makes me the happiest I've been in a long time."

"Okay, then." Daniel nods and closes the lid. The soft *thump* echoed in the quiet garage. "Then let's come up with a plan."

SAVANNAH

"Admit it," Becky says as the bell chimes, and the smell of freshly baked goods and coffee reaches my nostrils. "This was a fine idea."

I roll my eyes at my best friend. "You were right."

When Becky texted me this morning, suggesting we should have a girls' day, I was reluctant to leave, but Blake insisted and reassured me they'd be fine on their own and that I should go.

We had lunch with Kate, after which she had to head back to work while Becky and I went to get our nails done. And

Becky even insisted that we should stop at a boutique. I had to admit, it was nice to spend some time with my friends and just enjoy myself, but I was starting to miss my baby, and I couldn't wait to get back home so I could squeeze her.

"Of course I was right."

"What was she right about?" Jessica asks, smiling as Becky slips behind the counter and goes for the coffee machine.

"What am I *not* right about?" Becky smirks.

Jessica and I exchange a knowing look. "So you'd like to think."

"Did you guys have fun?"

"Yeah, it was nice to get pampered for a few hours, but now I feel wiped. You'd think I spent the day running errands instead."

"It's hard to relax when all you do is work."

Just then, the bell chimes, and as one, we turn toward the door only to spot Rose O'Neil coming into the café.

"Hey." She gives us a tentative smile as she walks to the counter.

"Hi." I give her a curious once over. "You look extra nice today."

"You think?" Rose smooths her hand over her skirt. "I'm going to a job interview, but I wasn't sure what to wear."

"What kind of interview?" Jessica asks.

"For an assistant position at a law firm. It's in the next town over. I figured I'd stop and grab a coffee on my way there."

"That's amazing." I shoot her an encouraging smile as Jessica starts working on her order. "I think this is a good outfit, you look professional but classy."

"Thanks." Rose ducks her head for a moment. "The other few interviews I had didn't really go well, then again, I never got around to getting my diploma so..."

I place my hand over hers. "Just keep trying. There has to be a job that values a good, hard worker over a diploma."

"She's right." Jessica slides a to-go cup of coffee on the counter. "Your usual."

"Thanks, let me just..." Rose starts to pull out her wallet, but Becky waves her off.

"It's on the house."

Rose's head snaps up, and she shakes her head. "I can't..."

"I'm the boss, so you sure can. For good luck."

"Thank you, I really appreciate it." She lets out a shaky breath and glances at her watch. "I have to get going. I don't want to be late."

"Good luck."

Rose gives us a grateful smile as she leaves, my gaze glued to her retreating form.

"*Ouch*," Becky hisses. "What was that for?"

I turn around just in time to see her rubbing at her elbow.

"You ever planning to post that job opening?" Jessica asks, which has Becky sighing.

"I'm going to do it. These last few weeks have just been busy."

Jessica smirks at her. "More like you've been busy with your husband."

Becky pokes her tongue out at the younger woman. "You're just jealous."

I stay at the café for a little while longer, the conversation shifting to our upcoming book club as I finish my coffee.

The late afternoon heat slams into me the moment I step outside, the fine hair at my nape sticking to my sweaty skin as I make my way to the car I parked on the street and slip inside, starting the engine.

This was the first time I'd been away this long from Poppy,

and while I knew Blake and the boys were more than capable of taking care of her, I missed my little girl.

Since I gave birth just before the holidays, I've decided to stay on maternity leave for the remainder of the school year. There was no sense in returning back to class mid-semester, and I considered myself lucky to be able to stay home with Poppy. Blake even suggested I didn't have to go back to work at all, but I love teaching.

Pulling in front of the house, I kill the engine and slide out of the car. We've been hard at work ever since we agreed to move permanently into Grams' house—our home. It's been a lot of work overall, with the boys moving the majority of their stuff just days before Poppy was born. We've put our focus into getting the boys situated, and since then, we've been slowly making improvements to the house. Just last week, Blake and Daniel painted the house, the bright white paint making the red shutters stand out.

"Hey, I'm home," I yell as I enter the house and put my stuff onto the table by the door.

"In here," Blake yells from the back of the house.

A smile spreads over my lips, excitement coursing through me as I make my way down the hallway toward the living room. "I have to admit it, you were right. I had fun—" I come to a sudden stop in the doorway when I spot Blake and the kids standing in the living room.

He smiles at me as I take in the space: candles and flowers. The four of them are side by side, from oldest to the youngest, with matching white signs in their hands. The boys are all dressed in a nice pair of slacks and matching red shirts, and they even dressed Poppy in a red dress with a tiny bow in her blonde hair. Definitely not what I dressed her in this morning, but damn, she looks adorable sitting in her bouncy seat.

I shift my attention to Blake, my tongue darting out to slide over my lower lip before I ask, my voice coming out shaky, "Wh-what's going on?"

"We have a question to ask you!" Levi immediately says as he bounces on his heels, buzzing with excitement.

A question—

Oh my gosh...

Nervously, I slide my hand over my skirt, my palms turning clammy. And why is it suddenly so hot in here. "You do?"

Levi nods eagerly and glances at his dad, his hands gripping the paper. "Is it time, Dad? Can we ask her? Please! Can we?"

"In a bit, buddy." Blake shakes his head at him before those bright gray eyes turn to me. They crinkle with amusement, faint lines appearing in their corners. And love, so much love, that it feels like I can't breathe.

"As Levi said, we have a couple of really important questions to ask you, Blondie. It's been over a year since I first saw you in that bar. You took my breath away that day and every day since. And I know we did a lot of things backward, but meeting you, getting to know you, getting to *love* you, and having a family together has been the best privilege of my life."

"Blake," his name comes out shaky, tears prickling my eyelids.

"I mean it, Sav. Things haven't been easy for us, but I'm grateful that I got to walk this path with you. And I want to keep on walking it until the very end. I want to marry you. I want you to share my name. I want to raise our family together, to laugh and to cry and to grow old together. I want it all with you."

Blake glances at his kids, and I raise my hand to wipe away the tears that slid down my cheek. "*We* want it all with you."

Before I get to say anything, he gets on one knee, and all the signs turn as one.

I let out a soft sob and raised my shaking hand to cover my

mouth as I stared at the words written on the paper, still in shock.

Will you marry us?

"I love you, Savannah. I love your fierce nature and your big heart. I love how you adore our baby girl, and I'll forever be thankful for the role you play in my sons' lives. I've watched them fall in love with you these past few months as much as I have. You gave me my boys back, you were the missing piece we never realized we needed, the glue that's holding us together. You're our family, Savannah, and now I want to make it official so there is no confusion. Marry me, Blondie. Marry me and make me the happiest man alive."

My heart squeezes tightly, and more tears start to slide down my cheeks as his words echo in my mind.

Our family.

Everything I've ever wanted. Everything I never dared hoping for, not really. But he was giving it to me.

A family to call my own.

Biting the inside of my cheek, I go to him. Blake's up immediately, his strong arms wrapping around me as I bury my head into his chest.

My rock.

His arms tighten around me, his mouth brushing against the top of my head. "Shh, it's good..."

"I'm sorry, I'm such a mess, but this..." I shake my head, unsure of how to explain it, but I don't have to. Not when it comes to Blake.

"I know, baby. I've gotcha."

"Why is she crying?" Levi asks, and I can feel his arms wrapping around my legs. "You shouldn't be sad, Sav. Don't you want to marry us?"

Brushing away my tears, I turn in Blake's arms to look at my beautiful, compassionate boy, who's anxiously nibbling at his lower lip.

"I do. These are happy tears." I place my hand on his back to steady us and blink my eyes open to find Blake watching me with all the love and patience in the world. "Because I do want to marry you."

"All of us?" he insists, a little bit of that uncertainty that was there when I met him written in his eyes. It's rarely present these days, which only shows how much this means to him, and my heart melts for this little boy as he purses his lips and nods. "Because we're a package deal, you know. If you marry Dad, you get all of us."

I brush my thumb over his cheek. "I wouldn't have it any other way, Levi."

And I meant it. They couldn't understand how much this meant to me. The little girl who never knew her father, who was left by her mother, and robbed of her grandmother, the only real family she knew way too soon, finally had a family of her own.

"Yes!" Levi fist pumps excitedly. "Show her the ring, Dad!"

"I was getting to that." Blake clasps my hand in his, his long fingers engulfing my palm. Patience and love, so much love, shone in his eyes as he slips his hand into his pocket and pulls out a ring that he slips in place, the warm band slipping easily onto my finger. I glance down at the ruby shining between four smaller diamonds and more tears start to fall.

My head snaps up. "Blake, this is..."

"You'll never, ever be alone, Blondie." His calloused hand cups my cheek. "We're your family. That's my promise to you. Today, tomorrow, and every day after that."

Grabbing his shirt, I tug him down, my mouth meeting him in a gentle kiss. Levi groans in protest, but I don't let it stop me. My lips sweep gently over his. "I love you, Blake Walker."

"I love you more, baby."

Poppy lets out an annoyed cry, done with being ignored. I turn to pick her up, but Daniel is already unhooking her from her bouncy seat and pulling her into his arms. "I think somebody needs attention."

He brings her to me, and I brush away her tears gently before picking her into my arms. Daniel takes a step back, but I place my hand on his arm. "Are you okay with all of this?"

Our relationship has been much better in recent months, but I knew this was a big step.

"Yeah." Daniel nods. "Dad loves you, and he's happy."

"I love him too." I give his arm a gentle squeeze. "The promise from that day still stands. I love you, and I love Levi. Whatever you need me to be, whenever you need me, I'll be there for you boys, no questions asked."

His throat bobs, but before I know it, he pulls me into his arms. I wrap my free hand around him, rubbing at his back.

"Thank you, Sav."

"No thanks needed," I reassure him softly before he takes a step back, and Blake's arm is around my middle.

"Just when I think I couldn't love you more, you show me otherwise."

I tilt my head back. "That's good. I like keeping you on your toes, Mr. Walker."

Something primal and possessive shines in those gray depths.

"And when do I get to call you Mrs. Walker?"

"Hmm... How about we do it before school starts? Something small, just for close family and friends."

"Hell yeah. A month."

I blink, unsure if I heard him correctly.

"Wait now, I don't think..."

Blake gives me a pointed look. "One month, Blondie. That's the most I'm willing to wait for you to choose me in front of the whole world."

"Fine," I let out a sigh and brush my lips against his. "But you don't need to wait. I choose you, Blake Walker. I choose you today, and I'll choose you for the rest of our lives."

Meeting Blake Walker was unexpected.

Falling in love with him was inevitable.

But loving him?

Loving him is effortless.

A soft tug at my hand has me looking down to find Levi watching me with big eyes. "Sav?"

"Yeah?"

He motions me closer, so I crouch down so we're at the same level. He's grown in the last year, and I was pretty sure sooner rather than later, he'd be towering over me too.

Levi leans down, his hand cupping around my ear as he whispers. "I want to ask you something too."

My gaze darts to Blake, who's just smiling at us.

"Okay, sure," I say tentatively and give him my full attention, unsure of where this is going. "What do you want to ask me?"

"I know you're Poppy's mom, but..." His grip on me tightens, his palms clammy with nerves. "Can you be my mom too?"

My eyes fall shut, my chest squeezing tightly as all the emotions and the weight of his request slams into me. My throat bobs as I try to swallow. Blinking my eyes open, I find him watching me. I cup his cheek. "If you want me to, yes. It would be an honor to be your mom, Levi."

"Really?" Levi blinks for a second, clearly surprised, as if I could ever tell him no, but then his arms wrap around my shoulders, and he buries his face into my neck. "Yes, I want to. I love you, Mom."

Mom.

Yes, I've been a mom for the last five months, but this was the first time somebody—my child—called me such.

I clutch him tightly, "I love you too, baby."

Acknowledgments

This one was a long time coming, huh? *Need You To Choose Me* ended up at just over 130k words, which is pretty standard for any of my books these days.

The number of deleted words, however? 135k. And that's not including small tweaks, and edits, only whole scenes that were deleted, cut, or completely changed from the original idea.

Let that sink in.

I wrote over 265k words for ONE book in 2024.

For a normal author who writes 85-90k words that would equal *three* books.

How crazy is that?

I had so many different ideas and directions I wanted this book to go. There are some scenes that had to be cut because it would mean going in a certain direction that would require me to add even more words in order to do this story and characters justice, and I knew I couldn't have that. Not because I didn't want that, but because there are certain standards and expectations that have to be met. Maybe one day, once I'm feeling better about this whole year, I'll go back, look at some of those scenes, and send them in my newsletter as a bonus chapter, so if you're not subscribed, make sure to do so!

The biggest shoutout goes to my very lovely and *extremely* patient beta readers – Nina, Anna, Nadine and Carrie. I've been bugging them for a whole year with all of my ideas and tweaks. They've read the mismatched scenes, and bits and pieces of this book to help me make it what it is today, so THANK YOU!

As always, I want to thank my team. Kate for squeezing me in for edits. My lovely cover designer Najla and her crew for bringing these covers to life, and the amazing Wander Aguiar for the stunning photo of Savannah and Blake!

Thank you to my street team, and all the bloggers who've helped me promote the book.

But most of all, THANK YOU, my readers. Thank you for being patient with me. Thank you for giving me grace and time to finish this book and trusting me to bring this story to life. I couldn't have been able to do any of this without you. This one's for you.

Until the next book,
Anna

Playlist

Jenna Kramer - Voices
Taylor Swift - Afterglow
Lady A - Bartender
Taylor Swift - I Almost Do (Taylor's Version)
Taylor Swift - Gorgeous
Tate McRae - messier
Taylor Swift - The Way I Loved You (Taylor's Version)
Jessica Baio - at least
Jessica Baio - trust issues
Nate Smith - Wildfire
Nate Smith - I Found You
Dasha - Share This City
Taylor Swift - The Prophecy
Gracie Abrams - Risk
Gracie Abrams - Let It Happen
Natalie Jane - Somebody to Someone (I Just Wanna Fall in Love)
Taylor Swift - Untouchable (Taylor's Version)
Kelsey Ballerini - I Think I Fell in Love Today
Thomas Rhett - After All The Bars Are Closed
Taylor Swift - You're In Love (Taylor's Version)
Nate Smith - Carry You Home
Taylor Swift - invisible string

Books by Anna B. Doe

Bluebonnet Creek

Small town sports romance

It Should Have Been Us

Need You To Choose Me

Make Me Trust Again

Blairwood University

College sports romance

Kiss Me First

Kiss To Conquer

Kiss To Forget

Kiss To Defy

Kiss Before Midnight

Kiss To Remember

Kiss To Belong

Kiss Me Forever

Kiss To Shatter

Kiss To Salvage

Kiss Me Tenderly

Greyford Wolves

YA/NA hockey romance

Lines

Habits

Rules

Greyford High

Sweet YA sports romance novellas

The Penalty Box

The Stand-In Boyfriend

New York Knights

NA/adult sports romance

Lost & Found

Until

Forever

Standalone

YA modern fairytale retelling

Underwater

Anna B. Doe is a USA Today and international bestselling author of new adult sports romance. She writes angsty, real-life romance featuring flawed, yet resilient characters. She's a coffee and chocolate addict. Like her characters, she loves those two things dark, sweet and with little extra spice.

When she's not writing her newest book you can find her reading books or binge-watching TV shows. Originally from Croatia, she is always planning her next trip because wanderlust is in her blood.

She is currently working on various projects. Some more secret than others.

Find more about Anna on her website: www.annabdoe.com

Join Anna's Reader's Group Anna's Bookmantics on Facebook.

Made in the USA
Columbia, SC
31 May 2025